Skinner's Rules

Skinner's Rules

Quintin Jardine

HEADLINE

First published in 1993
by HEADLINE BOOK PUBLISHING

First published in paperback in 1994
by HEADLINE BOOK PUBLISHING

15 17 19 20 18 16 14

ISBN 0 7472 4139 2

Printed and bound in Great Britain by
Mackays of Chatham PLC, Chatham, Kent

HEADLINE BOOK PUBLISHING
A division of Hodder Headline PLC
338 Euston Road
London NW1 3BH

Kate

Book One

Right and Righteous

1

As a city, Edinburgh is a two-faced bitch.

There is the face on the picture postcards, sunny, bright and shining, prosperous and smiling at the world like a toothpaste ad.

But on the other side of the looking glass lies the other face: the real world where all too often the wind blows cold, the rain lashes down and the poverty shows on the outside. That cold hard face was showing as Bob Skinner made his way to work.

The wind whistled down from the North, driving the rain across Fife, with the threat of snow not far behind. It was 6.43 a.m. on one of those fag-end of the year November days when it seemed impossible to relate the dull, grey city to the cosmopolitan capital of the August Festival weeks, or the friendly town invaded on bright, sparkling Saturdays in January by hordes of visiting rugby followers.

Detective Chief Superintendent Robert Skinner brought his Granada to a halt at the High Street entrance to Advocates' Close. The tiny gateway, unnoticed every day by hundreds of passers-by, led into one of the many alleyways which flow from the ancient Royal Mile, down to Cockburn Street, to the Mound, and to Cowgate.

Skinner stood framed in the entry, the disapproving bulk of St Giles Cathedral, the High Kirk of Edinburgh, looming behind him. He looked as grey as the city itself. Steely hair which sometimes sparkled in the sun now flopped lustreless over his forehead. The last of the summer tan was long gone, and the face bore the lines of one wakened too often from too little sleep.

He was dressed for the occasion, in a long leather coat, black and Satanic, over a grey suit. Only the shoes, light leather moccasins, were incongruous. But even in the ungodly gloom, there was no masking the presence of the man. Standing two inches over six feet tall, he filled the gateway as he surveyed the carnage in the Close. Skinner was forty-three years old, but he retained the grace of an athlete. Power was written in every

3

movement, and in the set of his face, where deep blue eyes, a classically straight nose and a strong chin seemed to vie with each other to be the dominant feature.

He stepped over the tape which had been stretched across the entryway. A group of men, some in uniform, stood around a huddled heap of something, lying where the Close emerged from the shelter of the building above into the open air. Daylight was only a vague promise in the eastern sky as he stepped forward into the poorly-lit alley, hunching his shoulders against the rain and screwing his eyes against the wind.

One of the kneeling men, his back to Skinner, looked over his shoulder, as if sensing his presence, and jumped to his feet.

'Morning, boss!' Detective Inspector Andy Martin used the form of address beloved of policemen and professional footballers. He was shorter than Skinner, but broader in build. He was fresh-faced, and looked younger than his thirty-four years. His hair, cut close, was unusually blond for a Scot, and his eyes were a bright green, accentuated by a tint in his soft contact lenses. He was dressed in black Levis and a brown leather bomber jacket.

Skinner nodded to his personal assistant. 'Morning, Andy. Just how suspicious is this suspicious death, then?' The whole force knew that the Head of CID did not like to be called in on obvious suicides by nervous divisional commanders.

Martin stood between him and the heap. 'You'd better prepare yourself for this one, boss. This boy's been chopped to pieces, literally. I never want to see anything like it again.'

Even in the dim light which crept in from the High Street, Skinner could see that Martin's face was paler than usual.

His expression grew grim. 'Just fucking magic,' he muttered, and stepped forward, past the younger man, towards the lamp-lit heap, which not long before had been a human being.

The first thing that he saw clearly was the face, which seemed to stare at the truncated body with unbelieving eyes. The man had been decapitated. Even as he saw the two pools of vomit on the slope below the corpse, his own stomach churned. In all his years on the force, this was as bad as anything he had seen.

But to his people he was the Boss, and the Boss could not show any trace of weakness. So, switching off the horror, he turned his eyes back towards the scene. The head lay about four feet away from the rest of the body. It had landed, or had been placed upright. Skinner noted that it had been severed neatly, as if by a single blow. He looked again at the

4

face and shuddered. The man, apart from the dull, dead eyes, bore a fair resemblance to Andy Martin.

'Is everything in the position it was when it was found?'

'Of course, boss.' Martin sounded almost offended. Then his tone changed, to an awed murmur. 'It's as if the bastard left the head like that on purpose.'

'Who found him?'

'Two polis from down the road. One of them, PC Reilly, he's in the Royal, in shock. The other, WPC Ross, she's over there. Tough wee thing, eh!'

'Maybe too tough,' said Skinner, almost to himself.

He forced himself to turn away from the staring eyes, and from the stream of blood which wound down the close into the darkness, to look at the rest of the body. The belly had been slashed open; the intestines were wound around the fingers of the bloody left hand, as if the victim had been trying to hold them in. The right hand had been severed and lay beside the body. It had been cut off, like the head, by a single stroke, the wound running diagonally from a point two inches above the wrist to the base of the thumb.

Because of the blood, and because of his soiling himself in death or in fright, it was difficult to say with certainty what the man had been wearing. Skinner forced himself to look closely and identified black flannel trousers, once supported by a black leather belt, which had been severed by the disembowelling stroke. The shirt was of a heavyweight woollen check cloth, and had been worn over a thick undervest.

'No jacket or coat found?' he asked, then failed to see Martin's shake of his head as he spotted the briefcase under the body. 'Did the photographer get all this?' He directed the question over his shoulder.

'Yes, sir!' barked a thin man, anorak-clad and carrying a camera.

Gently, taking care to spill no more innards into the close, Skinner drew the case out from beneath the corpse.

It was hand-stitched, in brown leather. The initials 'MM' were embossed on the lid in what looked like gold leaf. There were combination locks on either side of the handle. Skinner tried them. They stayed firmly closed.

'Bugger!' he swore softly.

He leaned over the body again. The check shirt had two button-down chest pockets. He undid the flap on the left side, and withdrew a small black calf-skin wallet.

A wad of notes was wound around a central clip. Four plastic cards,

5

two of them Gold, were held in slots to the left, and to the right, under a plastic cover, was an identity card.

MR MICHAEL MORTIMER
Advocate

Advocates' Library	67 Westmoreland Street
Parliament House	Edinburgh
031-221 5706	031-227 3122

'Christ, that opens a thousand avenues of possibility,' said Skinner, showing the card to Martin. 'If this guy was a criminal advocate, and from memory, I think he was, we'll have to check on every dissatisfied customer he's ever had, and their relations. If anyone did that for revenge, he must have had a hell of a grudge.'

'Too right!' said Martin.

Skinner's eyes swung toward him. 'Is the doctor here?'

A slim figure heard the question and detached herself from a group further down the alley.

Skinner watched her approach. 'Surely to Christ,' he said heatedly to Martin, 'they could have sent one of the old lags to a thing like this!'

The woman heard him. 'Hold on just one minute, Skinner. I am a medical practitioner with scene of crime experience. Since not even you would doubt my qualifications, you must be saying that this is no job for a woman. That is sexist!'

But Dr Sarah Grace's soft smile was at odds with her combative speech. As she came to stand beside Skinner and Martin, she said, 'I just happen to be on call this month. There are no favours in this job. But just to restore your belief in the weakness of women, one of those little pools of sick down there is my breakfast!'

The duty police surgeon was young for the job, at twenty-nine. She was around five feet six inches tall, with auburn hair and dark hazel eyes, in which, Skinner thought as he looked at her, a man could easily drown. She was American. Normally she dressed with all the sophistication of a New Yorker, but in Advocates' Close, in the chill November drizzle, she wore denims and a wraparound parka.

Skinner returned her smile. 'Sorry, Doc, I stand chastised. Now, can you give me an estimate on time?'

'He's still fairly fresh. He was found at 5.30, and I'd guess from the indicators that he'd been dead around ninety minutes by then. It's a wonder that no one found him earlier. I mean he's just yards from the sidewalk.'

Skinner shuddered slightly. 'Just as well. One of my lads is in shock. Imagine some poor wee cleaner on her way to work tripping over a bit of Mr Mortimer!'

He led her away from the body. 'Can I have a formal report as soon as you can manage, please, Doctor?' Skinner smiled again at Sarah Grace. The creases around his eyes turned to laugh-lines, and for an instant the steely hair seemed to sparkle.

She returned his request with a grin and a drawl. 'Double quick, Skinner.' She stripped off her latex gloves, stuffed them into a disposal bag and thrust that deep into a pocket of her parka.

Skinner looked back towards the mouth of the Close. At the entrance, one or two early morning passers-by had stopped to stare. 'Andy,' he called across to Martin, 'get a screen up there, will you, and move those gawpers on. And let's have a cover over the body. It'll be light soon; some clever bastard with a camera would get a fortune for that picture!'

Two constables, without a direct order, stripped off their long overcoats and spread them over the separate parts of Mr Mortimer, pulling the garments together so that they formed a single cover. Two more, the tallest of the officers at the scene, stood shoulder to shoulder at the mouth of the Close. The two who were stationed at the foot of the alleyway moved round the corner and took up position at the head of the steps which led down to Cockburn Street.

'Right, that's better. Now you technicians get finished and let's gather up this poor mother's son for the mortuary.' He turned back to Martin. 'Andy. No weapon at the scene?' Again, Martin shook his blond head. 'No, I thought not. Ask Doctor Sarah for an opinion. Whatever it was, it was bloody sharp and handled by someone strong, and an expert at that. A mug would have put a foot in all that blood, but this boy – there's not a sign he was ever here apart from that thing over there.'

As Skinner nodded over his shoulder towards the body, his eye caught a dark figure running up the alley towards him. He was waving something, something which shone, even in the poor artificial light.

'Sir, sir, excuse me, sir.' It was one of the two constables from the foot of the close. His voice was of the Islands, light and lilting, contrasting with the harder Central Scotland tones of Skinner and Martin.

The boy, for he was no more, rushed up to them. He brandished something which looked like a short sword.

'This was stuck in a door at the foot of the Close, sir. It's one of those

7

big bayonets from the First World War. I know because my great-grand-father brought one back with him. It's a sort of a family treasure now.'

Skinner looked at the constable, who stood panting, like a dog await-ing a reward for the return of a stick. Martin shook his head and sighed, waiting for the thunder which he knew was about to crash around the young man.

But the Chief Superintendent spoke quietly. 'Son, how long have you been on the force?'

'Nine months, sir!' The face was still expectant.

'Nine months, eh. And in all that time, has no one told you that if you're at a murder scene, and you find something that might be – however slight the chance – a weapon, that you leave that thing exactly where it is and summon a senior officer? Has no one told you that?

'Don't you even watch bloody *Taggart*?'

The young man's face fell. He looked down at his big feet. 'Och, sir, I'm very sorry.'

Skinner smiled for the third time that morning. 'Okay, son. Let's just say that this is your first really dirty murder enquiry, and you got excited. You've just learned lesson one: Keep the head.' Christ, thought Skinner, as the words left his mouth; what a thing to say. For a second, laughter, as it sometimes can in terrible moments, almost burst out. But he checked himself in time.

'That's lesson one. Here's lesson two. If you ever again come rushing up to me waving a bloody great bayonet, I will take it off you and stick it right up your bottom-hole, sharp end first. Is that understood also?'

'Yes, sir!'

'Right, now that it is, show Mr Martin and me exactly where you found the thing. What's your name, by the way?'

'PC Iain MacVicar, sir.'

PC Iain led them round the corner and across to a small doorway. 'It was sticking in here, sir, as if someone had thrown it away.'

'Try to put it back.'

Like a uniformed King Arthur, the young man slid the brutal knife back into a deep groove in the dirty, weathered doorframe. It stayed in place.

'Okay, Iain,' said Skinner, 'that's fine. Now guard it with your life until the photographer has taken his picture and until the technicians come to take it away.'

As they walked back up the steep slope, Martin spoke. It was the first time since the arrival of his Chief that he had offered an opinion. The care which he took in weighing up a situation was a trait that Skinner admired in his young assistant. It was one of the secrets of efficient detection.

'You know, boss, that's a big brutal knife, all right, and it could have done the job, but anyone who did all that damage with just three swipes wasn't just lashing out. We're not just dealing with another nutter with a knife here, but with someone with real weapons skills.'

'Aye, but that doesn't stop him being a nutter as well!'

An hour later, after easing an account of the discovery of the body from WPC Ross, who had begun to react at last to the horror, Skinner led Martin out of the Close on to the High Street. It was 8.10 a.m., the sun had risen behind grey watery clouds, and the morning traffic was building up. Buses boomed past, their wheels roaring on the ancient cobbles.

Weatherproofed office workers bustled grimly through the drizzle. Some were heading for the Lothian Regional Council headquarters, a building so out of synchronicity with the rest of the historic street that most Edinburgh citizens try to forget that it is there. Others walked purposely towards the magnificently domed Head Office of the Bank of Scotland which overlooks Princes Street from its perch on the Mound, and is dominated in its turn by the mighty Castle, secure on its great rock.

'Come on, Andy. Let's go across and see if Roy Thornton's in yet.'

2

The Advocates' Library is situated in Parliament House, on the far side of the Great Hall, the finest public room in Scotland. It is barely 200 yards from the mouth of Advocates' Close.

Skinner and Martin walked the short distance, entering the Supreme Court buildings through the unmarked, anonymous, swing doors. They had almost passed the brightly-uniformed security men – known colloquially as the High Street Blues – when Martin stopped. 'Hold on a minute, boss.'

He stepped over to the reception desk where a registration book lay open. Names, locations in the building, times of arrival and times of departure ran in four parallel columns. He scanned backwards through the list of signatures.

'Here we are. Mortimer signed in at 9.11 p.m. and out at 4.02 a.m. Signed off for good about a minute later, I should think. I wonder what kept him working all night.'

'It's not all that unusual, Andy. The Library's open twenty-four hours a day for advocates' use, and these are busy people as a rule. The younger ones often live in small flats, and like to use this as an office as well as just a reading room.'

They walked across the Great Hall, beneath the magnificent hammer-beam roof, and past the stained glass window which reminds visitors that the Hall was, in centuries gone by, the home of Scotland's Parliament.

The clock stood at only 8.22 a.m., but Roy Thornton, the Faculty of Advocates' Officer and front-of-house manager, stood in his box at the Library entrance, resplendent in the formal uniform which was his working dress. It suited him. He had been, in an earlier career, Regimental Sergeant Major of the King's Own Scottish Borderers.

He was a dark, trim man, with a neatly clipped moustache, and a face which gave a hint of his fondness for malt whisky. He and Skinner knew each other well, and the big detective respected the ex-soldier as the

10

fountainhead of all knowledge about the head office of Scotland's law business.

Thornton smiled in greeting. 'Hello, Bob. Bit early for you, is it no'. Or have you not slept since that football team of yours was stuffed on Saturday!' Thornton laughed. Football rivalry was another link between them. Roy Thornton was a Heart of Midlothian fanatic, while Skinner retained a boyhood loyalty to Motherwell. Both were Premier Division sides, and on the previous Saturday, Hearts had beaten Motherwell in a close and controversial match in Edinburgh.

Skinner grunted. 'Had the ref locked up. He's up in the Sheriff Court at ten o'clock. Charges are daylight robbery, high treason, buggery and anything else that I can think of between now and then.'

Thornton rocked back on his heels as he laughed. 'So what brings you here, big fella. Looking to nobble an Advocate Depute?'

Skinner dropped the bantering tone. 'No, Roy, what brings me here is bloody murder, most foul. Know a boy called Mortimer, one of yours?'

The term 'boy' is used widely in Scotland to denote any male person who is above the age of consent, but younger than the speaker.

Thornton nodded, his smile vanishing. 'Young Mike? Aye, he's a good lad. Why, what's up?'

'About four and a half hours ago, someone separated young Mike from his head – and I mean that – across the road in Advocates' Close.'

The colour drained in an instant from Thornton's face. 'Sweet suffering Christ!'

Skinner gave him a few moments to absorb the news. 'Listen, Roy, say no to this if you have any sense, but if you could make a formal identification now it could save the next of kin a load of grief.'

'Sure, I'll do that.'

3

Ten minutes later, they re-entered the building. As they crossed the Great Hall, Thornton said to Skinner: 'In the army once, in Ireland, I had to clean up after an explosion, so I've seen things like that before. But it's part of the scene there.

'This is Edinburgh. This is a safe, kind place. What sort of a bastard is there in this city that would do a thing like that. A loony, surely.'

Skinner looked sideways at him. 'I hope so, Roy. Because if whoever chopped up your boy Mike is sane, it doesn't bear thinking about. Tell me what you know about Mortimer.'

There was little to tell. Mike Mortimer had been thirty-four years old, and had been at the Bar for four years, after five years in the Procurator Fiscal service in Glasgow and Stranraer. He had grown a successful criminal practice quickly, from scratch. He was unmarried, but was widely believed to be sleeping with Rachel Jameson, an advocate a year or two his junior, both in age and in service at the Bar.

In common with most advocates, his family background was non-legal. His father, Thornton recalled, worked in a factory in Clydebank.

'Nice people, his Mum and Dad. I remember them at Mike's Calling ceremony. They were so proud of him.' He shook his head slowly and sadly.

'Look, Bob, you'd better see the Dean.'

'Of course, Roy. But give me a second.' He turned to Martin. 'Andy, will you talk to the security guards. The night shift will be away by now. Find out who they are, get their addresses and have someone take statements.'

Martin nodded and recrossed the Hall.

Thornton left Skinner for a few moments. On his return, he motioned to the detective to follow him, and led the way through the long Library, past rows of desks under an up-lit, gold-painted ceiling, to a door halfway down on the left.

David Murray, QC, recently elected as Dean of the Faculty of Advocates following his predecessor's elevation to high judicial office, was a small, neat man, with a reserved but pleasant manner, and enormously shrewd eyes, set behind round spectacles. He was a member of one of the legal dynasties who once formed the major proportion of the Scots Bar. He was held in the utmost respect throughout the Faculty and beyond, and his election, although contested, had been welcomed universally. He was a man of stature in every respect other than the physical.

While Murray's practice was exclusively civil, he had enjoyed a spell in criminal prosecution as an Advocate Depute. During that time Skinner's evidence in a number of spectacular trials had helped him to maintain an undefeated record as Crown counsel. He greeted the detective warmly.

'Hello, Bob, how are things. Thornton tells me you want to see me. None of my troops been up to mischief, I hope.'

'David, I'm sorry to have to tell you this, but one of your people has been murdered. It happened just a few hours ago. He seems to have been on his way home from the Library when he was attacked in Advocates' Close.'

Murray stood bolt upright. 'Good God! Who?'

'A man named Michael Mortimer. Roy Thornton just confirmed our identification.'

'Oh no, surely not.' Murray ran a small hand through what was left of his hair. 'You said murder. Is that what it was, strictly speaking, or do you think it was a mugging gone wrong?'

'David, not even you would have accepted a culpable homicide plea on this one, believe me.' Skinner shuddered at the memory, still vivid in his thoughts. He realised, with a flash of certainty, that it would never leave him completely.

'Listen, I know it's early, but do you have a spot of something? I feel the need all of a sudden.'

The Dean's room was lined with books from floor to ceiling. Murray walked over to a shelf and removed a leather-bound volume with the title *Session Cases 1924* printed in gold on the spine. He reached into the darkness of the gap that it had left and produced a bottle of Glenmorangie. He removed a glass bearing the Faculty crest from a drawer in his octagonal desk, and uncorking the bottle, poured a stiff measure.

'Thanks, David.' Skinner slumped onto the battered leather couch beneath the tall south-facing window. Outside the day was bleaker than ever.

'Bad one, was it?' said Murray. 'I thought Thornton looked drawn when he came in just then.'

Skinner described the murder scene in detail. When he had finished he looked up. Without a word, the Dean, now ashen-faced, produced a second glass and poured a malt for himself. His hand shook as he did so.

Skinner watched him drain the glass. 'David, can you think of anyone with a professional grudge against this man? Had he lost a case? Could this be a disgruntled ex-client putting out a contract from Peterhead?'

Murray thought for a moment. 'I can't see that. The fact is that Mortimer was very good. He's still a junior, but he's led for the defence in one or two quite big cases, and given the Crown a good stuffing in the process. I can think of a couple of Glasgow villains who would be doing serious time right now, but for Mike Mortimer. But do you really think that the perpetrator knew him? At 4.00 a.m., down a close, wasn't this just a random madman?'

Skinner nodded. 'In all probability that's exactly what it was. But one thing bothers me. The animal got away without leaving a single pawprint behind him, yet he tossed away this huge bloody bayonet where we'd be sure to find it. Still, you're right. Chances are it's a nutter. I only hope that he doesn't get the taste for it!'

'Indeed, Bob, indeed!'

The big detective stood up, towering over Murray. He was six years younger than the Dean, but at that moment he felt much older.

'Look, David, can I have your permission to talk to Mortimer's clerk, and to check on past and current instructions? Just to cover all possibilities.'

'Of course. Carry on whenever you wish. In the meantime, I'd better put a notice up in a public place. All your people across the way will have drawn attention, as will the closure of the Close. Gossip spreads like flame here, so I'd better let the troops know the bad news as soon as possible.'

The two shook hands, and Skinner left the Library. He walked back across the street, to the mouth of the Close. A group of journalists and photographers had gathered. They crowded round him as he approached, thrusting tiny tape recorders under his nose. A television camera and hand-lamp were trained upon him.

'Any statement yet, Mr Skinner?'

'Any ID on the victim, Bob?'

He held up his hand to silence the clamour. No point in delaying, he thought. He had always been willing to talk to the media, and this had won him their respect and their trust. It had also brought him the highest public profile of any detective in Scotland.

'Okay, gentlemen . . . oh, yes, and okay, Joan . . .' he began, spotting the Scottish Television reporter beside her camera crew.

'At around 5.30 this morning, two police officers discovered the body of a man in Advocates' Close. It was quite obvious that he had met a violent death, and a murder investigation is now under way.

'The victim has been identified, but the name will be withheld until next of kin have been informed. Once that has been done I will make a further statement.'

Alan McQueen of the *Daily Record* was first with a question. 'Have you found a weapon, Bob?'

'We have found something near the scene which could well be the murder weapon. We are talking here about severe wounds caused by a sharp-edged weapon. That's all I can say for now. Thank you all.'

He turned away and was about to enter the Close, when McQueen put a hand lightly on his arm. 'Any more you can tell us off the record, Bob?'

Skinner stopped and turned back. As he did so all of the tape recorders were switched off and pocketed, the television hand-lamp was extinguished and the camera was lowered from its operator's shoulder.

He was silent for a few moments, as if choosing his words. Then he looked at McQueen directly. 'Without quoting anyone, you can say this: senior police officers are agreed that this is one of the most brutal killings they have ever seen.

'You can say, too, that police are anxious to speak to anyone who may have seen a person in the High Street, Cockburn Street, or Market Street area between say 3.30 a.m. and 4.30 a.m., with what might have been blood on his clothing. I don't want to alarm the public at this stage, but I want this bastard caught and bloody quick, so any help you can give me in putting that word about will be much appreciated.'

'Any hint on the victim?'

'Male, aged thirties, unmarried. We should have broken the news to his parents and his girlfriend within the hour, so check with me at ten-thirty. I'm going to set up an incident room in the old police office across the road.'

'Thanks, Bob.' 'Thanks, Mr Skinner.' The group broke up, the journalists rushing off to file copy and to prepare broadcast reports. Skinner knew that his disclosure of the brutality of the killing had provided an extra headline, but if there was a maniac at large it would do no harm to put the public on guard.

He pushed aside the tarpaulin sheet which had been raised as a screen over the mouth of the Close and stepped inside. David Pettigrew, the deputy Procurator Fiscal, as Scotland's public prosecutor is known, awaited his arrival. He was a burly man with a black beard which, even in the poor light, accentuated the greyness of his face. I've seen that pallor a few times today, Skinner thought.

'Mornin', Davie. I can tell by your face that you've had a look under that cover.'

'Holy Christ, Bob! Who'd have done that? Jack the Ripper?'

'Don't. He was never caught.'

Pettigrew shot him a lugubrious look. 'I see you've found the murder weapon. Any thoughts on who might have used it? Former client connections?'

'That's the obvious starting point, but David Murray says no. Apparently the lad left a string of happy villains behind him. According to his description of Mortimer's career the Glasgow Cosa Nostra would help us find whoever did this. And I might have to ask them because, apart from a bayonet which I know even now is not going to give up a single finger print, I do not have a single fucking clue!'

4

The news of the murder broke first on the 10.00 a.m. radio news bulletin on Forth RFM, Edinburgh's commercial music station. By that time, David Murray had posted a black-edged notice at the entrance to the Library, having first sought out Rachel Jameson, and having broken the news personally. By that time, too, CID officers in Clydebank had told Mike Mortimer's stunned father that his brilliant son was dead.

As he had promised the press, Skinner set up a command room in the former police station behind St Giles Cathedral, across the street from the murder scene. The building had been converted to a District Court two years earlier, but there was still adequate office space available.

There, he and Martin stood looking at their two items of evidence. The technicians, with unprecedented speed, had confirmed his guess that the bayonet was absolutely clean of fingerprints. There was no sign of blood or bone fragments, but halfway down the blade its long cutting edge was slightly notched.

Carefully Skinner picked it up.

'Andy, I want Professor Hutchison, the Big Daddy pathologist, to do the postmortem, and I want a yes or no from him on whether this was the weapon. He'll want to run a test, so find the biggest, ugliest polisman in Edinburgh and have him ready to try to go through the equivalent of a human neck with that thing in a single swipe.'

Martin grinned. 'I know just the bloke. There's a beast down at Gayfield that they send up to the station when the Glasgow football crowds arrive for a Hibs game. One look at him and they're like sheep.'

Skinner looked at the briefcase. 'It's a bugger about this combination. Six digits, three either side. This is a valuable piece of luggage, so I don't want to damage it. We don't have any safe-breakers in court today do we?'

'Sorry, we don't. I've checked.'

'Right, let's try some of the obvious ones. What was Mortimer's date of birth?'

Martin checked a folder: '4-6-60.'

'Let's try that.' Carefully, he set the digits in sequence, then tried the locks. They remained immobile. 'Let's reverse it.' He reset the combinations to 06 and 64, then pulled the square raised levers, simultaneously, away from the centre of the case. The catches clicked open. 'Gotcha.'

He opened the case and, carefully, lifted out the contents. Briefs for two criminal cases in the High Court in Glasgow, one an incest trial, the other arson. Witness statements, and notes on each side. A Marks and Spencer sandwich wrapper. A Mars bar, untouched. Two green Pentel pens.

'Not a lot here,' Martin spoke Skinner's thoughts.

'No, there isn't.' Skinner hesitated. 'But you know, Andy, there's just something about this that doesn't quite square away; something about this situation that raises one wee hair on the back of my neck. It's niggling away at me, and I'm buggered if I can figure out what it is.'

Martin knew the signs. The Big Man was a stickler for detail. If anything in a situation was out of line with what he considered to be normal, he would gnaw away at it forever. But nothing here seemed out of the ordinary.

'I've got to say, boss, that I can't see anything odd.'

'No, and if it's there, you usually do. Maybe I'm still just a bit sick over this one.

'All right, let's get this enquiry properly under way. I want all the taxi drivers covered. Everyone at the *Scotsman* who was either going off or beginning a shift at that time. All the office cleaning contractors. Railwaymen. Coppers, even. Talk to them all, and I'll deal with the overtime bills later. We've got the Queen here in two weeks, and I don't want our nutter still on the loose by then!'

18

5

It is one of the great truths of crime, that in the majority of murders, the victim is known to the killer. But an exhaustive search of Mortimer's circle of acquaintances, professional and social, produced not a trace of a lead. And without that personal connection, which in many cases is as direct as the husband sat drunk in the kitchen, while his strangled wife grows cold in the bedroom, any murder is enormously difficult to solve... unless the investigating team has an enormous slice of luck. And luck was in short supply that week in Edinburgh.

In forty-eight hours every one of Skinner's targets had been covered. None of them had produced a lead towards the identity of the 'Royal Mile Maniac', as the tabloids had labelled the killer.

During that period, Skinner directed operations from his command centre in the High Street, interrupted only by a three-hour visit to the High Court to give evidence in a drugs trial.

Three men had been kept under observation in Leith, and a consignment of heroin had been tracked from a Panamanian freighter to a ground-floor flat in Muirhouse. The police raid had been well-timed and wholly successful. The three men had been caught 'dirty' and their distribution ring had been broken up. Skinner had been irked, but not surprised by the 'not guilty' plea. The Scottish Bench was commendably severe on dealers, and the three knew that they could be going away for fifteen years.

So it was that Skinner came to be side-tracked from the Michael Mortimer murder enquiry, and cross-examined by Rachel Jameson for the defence. She was a tiny woman, barely more than five feet tall. Her advocate's horse-hair wig hid most of her blonde hair, which was swept back and tied in a pony tail. Under her black gown she was dressed in the style required by the Supreme Court of lady advocates, a dark straight skirt surmounted by a high-necked white blouse.

As the Advocate Depute finished his direct examination, she rose, bowed to Lord Auchinleck, the judge, and walked slowly towards Skinner.

'Your information came from an anonymous source, Chief Superintendent?'

'That is correct, Miss Jameson.'

She looked towards the fifteen men and women who faced the witness box. 'Might the jury be told his or her name?'

'Miss Jameson, I will not reveal that unless I am instructed so to do by the Bench.'

She looked towards the judge, who sat impassively in his wig and red robe.

'Convenient, Mr Skinner. Mr or Mrs Nobody tells you about a stash of heroin. You kick the door in, and lo and behold there it is. Mr Skinner do you trust your officers?'

'Implicitly.'

'So what would be your reaction to my clients' claim that these drugs were, as they say, "planted" by your detectives?'

'I would say that it was preposterous, and wholly untrue.'

'So defend your officers, Chief Superintendent. Name your informant.'

Skinner leaned forward in the witness box. He looked deep into Rachel Jameson's eyes and held her gaze. 'Counsel may be aware that I have come to this Court from a highly-publicised murder enquiry. Earlier this week I saw a person who had been brutally killed. If I do as you ask, I might well have to look at another. I don't want that. Do you?'

Rachel Jameson paled. She nodded to the Bench and sat down. Lord Auchinleck thanked Skinner and excused him. He left the Court feeling a twinge of sympathy for the defence advocate, but only a twinge. Each of them had clients to protect.

6

The telephone, held in a cradle screwed to a post at the head of Skinner's pine bed, rang at 6.00 a.m. He struggled out of sleep, cursing softly. The slim figure beside him rolled over, grumbling. His groping hand found the receiver. The caller was Andy Martin.

'I'm sorry to wake you, boss, but there's been another murder. Jackson's Close this time. Some bastard's set a wino on fire!'

'Aw, come on, Andy. Those poor sods are always dropping matches on their meths.'

'No' this one. He had a gallon of petrol poured over him and was set alight by a piece of paper thrown on to a trail four feet away. Look, I wouldn't have called you, but with the other one so close by, and so recent . . .'

'That's okay; you were right. I'm on my way in.'

Martin hesitated. 'Eh, boss, you wouldn't happen to know where the duty police doctor might be. I can't raise her on the phone at home.'

'Andy, don't push your luck.'

With a soft smile, he replaced the telephone in its holder. 'Come on, gal. It's you and me for the early shift again.'

Sarah Grace sat up in bed and tried to rub the sleep out of her eyes. 'Shit. Do you want to go first in the shower?'

'Who says we have to take turns?'

Sarah stripped off Bob's Rugby World Cup tee-shirt, which had been her night attire, and together they stepped into the shower cubicle in the *en suite* bathroom. He chose 'champagne' from the range of options, and turned the shower to full power.

Her eyes were squeezed tight shut as he soaped her breasts and belly. 'Is it a bad one, Bob?' she asked quietly.

'Not now, sweetheart. Things like that don't belong in here. I'll tell you on the road.'

Sarah stepped first out of the shower. She looked back at Robert

Skinner, Detective Chief Superintendent, as he kneaded shampoo through his hair. Her professional eye told her that he had the body of a man younger than his forty-three years. One hundred and ninety pounds was spread evenly over his lean frame. Good muscular definition, there, she thought, clinically. His hands were slender. This, when he was clothed, tended to mask his strength, which was maintained by regular work-outs in the small, well-equipped gym alongside the shower room. Fresh from sleep, fitness shone from the man. Only those creased eyes offered a hint of the pressures of his job.

Twisting the valve to turn off the shower, Bob took the towel which Sarah held out to him. As she rubbed her auburn hair, he smiled at her slim brown body, its colour accentuated by the white bikini marks. Sarah's parents lived in retirement in Florida. In October, she had visited them to break the news of the widowed policeman who had come bursting into her life seven months before.

Sarah had met Skinner in her first week as a part-time police surgeon, introductions effected over the body of a middle-aged man, stabbed to death by his only son in a squalid house in Newhaven. At first she had been in awe of the famous DCS Skinner. A hard man, she had heard from colleagues. Perform well and you were okay. Slip up, and you'd never forget it.

She had done well, and she knew it. Skinner had been polite, even complimentary. And, Sarah thought, to her great surprise, a bit tasty for a Detective Chief Superintendent.

When he had telephoned a week later to invite her to dinner, she had been astonished. But she had said yes, pausing only so that she did not sound too eager, yet answering, she thought afterwards, more quickly than she should have. 'I didn't even ask if he was single,' she said to herself, but then she recalled the story. Skinner, widowed at twenty-seven by a road accident, was married to the job.

He had taken her to Skippers, ostensibly a dockside pub, but in reality, Edinburgh's finest seafood restaurant. The meal was relaxed; Skinner was charming, suddenly younger than he appeared at work. Her preconceptions of the man had been obliterated from the moment she opened the door of her Stockbridge flat, as Skinner had arrived to collect her. The copper's overcoat had been nowhere in sight. Instead, he had stood there, tall, lean and shining, flowers in hand, dressed in calf-skin moccasins, tan slacks and a soft brown leather jacket, with the collar of a blue and white striped Dior shirt, worn open-necked, spread wide on the shoulders. His only jewellery was an eighteen-carat gold rope neck chain.

Over their first meal together, Skinner, skilled and subtle interrogator that he was, had found out almost all there was to know about Sarah.

She had been born in Buffalo, New York, to a prosperous forty-year-old lawyer and his twenty-eight-year-old teacher wife. She had been brought up in a fine house with a pool and educated at the finest schools and colleges, where she had always achieved good grades and had been an enthusiastic member of the tennis squads. She had graduated from medical school six years earlier and had shocked her parents by turning down the local internship which her father had arranged for her, through what he called the 'Buffalo Magic Circle', in favour of a job in the wildest hospital in the Bronx.

Her first experience of what she soon learned to call the 'real world' had changed her life. She had remained on the staff of the hospital after her initial contract was over, and had undertaken post-graduate studies of scene of crime work. She had given her time voluntarily to clinics offering free medical care to New York's thousands of poor families, mostly black or Hispanic.

She explained that her move to Scotland had been prompted not by job dissatisfaction, but by the break-up of her three-year relationship with, and six month engagement to, a very earnest young Wall Street fund manager.

'What happened?' Skinner asked.

'I just realised that having my pants bored off wasn't necessarily the best way.' She had answered him naturally, without thinking, then had realised what she had said. Her mouth had dropped open, she had gasped, flushed and then they both had laughed. To her surprise, she had noticed Skinner blush slightly.

Before the evening was over, Skinner had known the story of the twenty-nine years of Sarah Grace, all the way up to her decision to find out what the world outside New York State was like, beginning with Edinburgh. It was only after he had dropped her off at home, declining her offer of coffee, and unknown to him, maybe more, that Sarah had realised that she still knew little or nothing about him.

That had changed four days later, on a bright spring Saturday. As arranged, Bob had picked her up at 1.00 p.m. When he had made the date he had said something vague about a football match, Motherwell versus Rangers. Great! Sarah had thought; just what I want – a sports freak.

But instead of joining the flow of football traffic, he had headed eastwards out of Edinburgh towards the East Lothian coast. They had stopped in Gullane, pulling up outside a grey stone cottage, set in what looked like half an acre of ground. In recent years the house had been extended, to the rear and into the attic, to provide more living space. A big wooden hut stood in a corner of the garden.

On the drive out, he had talked about his life; his Glasgow up-bringing, his education at a modest fee-paying school, his decision to join the police force, taken out of a desire for an ordered life. Then his tale seemed to become one of growing loneliness, as he spoke of the illness and death of his father, a lawyer like Sarah's, of the more recent death of his mother, and finally, painfully, of the loss of his wife Myra sixteen years earlier in a car crash.

'It was just here,' he said. They were taking a long left-handed curve between the villages of Aberlady and Gullane. 'We had just moved out here. I had just made Detective Sergeant, and Myra was teaching. We were comfortable and very happy. She had this Hillman Imp. It hit a patch of black ice, then a tree. Broke her neck.

'So that was me left with two jobs in life – policeman and single parent.'

And when he had opened the door, there she had been. Alex, at nineteen. Bob Skinner's secret, the daughter he had brought up alone, in the country, shielded from the reality of his work. Since his first days in the Edinburgh police, Skinner had kept a barrier between his work and his home life. He had always been seen by his colleagues as a private man, with an inner driving force. Very few colleagues knew what that force was; even fewer had met Alex.

The girl was stunning. She was taller than Sarah, and as slim. Long dark hair fell in ordered confusion on to broad shoulders, framing a perfectly oval face, which was lit by huge, soft blue eyes.

'Hi,' Alex had said with a sudden smile, putting her at her ease with an outstretched hand. They had shaken, formally, and then the jumble of words which was Alex's trademark had come pouring out.

'You're really a doctor, then. And a New Yorker. That's great. Pops thinks that Glasgow is on the other side of the universe. I'm at university there, doing Law, did he tell you? My greatest threat to him is that when I graduate I'm going to join the Strathclyde Force and set up in opposition.'

'The hell you will!' Skinner had snorted in a John Wayne drawl. Sarah had realised just then that she had never seen a man look so alive.

And so by that introduction to Bob's other life, their relationship had been put on a formal footing. It had blossomed at once. Sarah had found out from Alex the things which Bob hadn't said, and which she could not ask. She had found out that since his wife's death he had never had

24

a long-term relationship. 'A few dates, that's all. You're the first girlfriend who's ever been in this house.'

Alex had returned to Glasgow that evening in her silver Metro, pleading study. And Sarah had come into Bob's bed without a word of it being said. He was big, but he was gentle, and when they made love for the first time, Sarah had felt him explode inside her with the force of a bursting dam as if the years of loneliness were flooding away. She had drifted out of her own mind for a time, on the crest of the deepest physical sensation she had ever known. And afterwards, when they had returned to the present, she had nibbled his ear and said: 'Now, that's the way I've always thought it should be.'

From that moment on, their relationship, new though it was, had fitted around them like a well-worn pair of good leather gloves, and soon it had seemed as if it had always been. As it had developed, they had discovered the bonuses. They both loved movies, and shared a secret enjoyment of TV soap operas. Their tastes in music were wide and complementary. They played squash well together, and Sarah's golf was competent enough for them to reach the quarter-finals of the Golf Club mixed foursomes. But best of all the plusses for Sarah had been the friendship she had developed with Alex. There was nothing step-parental in tone about it. Alex was a mature lady for her years, and they had become solid, steadfast adult friends.

Marriage was not discussed. Sarah, having been engaged once, painfully, had no desire to rush back into that state. And in any event, it had hardly seemed necessary.

Their relationship, as they had agreed early on, was never discussed at work. But equally they had agreed that they would make no elaborate attempts to hide it. Her years in New York City had taught Sarah the value of privacy, but she realised that Edinburgh was a village by comparison, where secrets guarded too jealously rarely kept safe for long. And Andy Martin was too good a detective and too close to Bob not to have happened early upon the truth.

He had soon begun to notice his boss disappear more often at lunchtime than was natural for him, and had noticed too the new air of relaxation which he wore at work. However, when he had stumbled on the secret it had been by accident, calling in at Gullane one Sunday morning, with his wind-surfer strapped to the roof of his car. It was 11.00 a.m. The boss never, ever, slept late.

'Hello, Andy,' the big tousled figure in the blue silk dressing gown had said as he opened the door. 'You'll have had your breakfast, then?'

25

And he had called into the kitchen. 'Come on out, love, it's the polis!'

So Andy had been admitted into the secret circle, and when the two had disappeared together in July heading for L'Escala on the Costa Brava, where Bob had a small apartment, he had said not one word to encourage the one or two who remarked on the coincidence of the Big Man and the Young Doctor being on holiday at the same time.

July was a fond memory, and on that dark November morning it was still summer for Skinner and Sarah Grace, even as they drove into Edinburgh on their grim business.

On the road, Skinner repeated Andy's message, to prepare her for what she would see. He could sense her shudder in the passenger seat beside him. Nevertheless when they arrived at the scene of the murder, she was all professionalism. She approached the black thing huddled in the doorway, despite a combination of nauseating smells of squalor, abuse, decay and destruction.

She gave Skinner a running commentary as she worked. 'Almost total immolation by fire of the front part of the body. It's definitely male, but God knows what the age might be. It's hard to tell, because of the reaction to fire, but the hands look as if they were heavily arthritic. If that's the case, it would have been difficult, if not impossible, for this poor lump to strike a match.'

Martin broke in, 'In any event, look at this.'

Skinner followed his pointing finger and saw a five-litre Duckham's oil can which stood against the damp wall of the close. It was still possible to see where the fire had been started and to follow its course to the corpse, across the scorched flagstones.

'No doubt about it, is there? Who found it?'

'Young couple in a passing car. She saw the flames. The bloke had a fire extinguisher in the car. He put it out, but the poor bugger was a cinder by then. No reported sightings, but there were fewer people about than usual on a Saturday morning. The punters must be saving up early for Christmas.'

Skinner nodded in agreement. 'We've got no reason to believe that there's a connection between this and the Mortimer affair, but two murders in two closes in the same week is a Hell of a big coincidence. In any case I don't want us to be accused of trying less hard for a wino than for an advocate, so let's repeat everything we've done so far in the first one.

'Let's go up to the High Street office. Come on, Doctor, I'll treat you to breakfast.' He handed Martin a five-pound note. 'Here, Andy, you're a detective. See if you can detect some bacon rolls and coffee on a Saturday morning.'

7

The Edinburgh media were less equipped to handle a murder story on a weekend morning. Nevertheless, Skinner knew that the tip-off machine would make it necessary for him to issue a short-notice statement. The journalists who turned out to High Street at 9.30 a.m. were a mixture of freelances and evening and Sunday paper writers. There was no sign of television, but the diligent Radio Forth was present.

Roger Quick of the *Evening News* asked the only question after Skinner's brief factual statement. It seemed that no one, certainly not the Scottish weekend public cared too much about an incinerated wino. 'When do you expect an identification, Mr Skinner?'

'Quite frankly, Roger, I don't know. Some of these poor people can't remember their own names, far less those of the people around them in the hostels.'

And that was how it turned out. The body was too badly burned to be identifiable, and without a photograph, or any distinguishing feature, it was impossible to conduct a productive enquiry among the city's alcoholic drop-outs. The hostel wardens agreed to check on absentees from their usual list of guests, but none were hopeful.

Thousands of questions were asked, but no leads uncovered. The charred corpse remained stubbornly anonymous over the weekend.

On Monday morning, Skinner anticipated press requests and called a news conference to report no progress in either case, and to renew his request for assistance from the general public.

Douglas Jackson of Radio Forth asked for an interview. 'Chief Superintendent, do you believe that there is any connection between last week's two Royal Mile killings?'

'There is no proof of that at all. But I've been a policeman for a long time, and I have learned to mistrust coincidences.'

A few minutes later, Skinner sat at his borrowed desk in the old High Street office, studying once more the papers in the two cases. Professor

Hutchison had worked hard over the weekend to complete his examinations of both bodies. His notes were extensive. 'Yes,' they read, 'it is possible that the bayonet found at the scene of the crime could have inflicted Mr Mortimer's injuries, if wielded by someone of sufficient strength and expertise. However there is no physical evidence to confirm this, no blood, bone, or tissue adhering to the blade.

'In the second case, this unfortunate man died from shock as a result of immolation. However his physical condition was so low that the least exertion might have killed him. Had the man been *compos mentis* at the time it is possible that he could have beaten out the flames. I should have thought it impossible to categorise the crime from the circumstances. One cannot rule out the possibility that this was a youthful prank which went terribly wrong.'

'Bollocks!' Skinner shouted to the empty room. 'The poor bastard was doused in high performance lead-free and set alight. Not much bloody room for error there.'

He looked at the two files. Where to go from here? One man on the threshold of an outstanding professional career, the other in the poorest state to which it was possible to decline in society. Each killed, savagely, in the same week, not three hundred yards apart. That was a link, if nothing else, and experience was shouting at him that there had to be others.

The telephone rang four times before it registered in his brain.

It was Martin. 'Boss, are you free? I've just been given a lab report, and you'll want to see it.'

Minutes later Skinner's face wore an expression of triumph as he finished reading the report. The bayonet which had been thought to be clean had in fact yielded three black woollen strands, wedged in the finger guard. And on the handle of the Duckham's can, of which the most recent contents had indeed been high-grade lead-free petrol, a wedge of black wool had been snagged. A series of tests of the samples had proved that they were identical, and had come from the same gloves.

'That's it, Andy. It is the same bloke. My God, what do we have here? Look at the two victims. Picked apparently at random in the same public street. This looks like a homicidal maniac with a taste for the dramatic, and we don't have a fucking clue as to who he is. I want the patrol strength trebled after dark in the High Street, right down the Royal Mile. That Royal Visit is getting nearer, and we've got a guy leaving stiffs on the Queen's doorstep.'

8

November is the drabbest month of the year in Edinburgh. There are no tourists, little money in the shops, restaurants and pubs, and, as a rule, bitter weather, fit to freeze the bronze balls off the Duke of Wellington's horse, rearing on its plinth in front of Register House. But as December draws near, and the parsimonious merchants and benevolent City Fathers dig into their pockets to illuminate the Christmas message, 'Spend, spend, spend', the old grey city sparkles into life.

Looking along the mound from the pavement opposite the Bank of Scotland's modest front door, PC Iain MacVicar, preparing for his first Christmas away from Stornoway, thought that the silver-lit tree on the slope in front of the Assembly Hall of the Church of Scotland was just about the brawest thing he had ever seen. It gave Edinburgh character, he thought, marked it out as a good Christian place after all. PC MacVicar was a Free Presbyterian by descent and upbringing, but his months in the city had shown him that there were other things in life than the grim island Sabbath, and colours other than dark blue.

Surely God can't take exception to that, thought PC Iain, gazing at the silver tree.

The single scream seemed so out of tune with the moment that he almost thought that it had been a product of his young imagination, or the voice of God rebuking sinful thoughts. But as his attention returned to the job in hand, he knew that it had been real enough, and that it had come from somewhere down below.

The News Steps, a long open stairway turning through ninety degrees, run from the Mound down to Market Street. They are steep, and those who are less than fit think not twice but several times at the foot before beginning to climb.

PC MacVicar's heart was in his mouth as he rushed to the head of the stairs, straining his eyes for movement in the orange-lit shadows below. It did not occur to him to think that there might be danger ahead, and even if it had, he would still have leapt headlong down the Steps. That was a woman's scream and he was a policeman.

Iain screamed himself when he saw what was lying at the foot of the stairs. The woman had been short and dumpy, in her middle years. She still clutched a straw shopping bag in her right hand. The fingers were twitching slightly as the last motor messages reached them as she lay on her back.

A big kitchen cleaver had silenced the scream. It was embedded in the woman's skull, from between her eyes to the top of her head. A woollen hat, split almost in two, had fallen away from the grey hair. There was, he observed, feeling ludicrously proud of his professional reaction, very little blood.

PC Iain found that as much as he wanted to, he could not move his gaze from that awful sight. And so he only heard the slight sound as the black figure leapt from the shadow on top of the fence behind him. And he only felt the wool of the hard, gloved hand across his mouth, drawing his head back, and the cold of the knife across his throat. Somewhere he may have imagined that he heard the gulls crying over a far-away harbour, but all he saw, as he slumped to his knees, were the pretty Christmas lights, away up in Princes Street, as they winked and went out, one by one.

9

This time Skinner was alone when Martin's call came through. The Detective Inspector had just been told himself of the double murder, but the sergeant who had telephoned had neglected, amazingly, to inform him that one of the victims was a policeman.

Sarah arrived at the scene after the two detectives. She had been contacted while seeing a cardiac emergency to Edinburgh Royal Infirmary, not far away. She parked her Fiat in Market Street and turned into the Steps. When she saw Skinner there was a strange glaze in his eyes, and she recognised the tears held back.

Then she saw the policeman's cap on the ground and her gaze swept past the terrible thing that had been the woman, to the ginger hair, innocent eyes and opened throat of young MacVicar. She looked at Bob and was in tears herself.

She put her head on his chest, sobbing. 'Why am I crying for him, when I didn't for the others?'

'If you weren't, I'd have something to worry about. It's always worst when it's someone you know, or can relate to. It doesn't happen often, but it happens.'

Skinner realised that he had enfolded her, quite naturally, in his arms, and that one or two of the uniformed officers were glancing furtively in their direction. Then, because life is hard, and because coppers have to be even harder, he broke the mood and became Chief Superintendent Skinner once more.

'Come on, Doctor, let's go to work.'

And Sarah did just that. Her first, quick examination told her that both the woman, an office cleaner on her way to work she guessed – correctly as it turned out – and MacVicar had been taken completely by surprise. The woman might have had time to cry out as her attacker appeared in front of her, but the blow had killed her instantly. There were no marks on MacVicar's body other than the throat wound, which had been caused

32

by a knife or a razor, indicating that he too had been taken completely unawares.

She looked up at Skinner. 'The way the wound is, I'd say that the man pulled his head back from behind and cut his throat.'

Skinner nodded. 'That's how it looks. There are no other marks that I can see, or any other signs of a struggle. The poor laddie can't have had a chance to defend himself at all.' He looked at Sarah, a glance of enquiry. 'Can we make any assumptions about this guy's height?'

'I'd say that he would have to have been as tall as MacVicar to have cut him at that angle. He needn't have been a Superman though. If he caught him completely unawares it would all have been over in a second.'

Skinner shook his head sadly. He looked round towards Martin. 'Andy, what was the boy's last reported position?'

'He radioed in from the top of the Mound, boss. Said it was all quiet and didn't the Christmas tree look nice.'

'Well, my guess,' said Skinner, 'is that he hears something, maybe the old lady gets a shout off, and charges down the News Steps. Being MacVicar, he doesn't think to call in first for assistance.

'Now from past performance we can assume that our pal – or does anyone want to tell me that it could be someone else – is pretty agile, quick enough to have got off his mark before a big, blundering bobby, whose feet he must have heard from a mile off, could have got anywhere near him.

'That says to me that he was looking for, or at least wasn't afraid to chance, a double act. As you said, Sarah, our poor lad barely knew what happened to him.'

He looked around the scene, and at the high fence behind which the bulk of the Festival Office building cast a dark shadow.

'He probably hid up there after he whacked the woman. Maybe he heard MacVicar up there on the Mound. Maybe she did scream, and he decided to hide until he could be sure that no one had heard. Whatever it was, MacVicar appears and he jumps down and does the boy in.'

Anger blazed in Skinner's eyes.

'If that's right, then we surely don't just have a random loony here. We've got someone who moves and kills like a professional. Maybe a martial arts freak who's seen one too many Kung-fu movies, who knows. But whatever he is, he's here, and he's leaving the proof all over the Royal Mile!'

As Skinner finished, the Chief Constable arrived, called to the scene by Martin. One of his men had been killed. He should be there.

'Good morning, Bob, Inspector.' He nodded and smiled courteously at Sarah. Skinner took the cue. 'Chief, may I introduce Dr Sarah Grace, the duty Police Surgeon. She's picked the wrong month to be on call!'

The Chief Constable bowed slightly and removed his heavy glove to shake hands.

The Chief turned to Skinner. 'A word in private please, Bob.'

The two men, one heavily uniformed, stepped out into Market Street. Skinner had never managed to feel the bond of comradeship with Chief Constable James Proud that he did with other senior officers. He had always put that down to the burden of the highest rank in the police force, and he had afforded the man every respect, insisting that those under his command do the same. But he knew that many of his colleagues disliked the Chief, taking the view that he had reached his office by a political rather than by an active route.

James Proud, known universally as 'Proud Jimmy', was three years short of the official retirement age. He had been in the job for sixteen years, and even his critics still marvelled, grudgingly, at the skill with which he had achieved it. Cynics said that he had been picked because he looked the part. For that he surely did. In his heavily braided uniform, Proud Jimmy represented authority. And with his crinkly silver hair, peering from the sides of his uniform cap, and his bright blue eyes, he spelled out reassurance to the public that they were in safe, sure, hands.

It had once been said by a critic that the Chief was the incarnation of PC Murdoch, one of the many great creations of the cartoonist and genius Dudley D. Watkins, whose comic strips were part of the Scottish culture. The wit had gone on: 'Bet if his father had been Lord Provost of Edinburgh, and a member of the New Club, PC Murdoch would have made Chief Constable too!'

But Skinner knew that there was far more to the man than that.

Proud the Provost's second son, with no head for figures and no desire to enter the family bakery, had joined the force on leaving Edinburgh Academy. He had pounded an upper-class beat in the New Town for four years, before becoming, at twenty-three, one of the force's youngest ever sergeants. He had risen steadily through the ranks and had become Chief Constable on the long-awaited retirement of the venerable worthy to whom his career development had been entrusted by his father long before. Once in the post, he had been a staunch public defender of the traditional values of law and order, and an advocate in private of his force's case for more money, against a local authority whose commitment was to spending on social workers to treat the effects of crime and indiscipline, rather than on policemen to cure the problems at source. Yet while his views had irked the councillors, they had not filtered through to his men, to many of whom he seemed a remote, austere figure.

Skinner was a traditionalist at heart. He was grateful for the added resources which Proud had won through his battles with the Police Committee, and he had more respect than most for his instincts as a policeman.

Once he had defended him in public against a critic within the force. 'There may be things that the man hasn't done in his career, but he's done all he can in the job to learn about them, and to understand the problems of the guys on the ground. And he's made a point of going alone, on foot in uniform into every one of the toughest places on his patch, places where I would think twice about going. He may not have the sharpest mind on the force, but he's bloody shrewd, and he's loyal to his men.'

Proud's least noticed virtue was the skill with which he spotted potential in his officers, and advanced them, if necessary, ahead of the normal police promotion timetable. He had first noticed Skinner sixteen years earlier, as a recently promoted Detective Sergeant, when Proud himself had just become Chief Constable. He had been impressed by the young man's intellect, judgement, and most of all by his devotion to the job. He had sensed the driving force which set him apart from his contemporaries. He had made discreet enquiries into his background, and had learned of his widowhood, and the task with which he had been left, of bringing up his young daughter. From that time on Skinner had been his unsuspecting protégé.

Proud had determined that he should become Head of CID at the first opportunity. When the time had come for Skinner's predecessor, old Alf Stein, to retire, the Chief's tentative suggestion had met with a ready endorsement, although Skinner was still a relatively newly promoted Detective Superintendent, with only two years seniority in the rank.

'If you want CID to be tight, efficient and effective, Jimmy, then you'll give the job to young Bob, no doubt about it.' Proud had been happy to have his own judgement backed up.

So Bob Skinner had been appointed Head of CID, and as Stein had predicted it had run like clockwork, maintaining the highest detection rate of any Scottish force, and achieving reductions, against the national trend, in the crime figures.

But it was a rattled Proud Jimmy who now took Skinner for a walk in Market Street. 'Bob, what's the score here? What have we got on our hands?'

'Look, Chief, let's get into my motor. I don't want the *Record* to snatch a picture of the two of us.'

Proud nodded and the two men climbed into Skinner's Granada. The Chief was white-faced. Skinner was sympathetic, understanding that viewing the remains of butchered people was out of his normal line of duty.

'On the face of it, Jimmy, we have what the Yanks like to call a serial killer. My lads prefer to call him a fucking loony. He's killed four times inside a week, in the same area, in different ways, with no apparent motive other than bloodlust.

'I won't try to kid you about our chances of catching this guy from the evidence that he's left behind him. At best they're bloody slim. All that we can do for now is make sure, as best we can that he can't do it again, and be ready to nab him the moment he gets careless. But so far all the luck has been on the bastard's side; luck, I'm afraid to say, matched with some highly developed killing skills.'

'What are we going to tell the public?'

'We're not going to lie to them. But at the same time we have to try to keep them calm. I was only a wee lad in Lanarkshire when Peter Manuel was on the loose, but one of my earliest memories is of the fear in the air at that time. You remember what Gary Player said about luck? "The harder I work, the luckier I get." That's all we've got to show the people. Hard work by the police. Every door in this part of town is being knocked. Everyone who lives here, and who works here is being interviewed, then if necessary interviewed again. I'll have men on the street all night and every night, and I'll let it be known that some will be armed. The pubs'll hate it but I'm going to ask the punters to stay away from this area in the late evening, for their own security and to make our job easier.'

'What if he does it somewhere else?'

'We'll spread our resources as wide as we can, and bugger the overtime, and we'll appeal for general public vigilance, but we'll concentrate our effort here.' He looked the grim-faced Proud straight in the eye. 'Between you and me, I've got a funny feeling about this whole business.'

'What do you mean?'

'I've seen a lot of bad bastards in my time, and more than a few mad ones as well. There's something about this guy that makes me feel that he's in a category of his own. Something, but I can't figure out what it is.'

36

Proud looked at him for a long silent moment. 'So what's the next step?'

'I'm going to call another press conference, a full-scale one, back at Fettes Avenue this morning. We've got to make the media work for us all the way on this one; if they turn on us we're in real trouble. I was going to chair it, but if you like, I'll defer to your rank.'

'No, Bob, you're Head of CID; you do it . . . unless you want me up front, that is.'

Skinner smiled for the first time that morning. Suddenly, when the chips were down, he felt closer to this man than ever before. 'No, Chief, you trusted me when you gave me this job. I won't drop you into this one!'

10

Skinner's press conference began at twelve noon precisely, in a large conference room in the police headquarters, a 1970s building in Fettes Avenue.

Skinner, with Andy Martin for company, sat at a brown formica-topped desk, facing the biggest media audience of his life. With the double murder, media interest in the sequence of killings had mushroomed from the few reporters who had covered the Mortimer death five days earlier.

There were four television crews in the room, four radio reporters, and journalists from every daily newspaper and news agency in Scotland.

He held nothing back. He listed the four murders, beginning with Mortimer, on through the nameless derelict, ending with that day's news, the killings of Mrs Mary Rafferty, a Scottish Office cleaner, and PC Iain MacVicar, from Stornoway, just twenty-two years old.

For the first time, he described the injuries to each victim, choosing his words with clinical care. He explained that certain forensic evidence had linked the first two killings, and that there was no doubt that all four were the work of the same man. Every avenue, he said, was being explored. Mortimer's client list had offered no indication that a jailed villain might have sought revenge. He did not believe that the killing of a policeman had been planned by the attacker. MacVicar had been simply unlucky.

He repeated his plea to the public for any information that might be relevant. And he ended with a solemn warning. 'Until this man is caught, the Royal Mile area is not a place to go after dark without good reason. Avoid it if you can, and if you must go there stick to the broad, well-lit streets.'

Questions flew at him. The first which he took was from an old friend, John Hunter, a veteran freelance. 'Mr Skinner,' John was suitably formal, although they were occasional golfing partners, 'are you consulting other forces in the course of your enquiries?'

'Yes, we are looking, with colleagues in other areas, throughout the

UK, at the possibility that this might be a serial killer.'

He caught a few puzzled looks around the room.

'Since Saturday's murder we have been seeking information from other forces, checking for groups of similarly brutal unsolved killings in other communities. We have been in touch also with Interpol, and with the FBI in Washington. One or two lines of enquiry have emerged, but I have to say that none of them look promising.

'There's something else to remember. It's one thing knowing that you have a serial killer on your patch. It's something else catching him. As soon as an obvious pattern emerges in one area, he usually moves on. That's why some have lasted so long in the States. Strings of forty or fifty murders have come to light, but rarely more than four or five in a single location.'

'So are you saying that if we have had a serial killer here, he may have run his course?'

'It's possible, John. But no one should make that sort of assumption. It could be fatal.'

Skinner looked around the room.

'Groups of unsolved murders aren't as uncommon as people think. Look at the Rippers. The first one was never caught, and the second went on for years. So did Neilsen. And look at Bible John.'

One or two of the old lags nodded. Bible John was a mystery man from the early Sixties in Glasgow, who had murdered a number of young women. Several witnesses had spoken of seeing victims with a young man whose most memorable feature had been a readiness to quote from the Bible, a trait which still makes a man stand out as an oddity in a Glasgow disco.

'You don't think there could be a connection here, Mr Skinner?' asked John Gemmell of the *Express*, ever keen for an angle.

'Do me a favour! If Bible John is still around, and I hope fervently that he is not, he'd be well over fifty by now. These killings are the work of someone who is agile and pretty strong. Another thing: Bible John's method was the same every time. This guy varies his methods.'

An English TV reporter, a newcomer to Skinner, raised a hand.

'Chief Superintendent, are you checking on recent releases from secure hospitals?'

'Yes, we have done that, and we're looking further back. But the fact is that when people are released from a secure mental hospital, they normally take time to readjust to society. They are cautious, and tend to stay indoors most of the time. An orgy of violence such as this is most likely to occur in the course of an escape. But even then, few escapees get more than a few miles. They put all their efforts into planning the breakout, then once they're on the outside, they realise that they haven't a clue what to do. I have the feeling that we are dealing here with a man who plans every step he takes.'

John Hunter again. 'Does that mean there could be a motive?'

'On the face of it, no. But if there is, we'll find it.'

There were several more questions of detail, on timing, about the murder weapons and about the backgrounds of the four victims. The press conference was dragging naturally to a halt, when William Glass, of the *Scotsman*, raised a hand. Skinner considered Glass to be arrogant and pompous. He also admitted to himself, grudgingly, that the man was a first-class investigative reporter.

'Chief Superintendent, with due deference to you, might one ask why the Chief Constable himself is not here, and why he has not been seen to have taken personal charge of such an important investigation?'

There was a shuffling of feet among the other journalists. John Hunter looked across angrily at his colleague.

For a time it looked as if Skinner would ignore the question. He glared at the man with the same look he had fixed on hundreds of suspects as they protested innocence, until Glass broke the eye-contact and looked away, flustered.

'Mr Glass.' A formal address by Skinner was his form of rebuke to the media and they all knew it. 'The Chief is in charge of this enquiry. I report to him as Head of CID. I am also answerable to the public. That's why I'm here talking to you when I could be out knocking doors with my lads.

'I have been the spokesman since the first murder. The Chief Constable feels that it is important that I continue in that role, as the man with the most detailed knowledge of the enquiries. That is the channel of communication which he wishes to maintain.' His voice rose and hardened. 'If you want to maintain it you will oblige me by ensuring that your questions are relevant and pertinent.'

Skinner looked around the room. 'Thank you, ladies and gentlemen; this conference is closed!'

As the door closed behind him, Skinner heard John Hunter begin to harangue Glass, to murmurs of approval from his colleagues. He knew that he should have kept his temper in check, but it had been a hard week.

He was still seething quietly when he reached the gym. Since his teens karate had been one of his favourite sports. He had maintained it on reaching high rank, partly as an example to his troops, but also because it compelled him to keep up a high standard of fitness. He changed into his whites, tied on his black belt, and went into the gym, to the club which he had helped to found.

The instructor was a newcomer. He was an army drill sergeant who had been sent along, at Skinner's request to try to improve standards. Skinner was prepared to stay in the background, his normal practice, and work on coaching beginners, but the soldier, with a trace of cockiness, singled him out.

'Shall we work out, sir? Let's show these people what it's all about.'

Skinner sighed and nodded. They exchanged bows and moved to the centre mat, surrounded by a group of around twenty policemen and women in white tunics. Skinner was aware, suddenly, for the first time ever, that he was the oldest person in the room.

The thought was still in his mind when the man kicked him painfully on the left calf.

'Just trying to get your mind on the job, sir.'

Cheeky bastard, thought Skinner. But he did not react. The cocky look grew in the man's eyes. Another flashing kick caught the tall detective on the right thigh.

'Still haven't got your attention, sir.'

Skinner feinted to his right, then pivoted on the ball of his left foot. His right toes, bunched, jabbed the inside of the soldier's thigh, with force. The foot swept up, the outside edge slamming into the testicles. The leg retracted, then swung up and round, until the foot slammed into the soldier's left temple. Clutching his groin, the sergeant collapsed in a crumpled heap.

'You're wrong, son,' said Skinner to the white-clad figure. 'I couldn't take my bloody eyes off you. Class dismissed!'

He took a quick shower and caught up with Andy Martin in his office. One of the detective constables in the class had beaten him there from the gym, carrying the news that the boss had kicked the shit out of the karate instructor.

Martin eyed him warily. 'You all right? Or are you still in your Bruce Lee mode?'

Skinner cocked an eyebrow at his assistant. 'Never better, Andy. Let's drink some lunch. Fancy a pint in the Monarch?'

They found a Panda car heading out on patrol. It dropped them outside a big grey pub which was situated on the edge of one of the city's worst crime spots, and which boasted one of the biggest beer sales in the East of Scotland. Skinner had no doubt that the two statistics were related.

When the two policemen entered the public bar, several patrons drank up fast and left by the nearest available exit.

'Thanks very much, Mr Skinner,' said Charlie, the manager. 'Not even the Salvation Army can clear this place quicker than you can. Thought you'd be up the High Street the day, anyway.'

'We won't catch anyone up there in the daylight, Charlie. And the way our luck's been, we wouldn't spot the bastard if he was running down the High Street waving a chainsaw.'

'Naw, youse'd probably jist think he was yin o' thon Labour cooncillors. By the way, ah wis sorry tae hear on the radio about the young polis.'

'Thanks, Charlie.'

Skinner ordered and, despite Charlie's protests, insisted on paying for two pints of McEwan's 80 shilling ale. He took a bite out of the thick, creamy head, and motioned Martin over to a table. The inspector could see that the unaccustomed black mood had gone.

'You know, Andy, all of a sudden I feel optimistic. Daft, isn't it. Not a clue, almost literally, yet there's a voice in here that's telling me we're going to catch this guy. There's still something there that I'm missing, but I'll get it. And when I do, I'll get him.

'I think that this man's too intelligent to be killing just for fun. There has to be something behind it. Let's assume that neither John Doe the Wino, or wee Mrs Rafferty, or even Mortimer had stumbled over the truth behind the Kennedy assassinations. So what else can it be?

'I'm going back to square one, with Mortimer. I'm going to see David Murray, and go through his professional life, trial by trial.'

Martin looked at his boss. Bob Skinner's success was founded on intellect and powers of analysis, two of the three secrets of successful detection. The third, Andy knew, was luck, and history showed that Big Bob made his own.

Skinner had been Martin's role model almost from the day he had joined the force. He had shocked his parents, both doctors, by turning his back on Chemical Engineering, his original career choice, after graduating twelve years earlier from Strathclyde University with an honours degree.

Instead he had joined the Edinburgh police force, having seen enough of Glasgow, and had been thrown on to one of the toughest beats in one of those areas of which the City Fathers do not boast to tourists. He had pounded the pavements for a year and a half, before being allowed the luxury of a Panda car.

Community policing for Andy had meant putting a cap on vandalism, breaking up drunken domestic disputes, sorting out youth gangs, keeping an iron hand on solvent abuse and looking out for the introduction of cannabis and harder drugs into his patch by the capital's many pushers.

He was well equipped for the job, physically and temperamentally. He stood a level six feet in his socks. He was broad and heavily muscled, although he dressed to hide the fact. His eyesight had just been good enough to meet entry requirements, but equally, had he not been an outstanding candidate for the force, it might have been bad enough to fail him.

He had joined the force's karate club at an early stage in his career, when he realised that shift work would mean an end to his hopes of playing rugby at a high level in Edinburgh, and of carrying on what had been a promising career as a flank forward with the West of Scotland club.

As a beginner in his new sport, he had been taken under the wing of Detective Chief Inspector Bob Skinner, and had progressed speedily through the grading structure.

The two men had hit it off from the start. Martin had heard all about Skinner's war on drugs in Edinburgh and about his outstanding arrest record. Talking to the Big Man – an occasionally awarded Scottish nickname which has as much to do with leadership as with size – had convinced Martin that CID was for him. And Skinner had recognised in the younger man a commitment to the job and the simple desire to catch the bad guys which marks out good detective officers.

Two years after joining the force, Martin had been transferred to CID, on Skinner's drugs squad. From that time on their careers had progressed in parallel. After a further two years, Martin had been promoted to Detective Sergeant, just at the time of Skinner's appointment as Head of CID. Five years later, Skinner had chosen him as his personal assistant, with the rank of Detective Inspector and the responsibility of liaison with the various units which made up the Criminal Investigation Department.

Close as they were, when Skinner changed the subject in the Monarch, Martin was astonished.

'Andy, can I ask you to do me a couple of favours. The first is to do with the CID dance this Christmas. Sarah and I think that it's time to come out of the closet, and so we're going together. The other is maybe more difficult. It's about that terrible all-night piss-up that the students have in Glasgow. Daft Friday, they call it. It's at the end of the first term.

'You remember I took Alex to the dance last year. Well she's determined to go again, and to go to this Daft Friday thing. The only thing is, she needs a partner for both. She's still a bit shy, so she asked me if I would ask you if you'd like to take her.'

43

Skinner ended, awkwardly. Martin was at a loss for a word.

Skinner misunderstood his silence. 'Look, Andy, forget it. She's only a lassie yet. It's not fair of me to put you on the spot.'

'Look, Bob, don't be daft. I'd be honoured. And by the way, lassie or not, Alex is closer to me in age than Sarah is to you!'

Skinner looked at him in surprise. He grinned, then muttered: 'Just you remember that poor wee broken soldier boy back at the Karate Club!'

11

Later that afternoon, four men sat in the Dean's room within the Advocates' Library; David Murray himself, Skinner, Martin and a second advocate, Peter Cowan, who held the elected post of Clerk of Faculty. Before each was a photocopied list summarising every criminal trial in which Michael Mortimer had led for the defence.

Cowan explained: 'I've prepared this report to help you gentlemen determine whether you should continue to explore the premise that Mike might have been killed by or at the behest of a dissatisfied client. I imagine that subsequent events make this possibility much less likely, but let us proceed anyway with our analysis.

'My findings bear out the Dean's view. Mike Mortimer was a very good criminal advocate. That's a matter of record, not just of opinion. Even those who were convicted, tended to receive below-average sentences. Here's a good example. A man convicted of a series of mortgage frauds: sentence three years. Now I happen to know that the Crown took a very hard line in that prosecution. Mortgage fraud isn't common, but it's easier to bring off than most people think, and they wanted an exemplary sentence.'

'I know,' said Skinner. 'My fraud guys investigated that one. It involved obtaining twelve houses through fraudulent mortgage applications, renting them, often to DSS cases, to service the mortgages, and eventually selling on at a profit. The building societies were screaming bloody murder.'

'Right,' said Cowan. 'So there's the Crown, with a unanimous conviction, having dropped heavy hints to the judge, one of the harder Senators, by the way, that ten to fifteen years might be about right, and Mike gets to his feet. Next thing the Advocate Depute knows, the accused is a simple soul who had no real criminal intent, a poor chap whose wish to put roofs over the heads of homeless young people just got out of hand. The fact that he was enjoying their sexual favours as part of the deal was never

45

led in evidence by the Crown. They didn't think they needed it. By the time Mike has finished, there are tears in the eyes of the hanging judge, and his client goes whistling off to Saughton with only a three-stretch.

'Here's another: Strathclyde Police round up a really nasty tally man, a loan shark of the worst kind. The charges include serious assault, extortion, you name it. But the police witnesses were a bit sloppy, and one or two of the victims were clearly a bit wide themselves. Mike goes on the attack, and his client goes back to Castlemilk a free man, on a Not Proven verdict, to his astonishment and joy.

'Then there's the Chinese job. A young Japanese student at Strathclyde University – the daughter of an industrialist, resident in this country – is found raped and strangled. Two Chinese waiters are arrested. One of them has the girl's knickers in his pocket. Mike and Rachel Jameson defend one each. They put up a lovely impeachment defence. First, they claim that the girl was into group sex, and produce three witnesses to that effect, one Chinese, two white. Then their clients allege that there was a third boy involved. Neither of the other two knows his name. They claim that the girl was a willing participant, that they left her behind with this bloke, and that he must have done it. Forensic evidence – semen samples and so on – confirms that there was a third person involved and the two lads are acquitted, fifteen – nil.

'I've been through the rest of Mortimer's court work. There is nothing else of any significance. One or two small-timers in jail for shorter terms than they expected, others free and happy, and absolutely no sign of anyone swearing vengeance.'

Skinner and Martin sat deep in thought. Murray looked frustrated.

'Thank you, Peter,' said the Dean. 'Faced with that, we are forced more and more to the conclusion that Mortimer just happened to be in the wrong place at the wrong time. Such a damn waste. I almost wish you had found a link.'

But Skinner's optimism had not dissipated. 'I agree, David, I can't see anything there either. Still, there is something. I know it, and I'll nail it, and I'll nail him. Can you find me transcripts of those three trials?'

12

As Skinner's meeting was taking place, his team had their first small stroke of luck. An early-shift railway worker, interviewed by uniformed police at the end of his day's work, produced the first possible sighting of the quarry.

'Aye, it would be a bit before six o'clock. Ah wis on ma way to that early mornin' roll shop in Cockburn Street for ma breakfast. Ah was walkin' over Waverley Bridge when this fella goes tearin' off doon Market Street as if he had jist landed a big treble, then heard that the bookie was packin' his suitcase.'

'Can you describe him?'

'Well it wis dark, ken, but he looked like wan o' they ninja fellas. He wis wearin' a black suit and some sort of black bunnet. Ah couldnae see his face.'

'What happened then?'

'Well, like ah say, he goes tearin' off doon Market Street. Then a car starts up, and this big white motor goes shootin' back up the hill.'

'Did you get the number?'

'Gie's a break, lads.'

'Didn't it occur to you, after two murders that something might have been up?'

'Naw, wi' the shifts ah work, ah see odd buggers a' the time. And onyway, ah'd had a few bevvies the night before. All ah could think about was two fried egg rolls, a mug o' tea and a fag.'

Skinner seized the statement when it was put before him in his High Street office. 'Bring him in. Now!'

An hour later, Arthur Murphy, consenting but complaining, found himself in the High Street facing Edinburgh's most famous copper.

'Right, Mr Murphy, I've read your statement, and I thank you for it. Maybe you can recall a few more things if you concentrate, and put your healthy eater's breakfast out of your mind. For example, was the

47

fellow carrying any sort of weapon?'

The man knitted his brows and thought hard for a minute or so. 'Well he'd this sort of sheath or holster thing at his back, and there could hiv been somethin' in that.'

'That's a good start. Now what about the car? What make was it?'

'God, a dinna' ken yin frae anither!'

'Well was it a Sierra?'

'Naw, it wisnae yin o' thon.'

'Vauxhall?'

'Naw, no that either. Ah tell, ye,' said Murphy with a sudden flash of inspiration, 'it could have been yin o' thon German motors, an Oddy, is that it? Or maybe it was yin o' thon Jap jobs.'

Skinner sighed inwardly. That was as much as they were going to get from the man, and even that might have been dredged from his imagination.

'Right, Mr Murphy, that's all. Thank you for coming in, you've been a great help. We'll arrange a lift home for you.'

'Eh, could yis jist take me back tae the pub where ye lifted me from?'

'Fine.'

Skinner shook his head as their first witness left the room.

'Doesn't take us much further, does it, Andy?'

Martin had slipped into the room at the beginning of Skinner's questioning of the bewildered Murphy.

'A wee bit, sir. We can tell the troops to look out for a white vehicle, possibly an Audi. And for a man in dark clothing. But of course the driver of the car wasn't necessarily our man.'

'He had to be. If that had been anyone else getting into his car, he'd have been face to face with our man, and then he'd have been a goner. Tonight, we double last night's strength, in the area from the Castle to Holyrood Palace. Everyone warned about the car. And I want a dozen armed men in the area. That includes you and me.'

13

Rachel Jameson arrived home at 6.45 p.m. She still ached from the loss of Mortimer, but she had decided against asking the Dean to grant her leave from practice. Instead, she had chosen work as her solace. In her line of business, that had meant acting for the defence in a nasty rape trial in the High Court in Glasgow.

The first day had been taken up by the empanelling of the jury, and the opening statements of counsel. The second, which had ended that afternoon at 4.25 p.m., had seen the alleged victim spend four and a half hours in the witness box.

Patrick McCann, Rachel's client, was a dark man in his late twenties. The rape of which he was accused was particularly brutal, with the victim having been mutilated after the attack.

The trial troubled Rachel; she knew with utter certainty that her client was guilty. The girl, who had been attacked in her own home, had known McCann by sight and reputation. The weapon had been found, with blood patches, consistent with the victim's group, on the handle, and with clear prints of the accused's thumb and two fingers.

All the forensic evidence backed up the Crown argument. To cap it all, the victim, who had been forced to have every kind of sex with her attacker, had described in detail a brown mole on the right side of the man's penis.

Rachel's advice to her client, endorsed by the instructing solicitor, had been quite clear. 'Plead guilty. If you go to trial you will be convicted, and the judge will probably give you a life sentence. Plead, save the woman the ordeal of a trial, and keep detailed evidence from the Bench, and I might, just might, be able to keep it down to about eight years.'

McCann had looked at her with the arrogant eyes of a psychopath. 'No way, miss. She was wantin' it all. The stuff with the knife she made up.'

Occasionally, an advocate will come across a client who is pure evil. Rachel recognised this in Patrick McCann. She knew that at fifteen, he

49

had knifed a schoolmate to death in a brawl which had followed McCann's attack on the boy's sixteen-year-old sister. She knew also that he was the chief suspect in two recent, and still unsolved, murders of drug users.

But an advocate does not have the option of shunning such a creature. Justice and the Faculty regulations demand that any person on a criminal charge should have the benefit of the best available defence. Rachel's performance in the Chinese trial had added to her reputation as a High Court pleader. Her clerk's recommendation that she should be given the McCann brief was sound and natural, and she was available.

All that day, as the Advocate Depute had extracted skilfully from the terrified victim, an account of the night that had changed her life, Rachel had looked on, hardening her heart against thoughts of sympathy. Occasionally, she had glanced across at her client. All the while that the woman stood in the witness box, McCann had kept his dark gaze fixed upon her. The victim's evidence in chief had ended with the day's session. Tomorrow Rachel would cross-examine.

Normally she would have been preparing her examination in her mind. Instead, as she soaked her neat little body in her pink bathtub, sipping occasionally from a gin-and-tonic on the cabinet by her head, Rachel wept softly.

Everything about the trial reminded her of Mike Mortimer, with whom she had made love in the same bathtub only a week before. It reminded her of his style of advocacy, direct, yet sympathetic, in difficult situations like the Chinese trial, where he had been as kind as possible to the parents of the victim, while fighting as hard as possible for his client.

She knew that in the cross-examination to come she would be unable to mix consideration with effectiveness. That poor woman was in for a hard time, just as hard as Lord Orlach, the trial judge, would allow.

And even as she planned her strategy for the next day, the secret fear which had been growing in her all afternoon came to the surface. The Crown's proof was strong, but like all rape trials, the issue hinged on the credibility of the woman in the witness box, and on the jury being left in no doubt that she had been violated.

That woman today was a lousy witness, thought Rachel. It was natural enough, but if she was scared under the kindly eye of the old judge, and under the protection of the Advocate Depute, how would she react when Rachel went on the offensive in cross-examination?

Suppose, just suppose, that she won a Not Guilty, or even just a Not Proven, the third option in Scotland's unique trinity of verdicts. The animal

McCann would be out on the street, to rape again undoubtedly, and in all probability, to kill.

It was a dilemma which all advocates know they may have to face. It was worst for women counsel in rape trials. But even as the tears for her lost Mike trickled down her face, Rachel had no doubt. She would go all out tomorrow. Justice demanded it. That was what the job was about.

As the bath water cooled, and as the ice melted in her gin-and-tonic, another worry, forgotten earlier gnawed its way through to the surface of Rachel's thoughts. It centred around that stony, impassive Japanese figure sat on the back row of the public benches.

'What the hell was he doing there?' Alone in her bathroom, she asked the question aloud, as if Mike was still there to answer.

14

The night's stake-out in the Royal Mile produced nothing, or almost nothing. At 4.15 a.m. an armed detective constable came within two seconds of opening fire on a black cross-bred Alsatian Labrador which had ignored three commands to stand still in a dark corner of Gladstone's Land.

At 5.45 a.m. a uniformed policeman, the giant found by Martin to test the cutting edge of the weapon in the Mortimer killing, snapped a powerful armlock on a dark-suited man in Campbell's Close, dislocating the man's elbow. Detective Sergeant Brian Mackie, a firearms specialist called in for the night patrol, was taken for treatment to Edinburgh Royal Infirmary's casualty department.

As he switched off his radio after standing his men down for the night, Skinner muttered to Martin, 'Keystone bloody coppers, that's us!'

They were wearier than their men. They had been on the move for more than twenty-four hours, having broken off only for a quick meal.

'You know, Andy,' said Skinner, trapping a butterfly prawn with his chopsticks, 'the police who investigated the original Ripper murders claimed afterwards that they sensed when he had stopped. They said that the evil went out of the air in Whitechapel. I've always thought that was a load of fanciful shite. I've never accepted the Ripper mystique. He was just another bad bastard who didn't get caught . . . Or maybe he did!'

Martin's eyebrows rose over tired eyes. 'Oh yes, who do you think did it then?'

Skinner smiled. 'The novelist in me has always reckoned that it was the Duke of Clarence, and that the whole thing was hushed up. The Home Office was very careless with a hell of a lot of files, mind.

'But like everyone else who hasn't seen those files, I haven't a clue. I'll tell you what I wish, though. I wish I had ten per cent of all the money that's been made by clever people writing books and making films about old Jack. If he'd been nicked, tried and topped, and had turned out to be just another run-of-the mill sadist with a taste for human kidneys, then a whole industry would never have been born. But going back to what I said earlier. I've got a funny feeling that we won't see this fella back here.'

Martin looked at him in surprise. 'What, are you saying that "the evil has gone from the air"?'

He shook his head grimly. 'No, it doesn't smell like that. This guy's evil, okay. But not the black cloak, horns and tail type. At the moment we're the ones with tails. The bugger's got us chasing them and somewhere, he's loving it and laughing at us.'

Martin did not bother to ask Skinner about the basis of his belief. He knew that his style was to drum information, logic and careful analysis into all of his troops. Then every so often, if they were stuck in a rut and going nowhere on an enquiry, he would project himself somehow into the mind of the villains, follow a hunch and break the deadlock.

'So what about the stake-out, boss? Do we give it a couple of nights and scale it down?'

Suddenly Skinner was vehement. 'No. We've got a public duty, Andy. We keep them up, full strength, armed men and all, and we maintain them at that level for at least a week, or until I'm proved wrong and we nab this bastard. But not you, Andy, not you. I've got something else in mind for you. I'll tell you tomorrow.'

And after their night on the streets, as they sat in the High Street Office nursing huge mugs of hot tea, Skinner kept his word.

'You know Alec Smith? He's handing in his papers. Retiring after the New Year. He's landed a job with one of the big private security firms as their head bummer in Scotland. A fancy salary and a Jag, to top up his pension. I want you to take his place as Head of Special Branch.

'Mind you, this isn't an order. You've got to be willing. It means a rigorous vetting by outside people, and maybe even a few questions you won't like, but you'll understand why they're necessary. If the process seems like an invasion of privacy, maybe the promotion will make up for that.'

Skinner paused and looked Martin in the eye. 'Well, do you want the job?'

Contrary to popular myth, there is no centrally controlled organisation called Special Branch, with tentacles all over the nation, run from a false-front office by a man called X or Y or even M. But within each police force there are certain detective officers whose duties are not connected with routine police work, or in the normal course of events with the investigation of crime. Special Branch officers are responsible on their own territory for the physical security of royal and political VIPs, adding manpower and local knowledge to the permanent protection staff.

Special Branch officers also maintain a discreet surveillance over terrorist suspects, potential agitators, crackpot revolutionaries and general troublemakers. Their criminal investigative functions extend to offences against the State, or involving the security of the Nation.

In these and in some other circumstances, they will link with that genuinely secret apparatus of State known euphemistically as the Security Service. However on a routine basis, Special Branch officers report to their Chief Constable and Head of CID.

Special Branch activities in the Edinburgh area were under the command of Chief Inspector Alec Smith, a man of renowned judgement and unflappability. Martin was well aware that if he succeeded the veteran he would become the youngest officer ever to hold that private post.

He voiced this thought to Skinner. 'Do you think I'm ready for it?'

'Of course I bloody do, or I wouldn't be offering it to you. Look, Andy, you've got it in you to be Chief Constable of this or of some other force. On the way to that you're going to succeed me as Head of CID some day.

'You take this number, Andy. You're ready for it, it's bloody interesting and it'll do you the world of good in career terms.'

'I'll miss working with you, Bob.' The decision is made, thought Skinner.

'Don't worry. You'll still be working with me. What you, even you, don't know, is the amount of contact I have with Alec Smith. He reports to me and so will you.'

'Doesn't he report to the Chief, too?'

'In theory yes, in practice not too much. There are some things that the gaffer doesn't need to know about, unless and until they're likely to go critical. For instance, if he knew all there was to know about some of the characters on the Police Committee, he'd never be able to look them in the eye.'

With that, Skinner looked Martin squarely in the eye. 'Right, Andy, so the answer's yes, is it?'

'Of course it is, boss, and thank you very much. When do the snoopers start on me?'

'They started on you two days ago, as soon as the Chief had approved the appointment. It seems that your bank manager has done as he was told and kept his mouth shut. As of tomorrow you start a hand-over with Alec Smith. The Royal Visit that's coming up should give you a good start.'

15

The Japanese man was there as Rachel Jameson rose to begin her cross-examination.

As usual, the tight wig sat awkwardly on her head. She bowed to the Bench, pulled her gown further up her shoulders and walked towards the woman. The witness was stout, with dyed red hair. She was wearing an imitation fur jacket over a tight sweater and skirt. She had teetered into the witness box on pink high-heeled shoes. Rachel thought that she had never seen an alleged rape victim dressed less appropriately. But she knew that the vivid red scar running down the left side of the woman's face was likely to command all of the jury's attention.

'Miss X, you are twenty-four; is that correct?'

'Aye, that's right.' There was a new, aggressive edge to the witness's tone. She sounds stronger today, thought Rachel. Must have popped an extra Valium.

'Were you a virgin before the alleged attack?'

Miss X reddened. 'Naw. Were you when you were twenty-four?'

It was Rachel's turn to flush. Christ, she thought, that'll have done her no good with the jury.

Severity stirred in the kindly Lord Orlach. 'The witness will answer questions, not ask them. Madam, you must accept that counsel is entitled to examine whether your sexual history has a bearing on this trial. Hers most certainly does not.'

'Thank you, my Lord.' Rachel turned back to face Miss X. 'When did you have your first sexual experience?'

'Ye mean the full thing?' Rachel nodded. 'When ah was thirteen, with a boy at the school.'

'And since that time, how many lovers have you had?'

'God knows! Naw, wait a minute. Ah've had . . .' she thought for several seconds ' . . . eight steady boyfriends, and maybe twenty or so one-offs. Ah cannae remember.'

'So you like sex?'

'No' that much, tae tell you the truth, but the fellas expect it.'

'Have you ever taken money for it?'

'No way!' The woman shouted her answer.

Rachel rebuked herself mentally.

'Right, let's accept that. Do you ever make the running, make the first sexual advances?'

'In Barlanark, are you kiddin'?' One or two spectators laughed. Lord Orlach threw the witness a frown.

'So you didn't give Mr McCann the come-on?'

'That pig! No way.'

'You knew him by sight, did you not?'

Miss X nodded.

'Isn't it the case that you once told him you fancied him?'

'Never. I knew him by sight, but I knew about him an' all, that he was dangerous.'

Rachel's tone hardened as she moved quickly on to wipe that last remark from the memory of the jury. 'Did you not invite him into your mother's home while she was out?'

'No ah did not. Ah telt that other fella, ah went across tae the Paki's for a video, and when ah got back he was in the hoose!'

'Miss X, we have heard your account of the alleged sexual attack. I won't ask you to repeat it. However you did give a remarkably detailed description of the part of my client's anatomy on which this case hinges. Do you always notice things like that?'

Miss X looked at her grimly, and said without humour: 'Only when they're forced on me.'

And so it went on, Rachel pressing, hammering away at the witness, weakening her resolve, going over and over the account of the attack. Finally she turned to the wounding.

'Miss X, I put it to you that your injuries were self-inflicted.'

'No.' The woman was quieter now, her voice smaller.

'Is it not the case that McCann made fun of your sexual offerings?'

'No, that's no' true.'

' . . . and that when he did, you attempted to stab him with a kitchen knife . . .' She picked up the weapon, and held it up for the jury to see. 'This knife, which, it has been admitted, belonged to your household?'

Miss X shook her head. Rachel's voice was firm, but she did not shout.

'Is it not the case that McCann disarmed you, that your face was cut in the struggle, and that he threw the knife away as he panicked and ran from your house?'

The woman was shaking. All of her abrasive chemical confidence was gone. 'No, it's no' true. He raped me, then he cut me, now he's trying to lie his way out.'

'Miss X, there is a liar in this courtroom. I suggest that your whole demeanour indicates that you have concocted a story out of a desire to revenge yourself on my client for your own failure to satisfy him sexually.'

Rachel sat down. McCann's alternative version of the attack was the only card in her hand. But she knew that she could not counter medical evidence still to come of bruising on the woman's throat and of vaginal damage. All that she could do was try to win a concession that this could have been the result of normal, if rough, intercourse. Still, the woman's initial cockiness under cross-examination might just have given the jury – which Rachel had ensured had men in an eleven-to-four majority – the inclination to look for a reasonable doubt acquittal. She had no intention of putting McCann in the witness-box. It was up to the Crown to prove its case. To allow the jury to see the arrogant, psychopathic accused crossing swords with the Advocate Depute could only help it do so.

On the 5.30 p.m. train from Queen Street to Edinburgh Waverley, and during her evening bath, she went over the day in her mind. The rest of the Crown case had been clear cut. Her major success had been in winning a concession from one or two expert medical witnesses that the sexual injuries were indicative of violent activity by one or both partners, but were not, of themselves, conclusive proof of rape.

'Tomorrow's the day, McCann,' she thought aloud, draining the last of her gin-and-tonic as the bath foam dispersed, 'and you're in with a chance, you bastard. A slim one, but a chance.'

16

Summing up in the trial of Patrick McCann took only ninety minutes in total. The jury retired at 11.32 a.m.

The Court waited in readiness for a verdict, until 1.00 p.m., when the jury was given lunch.

Rachel ate in the Court restaurant with the Advocate Depute and with Sam Burns, the instructing solicitor.

The AD had looked sure of his success when the jury retired, but Rachel noticed him grow more and more edgy as time wore on. Anything longer than forty minutes normally meant disagreement. In a case like this, anything more than an hour could be ominous for the prosecution.

Rachel was nervous too. Suddenly, success looked like a real possibility. Soon, the evil McCann might walk free through the front door of the Court, instead of being hustled through the side exit, handcuffed to prison officers. She began to experience, truly, for the first time in her career, that terrible divide between elation and guilt. This was not the same as the Chinese trial. Her client then, Shun Lee, had been a simpleton, who, she still believed, had played no part in the girl's murder.

Lunch over, the jury remained closeted in its room.

Finally, at 3.52 p.m., a bell rang, summoning participants and public to the Court. The jury was on its way back.

McCann was brought up from the cells. And the eleven men and four women, unanimously, declared him guilty of both charges.

Lord Orlach wasted no time. After McCann's previous convictions had been read out by the Clerk, the old judge told the prisoner that it was clear that he had to be removed from society once again, and for a long time. He sentenced him to life imprisonment for rape, with the recommendation 'to those whose task it will be to consider your eventual release', that he should serve at least fourteen years. He also sentenced him to six years' imprisonment on the wounding charge, to be served concurrently.

Rachel Jameson's last duty after the trial was to visit McCann in the cells, as he awaited transfer back to Barlinnie, this time as a convicted prisoner, a sex offender, a prison pariah.

The man who had sat so calmly through trial and sentence was now in a rage. He sat at a plain table, a burly prison officer at his side, and swore savagely at Rachel. 'So you were clever, eh. You said ah'd get life and you were fuckin' right. If you hadna held back on that hoor in the witness box, ah'd be out now! Ah tell you somethin', hen. Fourteen years won't be long enough for you. As soon as ah'm oot, you're finished. In fact you're fuckin' finished now!'

Rachel screamed as McCann lunged across the table. The big prison officer thumped him on the side of the head. McCann swayed to the side, then suddenly swung back toward the guard, who had been thrown off balance by his own blow, and butted him savagely between the eyes.

The man went down poleaxed, just as his colleague threw the door open. The newcomer had no time to react as he was seized and shoved backwards. His head cracked loudly against the wall.

Smiling now, McCann released the unconscious man, and turned towards Rachel. She had backed into a corner of the white-tiled room, cowering and mute with fear, unable to scream or even speak. Her handbag lay open on the table. McCann saw the wallet inside. He snatched it up, clawed £55 from the notes section, and emptied the change pocket, then threw it into the far corner of the room. He looked back towards her. His face was calm, the eyes shining, the familiar arrogance back. He smiled. 'I'll see you again, Miss Jameson.' He looked out of the room, left and right, and then he was gone.

Rachel stood frozen in her corner. She heard, but she could not react to the sudden commotion as McCann crashed through the exit door. She did not move for almost two minutes, until the prison officer nearer to her on the floor began to come round. She crossed the room towards the man. His nose was pouring blood and there was a deep vertical cut between his eyes.

A young police constable appeared in the doorway. 'Oh Christ,' he gasped, then turned and ran. Seconds later an alarm blared. Rachel looked along the corridor. The exit door lay ajar. The feet and legs of a third uniformed man were visible, sprawled like his colleagues. McCann was free and clear.

17

Policemen filled the corridor, and the room. A man in plain clothes led Rachel back into the interview room, where first aid was being administered to the two stricken prison officers. The big guard was on his feet, but the other showed no response. He was grey-faced.

'Get an ambulance, quick.' The plain-clothes man snapped out the order. 'What happened Miss Jameson?' At last Rachel recognised Detective Inspector Strang, the arresting officer in the McCann case. She told him the whole story of the escape. The first prison officer, still bleeding, added his account.

'He made a dive for the lady, sir. I was sure he was going to do her in. I whacked him, then next thing I knew my lights were out.'

'Sounds like he put on a show for you, you big clown. What the f . . . , sorry miss; what were you thinking about, staying in here alone with that man?'

Strang turned back to Rachel. 'McCann's a clever bastard. Don't read too much into that threat, Miss Jameson. He'll be heading away from you as fast as he can. How much money did he take?'

Rachel looked at her wallet. 'I'm not sure exactly; around sixty pounds, I think. No more, certainly. At least he's left me my rail ticket.'

'Better use it, then. Formal statements can wait; for now, just you get straight home. As I said, I'm sure you'll be okay, but I won't take any risks. I'll have two of our lads run you to Queen Street and put you on the train. Then, just to be sure, I'll get on to Edinburgh and make sure that they keep a watch on your house. They'll love me for that, with all the bother they've got, but let's just play safe.'

Two young, courteous, uniformed policemen drove Rachel to Queen Street rail station, off George Square. They parked the police car at the taxi rank and made to get out, but she stopped them.

'Thanks, boys, but I'd rather not be escorted on to the platform. The train should be in by now anyway.'

The policemen looked doubtful, but after a few seconds' discussion, the driver smiled at her.

'Okay, miss. But don't tell anyone. We were given strict orders, see.'

It was 5.20 p.m. The Queen Street to Waverley service runs on the half-hour at peak times. On occasion it falls behind time. There was no train waiting on platform six.

Rachel crossed the forecourt to the newsstand, and bought an *Evening Times*.

'JURY OUT IN RAPE TRIAL,' the front page banner headline blared at her. She saw her own face staring out from the page. Scottish law forbids the publication, until after the verdict, of a photograph of any accused person. The *Times* picture editor had obviously chosen the stock shot of the attractive little advocate as an alternative.

In the distance, Rachel could see the lights of an approaching train, gliding in slowly and quietly. She walked towards platform six.

She stopped after only a few yards, just past the big hydraulic buffers. As she glanced again at her *Times* and at the stop press, which, badly out of date, proclaimed, 'McCann jury still out', most of her fellow passengers rushed past her. No one noticed the little lady in the dark overcoat, from which a high, white-ruffled collar peeked.

It was the flash of that white collar, as much as anything, that caught the driver's eye. As he said later, it was winter, it was after dark and the station lighting was patchy. People were rushing, and he was concentrating on applying the final touch to the brakes, to stop the train just short of the buffers.

And in any event, even if he had seen Rachel earlier, falling in front of his train, he could have done nothing but try not to listen to the thump as the body went under the wheels.

18

Detective Sergeant Brian Mackie, Andy Martin's provisional replacement as Skinner's personal assistant, his arm still in a sling after his mishap two nights before, received the request from Inspector Strang of Strathclyde CID, that officers be assigned to protect Rachel Jameson.

Skinner grumbled, but ordered Mackie to arrange for two plainclothes officers, one of them a woman, to meet Miss Jameson from the 5.30 Glasgow train on its arrival at Waverley, and to take her home. He instructed also that a uniformed officer should be stationed at her front door until further notice.

'And make sure that she's advised to take a taxi whenever she goes out.'

Forty-five minutes later Mackie was back to tell him of Rachel's death.

Skinner had a perfectionist's hatred of shoddy work. 'They've had a great day in Glasgow, Brian, have they not. First they let a newly convicted man do a runner from the High Court itself. Then they ask us to protect a threatened woman and allow her to go under a train before they can hand her over!

'What the hell happened?'

Mackie looked at his note of Strang's second telephone call.

'Nobody seems to have seen very much, sir, not even the engine driver. There were a lot of people milling about at the time. But,' he paused, 'the Transport Police have a report of someone answering McCann's description running from the station just after the incident. And, according to Inspector Strang, McCann could have seen the rail ticket in her wallet when he stole that cash from her.

'Mind you, sir, Strang said they think it was probably suicide. With this threat coming on top of Mortimer's death, they think she probably jumped.'

Skinner shook his head. 'Brian, this is Strathclyde we're talking about.

Strathclyde CID could find a man nailed to a cross in the middle of Glasgow Green, with a crown of thorns on his head, and they'd still not rule out suicide. As for the Transport Polis, show them a picture of a dog and they'll start barking themselves. They heard that McCann was on the run; they'll have seen a dozen McCanns in that station before the day's out.

'Think about it; there's McCann, sent down for fourteen long years, then, thanks to the biggest stroke of luck he's ever had in his life, he finds himself on the street half an hour later, still in his civvy clothes, with sixty quid in his hand. The last place he's going to head for is a bloody railway station. He's stowed away on a cargo boat by now, or hidden himself in a container lorry heading south, probably one with Continental plates, trusting his luck to hold out so that they don't find him at sea and chuck him over the side, or that he isn't picked up by the customs at Hull or the Channel.'

But even while he scoffed at Strathclyde's suicide theory for Mackie's benefit, he admitted grudgingly to himself that there might be something in it.

The incident report which was telexed to Edinburgh seemed to back that up. Rachel had just lost a high-profile trial. She had been badly frightened by McCann. She had reacted badly, Strang had reported, to his suggestion of police protection and had insisted that her escort allow her to go to the train alone. And thought Skinner, she had just lost her boyfriend in the most gruesome way imaginable. The mental picture of Mortimer's mutilated remains was still with him when he read the preliminary medical report and saw, to his horror, that Rachel Jameson too had been decapitated.

One thing did seem certain from the report. This had been no accident. The engine driver's fleeting recollection, and the position of the body made it clear that the woman had not stumbled and fallen. She had travelled outwards from the platform with some momentum, either having been pushed, or, as Skinner finally conceded was likelier, having jumped.

But he hated coincidence. Two people, romantically and professionally linked, die violently within days of each other, murder certain in one case and in the other, a possibility. Yet if they were both murdered, where was the link? And if there was a link between them, what about the other three killings?

Skinner hung on tenaciously to the idea of a connection. A nagging feeling that he had missed something important in the Mortimer enquiry, remained with him. But reluctantly, his mind began to separate Rachel

Jameson's death from the others, expecting soon to see a witness statement confirming that she had jumped in front of the train.

He wrote, *Noted, RS.*' on the Strathclyde telex and tossed it into his filing tray.

19

Two days and two miserable, barren night watches later, Skinner attended the first of the funerals. Mike Mortimer was cremated at Old Kilpatrick, a bleak post-war funeral factory standing behind Clydebank, where staff struggle with a crowded timetable to allow families to bid a dignified farewell to their departed. Skinner hated crematoria, the speed of the service, the euphemism of the curtains closing over the coffin, the theatricality of it all. Once he had said to Alex that when the time came for him, he was to be planted, like his wife, in the old-fashioned way in Dirleton Cemetery.

Waiting outside the chapel in the cold clear winter sunshine, he cast his eyes around for a familiar face. David Murray stood, almost hidden, in the midst of a group of middle-aged and elderly men in Crombie overcoats, some wearing bowler hats. Among them Skinner recognised two judges, one of them Murray's predecessor as Dean. Peter Cowan stood slightly apart, wearing the black jacket, waistcoat and pin-striped trousers that are the advocate's trademark. Skinner caught his eye, and the two men ambled slowly towards each other.

'Morning, Bob. Is this part of the investigation?'

Skinner nodded. 'I'm afraid it is. Don't look in his direction, but I've got a photographer in that out-building over there, just on the off-chance that we pick up someone in the crowd who shouldn't be here.'

'Will you go to the other funerals?'

'Yes, we will. Even to poor old Joe the Wino's. Doubt if we'll see too many judges there!'

The Clerk of Faculty chuckled quietly. Still short of the years at the Bar necessary to take silk – to be appointed Queen's Counsel – he retained an irreverence not found as a rule in seniors, many of whom were en route for the Bench, and comported themselves with that in mind.

Quite suddenly Cowan's smile faded. 'That was an awful business about poor Rachel.'

'Yes, Peter. Just terrible. And preventable, if those buggers in Strathclyde had followed orders and seen her right on to the train, instead of allowing her to go under it.'

As the mourners from the previous funeral filed out of the chapel, and made their way towards the busy car-park, the Mortimer congregation moved forward to take their places. The cortège had arrived and was parked in the driveway, waiting for the moment to draw up to the door. A light-coloured wooden coffin, topped by a single wreath, lay in the hearse. Through the windows of the first limousine, Skinner saw a silver-haired man, and clutching his arm, a woman in black, her head on the man's shoulder.

The gathering stood around while the family mourners were shown into the building, and led to the front two rows facing the pulpit. Then quietly, they followed, shuffling into rows of hard wooden benches on either side of the central aisle.

As they sat down, Cowan whispered to Skinner. 'I gather that the verdict on Rachel will be suicide, not accidental.'

'There's no way that it was accidental, Peter. Since no one's come forward to say that she was shoved, that's the way it'll go down. That McCann sighting . . . You heard about that?' Cowan nodded. 'That was a load of cobblers. McCann was sighted for real last night, robbing a filling station in Luton. He pinched a car, and the Met. found it abandoned three hours later at Brent Cross. So he's in London. I believe they're releasing the story about now.

'All the indications are that the girl was a bag of nerves after Mortimer's death and after that threat. It probably wasn't planned, just a spur of the moment suicide.'

'Mm, sounds like it.'

The congregation rose slowly and solemnly to its feet as the coffin was borne to the altar on the shoulders of the undertaker's assistants.

As they resumed their seats, Cowan whispered again to Skinner. 'I was speaking to George Harcourt yesterday. He was the Advocate Depute in the McCann trial. He said that Rachel was very shaky before the jury came in with its verdict. Oh yes, and he told me a funny thing, too. He said that she was upset by a Japanese bloke who sat all the way through the trial.'

Skinner's eyes widened. 'You what . . . !'

'Brothers and sisters in Christ . . .' The Faculty chaplain cut the conversation short as he began the funeral service.

Fifteen minutes later as the family party filed out to a background of solemn organ music, Skinner was able to speak again. 'You said a Japanese bloke?'

Cowan nodded.

'Peter, have you got a car here?'

'No, I came with David.'

'Right, if you don't mind, you're coming back with me. I want to have another look at that so-called Chinese trial. I smell something here.'

20

Skinner rarely used a police driver. He believed that he thought better at the wheel. And so, on the way back to Edinburgh, cruising along the M8 at just under eighty miles per hour, he and Cowan exchanged few words.

Once the advocate broke a long silence. 'Look, Bob, you don't jump in front of a train just because you don't like someone's face in the public gallery.'

'Granted, Peter. But one of the few visible links between any of the people in this whole series of deaths is the Japanese involvement. Now you've brought it up again, I've got an itch, and I want to get back to Edinburgh to scratch it.'

The Library was busy when Skinner and Cowan returned to the capital city. More than a dozen advocates, some in casual clothes, sat working at the rows of desks set beneath the magnificent gold-painted, panelled ceiling. They went into the Clerk's office, alongside that of the Dean, and closed the door behind them.

Cowan dialled an internal number, and issued instructions to his secretary. Soon afterwards she appeared carrying two folders. Each contained a set of the papers in the Chinese trial.

They read through the notes and transcript in silence. Then Skinner went back to the beginning and listed the facts, point by point.

'The victim. Shirai Yobatu. She's twenty, and she's at Strathclyde University. She's found strangled in Kelvingrove Park. There are signs of sexual activity which could be rape. Forensic establishes that three men had intercourse with the girl immediately before her death.

'She was seen earlier from across the street in Park Circus, by another girl student. She was in the company of three oriental men. The girl recognises two of them as waiters in the Kwei Linn Chinese Restaurant off Sauchiehall Street. A lot of the students have eaten there and know the two lads. The witness doesn't know the other one. No one does. He's never been found and the other two wouldn't name him. It didn't occur to the witness that Shirai might not have been going willingly with them. She didn't look under duress.

'Christ, Peter, the Crown Office made a balls of this, and no mistake. If they'd left out the rape and just gone for a murder conviction they'd have got it no bother. As it was Mortimer and Jameson were able to take the rape charge apart, and to lull the jury into acquitting on both counts.'

Skinner went back to the notes. 'The accused: John Ho, defended by Mortimer; and Shun Lee, defended by Jameson. They deny the rape charge and it falls apart. They say they didn't know the third man. They claim that he had just started that day as a dishwasher at the Kwei Linn, and they didn't know his name. The owner says he only gave the guy a few hours' work, and he didn't know it either. He says that the boy was a deaf mute.

'The lads claim that they had a date for a threesome in the park with Shirai, who, they allege, is a student nymphomaniac likely to graduate with honours – there's absolutely no evidence of that; her flatmate said she was a quiet girl – and the third guy came along as a spectator. They say that Shirai fancied mystery man too, and that they went off in a huff, leaving her to get on with it.

'That evening they hear on Radio Clyde that a girl has been found strangled in the park. Mystery man doesn't show up to wash dishes, and John Ho and Shun Lee decide to do a runner. They separate and go home, but each one is lifted by Strathclyde CID in the act of packing his bags.

'Mike and Rachel plead panic. The guys are good witnesses; the jury believes them and they walk. So once again, we've got two very satisfied clients. Agree?'

Cowan nodded emphatically.

'But not everybody's going to be happy with that, are they? What more do we know about Shirai?' Skinner flicked through the papers before him and found a two-page document, the A4 sheets stapled together. 'This is the Strathclyde Police report on her background. Let's see what it says.'

Cowan found the same document in his sheaf of papers; each read quickly.

Skinner summarised aloud as he went along. 'Interesting. Comes from an above-average family background, even by Japanese standards. And interesting too, she's not an overseas student, as such.'

The shadow of a smile crept across his face.

'Her father and mother live in Balerno, of all places. He's forty-four, managing director of a Japanese pharmaceuticals company in Livingston.'

Cowan looked at him. 'So he could be a man with a grudge? Not a dissatisfied client, but the father of a victim. Is that what you think?'

Skinner shrugged his shoulders. 'It's the only lead I've got, so I'll have to follow it up. Tell you one thing, I'll be interested to learn what John Ho and Shun Lee are doing right now. And I can't wait to show a photograph of Yobatu *san* to your Advocate Depute pal Harcourt.'

Cowan held up a hand. 'Hold on Bob; you can link this man to Mike and Rachel through that trial, fair enough. But how can you connect him with the other three murders?'

'I'll worry about that later. This is the only bone I've got to gnaw on at the moment, and I'm going to give it a bloody good chew.'

Skinner closed his folder. 'Come with me when I pay a call on Harcourt, once I lay hands on that photo.'

21

Detective Sergeant Mackie had just returned from hospital, where his injured elbow had been pronounced sound, when Skinner buzzed from his office.

Mackie went through to the inner sanctum. 'Hello, sir. I didn't know you were back. Did our man put in an appearance at the funeral?'

'I won't know for sure till I've seen the photographs. That's the first thing I want you to chase up for me. These are the others.' He issued a series of clear concise orders. 'And I want them now!'

The funeral photographs arrived two hours later.

Skinner sifted carefully through the blown-up prints. Some of the people, he recognised, but most, he did not. However the most telling thing was that no one seemed to be out of place, or standing in isolation, other than, in one photograph, himself.

'Christ,' he muttered aloud. 'No one would ever know I was a copper from that! Not bloody much!'

Skinner scanned the prints again, to confirm his first impression. There were no oddfellows there. And no one in the gathering looked in the slightest oriental.

The photograph of Toshio Yobatu, Managing Director of Fu-Joki Blood Products plc, arrived half an hour later. Mackie brought it, having been handed the print in a brown envelope, in a pub behind the *Scotsman* office, by a photographer with whom he maintained a mutually beneficial acquaintance. Mackie had agreed that his friend's lack of curiosity about the reason for the request would earn an extra favour at some time in the future.

Skinner tore open the envelope and withdrew the photograph. He looked at it and caught his breath. Alongside him, Mackie gave a soft whistle.

The picture had been 'snatched' as Yobatu left the High Court in

71

Glasgow, following the acquittal of the two Chinese youths. It had been blown up until most of the features were fuzzy, but nothing could dim the ferocity of the eyes which blazed out at the two detectives.

Nothing could have been further from the image of the smiling Japanese businessman. Even in a bad photograph, Yobatu's ferocious gaze had an almost hypnotic effect. Not a hint of humour or compassion lay there, only a burning anger, accentuated by a tight mouth, which seemed to have been slashed across the man's face.

'Jesus, boss,' Mackie whispered, 'if this character had sat staring at me for three-and-a-half days in a High Court trial, I think I'd have jumped under a bloody train as well!'

22

Like many advocates, George Harcourt lived in the network of streets which stretches downhill and northward from Heriot Row, in grey and ordered simplicity.

'*Mr Harcourt. Advocate*,' the brass name-plate announced. However its portent of aloofness was not borne out by the man who answered the door to Skinner and Cowan, and who invited them into a book-lined drawing-room.

George Harcourt was a slightly rumpled Glaswegian, with a round head, set on a stocky frame. He had a voice which seemed to echo from the depths of a well, and which in court had the effect from the outset of his trials, of convincing juries that they were there on serious business.

Skinner had encountered him twice professionally; on the first occasion Harcourt had been acting for the defence, and on the second he had been prosecuting. He had been impressed by the man, in each role. A judge in the making, he had decided.

Harcourt poured each a Macallan, and offered them seats in red leather Chesterfield chairs.

Skinner took a sip from his glass. 'George, I'm going to ask you to look at a picture.' He drew Yobatu's photograph from its brown envelope and handed it to his host.

Harcourt looked at it and gave a start which in other circumstances would have seemed theatrical. Skinner did not doubt its sincerity for a moment. The stocky advocate looked towards Cowan.

'That's the guy, Peter. That's the guy I was telling you about. I'd know that face anywhere. That's the guy who sat through the McCann trial, staring at Rachel. If she'd asked me, I'd have had the judge throw him out. As it was, she never said a word, but I could tell that she was aware of him, and that she was rattled. And no wonder. Look at those eyes!'

23

When Skinner returned to his office, at just after 9.00 p.m., he found in his in-tray another telex from Strathclyde CID. It was marked, 'Urgent. FAO DCS.'

He picked it up, switched on his desk lamp and read quickly.

The report told him that at that moment, John Ho, one of the two accused in the Yobatu trial, was safely locked away in Peterhead Prison. While Mike Mortimer's excellent advocacy had seen him acquitted of the rape and murder charges, it had been unfortunate for Ho that when he was arrested following Shirai's murder, the police had found, hidden in his apartment, heroin with an estimated street value of £100,000.

The case had been tried a week after his acquittal of the murder. Ho, represented by a different advocate, since Mortimer's clerk had arranged, skilfully, for him to be elsewhere, had pleaded guilty. The judge had sentenced him to twelve years.

Shun Lee too was out of circulation: permanently.

In October, ten weeks after the murder acquittal, he had been found hacked to death outside his home in Garnethill. The killing was brutal, and fitted the pattern of a Triad assassination.

Shun Lee's murder was still unsolved, but an informant in the Chinese community had suggested to Strathclyde CID that he and John Ho had stolen the drugs found at Ho's flat, to sell for their own profit. According to the story, which Strathclyde believed to have the ring of truth, the Triad gangsters who had owned the heroin had been mightily put out. Shun Lee had been killed by a ritual execution squad recruited from London. It was said that a bounty of ten thousand pounds had been offered on the prison grapevine to anyone who would assassinate Ho in jail.

While there was no hard evidence to back up the informant's Triad story, it had been taken sufficiently seriously for John Ho to have been removed from the main prison and placed in solitary for his own safety.

Skinner buzzed the outer office. To his surprise, Mackie answered.

'Brian? I thought you'd gone home.'

'Not me, boss. Just nipped out for a fish supper. We're on stake-out tonight again, remember.'

'Could I forget? Look, since you're here, would you try to get hold of Willie Haggerty for me. He's the investigating officer in the Shun Lee killing.'

'What's that, boss?'

'Those two Chinese lads I asked you to check on – seems that one of them went to join his ancestors a wee while back; courtesy of the Triads, so they say. The other's in solitary in Peterhead, in case he's next on the list.

'I've read the report; now I'd like to hear the story from Haggerty.'

Five minutes later he was back on the line. 'I've got Detective Superintendent Haggerty now boss. He's off duty, but I told them it was urgent.'

'Thanks, Brian.' The line clicked. 'Willie? Bob Skinner. How are you? It's been a year or two. Superintendent now, eh.' Skinner and Haggerty had worked together in the past, on an inter-force investigation of a country-wide stolen car racket.

'Aye, it's going well for me, Mr Skinner. I see you're having a busy time though. Is that what this call's about?'

'Could be, Willie, it just could be. But it all depends on the strength of your Triad information in the Shun Lee business. Is it cast-iron?'

There was a pause at the other end of the line. 'If you want the official answer, it's yes; our information is believed to be accurate. If you want the Willie Haggerty view, it's a wee bit on the iffy side. Ever since that film – what was it called – *Year of the Dragon*, Triad gangs have been flavour of the month. A Chinese cook gets drunk and chops off a finger, and the gossip machine has it worked up to a Triad punishment.

'Okay. They do exist. There was an execution – if that's the word for it – a couple of years back, but most of the talk's just bullshit.

'Now my informant on the Shun Lee job – no names no pack drill, but he's a restaurant owner with a real Triad phobia – he hears about Ho gettin' caught with all that smack, then he heard about Shun Lee gettin' done not long after he was back on the street from his murder trial, and he comes to me with the word that the two of them were in the drugs thing together and that the hard men put them on a hit list.

'Maybe he's telling the truth, but there's another possibility, and one that I fancy, that Ho wasn't a wide-eyed innocent who took a chance and nicked some smack, but that he was part of a drugs operation all along, one that our Squad didn't know anything about. As for Shun Lee, well he was just a horny wee waiter!

'Those boys worked together, right. Well they didn't live the same way. Shun Lee stayed in a pit in Garnethill. John Ho was nicked in a nice wee flat in the Merchant City. The tips must have been good for him to afford that.

'Another thing. Shun Lee drove a clapped-out Mini van. John Ho drove one of those big Nissan shaggin' wagons. If Shun Lee was into drug money he must have been sending all of the profits home to feed his starving brothers and sisters.'

'Any chance of that?' Skinner asked.

'Not much. He was born in Drumchapel, and there's no' too many signs up there of a rich benefactor sending pound notes home to the poor folk!'

Skinner laughed. 'So your informant's tale, that Shun Lee was belted because he and Ho stole some candy from the big boys, is thrown into doubt because Ho could have been one of the big boys himself, and had the stuff on him as a matter of business.'

'That's the idea.'

'Has Ho said anything?'

'Not a dicky bird, and he won't. It's quite a cushy life being banged up in solitary in Peterhead, compared with the rest of the place. Especially when you're Chinese. There's some nasty racist people up there, and one or two who might just take a fancy to a nice wee yellow boy.

'What it comes down to is this. If the Haggerty notion is right, and Shun Lee wasn't into Ho's smack, then he was done for some other reason. But the Triads could still be the bookies' favourites, because there were similarities between Shun Lee's murder and the few Triad hits that are on record. Several people involved, and several weapons used.'

'You've no fingerprints, no footprints? No forensic leads?'

'Next to nothing. We've got a machete that was left stuck in the guy's collarbone. Other wounds include two different-shaped axe cuts, and knife punctures. Oh ay, and they cut his balls off.'

Skinner felt his scrotum tighten at the thought. 'Were they left at the scene?'

'No, they'll be in someone's trophy case somewhere. That happens in Triad hits, by the way. So what about it, Mr Skinner? Does that help?'

'It's possible. I've got to think this one through. Did you hear about that advocate going under the train in Queen Street?'

'The suicide? Aye.'

'She defended Shun Lee in his murder trial. Ho's advocate, Mortimer, he was the first one killed through here.'

'Jesus Christ!'

'Look, Willie, not a word about this for now. I'll pursue my lead through here, and obviously if I get anything that has any bearing on your enquiries, I'll be in touch. Sit tight till you hear from me.'

24

'No, Brian, we will not scale down the Royal Mile patrols, even though the Queen has gone. It's what, only ten days since the last murders, it's Friday night, and we don't have an arrest yet.' Mackie could see that his boss was adamant, and dropped the subject.

'But I am having a couple of nights off. Your arm's fine now. You can take charge on the streets.'

'With respect, sir, I'm only a detective sergeant, and this is a big operation.'

Skinner smiled. He picked up a sealed white envelope from his desk and handed it to Mackie.

'With respect, Brian, as of this moment you are promoted to Detective Inspector. That letter confirms it. Now I'm off to think about tackling Toshio Yobatu.'

It was 7.30 p.m. When he arrived at Stockbridge, Sarah was waiting for him, dressed casually, as usual. She was barefoot; a big, bright, loosely buttoned shirt hung down to her knees. She opened the door, grabbed him by the lapels, pulled him inside, and kissed him. 'Here,' said Skinner, gasping, 'does everyone who rings your doorbell get this treatment?'

'Only policemen and insurance salesmen.'

'Milkmen too low-caste for you, are they?' They kissed again, longer this time. Her body moulded with his; he felt himself stir as she rubbed her belly against him. 'Hey!' he murmured in weak protest. 'I told Andy to get there for about 8.30.'

'Alex'll be home by now. She'll look after him if we're late.'

Sarah looked at him, her hazel eyes filled with what he recognised by now as her bedroom look.

'You've had a hard week, Chief Superintendent. I can feel the tension in you. And that's not good for a man of your years. Lucky for you that Doctor Sarah is on hand with her amazing device for the relief of stress.'

She stepped back from him and wriggled her shoulders. The loosely-buttoned shirt slipped from her shoulders, and floated gently down to settle at her feet.

25

'So this is what they mean by being under the doctor!' Skinner murmured softly in Sarah's ear. She lay on him, stretching down his lean body, her legs wrapped around his. As she moved against him she was still smiling, but the look in her eyes had changed from anticipation to satisfaction.

'You know,' she whispered, 'there is absolutely no medical justification for the notion that men are sexually over the hill once they leave forty behind. And you are living proof of the opposite.'

'This isn't something that hard-bitten detectives are supposed to say.' She bit his shoulder, gently. ' – Ouch! – but I love you, Doctor!'

'That's as well, my man, because I couldn't live any more without your taste in music.'

On Sarah's CD player, Joe Cocker, set on repeat programme, sang 'We are the One', for the eighth, or it could have been the eleventh, time. The choice had been Bob's from a disc he had bought for her. One of the things that Sarah had discovered about her policeman lover was his remarkable talent for creating a mood.

Later, just after 9.00 p.m., as they drove down to Gullane, Bob slipped a cassette of Mendelssohn's Scottish Symphony into the tapedeck. 'Just to remind you where you are,' he said.

They drove mostly in silence; Sarah was almost asleep by the time they reached their destination, lulled by the richness of the music.

They were smiling and completely relaxed when they arrived at the cottage.

'And where the hell have you been?' said Alex, rising to her feet as the living room door opened. Then she looked at the pair, Bob's arm round Sarah's shoulder. 'On second thoughts, don't answer that. There are certain things a father should not discuss with his daughter.'

Andy Martin sat stiffly on, rather than in, a big recliner armchair, managing somehow to make it look uncomfortable.

'Sorry we're late, Andy,' Bob volunteered, still smiling. 'Traffic was murder tonight!

'Let's go. The chef will be getting anxious.'

Alex drove Bob's car on the ten-mile journey from Gullane to Haddington. They had reserved a table in a riverside restaurant. The proprietor wore a relieved smile as they entered.

'Sorry, Jim,' said Bob. 'This lot kept me back!'

The meal was superb. King scallop chowder was followed by three fillet steaks, with Alex opting for baked sea-trout. As Bob finished off the second bottle of Cousino Macul, Sarah was happy to note that the unwinding process was almost complete.

They talked of music and movies, or rugby and royalty, the light, amusing conversation of a close group on an evening out.

Just before midnight, Alex, who had restricted herself to mineral water, pulled the Granada to a halt outside the friendly, family-owned hotel in Gullane which Bob had adopted years before as his local pub. It was one of his special places, and one in which Sarah felt completely at ease.

They settled into a table in the broad bay window.

At the restaurant, Andy had insisted on paying for the meal. 'This is my celebration,' he had declared. In the bar, Bob countered, astonishing Mac, the laid-back barman, by ordering champagne.

'Christ, Bob, is it your birthday or something?'

'No, you bugger, at the prices you charge, it's yours!'

An hour later, with the car secured in the hotel park, the foursome walked home under a clear crisp winter sky. In the cottage, as Alex made up the bed in the guest room, Bob poured three glasses of Cockburn's Special Reserve port. As Andy accepted his nightcap, he looked hard at his host.

'Are you going to tell me, or not?'

Skinner smiled expansively. 'Tell you what?'

'You think you might have cracked it, don't you? You think you've nailed our man.'

The smile grew even wider.

'Well, since you've been vetted, I will tell you.

'Even as we sit here sipping this fine port, two of our colleagues are out in the cold watching a certain house on the outskirts of Edinburgh, the occupant of which has been under constant observation for the last few days.

'And once the Sheriff gives me the necessary warrant, as he will tomorrow – sorry, this morning – you and I, you for old times' sake, will

81

pay a call on the gentleman. There we will interview him in connection with the four Royal Mile murders, the murder of Rachel Jameson . . . '

'But that was a suicide, wasn't it?'

'Don't you bloody believe it . . . and the murder in Glasgow of a certain Shun Lee.'

'Who the hell is Shun Lee?'

'Before he was axed, stabbed and castrated, he was a Chinese waiter, and a client of Miss Rachel Jameson.'

The revelation hung in the air for almost a minute. But even through the Cousino Macul, the champagne and the port, Martin's mind was working. His face lit up in comprehension. 'Not a client with a grudge. A victim.'

He looked sidelong at Skinner, with a quizzical smile.

'The guy we're going to visit. He wouldn't be Japanese, would he?'

26

Skinner had decided to take Yobatu by surprise. There would be no preliminary visit, but a full scale raid and interrogation.

Sarah awoke at 10.00 a.m. to find herself alone in Bob's king-size pine bed. There was a note on the bedside table. Robert, she thought, your handwriting is bad enough for you to have made it big in medicine.

The message was brief but multi-purpose: '*Morning, love. Tell Andy for me I've gone to see the man about a warrant for our visit tomorrow. I'll be back for one o'clock. I've booked a starting time on No. 2. We tee off at 1:36. Tell Alex she's partnering Andy. Luv, B.*'

'That's great,' Sarah muttered, but with a smile on her lips. 'I've got either a migraine or a hangover, and he wants to play golf.'

Alex's head appeared round the bedroom door. Her big eyes were clear, and her hair was as tousled as ever. 'Hi, Sarah. You awake? I'm doing a fry-up.'

Sarah's head was clear and painless by the time Bob returned. The healing process had been helped by a brisk walk along Gullane beach, a great mile-long stretch of golden sand. The weather continued cold, crisp and bright, with a light breeze blowing from the north-west.

They drove off from the first tee of Gullane Golf club's number two course at 1.36 p.m. precisely, Bob and Andy hitting drives across a wind which was refreshing and just beginning to swing round from the north.

By the time that they holed out on the exposed twelfth green, the most distant part of any of the three fine links courses laid out on Gullane Hill, the blue sky had gone. The wind had risen and the clouds looked to be heavy with snow. As Alex sank the winning putt on the sloping eighteenth green, the first flakes were beginning to fall.

Later, Bob and Andy, each of whom had been forced by circumstances to become expert in the kitchen, prepared dinner. Alex offered to help but was banished by a wave of her father's hand.

'Just don't get too close to him, Andy,' she said as she left. 'Pops isn't exactly the handiest man around the house.' She pointed to a crockery shelf which hung at an odd angle on the wall. 'He's been promising to fix that for years. Don't stand underneath it. The lot could come down on you!'

The meal, when it came, was dominated by seafood. Langoustine bisque, cooked and frozen two months earlier, was followed by four thick salmon steaks baked with prawns and served with courgettes, baby corn and a tossed salad of iceberg lettuce, peppers, tomatoes and olives.

Instead of dessert, Bob produced a wheel of Stilton, and a bowl of black grapes on ice. He programmed the Amadeus recording of Haydn's 'Emperor' quartet on his CD player, and as the glorious strings swelled from the Cyrus speakers, he smiled around the table.

'You know,' he said, squeezing Sarah's hand, 'this is turning out to be the best weekend I've had for a long, long time. And if tomorrow goes the way I think it might, well it could, just about, top the lot.'

27

Sarah, Skinner and Martin left Gullane just after 10.00 a.m. next morning, Andy in his own car, each driving carefully through the newly fallen snow. The two policemen met up at Fettes Avenue, after Bob had dropped Sarah at her surgery, where she had left a pile of paperwork.

A twelve-strong team was assembled in the briefing room, awaiting instructions. Skinner strode to a table at the far end of the room. Martin took a seat in the corner nearest the door. The Chief Superintendent looked refreshed and very formidable.

He looked around the room. 'Good morning, gentlemen, lady. Today we are off to an unusual place for us, Balerno. Very up-market.

'We are not going up there to knock on a steel door with a big hammer, but we are going on serious business. This is the gentleman we are going to visit. Brian, please.'

Mackie handed each officer a print of the Yobatu photograph. One or two started as they looked at it.

'That is Mr Toshio Yobatu, a Japanese industrialist resident in this country. A very respectable type indeed, upper-crust in Japanese society. But at this moment, we are investigating six violent deaths, yes people, six, and this gentleman has a very respectable motive in three of them. So we have to talk to him. And because he's a prime suspect in these serious crimes, the nice Sheriff has furnished me with a warrant to enter and search his premises.

'We are looking for a number of specific items. One, a black balaclava, or similar headgear. Two, a pair of black woollen gloves, almost certainly purchased from Marks & Spencer. Three, a black tunic, possibly one-piece. Four, sharp weapons, including axes, knives and possibly a sword. Five, human remains. It's most unlikely that we will find these last items, and I won't describe them. Suffice it to say that one of the male victims had some important bits missing.

'Now, as I have said, this is serious business, and our reasons for calling upon Mr Yobatu are strong. But the evidence is not yet conclusive, and on the basis that Mr Yobatu may well be innocent, we don't want to embarrass him unnecessarily in front of the neighbours. So we will go in at 1.00 p.m., when most people will be at lunch. Given the weather today, the snow will be thick up there, and so I don't anticipate there being too much traffic about.

'Those of you in uniform will wear overcoats, and no caps. We will travel in unmarked vehicles. When we arrive at the scene, Chief Inspector Martin, Inspector Mackie and myself will enter the house and show Mr Yobatu our warrant. Inspector Mackie will then come outside and fetch you gentlemen, and you, Miss Rose. You will enter the premises quietly and will conduct the search efficiently and neatly, inconveniencing Mrs Yobatu and her children to the minimum extent possible. DC Rose will remain with the mother and children while Mr Martin and I interview Mr Yobatu.

'The search will be coordinated by Inspector Mackie. You will work in pairs in areas designated by him. Should you find anything that you think may be relevant to our enquiries, you will not shout out but will summon Mr Mackie and point out the object to him. Whatever it is, you will not touch it. He will make an assessment, and I will be summoned if necessary.

'That is the operation. Any questions?'

A fresh-faced uniformed officer in the second row of seats raised a hand. 'What if he's no' in, sir?' He smirked as he said it.

One or two members of the group choked off laughter. Mackie looked at the ceiling.

Skinner nodded. 'Thank you, constable. I take it that your present rank represents the height of your ambition in this force. I'll say this just once more. This is serious business, potentially the most serious any of you have ever been on. I will come down like a ton of soft shit on anyone who treats it in any other way, or who is in the slightest bit disrespectful to any member of the Yobatu family. Now, are there any sensible questions?'

Detective Constable Maggie Rose raised her hand. 'Sir, can I ask, whether Mr Yobatu has done anything while under observation to support the possibility of involvement in these crimes?'

Skinner's eyebrows rose slightly. He knew Maggie Rose slightly. She had three years' experience in CID, and her DI had marked her highly in her performance reviews. He made a mental note to consider her for the vacancy caused by Mackie's promotion.

'Thank you, Miss Rose. The answer is no. Since we put a team on him, Mr Yobatu has done nothing at all out of the ordinary. He goes to work, he goes home, and he doesn't go out till he leaves for work again. There's an expensive TV dish on his house. He may watch a lot of telly, I believe there's a Japanese satellite channel these days.'

Skinner looked around the room again. 'Right. Time for a coffee or whatever, people. Carriages at 12.15, prompt.'

28

Home for Toshio Yobatu was a large secluded villa in a cul-de-sac off the main road which headed out of the city towards Lanark. The two-storey house was faced in light-coloured sandstone. An arched entry porch jutted out between two broad picture windows. Four more, smaller, windows ranged across the width of the second floor, and a big dormer was set in the roof.

To the left of the house stood a double garage with its up-and-over door raised, revealing a white BMW 535i and a black Nissan Sunny Gti. The snow-covered drive curved past the garage to the front door. Facing the entrance, a flight of three steps led down to a lawn, fringed with shrubs and flower beds, which ran under its unbroken white mantle to a high privet hedge. The snow on the path leading up to the house was undisturbed.

The three senior officers sat in Skinner's Granada as it turned into the wide driveway, with a uniformed constable, hatless, at the wheel. The search squad, in two anonymous minibuses, remained at the entrance to the cul-de-sac, out of sight of the neighbouring houses.

'Very nice,' said Skinner, surveying the scene. 'I don't see many signs of Japanese influence, though.'

'It's quite a big house, boss,' Brian Mackie remarked. 'I'm glad we brought a dozen with us. Even at that it'll take a while.'

The driver pulled up in front of the open garage, and the three detectives crunched round the snowy path. They stepped into the porch, kicking the snow off their shoes as they did so and wiping them on a large doormat. A big brass knocker hung between two stained glass panels set into the upper part of the heavy wooden door. Looking for a bell, but seeing none, Skinner seized it and rapped loudly, twice.

After perhaps thirty seconds, the door was opened by a black-haired Japanese woman. She was, Skinner guessed, not much more than forty years old but had the air of someone much older, someone who had seen too many sorrows. She was dressed casually, in Western style, her slacks emphasising her height, over five feet six, and a close-fitting black sweater emphasising her slimness.

'Yes, gentlemen?' The accent was flat.

'Madame Yobatu?' Skinner asked. The woman nodded. 'We are police officers; we wish to speak with your husband. Is he at home?'

'Yes. What is wrong? Has something happened at the factory?'

'Please fetch him.'

'Of course. I am sorry. I am being rude. Please come in.'

They stepped into a wide hall. Rugs were strewn on a polished oak floor. Five glass-panelled doors led on to different parts of the spacious house. From the centre, a stairway rose. The woman left them, they heard voices, and a few seconds later she reappeared.

'Please enter.'

They stepped past her. Again, the room was furnished in Western style, with an oatmeal-coloured Wilton carpet, and a black leather suite of settee and two chairs ranged around a big stone fireplace, in which sweet-smelling logs burned. At the far end of the long room, two sliding glass doors stood apart, framing a tall broad man.

'Come in, gentlemen.'

Yobatu turned, and led the three policemen into a spacious glass conservatory, walled to a height of three feet. A door on the right of the room led out into a large garden, enclosed by high fir trees. Shrubs and heathers ranged around a central lily pond, its frozen surface covered with snow.

The peaceful setting was wholly at odds with the blazing eyes of the man who turned to face them, his back to a gold upholstered swivel chair.

Coolly, Skinner looked around the room, and saw, for the first time, a sign of Japanese influence. At the far, curving end of the conservatory, behind a leather-topped, two-pedestal desk and green captain's chair, a full set of samurai armour stood on a frame. A short sword was tucked into the sash which was tied around the waist.

Skinner returned his gaze to the waiting man. Formally, he introduced himself, Martin and Mackie.

Yobatu nodded his head briefly towards each in turn. Then he spoke, and in his voice, Skinner caught an unmistakeable edge of contempt not far beneath the veneer of courtesy.

'Gentlemen, what is it that brings three so senior policemen to my home on a Sunday? This is my day of rest; I would have thought it was yours also. So tell me, what has happened to my factory?'

'Yobatu *san*,' said Skinner. Mackie's head turned in surprise at the greeting. 'Nothing is wrong with your factory. We are here to speak with you about other matters.

'In recent weeks there have been a number of violent deaths in Glasgow and in Edinburgh. We have looked for a link between these crimes, and in our investigation certain facts have come to light which indicate that such a link may possibly exist through you. This evidence is sufficiently strong for the Sheriff to have agreed to provide us with a warrant to search these premises for certain items which may have a bearing on these crimes.'

Yobatu's eyes burned even more angrily. He drew himself stiffly to his full height. He was almost as tall as Skinner.

'But this cannot be!' he exclaimed, his voice not far below a shout.

'I am sorry, sir, but it is.' Skinner turned to Mackie and saw that Madame Yobatu was standing in the sliding doorway. 'Inspector, please call our people. Madame, where are your children?'

'They are in the playroom in the attic.'

'Perhaps you will go to them. I will send a woman officer to you. She will ensure that you are not disturbed.'

Mackie left the room, and the house. He trudged through the snow to the end of the drive. Stepping into the road, he waved to the team. Quickly the two minibuses drew into the drive.

The officers climbed out, and entered the house, wiping their shoes on the mat as they were ordered.

In the hallway, Mackie split the group into five teams. He sent DC Rose to join Madame Yobatu, with orders to search the playroom without fuss. Then he allocated an area of the house to each team.

The search began.

29

In the conservatory, Yobatu had recovered his composure. He was seated in the gold chair, faced by Skinner and Martin, side-by-side on a Chesterfield which matched the captain's chair behind the desk.

Skinner maintained the formality of his tone. 'Yobatu *san*, I am required to begin by advising you that you are not obliged to answer our questions . . .'

For the first time the flicker of a sardonic smile crossed the brown face. 'I know.'

' . . . but that should you choose so to do, any answers that you might give could be used against you.'

Yobatu did not react again; Skinner began his interrogation.

'Yobatu *san*, what were your feelings when the men accused of killing your daughter were acquitted?'

The man sat bolt upright in his chair, rocking it forward. 'I was outraged. Those boys were guilty. My daughter was a fine girl, a good girl. She did nothing wrong, and your courts denied me revenge on the animals who took her life.' Again the voice had risen. The savage eyes were incandescent.

'Sir, what would be your reaction if I told you that one of the two men who stood trial is now dead?'

'I would say that that was just. And I would add that it is a pity that it was only one.'

'And what would you say if I told you that the man was murdered?'

'I would say – justice!' Yobatu spat the word.

'So you would be even more pleased if I told you that the man was hacked to death with axes and knives. Killed like a dog.'

Yobatu's laugh startled both Skinner and Martin. The man clapped his hands, and the eyes twinkled with a terrible pleasure.

'Just so. Before he died he will have shared my daughter's pain and terror, and known what he had done, and why he was not fit to live.'

'Are you a swordsman, Yobatu *san*?'

Again the man stiffened in his chair. He nodded towards the armour. 'I am samurai, like all my ancestors. Of course I am a swordsman.'

Skinner rose from the Chesterfield and walked across to the display. He took the sword and scabbard from the sash.

'Is this your weapon?'

Yobatu nodded. Skinner drew the blade, laying the ornate scabbard on the desk. Holding it in his right hand, he picked up a sheet of note-paper with his left and drew it edge-first downwards over the blade. Like two leaves, the paper, split, fell to the floor.

'Has it always been kept so sharp?'

'To do otherwise would be to do it dishonour.'

Carefully, Skinner resheathed the sword and returned weapon and case to their place in the armour display. He turned again and looked at the desk. A single, framed photograph was positioned on the right of a brass inkstand. It showed Yobatu, his wife, and three children, the eldest a girl in her mid-teens. An ordinary, happy family photograph. Madame Yobatu looked beautiful, carefree and radiant. Her husband's eyes were crinkled with laughter.

Skinner returned to his seat.

'Before the terrible thing that happened to your daughter, Yobatu *san*, were you happy in this country?'

Even seated as he was, the man's shoulders seemed to droop. His voice fell. 'I came here by choice. I saw Great Britain as a good place to bring my family, so that they could learn of the wider world and escape the insularity from which our culture has always suffered. I came here, I embraced your ways, I tried to become as you. And then my daughter was taken from me in, as you say, a terrible way.

'But I believed what I was told about your justice. I believed the policemen who said to me that the men who did this thing would be punished. I was betrayed. The jury, all-white, saw a Japanese victim and two Chinese, our traditional enemies, in the dock. They were guilty, but the jury was indifferent. Because my daughter was Japanese.

'They believed the lies that were told about her. They listened to the tricks and deceits of the two lawyers. They chose to accept the fairy story of those two men. They seemed to overlook the fact that she had been murdered. If it had been a white girl who had been slaughtered by those Chinese pigs, do you believe that they would have been found innocent? Do you believe that for a single moment?'

Skinner accepted the challenge. He returned Yobatu's stare. 'In all honesty, sir, having studied the evidence I think it unlikely.'

The frankness of the admission seemed to take Yobatu by surprise. For the first time, his anger softened slightly.

'But are you saying, Yobatu *san*, that the advocates who defended John Ho and Shun Lee used your daughter's racial origins to secure their clients' acquittal?'

The anger in the eyes flared again. 'I am saying that they invented stories about my daughter. If they had suggested that a white girl of good family would go off with three Chinese boys, the jury would not have believed them for an instant. I am saying that the lawyers of my daughter's murderers conspired to deny me justice, and revenge for her death.'

'Yobatu *san*, where were you last Thursday?'

Skinner caught what could have been a flicker of comprehension in the eyes.

'I was in the Court in Glasgow, watching one of the people who cheated me trying to free another guilty beast.'

'How did the case end?'

'This time the victim was white. This time the jury did not believe the lies.'

'How did you return to Edinburgh?'

'By railway.'

With an effort, Skinner managed to conceal his surprise.

'By which train?'

'The 5.30, but it was delayed by an accident in the station.'

Now Skinner's eyes grew hard.

'Not an accident, Yobatu *san*. Not an accident. A woman was pushed in front of the train.'

'I did not hear that said.'

'Do you know who that woman was?'

Yobatu sat motionless and impassive for several seconds.

Eventually Skinner filled the silence in a hard-edged voice. 'I believe that you do. I believe that you know that she was the woman whom you had watched that day, and throughout the trial.

'And where were you on the night of November the seventh, and on the next night, and two nights after that?'

Yobatu sat silent as a statue.

'Where were you on the night that the other advocate in your daughter's trial was butchered – with a sword – and on those other nights when three other people were done savagely to death?'

Still the man sat, and silent, but the anger in his eyes seemed to be joined by something which, Skinner thought, resembled frustration.

'I will tell you how it looks to me, Yobatu *san*. It looks as if you were so thirsty for justice that you decided to administer your own. That you killed Shun Lee and made it look like a Chinese quarrel. That you killed Michael Mortimer, and then, in the same part of the city, you slaughtered three other people, at random, to make it all look like the work of a maniac. And, finally, that you killed Rachel Jameson, quickly, in a moment of opportunity, and made it appear like suicide.

'That is how it looks to me, Yobatu *san*. Perhaps to you it looked, and still looks like an honourable thing to do. Perhaps those three random victims, being Westerners, and one a policeman, you saw as sharing the guilt.

'I have sympathy for someone who has lost as you have. I have a daughter myself. If you killed Shun Lee, I will lock you away, but I will understand. But if you killed those five other people – three, simply to help you avoid detection – then I will lock you away as I would a dangerous animal, one with nothing in its heart but death. What do you say, Yobatu *san*? Are you such an animal?'

Yobatu sprang out of his chair. Skinner, who had been leaning forward, his right forearm on his knee, fixing the man with his glare, was on his feet in a flash. He stared into the eyes and saw something beyond comprehension, something that seemed to transcend fury. Martin was on his feet too, watching, waiting, as lightning seemed to flash between the two men.

Now the challenge was in Skinner's eyes, facing down the flame in Yobatu's.

And then the silence was broken.

'Excuse me, sir.' It was Brian Mackie, stiff and formal, but insistent. 'Would you come with me, please.'

The tension did not evaporate; it was too high for that. It simply eased a little, and Martin found to his relief that, after all, he was still able to breathe.

Skinner nodded. 'You too, please, Yobatu *san*,' he said, curtly this time. 'Andy.' He signalled Martin to bring up the rear.

Mackie led the way into the hall and out through the front door. They walked in single file towards the double garage, with its door still raised.

Even with two cars inside, there was still room for a wide workbench, with four drawers running along its length. The third of these was lying open.

'Nothing has been touched, sir,' said Mackie. Wearing a pair of cotton gloves, he slid the drawer from its runners and placed it carefully on the workbench.

To the front of what was now a wide shallow box, Skinner saw a jumble of twine and two tins without lids, each full of nails. To the rear, he saw two short-handled axes and a heavy hunting knife. Mackie withdrew each object in turn for inspection, held it up before Skinner, Yobatu and Martin, and replaced it carefully in its original position.

Along the back of the drawer was a black bundle, tied with string. Mackie withdrew it and released the slip knot. The bundle unrolled into a light-weight one-piece tunic, topped off by a balaclava-style hood. As it did so, a pair of black woollen gloves fell to the floor.

Again, Mackie held the objects up in turn for inspection. Again he replaced them, bundled and tied, in their original position.

And last, pushed into a corner of the drawer, they saw a small card-board box, the kind used to gift-wrap special confectionery. Skinner saw Mackie's hand tremble as he reached out to pick it up. For the first time, he noticed that his assistant was deathly pale.

Oh Christ, he thought, as the box was lifted from the drawer, knowing – without needing to see – what it contained. Mackie raised the lid and held it out towards them. And as Yobatu looked into the box, so Skinner looked at him. For the merest second he thought that he saw a flicker of confusion in the eyes. Then as quickly as it had come, it was gone, replaced by a look of terrible exultation.

Finally, Skinner forced himself to look, and as he did so, he became aware of the odour of decay, dissipated by time. Shun Lee; or at least the missing pieces. Martin turned away and retched. Still trembling, Mackie returned the box to its position in the drawer.

30

When Skinner spoke he was suddenly hoarse. 'Toshio Yobatu, I am arresting you in connection with the murder in Glasgow of one Shun Lee. You have already been advised of your right to remain silent. You will accompany Mr Martin and me to police headquarters at Fettes Avenue, to assist us with our enquiries into several incidents which we believe are related to this murder.

'Let's go, now. Mackie, complete the search and advise Madame Yobatu of what has happened.'

Without a word, Yobatu accompanied the two men to Skinner's car. He sat silent in the back, between them, as the capless constable drove back into the centre of Edinburgh. It was Sunday, and so they arrived unobserved.

Martin signed them in, with their prisoner.

'Sergeant,' he instructed the duty officer, 'take Mr Yobatu to the interview room. He is to be accompanied by two men at all times. And make sure they're big guys.'

He and Skinner went upstairs to the Chief Superintendent's office, where they collapsed into chairs.

'Good thinking down there, Andy. I don't want an escape, and I don't want any bloody *hara-kiri* either. This man has to be as dangerous an individual as we've ever seen, so make sure that the guys on guard duty are up to it.'

Suddenly Skinner sighed. 'Let's have a coffee, and wait for Brian to get back. Then he and I will get a statement out of the guy. You can get back to spycatching.'

Martin noticed a change in Skinner. With the adrenalin surge of the confrontation dissipated, he looked spent.

'Boss, I should be saying "well done", but instead I'm thinking, "what's up". You should be doing handsprings, but you're not. Don't tell me that bloke got to you.'

Skinner shrugged his shoulders. 'I don't know. It's just a bit of an anti-climax, I suppose. I was expecting some master criminal, and all we wind up with is some poor bastard who's been driven stark raving mad by his kid's murder. He is a loony, Andy. After all that, he's a loony. He just sat there and took it. No bluster, no denial, no nothing. I'll bet you he'll turn out to be unfit to plead.

'I didn't expect that. My famous instinct told me that if we found anyone at the end of the day, it wouldn't be someone like that. An evil sod, yes, but sane, and with some sort of a purpose. Well, I was wrong.' He shook his head. 'I shouldn't care. It's catching him that counts. But I feel let down. Maybe I wanted him to have a go, to have a physical confrontation with the dark beast. As it is, I just feel empty. We've got him bang to rights and I don't feel a thing.'

Martin leaned towards him and spoke gently. 'Bob, this has taken more out of you than you realise. If Sarah was here she'd say you were reacting naturally to extreme stress.'

Skinner looked at him and smiled. 'Sarah. Yes, I'll call her. Alex too. She'll be in Glasgow by now.'

31

When Mackie returned an hour later, Andy had gone. The newly promoted inspector told Skinner that nothing else had been found, other than the incriminating drawer.

Madame Yobatu had been stunned by her husband's arrest.

'Did she say anything when you told her?' Skinner asked.

'Nothing at all, boss. I told her that her husband had been arrested, and why. I told her about the weapons – not about the other, of course. She didn't say a word. Just nodded, and went back to her children. I offered to leave Maggie Rose there, and she agreed.'

'Okay, Brian, that's fine. I didn't really expect anything else. Right, I'll call Willie Haggerty now, in Strathclyde, and tell him to get his arse through here, pronto. Then you and I will go and take a statement from our man, and wrap this thing up.'

But Skinner's earlier assessment of Yobatu had been all too accurate.

The two detectives entered the drab, windowless interview room and signalled the uniformed guards to leave. Yobatu sat at a table in the middle of the room, his forearms on the surface, his head bowed. A mug of tarry black tea sat untouched before him.

The detectives sat down on two hard chairs opposite the man. Mackie slipped two cassettes into a tape-recorder on the table, and switched it to RECORD.

Skinner faced the microphone and spoke formally. 'I am Detective Chief Superintendent Robert Skinner, with Detective Inspector Brian Mackie. It is 5.30 p.m. on Sunday, November the twenty-fifth, and we are here to question Mr Toshio Yobatu, a Japanese citizen, in connection with the murders of Mr Michael Mortimer, of a person as yet unknown, of Mrs Mary Rafferty, and of Police Constable Iain MacVicar.

'Mr Yobatu is also being held in connection with the deaths in Glasgow of Mr Shun Lee, and Miss Rachel Jameson. Later, officers from Stathclyde CID will arrive to question him about these events.'

He repeated, for the tape, the formal caution given to Yobatu earlier in the day. Then he turned towards the figure opposite.

'Yobatu *san*, you were present today when we found, in your garage, certain items which could be linked to the events I have described. You admitted to me earlier that you were present at the scene of Miss Rachel Jameson's death, and that you held her and Mr Michael Mortimer responsible for a slur upon your late daughter's honour.

'You said also that you held Mr Shun Lee to be guilty of your daughter's murder, and that you were pleased that he had himself been killed. Do you now wish to make a full statement describing your part in these murders and explaining your reasons?'

Since they had entered the room, Yobatu had not moved a muscle. While Skinner spoke, and for several seconds afterwards, he sat with his head bowed, his gaze fixed on the space within the 'V' of his arms on the table.

Then, slowly, he raised his head. His eyes, unblinking, tracked across the table, but rose no higher than Skinner's chest.

The big detective looked into the man's face, and winced at what he saw.

The unforgettable fire that earlier had burned so fiercely was gone completely. The eyes were empty, devoid of expression, dead, and pitiful.

Speaking carefully, Skinner invited the man, for a second time, to make a statement.

There was no response. No movement. Not a flicker in those blank and awful eyes.

Skinner spoke again to the recorder. 'The subject has declined to answer. I am now instructing that he be medically examined. This interview is at an end.'

Mackie switched off the tape. He followed Skinner from the room and sent the two constables back in.

Skinner went back to his office and called Sarah again. 'Business this time, love. I'd like you to come up and take a look at Yobatu, to examine him physically, and then, if you agree that it's necessary, to call in a psychiatrist.'

'What are the symptoms?'

'He's withdrawn, gone away deep inside himself. He could be putting it on, but I don't think so. He looks as if the soul has left his body, if that's not too melodramatic a description for you.'

'I'll be right along.'

She arrived ten minutes later. Before taking her into the interview room, Skinner showed her the photograph of Yobatu, and described in detail their confrontation earlier in the day.

Yobatu did not resist as Sarah carried out a swift but thorough physical examination. Blood pressure, respiration, pulse and reflexes, all were normal, indeed better than average for a man in his forties.

During the examination Sarah asked Yobatu several questions. He responded to none and his expression remained fixed.

When she was finished, Sarah motioned Skinner outside.

'Physically he's fine. In some ways he's a marvel. But you'd better get the head specialists in here now. This man is definitely not open for business. All the time I was working on him he didn't blink once. He's in as deep a trance as I've ever seen. Maybe it's self-induced, but I doubt it. It's more likely to be an extreme reaction to the shock of discovery, after what he thought was the perfect revenge. You've handled a few psychopaths, you must know how volatile they can be.'

Skinner nodded. 'Yes, too true. Brian, call Kevin O'Malley at the Royal Edinburgh. Ask him to turn out, and to bring a trusted colleague. We'd better double up on this one.'

'Very good, boss. There's one other thing. The tip-off machine's been at work already. The desk has had calls from the *Scotsman* and the *Record*.'

'Bugger it! I'd hoped to avoid that for a few hours, at least. Some day I'm going to take the time to find out who that tip-off mechanic is and disconnect him, permanently.

'Deal with it this way. Don't put out a general statement, but say in answer to calls that a man is helping us with enquiries into recent incidents. Don't mention Glasgow. They'll ask if charges are imminent. You can say "no" with a clear conscience. We can't do that till we know he can understand us.

'We'd better tell the Fiscal too. Give him a call and get him, or the Depute, up here. And get Maggie Rose to ask Madame Yobatu who the family lawyer is. Chances are it'll be one of the big firms.

'Once you've got that sorted out, I'll give the Chief a call. It's time he was brought up to date.'

32

When Mackie returned to the outer office fifteen minutes later, Sarah was about to leave. As she closed Skinner's door behind her, Mackie could have sworn he heard her say: 'See you later then.'

He paused, then shook his head. 'Nah, I'm hearing things.'

'All done, sir,' he reported to Skinner. 'The answer's going to the *Scotsman* and *Record* through channels, and anyone else who comes on will get the same story.

'The shrinks are on their way. As far as Yobatu's lawyer's concerned, Maggie says that Madame doesn't want to involve him, but she's called the Japanese Ambassador instead.'

Skinner whistled. 'Has she indeed! We always knew this was a high-toned bastard. Now we know how high-toned. Right, now I can phone the Gaffer.'

Skinner interrupted the Proud family's evening meal. The Chief Constable's wife answered the telephone. All coppers were like sons to her, Skinner often thought.

'Hello, Bob, haven't seen you in long enough. You must be having a terrible time of it with all these murders and so on. Hold on. I'll get Jimmy.'

The Chief Constable was still chewing something when he took the telephone. Skinner allowed him time to finish. Might choke when he hears what I've got to tell him, he thought.

He explained what had happened over the past few days, told of the raid on Yobatu, and of the arrest.

Relief swept down the telephone line. 'Well done, Bob. Bloody good work. I'm happy for you, and for me, I don't mind saying. For a while there I could see the knighthood going out the window!' The man's frankness was one of his best qualities.

Skinner laughed with him. 'I hope you don't feel I should have told you earlier, but it might have been a wild goose chase. If I brought you in on every bum lead you'd never finish a meal.'

'That's fine by me. Where is the man now?'

'I've got him locked up at Fettes, Chief. But there's a problem. Maybe two.'

He told Proud of Yobatu's collapse, and of his wife's subsequent telephone call to the Japanese Ambassador.

'I see. When are the shrinks due?'

'Any minute now.'

'Well let's see what they say. Do you want me to come in?'

'No, better not. There's just a chance that the papers might have this place staked out. If you arrive on a Sunday night, they'll know it's something big.'

'Fair enough. Well look, keep me in touch. Do you think you'll get a confession tonight?'

'Not unless someone's come up with a miracle cure for catatonic withdrawal. This bugger's not kidding. There is nothing going on in his head . . . nothing at all.'

'What about the press side of it?'

'I'll play that by ear. I'm not issuing any further statement till I have something to say. If I feel that I need to have a press conference, I'll consult you first.'

'No, just do what you think best. But let me know if you hear from this Ambassador fella.'

'Okay, boss.'

Skinner had just replaced the receiver when Willie Haggerty arrived, with another detective. The two shook hands, and Haggerty introduced his colleague. 'This is Detective Sergeant David Bell.' The other man was much taller than Haggerty, taller even than Skinner.

'Where's our man then, Mr Skinner?' Haggerty was breezy and ebullient, typically Glaswegian.

'He's in a room of his own, with two big polismen, but for all he knows he could be on a South Sea island, or back in Japan in a rice-paper house.

'You see, Willie, our man Yobatu has gone quietly out of his tree.

'I'm just waiting for two eminent practitioners to arrive, to take a look inside his head. I'll be bloody surprised if they find anything, though. So I don't think you should see him right at this moment.' Skinner's face split into an untypically mischievous grin. 'I'll show you Shun Lee's nuts, though, if you like!'

The stocky detective grimaced, throwing up his hands in mock horror. 'Aw yous're all fuckin' heart and generosity through here in Edinburgh!'

When the laughter had subsided, Skinner told Haggerty, from the beginning, the story of the Yobatu connection, taking it through to the confrontation in the Balerno conservatory, to the discoveries in the garage, and to the abortive interview.

'Christ,' said Haggerty, 'it all fits, but it's all so bloody bizarre. He does Shun Lee, then Mortimer, then the girl. But along the way, after Mortimer, he does in three innocent punters here in Edinburgh, one of them a copper, to blind you to the link between those three murders. We think that the Triads did Shun, and that the girl was a jumper. You're supposed to think that Burke and fuckin' Hare are back in business.'

'That's how it looks, Willie.'

'Jesus, it would chill you to the fuckin' marrow, would it no'? And you didnae even know he was at Queen Street till he told you?'

'No we did not. I don't know how I kept a straight face when he came out with that one.'

As Haggerty shook his head in wonderment, there was a quick soft knock on the door. Mackie stepped into the room.

'Two things, sir.' Things often came in pairs with Mackie, Skinner had noticed. 'One, Mr O'Malley and the other nutcracker have arrived. Two, Mr Martin's on the phone.'

33

Andy and Joanne, his lady of the past six months, had just settled into their table in the plush, red-upholstered Asian restaurant in Frederick Street, when Andy bleeped.

'Pardon me?' said Joanne.

'Sorry,' he said, his blond hair emphasising his sudden blush. 'It's this new job. I've got to carry one of these pager things with me everywhere.'

'Everywhere?'

'Everywhere!' He reached behind his back. Clipped into his belt was a box smaller than a cigarette packet. 'Can't be out of touch, you see, in case the balloon goes up, or whatever. Alec Smith is still in post, officially, but the first thing the sod did in our handover was to give me this gizmo here.' The little box bleeped again. 'Okay, I'm coming!'

Martin looked at the small screen. His expression grew serious. 'You're back at work,' said Joanne accusingly.

'Look, I'm sorry, but I'm going to have to make a phone call. Not from here, but from the car. Will you excuse me for five minutes?'

'Once more, Andy, just once more!'

'Thanks. Sorry. Back soon.' He rushed out of the restaurant and across the street to his car.

The message on his pager told him to call a London 071-number. Martin had a photographic memory for such details and he recognised it as one of a series which Alec Smith had given him during the handover, unlisted numbers connecting to people in and around Whitehall who were not listed in any directory. Some were security-related. This was diplomatic. He switched on the car telephone and dialled the number.

Three minutes later he was back in the restaurant. The elegantly dressed waiter was hovering over Joanne, who was making a show of studying the menu.

'Give us a minute,' Andy told the man, who nodded and backed away.

'Listen, Jo, I have to go back. I'll take you home for now, and pick you up later.'

He made their excuses to the waiter, pressing two crumpled Royal Bank of Scotland pound notes into the man's hand.

'Thank you, sir,' the waiter said with an understanding smile.

He dropped Joanne in Marchmont Road. 'About later, Andy. Just forget it!' She slammed the door and stormed into the dimly lit close of the tall grey tenement.

'Fuck it!' He snarled through narrowed lips. 'Never changes, does it.'

Before moving off he dialled the Fettes Avenue number. As he swung the Astra away from the kerb, he pressed the send button.

The ringing tone boomed out of the system's speaker. After three rings, a clear male voice answered: 'Police Headquarters.'

'This is Chief Inspector Martin. Please connect me with Chief Superintendent Skinner, right away.'

34

'What the hell does Andy want?' Skinner asked the question aloud, but to no one in particular. He looked up at Mackie from his swivel chair. 'Okay, tell them to put him through here.' Mackie disappeared, and a few seconds later, the telephone rang.

Skinner picked it up on the first tone. 'Hello, Andy, what's up? Was the Pakora too spicy for you?'

'I didn't get that far, boss.' Skinner could tell from the booming tone that the call was coming from Martin's car.

'Look, I can't explain over the phone, but I've had a message from an outside agency. They ask that there should be no further questioning of our guest at this time.'

In the car, Martin felt awkward, and on the spot. He had never heard anyone give Skinner an order before; now he was doing it himself. The message was second-hand and courteously phrased, but it was an order, and they both knew it.

Haggerty and Bell saw Skinner frown. 'I hear you, Andy. The request,' he leaned heavily on the word, 'is academic.' Now Martin was puzzled. 'However, we will comply. See you when?'

'Ten minutes, tops.'

'Okay.' Skinner replaced the receiver, slamming it into the cradle. Haggerty cast him an enquiring look.

'What's up?'

'Dirty work at the bloody crossroads, perhaps. It seems that our silent pal might have friends in high places watching over him. Whatever it is, it's too secret for an open telephone line. Andy'll explain when he gets back. In the meantime, if you need to brief your gaffer, there's the phone.'

'Bugger that, sir, have we got time for a pint?'

'You Glasgow boys get your priorities right, don't you. Come on. Andy can wait!'

106

* * *

When they returned, the two psychiatrists were waiting in the CID office, drinking bad coffee and completing their assessment of Yobatu.

Kevin O'Malley looked up as Skinner came into the room. 'Hello, Bob, how are you?'

'I'm in better shape than Yobatu, I reckon. What d'you think?'

'Complete withdrawal. The man's had a massive shock. It could be guilt. It could be the fact of his daughter's death getting through to him at last. As far as fitness to plead is concerned, let me have him in hospital for a week and I'll give you a considered view.

'On the face of it, from the information that your man Mackie gave us, we think he's probably a psychopathic personality with two extremes of behaviour, huge energy or total depressive introspection. When the top end reaches a critical point, a mental fuse blows and he collapses into the state he's in now.'

'Can you fix the fuse?'

'Maybe we can, maybe we can't. But we'll begin by putting him to sleep for a few days, with your agreement.'

'I might not have a choice. There's something funny about this one. In fact, Kevin, there's a lot funny about it. I'm a guy who's suspicious by nature of things that fall into place too easily.'

107

35

Martin was waiting in Skinner's office. He rose as the Chief Superintendent rose as he entered the room. 'Hi, Andy. You don't know our Strathclyde colleagues, do you?' He introduced Haggerty and Bell.

For Andy, the new title still had an awesome ring. 'Good evening, gentlemen. Pleased to meet you. My message has implications for you too, so it's as well that you're here.

'Just over an hour ago, my office had a "most urgent" call from a bloke called Allingham. He's a Superintendent in the Met, but on secondment to the Foreign Office. I suppose you'd describe him as part of the Diplomatic Service. His job is to deal, as quietly as possible, with awkward incidents involving foreign embassies and nationals.

'It must keep him busy, for he was in his office this evening, when he had a call from the Japanese Ambassador. According to him, the Ambassador was well upset. He had just been told by Madame Yobatu of her husband's arrest, of the things we found, and of the likelihood of murder charges. The Ambassador's on the spot, boss, and so are we all.

'What we didn't know, and what Yobatu and his wife didn't choose to tell us, is that the guy has vice-consular status.'

He paused only for breath, but that was time enough for Skinner to explode, 'Jesus Henry Christ! You know what that means don't you.'

'Exactly, boss. Yobatu has diplomatic immunity!'

'Marvellous, just fucking marvellous!' It was one of the few times that Martin had heard Skinner really raise his voice in anger. He decided, very quickly, to wait for the storm to blow over. Even the case-hardened Haggerty looked awed.

'So what does Mr bloody Allingham want us to do? Turn this murderous lunatic back out on the street?'

'No, boss. He hasn't asked that, not yet anyway. The Ambassador wants to talk to you, face-to-face, before deciding what should happen. But he can't order Yobatu to waive immunity, nor can he sack him retrospectively. Anyway, the Ambassador, whose name is Shi-Bachi, is flying up himself, tonight. He'll be on the 8.40 British Midland, arriving here about ten o'clock. Allingham is coming with him, and it was him who asked that there should be no further questioning until they arrive.'

Skinner laughed, a short laugh without humour. 'That's no problem at all.'

'What do you mean, boss?'

'The man's a vegetable, Andy. He's had a complete mental collapse. Kevin O'Malley's just gone off to arrange for his admission to the Royal Edinburgh, and Brian Mackie's away to get Madame Yobatu, so that she can sign him in.'

Martin whistled. 'That could be dicey. What if Madame decides to cut up rough, and starts denying everything on her old man's behalf. Could we wind up being the bad guys here?'

The hard edge had gone from Skinner's voice. He laughed that odd laugh once more. 'She can say what she likes, Andy. But there's one thing, or rather two, that she can't talk her way round. Remember what was in that toffee box in her old man's garage!'

He turned to Haggerty. 'Willie, you've got an interest in this. You'd better stay here to see the Ambassador. Get your boss through if you think it wise. Don't worry, though, if the shite does hit the ventilator over this, I'll make sure that none of it splatters on you.'

He looked over to Martin. 'I want you here too, Andy. Allingham's your pigeon. I'm going to talk to the Ambassador directly, not through him. So you be here to look after him. I won't have time. Besides, it'll be worthwhile experience for you; might teach you to store the names of all resident diplomats, honorary or not, in that photographic memory of yours.'

He picked up the telephone and called Sarah. 'It looks like being a long night, love.'

'Can I still expect you?'

'Yes, but I've no idea when I'll be through here. Things concerning our Japanese guest have taken an unusual turn. If I'm not there by midnight or so, you can start without me.'

36

Martin returned to the Fettes Avenue office at 9.45 p.m., after failing to make peace with Joanne. Skinner, Haggerty and Bell were still there. Three empty pizza boxes and three plates with cutlery lay on the table.

'You didn't see Proud Jimmy on your way in, did you?' Skinner asked. 'I called him earlier on. Ambassadors are right up his street.'

'No sign when I came in. Who's collecting the Ambassador and Allingham?'

'Brian's gone to pick them up. I gather the plane was on time. They'll be brought here, then we'll go up to the Royal Edinburgh. Yobatu's there now, under guard, with his wife. I've asked Kevin O'Malley not to sedate him until the Ambassador's had a chance to look at him.'

'How's Mrs Yobatu bearing up?'

'Okay. Brian asked her if she could account for the things we found. She said that she didn't have a clue. All that she could say was that her husband was and had always been a man who put great store in honour.'

Martin grunted his disapproval. 'That'll be a great source of comfort to Iain MacVicar's mother!'

As he spoke, Chief Constable Proud swept into the room, resplendent in full dress uniform and radiating authority. The Strathclyde detectives looked hugely impressed, almost bowing as they were introduced. Proud nodded to them, then turned to Skinner.

'He's not here yet, is he?'

'Not yet, Chief. Let's go out front to meet him.'

'Yes, let's be a welcoming committee.' He bustled out, all epaulettes and silver braid, with Skinner and Martin following.

They stood behind reception for five minutes before Mackie's car drew up at the main entrance. When he appeared in the hallway, the Inspector led an elderly, balding Japanese, and a tall man with a thin, sallow face and a dark moustache. They were dressed for the frozen North, in navy blue overcoats with a Savile Row look. Snowflakes melted on the dark cloth.

Proud shook the Ambassador's hand, and nodded in Allingham's direction. Shi-Bachi bowed slightly, and he and the Chief exchanged pleasantries as Proud led the way to his office. Skinner, following behind, attempted small-talk with Allingham. The man did not respond.

There was a pot of coffee on a tray on the big rosewood table in the Chief Constable's office. Proud poured six cups and handed them round.

'Well gentlemen, shall we get down to business. Bob Skinner has charge of this investigation, and enjoys my complete confidence; I suggest that he leads off.'

Shi-Bachi smiled and nodded his assent. He looked across the table towards Skinner, who put down his cup.

'Thank you, Chief, and thank you, Your Excellency, for coming north so quickly to help us with this difficulty. Now, where shall I begin?'

To his astonishment, even as the Ambassador opened his mouth to reply, Allingham cut in, brusquely.

'You can begin by telling His Excellency how a Japanese vice-consul, with full diplomatic immunity, comes to be locked up in your nick!'

Skinner turned on the man. He glared at him and said in a hard, even voice, 'Listen here, Mister; Superintendent is it? I don't know who the hell you are, I don't know what the hell you are, and guess what, I don't care about either! But I know where the hell you are. You're on my patch, interfering with my investigation, with no locus or authority. So before I go any further, you will go somewhere else with Mr Mackie, and make the Ambassador's hotel arrangements. That's what you're here for. That will allow His Excellency and I to discuss this matter without interference. Brian, take this man away!'

Allingham looked to Proud for protection, but was met by silence and an angry glare. He turned back towards Skinner, blustering. 'If that is what the Ambassador wishes . . . '

'It is.' Shi-Bachi cut him short. The man flushed, but rose without another word and left the room, with Mackie on his heels.

Skinner turned back to address the Ambassador. 'As I was saying, sir.'

Shi-Bachi nodded. 'Now that my guard has gone,' he said with a smile, 'perhaps you would simply tell me why you believe that Yobatu *san* may have done these terrible things.' He spoke in perfect, if slightly clipped English.

And so Skinner led him through the whole terrible story, beginning with the brutal murder of Yobatu's daughter and ending with the man's mental collapse earlier that evening. He missed no detail, and it was fully half-an-hour before his account was complete.

'So, Your Excellency, you will see that we have the strongest evidence of Yobatu *san*'s guilt. But as a diplomat, even an honorary one, he cannot be prosecuted, or brought to account for himself in any way. He is known here as a respectable businessman. If he is simply declared *persona non grata*, people will want to know why. If the story should emerge there will be embarrassment, to say the least. How do you suggest that the matter should be settled?'

Shi-Bachi looked grave. And then, after deep thought, he said, 'Let me see him. Let me try, at least, to speak with him. Then, as you say, we will sleep on it, and decide upon action in the light of the new day.'

Skinner nodded in agreement. 'Then let's go to the hospital.'

When they arrived at the Royal Edinburgh Hospital in Morningside, they were directed to a first-floor room. A uniformed policeman stood outside the door.

Inside, a second constable sat facing the bed on which Yobatu lay. His wife was at his bedside. The woman rose to her feet the moment the Ambassador entered, preceding Skinner, Proud and Martin. She bowed in respect. Shi-Bachi, smiling, walked to her. He spoke softly in Japanese and pressed her gently back into her seat.

Yobatu lay propped up by pillows, staring fixedly at a point on the wall. Shi-Bachi leaned over him and spoke clearly in Japanese. There was no reaction.

'I am sorry, gentlemen,' he said to the policemen. 'For your convenience, I will speak in English.'

He turned again to face the bed. 'Yobatu *san*, you know me well.

'You have been accused of terrible crimes. Do you have any defence, or any answer to these charges?' His tone was stern, but it brought no movement, no reaction of any kind.

Shi-Bachi repeated his question, louder the second time. But Yobatu continued to stare at his piece of wall.

The Ambassador looked at the man for some time. He placed himself in his line of sight. Still Yobatu did not react, or move a muscle. Shi-Bachi turned to the group of policemen.

'We have a problem, you and I. Let us go away to think about it.'

They left the hospital in silence. Skinner drove Shi-Bachi to the Caledonian, one of the two massive hotels which stand like bookends at either end of Princes Street. A subdued Allingham met them in the foyer. They arranged to meet at Fettes Avenue at 9.30 a.m. next day.

Skinner arrived at Sarah's flat just five minutes before midnight. She met him at the front door. 'Bob, you look exhausted. What a day you must have had. Come on, let's not bother with a night-cap. Let's go to bed.'

As they undressed in silence, Sarah looked beneath the tiredness, and saw that Skinner the detective was still mentally at work.

'Come on then, darling, tell me what's wrong.'

'I'm not exactly sure. I have a feeling that I'm going to lose this guy to the Japanese, and that's eating at me. But there's something else, too. It's been niggling away since the start, and I can't nail it down.'

'Look, Robert, you've got the right man, yes?'

'Look at the evidence. And he as good as admitted it before his mind went on its holidays.'

'Then does it matter whether he spends the rest of his life in a secure mental hospital here, or in one in Japan. Because that's the likely outcome, as Kevin O'Malley would tell you right now, if you really pressed him.'

'It matters to me that people know that we've caught him, that they can feel safe again. That's what really matters.'

'Then that's your deal with the Japanese. They can have him without protest, but the story is told.'

'My lovely Doctor, you are too sensible for your own good. Come here.'

'Skinner, you must be joking! Sleep – now!'

And almost instantly, involuntarily, he obeyed.

37

The meeting with Shi-Bachi and Allingham took place once more in Proud Jimmy's fine, oak-panelled office. Tea was served in delicate china cups, and two plates of MacVitie's chocolate digestive biscuits, obligatory at such meetings, even at 9.30 a.m., were placed on the highly polished table, around which seven men sat.

Skinner was on the Chief Constable's right, with Martin beyond him. On Proud's left, sat Assistant Chief Constable Graham Parton, Strathclyde Constabulary's Head of CID, with Willie Haggerty by his side.

Shi-Bachi and Allingham sat opposite the group of policemen, giving the meeting a suitably formal air. As soon as his secretary had poured the tea and left the room, Proud took the initiative.

'Your Excellency, I do not propose that a written record be kept of this meeting. But, I would ask you to agree to the attendance as an observer of Mr John Wilson, who is Private Secretary to the Lord Advocate, our senior Law Officer. In suggesting this, I recognise formally that our courts do not have jurisdiction over Mr Yobatu in the matters which we are here to discuss.'

The Ambassador returned Proud Jimmy's cool gaze. He nodded briefly. 'I have no objection, Chief Constable.'

'Thank you, sir.' Proud turned to Martin. 'Chief Inspector, you should find Mr Wilson in my outer office. Would you please invite him to join us.'

'Sir.' Martin left the room.

Skinner was surprised. The Chief had not told him about the Lord Advocate's observer. However, he supposed to himself that it was only natural for the politicians to want to keep an eye on a sensitive matter which was, not only in theory, but in all probability in practice, out of their hands.

Martin reappeared a few seconds later. He held the door open to admit a tall man in his early forties, with thinning hair and a sharp face. Wilson took a seat at the table, midway between Shi-Bachi and Martin, symbolically at least, a member of neither camp.

Proud Jimmy nodded towards the man, 'For your benefit, Mr Wilson, and, to an extent, for that of ACC Parton, I will ask Chief Superintendent Skinner to give an account of his investigation, and of the events which have led us all to this meeting this morning.'

Skinner looked to his right, making full eye-contact with Wilson. The man dropped his eyes after only a couple of seconds. In a far recess of Skinner's mind an alarm bell sounded, faintly. He ignored it and began to speak.

Once again, he went through the story stage by stage, looking at Wilson frequently as he did so, as if the man was a juror, and he was in the witness-box. As he reached the climax of his tale, he described in detail the encounter with Yobatu, citing the man's delight at the manner of Shun Lee's death, and his silent reaction to the discoveries in his garage.

Turning from witness to prosecutor, he began to sum up. 'So where does that leave us, gentlemen?

'It brings us to a position where we have motive, opportunity and hard evidence, all pointing to the guilt of Yobatu *san* of the murders of Shun Lee, Mortimer and Miss Jameson, and forensic evidence which proves categorically that the killer of Mortimer was responsible also for the murders of the unknown man, Mrs Rafferty and PC MacVicar.

'On the basis of our evidence we believe that we would undoubtedly gain convictions on the four Edinburgh murders, at the very least, were Yobatu *san* fit to plead. At the moment he is not, but the opinion of two psychiatrists who have seen him is that should he recover from his present collapse, his mental condition at the time of the murders would be a matter for the judgement of a jury.

'But all of this, Mr Wilson, is academic. As an honorary vice-consul of Japan, Yobatu *san* enjoys diplomatic immunity, and could not be prosecuted for these crimes, even if he were fit to plead. That is the situation which we are here to discuss.'

Skinner looked across at Shi-Bachi. 'Your Excellency, you can see my – our position. We have had a series of brutal murders which have caused great public concern.

'We believe that we have caught the perpetrator. But we can't tell the public, to allay their fears, and we can't charge the man because of his status.'

Skinner sat back in his seat and looked at Shi-Bachi.

But before the Ambassador could speak, Allingham broke in. 'Correct me if I am wrong, Chief Superintendent, but Yobatu *san* has not admitted these crimes.'

Skinner looked at him, mastering his dislike of the man only with an effort. 'Superintendent, listen as a policeman to what I am saying to you. The evidence here is so strong, that in all my experience, I have never encountered a jury which would have acquitted after hearing it.'

Shi-Bachi waved Allingham to silence. 'Gentlemen.' He looked directly at Parton, then Proud, and finally Skinner, upon whom his gaze settled as he spoke. 'I grieve for what has happened in your cities. I grieve for the people who are dead. But what can I do? We have a man suspected of vile crimes who is under the protection of international law. I cannot remove his status.

'However, Yobatu *san* himself can elect to stand trial and face the consequences if he is convicted. In theory, I cannot force him to make that choice. Nevertheless, I am of the Japanese royal family; he is samurai. In practice, I can order him, and he will obey. Should his condition improve so that it becomes possible, that I will do.

'In the meantime, you may keep him in your hospital for as long as is necessary. My Embassy will pay for his treatment, and will fly over the best available man in Japan to assist. For the present, I suggest that you tell your newspapers that you have arrested a man, who is for the moment too ill to be charged or to stand trial, but that you are looking for no one else. Then your people can feel safe again.'

Skinner's face brightened as Shi-Bachi spoke.

'Your Excellency, that is a most generous proposal.'

Proud and Parton nodded in support. The Chief Constable spoke for the first time in twenty minutes. 'Yes, Mr Ambassador, thank you indeed. We will discuss the wording of our announcement with our Crown Office and with you before any statement is issued.'

'One moment please, gentlemen.' Wilson's soft voice broke in. The policemen turned to look at the man in surprise, and with the beginning of annoyance. A second alarm bell sounded in Skinner's mind, louder this time.

Wilson's eyes were fixed on the table in front of him. He spoke slowly, choosing his words with great care. 'While I am only an observer here, I am, none the less, privy to the views of the Lord Advocate. Therefore I have to tell you that I have reason to believe that he would not concur with the course of action which the Ambassador has proposed.'

'Why?' Skinner barked the word.

'Only this morning I discussed with Lord Muckhart the question of the possible renunciation of the right to diplomatic immunity. It is the Lord Advocate's view that such a step would set a dangerous precedent. For example, circumstances might arise involving one of our own nationals, in a situation where that person might be placed under physical pressure to forego diplomatic status.

'I would even suggest that in this case there might be nations, and who knows, even people in your own country, Your Excellency, who would allege that Yobatu *san*'s revocation was the result of physical duress.'

Skinner thumped the table. 'Don't be so fucking stupid!' he shouted at the man. But Wilson did not flinch.

'Chief Superintendent, I can see why you are angry. I know that the Lord Advocate will understand too. But it is not going to change his view that the prosecution of Yobatu could undermine the whole principle of diplomatic immunity and could place certain of our nationals . . . '

'Our diplomatic spies, you mean,' Skinner fired at him.

'Yes, it is possible that people involved in the necessary gathering of intelligence might be placed in jeopardy.'

As Wilson finished Allingham coughed quietly and spoke. 'Gentlemen, I should tell you also that I have been instructed personally this morning by the Foreign Secretary. You will find that he shares the Lord Advocate's view. He believes that it would not be in the national interest for us to seek the removal of Yobatu *san*'s diplomatic immunity. It was his hope that this meeting would result in the immediate repatriation of Yobatu *san* to Japan, on a voluntary basis of course. Your Excellency will understand that the Foreign Secretary wishes to avoid the necessity of declaring him *persona non grata*.'

Four of the five policemen sat shocked and silent.

Only Skinner hurled a response back across the table. 'And has your Foreign Secretary told our Secretary of State that he intends to interfere in his territory? Poor wee Mrs Rafferty was his constituent. Does your man know that?'

Wilson replied for Allingham. 'Mr Fairchild has been told, Chief Superintendent. As far as territory goes, when a person has a diplomatic passport, technically the ground on which he stands becomes foreign soil.'

'Don't lecture me on the law, mister!'

'Please don't take it personally, Mr Skinner. The Secretary of State accepts the fact of the matter.'

'So did Pontius fucking Pilate!'

Gently, Proud placed a hand on Skinner's sleeve.

'So what do we tell our people?' the Chief Constable asked. 'That we've caught the bogeyman but that the politicians won't let us touch him?' His tone reassured Skinner.

Allingham and Wilson began to reply in duet. Allingham nodded and Wilson went on. 'You're not going to tell the people anything, Mr Proud. We, and I speak here with the authority of the Lord Advocate, and through Mr Allingham, the Foreign Secretary, do not wish this to become a public issue.'

Skinner laughed harshly. 'Look, pal, six dead people make it a public issue!'

'And one which will remain unresolved. We do not wish to see pressure growing for Yobatu to be tried. As we have said, ministers are determined to protect the principle of diplomatic status.'

Skinner looked from Allingham to Wilson and back again.

'This whole meeting has been a sham, hasn't it. You two bastards have had your heads together earlier on, to ensure that your bosses get the result they want. You've conned us, you've conned the Ambassador, and now you're proposing to con the people. Just who do you think you are? How do you think you can stop us from going public on this. I answer to my Chief, and he answers to the Courts, not to you. How can you stop him, or me, from walking out of this room and making a statement to the press?'

But even as he threw down the challenge, turning to find a look of furious defiance in Proud's eyes, Skinner knew that it was a bluff. And even as the Chief opened his mouth to back him, Wilson called it.

'Come on now, Chief Superintendent, I see that I do have to remind you of the law. You must know full well that in criminal investigations you are the agents of the Lord Advocate. You answer to him, not the Courts, and I have just told you what his instructions are, or at least what they will certainly be. I'm sorry, Chief Superintendent. There it is. Ministers have reached a clear view; we all will have to live with it.'

'Sure,' said Skinner his voice laden with contempt, 'unlike Shun Lee, Mike Mortimer, John Doe the Wino, Mary Rafferty, Iain MacVicar, and Rachel Jameson we'll have to live with it. And in five years or so, when people see a few quid to be made from a nice gory book about the Royal Mile murders, and point the finger at us as the idiot coppers who couldn't catch the maniac, we'll have to live with that, too.'

He looked across at Allingham. 'What will you boys do when some clever journalist follows the trail we've followed, comes to the same conclusion, and makes it the last chapter of one of those books?'

'It won't be published.'

'Or if an MP is persuaded to put down a question?'

'It won't be accepted.'

'And if there's any other way you'll block that up too. Right?'

'Yes, Mr Skinner, that is correct. We have the power to do all that and we will use it should it ever become necessary. This is a story that will not be told.'

Skinner glared at Allingham. Silence hung over the table.

It was Shi-Bachi who broke it. 'But can you stop me from telling this tale in Japan, Mr Allingham?'

Everyone, including Wilson, whose expression was suddenly shocked, looked at the Foreign Office man.

Allingham raised his hands from the table, steepled them and looked closely at his finger tips. After what seemed like an age, he turned to Shi-Bachi and answered him in a voice so low that it was as if he was afraid that he might be overheard. 'Yes, Your Excellency, I think that you would find that we can.'

Shi-Bachi shook his head, but it was in recognition of the certainty with which the man spoke, rather than in disbelief. He looked Skinner in the eye, and said sadly, 'Then I am afraid, gentlemen, that there is no more to be said. I am sorry that you are so badly treated.'

He rose, and the policemen opposite rose with him. He bowed shortly. Only Skinner returned the salutation as the Ambassador turned, opened the brass-handled door behind his chair, and walked out of the room. Without a word, Allingham turned and made to follow.

'Hold on, you!' The Chief Constable's voice boomed like thunder, ahead of a gathering storm. Skinner had never heard that tone from his boss before. He guessed that Allingham was about to discover how Proud Jimmy felt about being shown by an interloper, in his own office, the limitations of his power.

Allingham stopped in his tracks.

'You've made this mess. You clean it up. I want Yobatu *san* off my patch and on his way back to Japan, asleep or not, before this day is out. You will make that happen.

'If you try to leave Edinburgh before the arrangements are made and under way, I will have you arrested. And in this city, I have the power to do that.

'Martin, go with this man, and make sure that he does what he's told.'

Allingham's face flushed but he said nothing. He left the room with Martin, purposeful, at his heel. The Strathclyde detectives looked at

Proud in undisguised admiration. He thanked them as they left. For Wilson he had only a glare of dismissal.

38

Skinner turned to go, but Proud stopped him. 'Hang on a minute, Bob. Sit down.' He settled into one of two leather armchairs set on either side of a coffee table in the middle of the big room, and motioned Skinner towards the other.

Proud hesitated, as if considering his choice of words very carefully. At last, he said, 'Bob, you and I are different sorts of policemen. Let me put it this way. I'm a policeman, but you're a copper, in the best sense of the word. You have an understanding of the job and a feel for it that I, even at my exalted rank, have never had. I see it as something that is necessary to society, and I tend to approach it dispassionately. That works for me. But you, you care so much.

'I'm an administrator, you're a motivator. I feel bad enough about all this, but I can only imagine how gutted you must be at the way it's turned out. You've been a detective for most of your career. That's a dirty job, but there are times when my job can get dirty too; you've just been involved in one of them. I hate creeps like that man Allingham, but believe me, there are worse than him about. You'll find that out when you're sat behind that desk over there.'

Skinner looked at him in astonishment. Proud Jimmy had never talked to him like this before, had never mentioned him as a possible Chief.

'Maybe I don't want that,' he began, cautiously.

'Don't kid me, and don't kid yourself. Whatever you say, or allow yourself to believe, you want it all right. You can't criticise the man if you're not prepared to have a go yourself, and I know that you don't agree with everything I do.'

Now it was Skinner's turn to flush under the gaze of this new, and wholly unexpected, James Proud.

The Chief laughed. 'Don't worry, you're right, and more so after this morning. I must be getting past it, if I can allow myself to be set up like that, in my own bloody office no less, by those two slimy twats. When

121

Wilson told me that Pringle Muckhart wanted him here just as an observer, I actually believed the lying bastard.

'I'll tell you one thing, Bob.' Proud's tone changed, and his face was suddenly fierce. 'If Mr bloody Wilson goes just one mile over the speed limit anywhere on my patch, he'll have his fucking collar felt. Our Mr Wilson is about to become the best motor insurance risk in Edinburgh, and he doesn't even know it.'

Proud, who rarely swore, was deadly serious. Skinner looked at him in amazement, then threw back his head and laughed. 'But the Crown Office will drop the prosecution!'

'The Crown Office will move to bloody Stornoway by the time I've finished with it!'

His stern face broke into a smile once more.

'Anyway, about my desk, and the chair behind it. I haven't got that long to go, and I want you to be in a position to succeed me. I've felt aggrieved for a long time that Jock Govan in Strathclyde has an ACC as his Head of CID, while I've only got a lowly DCS. Well, finally I've managed to persuade those Bolsheviks on the Police Committee to authorise one extra Assistant Chief Constable on the establishment. They'll approve it today; and you, my son, are it. Congratulations.'

Once again the Chief left Skinner dumbfounded. When he could speak, he said, 'Sir, you've taken my breath away. Does that mean that you want me out of CID?'

'Good God no! You're the best detective in the country, you'll stay as Head of CID, but with ACC rank. You won't even have to wear uniform dress.'

'That's a pity. I've always had a thing about silver braid and Sam Browne belts!'

Proud laughed at Skinner's jibe at his formality of dress. 'I'm the last of the dinosaurs, Bob. Most chiefs these days dress like managing directors, and keep the uniform for ceremonial.' Skinner caught a change in his tone and looked at him curiously, but Proud went on. 'I've always believed in being seen for what I am, even in the New Club. It helps keep the aloofness which the job forces on you.

'By the way, that's another part of your grooming for office that I've taken care of. I've put you up for membership of the Club.'

'Oh Christ, not me, surely!'

'In Edinburgh, it goes with the job. You've just seen politics in action. Well, politics is what the Club is about, in part at least. I'll find a way to sort out Pringle Muckhart for what he's done to us today, and the Club will help me do it. If he's wise, My Lord Advocate won't waste any time in promoting himself to the Bench!'

'You're a deep one, all right, Jimmy,' Skinner mused inwardly. 'Too good at playing the caricature policeman, that's your trouble. So good that most people believe it, me included up to a point. Until today.'

Aloud he said, 'What a morning. Stuffed by the mandarins, now my whole life takes a new turn. Me in the New Club!' He shook his head in mock disbelief.

Smiling, Proud rose to his feet. Skinner took the signal, and stood up with him. 'I must get off to the Committee to have your appointment ratified. It's a formality, though. It'll be effective from tomorrow, but you can tell Alex now. And your Doctor, of course.'

Skinner's eyebrows rose in surprise.

Proud chuckled. 'When you're Chief Constable, you know everything!

'Take some advice, Bob. Clear your desk and take your wee girl away on holiday. It'll let you think about the future, and get Yobatu off your mind.'

'Thanks, Chief. I'll do that, just as soon as Sarah can get away.'

39

December, normally a month of mounting excitement, was relatively quiet after the uproar of November. Peace returned to Edinburgh. The press follow-up of the Yobatu arrest was deflected by a simple statement that the person interviewed had been eliminated from the enquiry. The officers in the search team were told that Yobatu was hopelessly insane, and that the arrest was not to be discussed with anyone, not even wives or partners. The vigils in the Royal Mile were continued for a time, but were scaled down, and eventually stopped, although a public pretence was maintained that they were still continuing at an appropriate level. Eventually, with other, newer stories to entice them, and with no further killings, the media lost interest.

The loss of Yobatu, and the unscratched itch, still rankled with Skinner, but four things happened to make them more bearable for him.

First, Sarah and Alex were joint belles of the annual CID dance – never referred to as a ball. The doctor's arrival on the ACC's arm finally allowed the force to discuss in public what it had been discussing in private for weeks.

Second, he became a member of the New Club, and found that the institution, in its bizarre home in Princes Street, was much less stuffy and austere than he had imagined. Quickly, he came to appreciate its value as an information exchange, and as a place where business could be done discreetly, if technically against Club rules.

Third, he noted on a routine report, the pending prosecution of one John Wilson, of Liberton, on a charge of driving with excess alcohol in his bloodstream.

Fourth, the Lord Advocate, Lord Muckhart, resigned suddenly and mysteriously, citing 'personal reasons'. Later he was forced to admit that he was involved in an adulterous relationship with the wife of a leading Scottish politician, after the *Scotsman* newspaper, having received information from an anonymous source, broke the story. 'That,' Skinner said to Sarah, 'is what I call getting even!'

40

The detective and the doctor flew to Spain on Boxing Day, on a tourist flight from Manchester to Gerona. They were the only people on the plane who were not bound for the Andorra ski slopes. The Catalan weather was mild and sunny, and the absence of heavy tourist traffic allowed them to make more use of their hired car than had been possible earlier in the year.

They spent hours poring through the maze of streets and alleys that was old L'Escala. Most of the businesses and shops were still open, reminding visitors that this was a working town first, a resort second.

Their week passed too quickly, as they relaxed in each other's company. Soon it was New Year's Eve. In common, it seemed, with much of L'Escala, they had made a reservation in their special restaurant in St Marti, where a gala supper was advertised to see out what had been for them a momentous year.

As usual, the food was superb. A feast of calcots, the unique Catalan vegetable, was followed by thick, creamy tomato soup, before the arrival of the main course: a spectacular baked fish-pot. The meal drew to its leisurely conclusion before midnight.

Suddenly Skinner took an envelope from his pocket and handed it to Sarah.

Puzzled, she tore it open. Inside was a pale blue card, with a gold question-mark on the front. She opened it. Inside there was a second question-tion mark, in Bob's scawled style.

She looked up at him, and as she did so, he placed a small box before her on the table. Embossed on the lid, in gold leaf, was 'Hamilton & Inches, Edinburgh'. She lifted the lid and a large single diamond set on gold sparkled out at her.

'Well,' said Bob, in a voice she had never heard before, 'are you daft enough to marry a copper with very limited promotion prospects?'

'My love,' she answered, twin tears tracking down her cheeks, above her shining smile, 'I'd be daft not to!'

Bob took the ring from the box and slipped it on to the third finger of her left hand. It was, of course, a perfect fit.

As Sarah stared at the diamond on her finger, parties at the three surrounding tables, who had been watching breathlessly, broke into applause. A dark Spanish man came over, smiling, and shook Bob's hand. His wife embraced Sarah. And just at that moment, midnight began to strike.

Bob reached across the table and took both of Sarah's hands in his. 'Happy New Year, my darling. You know, since Alex was born, this is the first one I haven't brought in with her. Once, even, I was on duty, in the office, and I took her in with me. But things change and lives move on. Now I don't intend ever to bring in another without you by my side.'

Normally, Bob danced only under extreme duress. But that night, as he and Sarah drifted around the floor to the music of the small band, it was as if they were waltzing on air, above the stone floor of the terrace restaurant.

At 1.00 a.m. local time they used the pay-phone in the corner to call Alex. To their surprise they connected first time. The background noise confirmed that it was midnight in Scotland, the sacred hour of 'The Bells', and that Alex had a full house.

'Happy New Year, love,' Bob shouted into the telephone.

She bubbled down the line. 'Happy New Year, Pops! Are you having a terrific time?'

'Yes, pretty terrific.

'Listen, baby, hold on to a chair for a minute, we've got something to tell you. You're going to have a stepmother!'

Twelve hundred miles away, Alex said, 'Yeah, wonderful. About time, too. Put Sarah on. Oh, look at me, I'm crying.'

Sarah took the telephone from Bob. She tried to imagine what a stepmother tone should sound like.

'Right, my girl. Are you behaving yourself?'

'Of course not, are you? Sarah, that's wonderful. Did he manage to propose without making it sound like he was charging you with something?'

'Listen kid, your old man's got style. It was wonderful. Right on the stroke of midnight he pops the question. When we get home I'll tell you all about it.'

The cut-off noise began to sound.

'Have a great time. See you soon!'

Sarah replaced the receiver and turned to Bob. She threw her arms around his neck and kissed him.

'You've no idea how good it feels to be official.'

'Oh yes, I have. You'd better start planning. Your track record shows that you're not very good at being engaged, so I don't intend for this to be a long one.'

Sarah took him at his word. As the taxi wound past the jetty where the Olympic flame had landed in 1992, and along the dark beach road to L'Escala, their plans took shape. It would be an Easter wedding, in Edinburgh. Alex would be maid of honour, Andy would be best man. If his uncertain health allowed him to travel, Sarah would be given away by her father, who had talked of a trip to Scotland when she had visited her parents in Florida.

'If he can't come maybe Andy could do that too,' she said.

'Can he do both?'

'Why not? Or maybe the Chief, what is it you call him, Proud Jimmy, maybe he could do it.'

'Steady on. We're not that chummy!'

It was 3.15 a.m. on New Year's morning when they returned to the apartment. They tumbled into bed and made love with a special unhurried air of relaxation which they both recognised was something new. Sarah's orgasm happened quickly, and went on and on. Bob, when he came volcanically inside her, cried out as every inch of their bodies seemed to fuse together.

When she could speak, Sarah whispered in his ear. 'If that's what being engaged does for you, I don't know if I'll survive marriage.'

'Nnnn.' Bob nuzzled his face into her neck, closed his eyes and, smiling, settled down to sleep.

He was still smiling next morning on the terrace, as they ate breakfast in the perfect sunshine. So was Sarah.

'That was a pretty high standard we set ourselves last night, boy. Tell me, Assistant Chief Constable Skinner, do you get as intense as that when you're working on your cases?'

He nodded at the recollection. And then it was as if his face had been flooded with light.

He seized her shoulders in each of his lean hands and kissed her, taking her by surprise and astonishing the English emigré neighbour who happened to be walking past with his black labrador.

'Dr Sarah Grace Skinner to be, you are a genius. That's it! The word you used last night. The word coppers never use.

'Cases!'

41

'That's it. That's the itch I've been trying to scratch! That's what was wrong with the Mortimer and Jameson situations . . . their cases.'

Bob was so excited that Sarah forgot to be annoyed that his mind had gone back to work, and to the Yobatu Affair.

'What do you mean?'

'Look, Mortimer's case was one of those combination jobs. And when we found it the lock was set. I've got one of those things. So have you, and so have quite a few other people we know. Do you ever set the combination for short journeys like office to home?'

'No, I don't suppose I do. I can never remember combinations anyway, I just keep it zeroed.'

'Right. So there's Mike Mortimer, on a short walk home in the middle of the night, yet the locks on his case were set!'

'Come on, Bob, that's a long shot.'

'No it's not. It's an unusual circumstance, and they're the first things you look for in a criminal investigation. Things, even tiny things, that don't fit a normal behaviour pattern. And even if it is a long shot on its own, taken with the Jameson situation it adds up.'

'What about her?'

'Her case wasn't there! The report of her death listed everything she had on her, yet there was no mention of a case. And I didn't pick that up. I'm so dumb I should be a Transport copper. The woman had just finished a major criminal trial, away from Edinburgh. Of course she would have had a document case with her, and probably a big one at that.'

'But what does it all mean?'

'Christ alone knows, but I'm going to find out.'

'Isn't it all closed. Official Secret and all that?'

'That's not going to stop me. I'll just have to play it a bit quiet, that's all. Poor old Andy! What's her name'll give him hell when he tells her he's working on New Year's Day!'

Book Two

Adapt and Survive

42

It was 11.53 a.m. on 1 January, when the telephone rang two feet from Martin's left ear. He opened his eyes blearily, and reached for the telephone on the bedside table.

'Hello; 747 3781. And a Happy New Year, whoever you are,' he mumbled into the phone.

'And the same to you, lad.'

Martin was suddenly wide awake. 'Bob, I didn't expect you to call. How's Sarah?'

'Great. We're getting married.'

There was a pause while the news sank in. 'Bob, that's great. Congratulations, you lucky sod.'

'Thanks, Andy; now you're going to hate me. Hope you're up to driving, 'cause I've got a couple of jobs for you. I want you to find Mike Mortimer's briefcase, wherever it is. I know our property people, and the time they take to process goods. So chances are it'll still be in police hands. Then I want you to find the property report on Rachel Jameson, and check for any mention of a briefcase. If there isn't one, and I don't think there is, get Willie Haggerty in Strathclyde – quietly, mind you – to check whether there's a case stashed in the office that dealt with her death.

'If there's still no sign, get on to the next-of-kin, her mother I think it was, and ask if she's got it, or knows where it is.'

'What if she didn't have a briefcase?'

'Don't be bloody dense, Andy. Where else would she carry her papers?'

Martin grimaced. His head was throbbing, and his concentration was not helped by Joanne's successor, Lucy, sliding down the bed to grasp him, as he spoke, in both of her long-fingered hands. Oh Lord, he thought, if You are just, I'll die now.

With masterful control he said, 'When I've done all this, boss, what then?'

'Nothing. Lock everything away and wait for me to get back. Don't tell anyone what you're doing. Just do it very quietly, and say nothing, not even to the Chief.'

A soft moan escaped Martin's lips.

'What was that?'

'Sorry, boss, just yawning. OK, that's understood. See you on Thursday, then.'

'Fine. Need to go now, the change is running out. Remember: quietly.'

The line went dead. Martin replaced the receiver. And screamed. Quietly. From beneath the humped duvet, Lucy grinned up at him.

43

The Fettes Avenue Headquarters were on skeleton staff when Martin arrived. The Yobatu papers were kept under lock and key in a restricted access area on the ground floor of the four-storey building. As Head of Special Branch, Andy Martin had access.

Quickly he found the files which covered the death of Rachel Jameson. He noted the telephone number of Rachel's mother. Then he scanned the list of effects for any mention of a briefcase. There was none.

He replaced the brown file, and walked quickly down to the Productions Store, in the basement of the building. The civilian clerks who normally staffed it were among the New Year's Day absentees, and the heavy door was locked. Martin opened it with a master key.

The big room was crammed with an incredible range of objects, arranged in an order which was logical only to the permanent clerks.

'Like bloody Alladin's cave, this,' Martin muttered to himself.

Video recorders, television sets and tape recorders were stacked alongside a wheel-chair and an artificial limb. Cash, in plastic bags, sat on a shelf, beside packages of hard drugs. Each item was labelled with details of the time of its lodgement, and of the case in which it was a production in evidence.

Martin went from shelf to shelf, from rack to rack. His eye lighted on a number of suitcases piled one on top of the other. He checked the labels. They were dated six months before the Mortimer murder. There was no sign of a briefcase anywhere near. His eye scanned along the row, to where a pile of documents lay clumsily stacked. Again he checked the label. They had been there for a week. In the rack behind, polythene wrappers reflected the light into his eyes. He stepped round for a closer look. It was a haul of three dozen tracksuits, recovered from a man arrested for breaking into a sports shop.

The back of the room was filled with cases of beer, lager and liquor of all descriptions. December was boom time for pub and off-licence break-ins, Martin recalled. As he glanced towards the store of drink, his eye was caught by a dark object, on a shelf near the floor. Crested, silver buttons gleamed. He looked closer. It was a policeman's uniform jacket. The breast was marked by a rusty stain that could only be one thing. Martin knew that it was MacVicar's uniform.

He knelt down, and, with a sort of reverence, withdrew the garment from the deep shelf. He looked into the dark space behind. There, leaning against the wall, was a hand-stitched brown leather briefcase. He reached in, and retrieved it.

It was wrapped in clear polythene; another dark stain, similar to that on the uniform coat, showed clearly on the lid, on which the letters 'MM' were embossed in gold leaf.

Martin looked at the briefcase, and as he did so his mind flashed back to that awful morning in Advocates' Close. A wave of revulsion swept over him at the recollection of the savaged corpse, its dead eyes staring pitifully at him from the severed head. As he locked the store and left with the briefcase, he was still white-faced. Sweat glistened on his forehead.

He went to his office, located Willie Haggerty's home number in his personal organiser, and dialled.

'Mr Haggerty? Remember me, Andy Martin, Special Branch in Edinburgh. Look, I hate to bother you on New Year's Day, but a question's come up on Yobatu. Just something we've got to tidy up. I wonder if you could have it checked, with maximum discretion.'

He explained that he was trying to locate Rachel Jameson's briefcase. 'It's a family request. They can't find it, and they asked us if we had it. I wondered if it was still in Strathclyde.'

Haggerty grunted. 'A family request! On New Year's bloody Day! That'll be right. You're up to something, son. But don't tell me, if Bob told you not to.'

At the other end of the line, Martin grinned. Crafty old bastard, he thought, almost aloud.

'Okay, Andy, I'll check it out. Since you're asking if rather than where, I'll assume that it's no' on the property list that's on your files. Gie's a phone number. Ah'll call you back.'

Martin gave Haggerty his home telephone number. 'Thanks, Mr Haggerty. Chances are this won't amount to anything, but if necessary we'll keep in touch.'

He kept the receiver in his hand, pushed the recall button and dialled the bereaved Mrs Jameson. He knew that Rachel's mother was a widow, and so he was taken slightly by surprise when the telephone was answered by a man. Voices sounded in the background. 'Good afternoon, sir,' he said. 'I wonder if I might speak with Mrs Wilma Jameson.'

'That depends. Who are you?'

'Chief Inspector Andrew Martin. And you are, sir?'

The voice at the other end of the line suddenly became respectful. 'Me? Oh, I'm Harry Peebles; Mrs Jameson's my sister. Hold on please. Wilma!' He bawled over the voices in the background.

'Christ!' Andy chortled to himself, with his hand over the telephone. 'I think I've got Fred Flintstone here!'

He heard Peebles mutter to his sister, then a strong female voice came on to the line. 'Mr Martin. What do the police want, today of all days?'

'It's just another day for us, I'm afraid. I'm sorry to interrupt your party, Mrs Jameson, but it's a matter relating to your daughter's death, and some of her legal papers which may be missing. By any chance, do you have her briefcase?'

For a moment Mrs Jameson sounded guilty. 'I'm not really having a party, Chief Inspector. My brother and his family have come round to cheer me up. You see, I always spent New Year's Day with Rachel. I wouldn't have known what to do with myself but for Harry, Cissie and the family.'

It was Martin's turn to feel guilty. 'Of course, Mrs Jameson.'

'Yes, but one must be strong. Now, Rachel's briefcase; I thought that you had it, or perhaps her Clerk, or someone else up at the Library. I certainly don't. I've been wondering about it, in fact. You will let me know when you locate it, won't you?'

'Yes, of course. I'm sorry to have bothered you.' He ended the call and replaced the receiver.

He pulled open a cupboard, rummaged around in the darkness for almost a minute, and emerged, holding an A5 handbook, with a pale blue and gold cover. It was a directory of practising advocates, listed alphabetically and by stables, each group headed by the name, address and home telephone number of its clerk.

He found Rachel's entry in the group serviced by Miss A. E. Rabbit. He picked up the telephone once more and dialled the number shown.

Angela Rabbit was used to calls at odd hours. Willingness to accept them was one of the requirements of the job, as was a total recall memory.

'Rachel's briefcase? Big black thing. No it never came back. I really should have the McCann papers as well. You don't suppose Strathclyde have lost them do you?'

Martin laughed, thanked her, and rang off.

He locked Mortimer's case in his security cabinet. As he stood up he spoke to the empty room. 'God knows what Bob'll make of it, but I have a feeling that there's trouble for someone on its way back from L'Escala.'

44

Unusually for a charter, their flight from Gerona to Manchester arrived on time. The big baggage hall was quiet, with only two of the six carousels in use.

The drive home took three and a half hours. They followed the M6 then the A74 to Moffat, cut cross-country to the Edinburgh by-pass and headed eastward to Gullane. It was just after 7.00 p.m. when Bob drew the car to a halt outside the cottage, beside Alex's ageing Metro.

The entrance hallway was dark. The cottage was silent. Sarah flicked on a light. Nothing happened. Skinner swore softly. Sarah found the handle of the living room door and opened it.

'Surprise!' forty voices shouted in chorus.

Sarah's jaw dropped. Alex and Andy stood in front of a host of friends, from Gullane, from the force, and from Sarah's practice.

Andy pressed a button on the CD player. Cliff Richard boomed out his congratulations through the powerful speakers.

'What the hell is this?' Bob said to Sarah, who looked equally stunned.

Alex answered. She stepped up to them with eyes shining. She hugged Sarah first, then Bob.

'This, my naive old parent, is Alexis Skinner's luxury-model surprise engagement party!

'Have a glass.' She pressed a champagne flute into his hand. Andy handed one to Sarah, kissing her on the cheek. Alex looked towards the corner of the room. 'Come on, Chief, do your duty!'

To Skinner's added astonishment, Proud Jimmy stepped forward, out of uniform for once. He raised his glass. 'Ladies and gentlemen! I am here to propose a toast to which I have been looking forward for some months now. I give you the happy couple, Bob and Sarah!'

'Bob and Sarah.' The toast rippled round the room like a Mexican Wave. Glasses clinked. Bob hugged Sarah to him. Alex grabbed her left hand.

'I've always known you had class, Pops, and you've really shown it this time!'

45

The party started to break up around 1.00 a.m., and the last of the guests left an hour later.

Bob and Andy were both signed off on leave until the following Monday.

Fat chance! thought Martin as he snapped off the table lamp in the small guest bedroom.

Inevitably, the door opened just after 9.00 a.m. Skinner, wearing track-suit trousers and a tee-shirt, came into the room. He was flushed and perspiring. 'You don't mind if I drip on you, Andy?'

Martin made a face. 'No, not at all. How far have you run?'

'Along to Dirleton and back past the farm. The usual circuit. Remember, you did it with me once.'

Martin recalled only too well the punishing pace that had been set on the five-mile lap. The experience had confirmed his preference for running alone.

Skinner sat on the floor, and came straight to the point. 'Did you take care of that job for me?'

'Yes. No problems other than breaking into New Year's Day in the Haggerty household. You were right about our Productions Store. You could lose a corpse in there. Mind, I still managed to find Mortimer's case, by luck rather than judgement. There's no sign of the other one. Not in Glasgow, not in the Advocates' Library, and not with her mother. It does exist though. Great big black thing apparently.'

'Did you check with the Transport Police?'

'Willie Haggerty did. Nothing there though. Some passer-by probably nicked it at the scene. They'd steal anything in Glasgow.'

Martin lay in bed, propped up on an elbow. Skinner looked at him, with perspiration running in a line down his temple.

'Casual theft is one explanation, but not the only one. Someone nicked it all right, but was it someone with a motive other than simple theft?

141

'Where's Mortimer's case?'

'Locked up in my security cabinet. But listen, boss, what is all this? The Yobatu enquiry is over and done with, isn't it?'

'Maybe; but in the middle of it all, there's something out of place. It has to do with those two advocates, or at least with their cases. Let's go and take a look at Mortimer's.'

Driving into Edinburgh half an hour later, Skinner explained his unease over the combination locks on Mortimer's case. Unusually, Martin was sceptical. 'OK, so if you're right and Yobatu took a look in his briefcase, what will that prove?'

'Why the bloody hell should Yobatu do that? He's in the frame because we see him as a madman out for vengeance. Once he's killed his target, he's not going to stay around to search his briefcase. But even if he did, why shove it under the body to hide the fact from us. That doesn't fit Yobatu. Theft was not his motive.'

'He stole something from Shun Lee, remember.'

'Then why didn't he take the same bits from Mortimer? Or maybe even his head? Andy, if he stole from Mortimer and Jameson, why didn't we find those things in our search? I tell you, it doesn't fit. If your killer took something from Mortimer's case, and then stole Rachel's, having heaved her under the train, then that person wasn't Yobatu.'

'So what are we going to look for in Mortimer's case?'

'Proof that someone did look inside.'

The police headquarters building was still on a care and maintenance basis, three days into the New Year. The Special Branch office was manned by a single detective constable, who stood up when Skinner and Martin entered, trying unsuccessfully to conceal an Ed McBain novel.

'Morning, Jimmy,' said Martin. 'Pretend we're not here.'

'Very good sir.' He sat down, but did not go back to the 87th Precinct.

Martin's office was beyond the main room. They went in and closed the door behind them. Martin took a bunch of keys from his pocket and unlocked the cabinet. He took out the case and put it on his desk.

Skinner picked it up. He held it up and looked underneath. He looked closely at the sides. The twin locks were still set at the combination they had discovered. Skinner pulled the catches outwards with his thumbs, and again the clasps sprung open.

Several pockets were set in the lid. He went through them one by one, finding only a red electricity bill, and an American Express Gold Card debit note. He skimmed through the documents in the case. They were depositions relating to a criminal trial in which Mortimer had been instructed for the defence. He switched on Martin's hooded desk lamp and held the papers in its light, one by one, front and back, keeping them in their original order.

As he turned over the last sheet, Skinner's eyes widened. He motioned to Martin. 'Look at this.' The younger man leaned over and looked at the sheet of paper, blank, save for a faint rusty smear which stretched up to the top right-hand corner. 'Let's have that checked. Remember, those gloves that we found were caked in blood.'

Skinner picked up the lamp and shone it inside the case. The lining was cream pigskin. A gold leaf rectangle, traced on its base, reflected the light from the lamp. Inch by inch he shone the light on the lining, until at last, his eye caught a faint brown circle in the centre.

'Check that, too, Andy, but I'll bet you now that it's blood and that it matches Mortimer's group.'

He put down the lamp and took from a pocket of his heavy windcheater jacket, a small chisel with a fine blade. He picked up the case and looked again at the locks. The three numbered wheels in each were set in a rectangular brass face, with the head of a rivet showing in each of the four corners.

Skinner slid the chisel's edge between one of the rivets and the facing. Holding it steady with his left hand he gave the wooden handle a sharp downward blow with the heel of his right. The brass rivet head flew across the room. He repeated the process with the other seven rivets. Finally he levered off the two square sliding catches which released the locks. As each one came away, so the brass facings fell on to the desk, exposing the inner mechanisms.

He bent the flexible shaft of the table lamp so that it shone straight down on the desk. Carefully he eased the right hand lock from its casing and placed it in the beam. Reaching once more into his pocket, he produced a small square magnifying glass with a swivelling leather cover, and a pair of philatelist's tweezers. As Skinner peered through the glass into the lock, Martin realised suddenly that they were both holding their breath.

Suddenly Skinner's face was lit with triumph. 'Got you, you bastard!'

In the outer office, the slumbering detective constable jumped in alarm.

Skinner handed Martin the glass. He leaned across and peered at the magnified image of the locking mechanism, in the bright light of the lamp. There, at the back of the device, four black strands of fibre were trapped between the numbered combination wheels.

'Get me an envelope please, Andy.'

Martin pulled open a drawer in his two pedestal desk, and took out a small folder, made of clear plastic, with a self-sealing strip along the top. He pressed its edges to force the envelope open, as Skinner picked up the tweezers and inserted them carefully into the lock. The strands came clear without breaking, and he placed them gently in the clear container.

Quickly, he examined the other lock. A single strand was trapped there. He put it beside the others and sealed the envelope.

'We'll get confirmation from the lab. tomorrow, but we know for sure now. The man who killed Mortimer looked in that case. And, certainly, he looked in Rachel Jameson's as well, only he couldn't do it at the scene.

'I ask you again, why would Yobatu do that?'

'But what about all the evidence pointing to him?'

'I know. Motive and opportunity. He's unstable after the death of his daughter. He kills his three targets, each in different circumstances, and along the way commits three smokescreen murders to lead us away from the link, and from him. It's incredible, but its a perfect fit. And like a Marks & Spencer suit, I bought it. An off-the-peg solution. A crazy avenging angel, dropped right in my lap.

'I bought it then, but now I'm taking it back to the shop.'

'Come on, boss! What about the stuff in the garage?'

'Andy, son, all that was planted. Whoever did all this had Yobatu picked out as Mr Lucky.

'Listen, when he looked in that drawer, I was watching him. Just for a second his expression changed. I didn't know what it was at the time but I know now.

'He was astonished. He was seeing those things for the first time.'

'But why didn't he say that? He had the chance, but he didn't deny any of it. None of our accusations. He virtually admitted killing the Chinese boy. Why would he do that?'

'That, I'm going to find out. He is deranged, remember. Maybe when we told him about the murders he even imagined that he did them. But the fact is, we've been fed this poor guy.'

'So there's another crazy, and he's still out there? Is that what you're saying?'

Skinner paused and settled back on the edge of the desk. His eyes were level with Martin's, and he gazed steadily at him.

'Yes, Andy, this is a very dangerous man, and he's still out there. But he's no lunatic; at least not the sort you're thinking about.

'For a while I was prepared to believe the Yobatu solution, and accept the idea of the three smokescreen killings, meant to steer us away from the real story. Now I'm even more ready to believe that someone else committed not three, but four side-track murders – yes that's right, Shun Lee as well – to set up Yobatu, and to stop us looking for a link between Mortimer and Jameson and whatever is the real cause of all this blood-letting.

'Let's forget Shun Lee. Maybe the Triads did whack him. Let's forget John Doe the Wino, Mary Rafferty, even for the moment young MacVicar. Let's concentrate on Mortimer and Jameson. They were the targets. They were involved in something we don't know about, and they were killed for it.'

'Suppose they weren't the only advocates involved,' said Martin quietly.

'That's another ugly thought; but yes, let's just suppose that they weren't. We'd better check with our friends at the Faculty whether any other advocates have met their Maker lately; and let's run a quiet check on anyone who might have instructed the late Michael or the late Rachel. At the same time I want a full search of all their effects, personal records, professional and social, and anything else that might give us a start on this.'

Martin nodded. 'I take it you want Special Branch to handle this, boss.'

'Too right I do. Think back to our friends Allingham and Wilson, and remember how eager they were to see Yobatu off our national premises. We could be involved in something here that goes far beyond our wee city, something that reaches up to Government itself.'

'Jesus Christ,' Martin muttered softly.

'You start searching through the personal effects. Brian Mackie's due back on Monday, but bring him in tomorrow. Brief him, then put together a small team of good people who'll keep their mouths shut. Use Maggie Rose as your sergeant if you like. I'll square it with her boss.

'In the meantime, I'll find out if the Faculty has lost any other advocates lately. Then I'm off to London. I want to see Shi-Bachi, to find out a bit more about what makes a man like Yobatu tick, and why he might have been willing to carry the can for something he didn't do.'

46

Cold rain was beginning to fall on the dimly lit Morningside Street as Skinner pulled his Granada to a halt outside Peter Cowan's solid, grey, terraced home. Internal wooden shutters, an original feature still in use in many of Edinburgh's elegant Victorian homes were pulled across the ground floor windows.

The Clerk of Faculty answered Skinner's knock on the door. 'Hello, Bob. Good to see you. Congratulations are in order, I hear.'

Faster than a speeding bullet, that's the Edinburgh grapevine, thought Skinner.

'Thank you, Peter. Yes, I'm a lucky man. Happy New Year, by the way.'

'Same to you; many of them. Come away in. Now what's the mystery?' He led the way into a comfortable family sitting room, with heavy velvet curtains and a chintzy suite, set around a coal-effect gas fire.

'Deep and dark, my friend, deep and dark,' Skinner replied. 'Look, don't over-react to this, but I want you to think carefully. Have there been, since Rachel Jameson's murder, or before Mortimer's, any other deaths in the Faculty of people who might have been close to either of those two?'

Cowan's expressive eyes widened. 'Rachel's murder! You know that the Crown Office has it labelled SUICIDE in big black letters. That's how the evidence will look at the FAI.

'I thought your Japanese connection had fallen through. Hasn't it?'

'It's a long story, Peter.' He explained how the Yobatu lead had developed, and how it had ended with the intervention of Allingham and Wilson.

'Now after being convinced, I've got reason to think that Yobatu didn't do it. If Mike and Rachel were killed by the same man – as I'm bloody sure they were – and it wasn't Yobatu, then there's another reason for their deaths, and maybe, other people involved and at risk. That's my concern.'

'I see.' Cowan's face took on a troubled look. He thought in silence for a few moments. 'No. There's been no one, no deaths. Not since Rachel, and not for more than a year before Mike. And I would know. As Clerk, I have to arrange wreaths, letters of condolence, that sort of thing. We're a relatively small club, and so deaths of practising members are not exactly common. The last one before Mike was two years ago, one of our most senior seniors, and he died of cancer.'

'That's something to be going on with. How about associates? Were Mike and Rachel part of any group?'

'Not that I've ever heard of. We have some special interest groups in the Faculty, but neither Mike nor Rachel belonged to any of them.

'Apart from the Chinese business, I don't recall them ever appearing together professionally. Everyone knew they had the hots for each other, but they kept their private lives well out of the Library, as we all do.'

'What about instructing solicitors? Could there be a link there?'

'I don't see it. They both had largely criminal practices. As you know, that means that most of their work would come from the West of Scotland. I can't recall any of the Glasgow solicitor mafia having come to a sticky end in the time-scale we're considering.'

Cowan walked over to a drinks table beside the door. He picked up a decanter and a glass, and looked at Skinner, raising his eyebrows.

'No thanks, Peter,' he replied to the unspoken offer. 'It's a bit early. Anyway, I'll need to get home to break the good news to Sarah that I'm going to London first thing tomorrow.'

'To do with this?'

'Yes. I'm off for another chat with the Ambassador. There's one other thing I'd like from the Faculty. Can I have your cooperation in a very discreet check on Mortimer and Jameson? I want to go through their lives with a toothcomb, from university on. For example, I want to find out if they knew each other then.'

'I can tell you that. They didn't. Mike was Glasgow, Rachel was Edinburgh. They worked in different cities until they came to the Bar. As a matter of fact I introduced them, and they were definitely meeting for the first time.'

Cowan put the decanter back on the table, unbroached, and turned back to face Skinner.

'Bob, I'll give your people every facility. I'll find somewhere private for them to work. But we'll need a cover story. Our place is a rumour factory. Who's going to be in charge of your team?'

'Andy Martin's putting a squad together. There'll be one or two on the premises, but I'll make sure that they're not known to any of your people, and if possible – though this will be more difficult – that they don't look like polis!'

'You can pretend they're auditors. No one ever goes near them!'

Cowan chuckled. 'When do you want to start? Monday OK? I say that because I'll need to brief my secretary to sort out all of Mike and Rachel's papers without attracting attention. What about the rest of their things? Personal stuff.'

'I'll need to talk to next of kin about that. With a bit of luck it'll all still be in their flats, or in the hands of executors.'

Cowan looked at him. 'That's if they left wills. They were both young, and lawyers are as bad as any professionals at following their own advice!'

47

Leaving Gullane at 6.05 a.m., and using the Edinburgh by-pass, Skinner arrived at the airport with twenty minutes to spare. He bought a ticket and boarded the half-empty flight. The 757 took off on time, and landed without the almost obligatory wait in the Heathrow stack.

The tube was quieter than usual, free on a Saturday of the hordes of office workers. He read the Weekend section of his *Scotsman*, and passed the journey in relative comfort.

He left the tube at Green Park and walked towards Piccadilly Circus until he found the Embassy, entered, and announced himself. The young Japanese receptionist checked a sheet of crested paper on his desk, and rose from his seat. 'Please follow me, sir.'

He led Skinner up a flight of stairs and along a thickly-carpeted hallway, at the end of which double doors opened into Shi-Bachi's outer office. 'Please be seated,' the young man invited, indicating a high-backed chair.

The receptionist whispered to a middle-aged man who sat in a red leather chair behind a dark wood desk. The man looked up from his papers and replied in Japanese. The youth withdrew, and the aide turned to Skinner. 'Good morning, sir. I will see if the Ambassador is free.'

He picked up one of three telephones on his desk, pressed a button, and spoke. In the flow of Japanese, Skinner recognised his own name. The man replaced the phone. 'The Ambassador will see you at once,' he said, indicating by his tone that the speed of the audience was something of an honour.

He escorted Skinner through a second set of double doors into a long room. The wall facing the door, was almost completely window, shrouded by heavy blast curtains in white net. The Ambassador's vast desk was set to the left, away from the windows. A portrait of the Emperor hung behind the swivel chair, with another of his late father above the fireplace opposite.

Shi-Bachi rose and walked towards Skinner, extending his hand in Western-style greeting. 'Good morning, Assistant Chief Constable. I am glad to see you again.'

Skinner bowed briefly and shook the extended hand. 'And I to see you, sir.'

They settled into two soft armchairs. The man from the outer office reappeared with a tray, on which were set a silver tea-pot, two china cups, a small jug of milk, and to Skinner's private amusement, a large plate of chocolate digestive biscuits.

Shi-Bachi pointed to the plate and laughed. 'Some things are common to both our cultures!' The Ambassador's aide looked puzzled as he poured.

Each sipped his tea in silence for a moment. At last Shi-Bachi spoke. 'So, Mr Skinner,' he asked softly, 'what is it that you wish to tell me about Yobatu *san*?'

'I have something to tell and something to ask, Your Excellency. New evidence has been discovered. We now know that the person who killed Mortimer looked inside his document case after the murder. And it appears that Miss Jameson's business case was stolen at the time of her death.

'The motive for the killings of the Chinese and the two advocates was a very strong part of the case against Yobatu *san*. What possible reason could he have had, once he had killed, for stealing the papers of his victims? And the second theft, from the platform, after Miss Jameson had been pushed under the train, was incredibly risky.

'No, Your Excellency, if theft was the real motive for the killings, and it now appears that it may have been, then the circumstantial case against Yobatu *san* is destroyed.'

Shi-Bachi held up his hand. 'But there was certain, er, physical evidence, was there not?'

'Which could have been planted for us to find. If that was done by someone who knew, or could guess that we were about to search, it would have been easy to time it so that there was little risk of Yobatu finding the evidence before we did. What better way of concealing a motive for murder and the identity of a killer than by framing an unstable man with a strong reason to kill, and one who, as an added bonus, could not be tried, only removed from the country?'

'But I would have seen to it that he stood trial.'

'Remember Allingham and Wilson. They were there to see to it that he did not.'

Shi-Bachi's small eyes twinkled. 'You believe that they are involved in this conspiracy, that your government is involved?'

'No, sir, I don't say that. The fact is that there was some political force to Allingham's argument, and Lord Muckhart may well have wanted to have avoided such a high-profile prosecution.'

Shi-Bachi nodded. 'I can see that. You have told me something that has eased my mind of a burden. What was it that you wished to ask me?'

Skinner sat forward in his chair, his elbows on his knees and bunched his hands together. 'It's your opinion as Yobatu *san*'s countryman that I need. The man had every chance to deny these crimes before he became ill. Why didn't he? His silence is my last reason to believe in his guilt.'

Shi-Bachi also perched on the edge of his chair.

'Mr Skinner, I have to tell you this. I have never believed that Yobatu *san* did these things. To be frank, that was why I was so keen that he should be made available for trial. Your evidence was strong, but I knew the man. He was of a samurai family, yes, and he boasted of it. But it was an empty boast. Yobatu *san* may have looked impressive, but it was all show. He may have had the blood of the samurai, but he was no warrior.

'He was sent to Scotland by his family to run an off-shoot company because he lacked the nerve to take essential but difficult management decisions at the centre. His business policies were laid down by Japan. His diplomatic status was gained through family influence, as a favour to them, and as a means of giving face to him. But he never actually did anything official. In his behaviour, Yobatu *san* deserted Japan. He adopted the ways of the West completely, keeping only the posturings of the Samurai to remind him of his heritage.'

Skinner held up a hand. 'In that case, sir, why did he not deny the murders from the outset? And why did he collapse after being arrested?'

'Here you can have my educated guess. When you told him what had happened to those people, the posturing samurai took over. His first reaction was to pretend for a while that he had done as his ancestors would have.

'His collapse? When it dawned on him that someone had done those things for him; that because of his weakness, his revenge had been taken by someone else, then laid at his door along with other bloody deeds. I would guess that his collapse was caused in part by his fear of the consequences for him of these things that he had not done, but also by his shame that he had not done them.'

Shi-Bachi sat back in his chair. He looked tired.

Skinner smiled slightly at him. 'Your Excellency, we have a psychiatrist in Edinburgh named O'Malley. I think he could learn from you.'

The Ambassador chuckled. 'I am glad to hear you say that. You see, I too am a psychoanalyst by profession.'

Suddenly something clicked in Skinner's mind. 'Sir, earlier you spoke of Yobatu *san* in the past tense. Was that unintentional?'

Shi-Bachi looked grave again. 'You are a thorough and perceptive man. When Yobatu *san* went back to Japan, I sent him to my clinic. There, my colleagues worked hard to bring him back into contact with the world. Gradually they began to succeed, although he never spoke. Three days ago, he dressed up in his Western clothes to meet his wife. When she came into his room, she found him hanging by his tie.'

48

The meeting with Shi-Bachi lasted for just over forty-five minutes. When Skinner emerged from the Embassy into Piccadilly, the morning was still fine. He strolled back towards the Circus, and turned past the restored Eros into Regent Street. As he walked a wave of depression settled on him. The Ambassador had removed any last thought that Yobatu might after all be guilty.

He was back to square one, starting an investigation into a possible murder conspiracy on the basis of evidence which, to others, might have seemed shaky. What if Mortimer had nicked himself shaving, and a drop of blood had fallen into the open case? Did he own black woollen gloves? Could the strands have come from them? What if Jameson's case had indeed been stolen by a casual thief? The murders had stopped, the affair was closed. Should he leave it that way?

'The hell I should!' Skinner exploded aloud, startling a street corner news vendor.

He arrived back at Fettes Avenue just after 4.00 p.m. Brian Mackie sat in the outer office, casually dressed, working his way through a pile of papers. The second desk, occupied during the week by a secretary, showed signs of use. Skinner jerked a thumb towards it and raised an enquiring eyebrow.

'Maggie Rose, sir.' Mackie answered the unspoken question. 'She's helping me with this lot. Statements from Mortimer's family and closest friends, and from those who saw him in the Library before he was killed. So far there's nothing. No one can think of anyone with a grudge against him, or can credit that he might have been involved in anything at all dodgy.'

'Is there a statement by Rachel Jameson there?'

'First one I studied, boss. There's nothing in it. Not a hint of anything like a lead. And she must have known him better than anyone.'

Skinner looked hard at Mackie.

'This won't be easy, Brian. If there's something there waiting to be found, we'll find it, but it'll take balls-aching hard work. Go over everything, and then go over it again. Glamorous job this, is it not?'

Maggie Rose came into the room, carrying two mugs of coffee. She started in surprise when she saw Skinner. 'Afternoon sir . . . and a Happy New Year.'

'Thanks, Sergeant.' He smiled at her. 'Same to you.'

He turned back to Mackie. 'Andy in?'

Maggie Rose answered. 'I think he's in his office, sir. I saw a light under the door when I was out for these.'

Skinner walked the few yards along the corridor to the Special Branch suite. Martin was at his desk, making a telephone call. He waved his free hand in a wind-up motion as he saw Skinner enter, and terminated the call after a few seconds.

'Hello, boss. London didn't take long. What happened?' In detail, Skinner told him. Martin grimaced at the story of Yobatu's suicide.

'So he really wasn't our man.'

'No Andy, not a chance. The poor bastard was trussed up like a Christmas turkey and set out before us. And we, greedy and gullible coppers that we are, we did the carving.

'Right, so what are we doing here?'

'Well, boss, we've started on all the available papers – statements that sort of stuff – in the Mortimer job. And the Transport plods are sending us through all their witness statements – such as they are – on Jameson.

'I've also spoken to Rachel's mother again this morning. We've had a bit of luck there. It seems that Mortimer and Rachel were planning to get married next summer. In advance of that, they'd bought a new house together. It's not built yet, but they'd signed up for mortgage, insurance and all that. When they did that, they each made a will naming the other. And each of them specified the same guy as executor; Kenny Duff of Curle, Anthony and Jarvis, in Charlotte Square. I've spoken to him.'

'Good day's work. What'd he say?'

Martin took a sip of coffee from the big white mug before him.

'Well for openers, neither Mike's nor Rachel's flat has been put on the market yet. Wrong time of year apparently. The new house wasn't to be ready until next September or October. So both places are lying there virtually as they were at the times of the murders. The only papers that have been disturbed are those to do with insurance, property and that sort of thing. All their personal and business documents will still be there.

'That's the good news. Now here's something that you're not going to like. Kenny Duff found definite signs of entry at each flat. There were indications that they had been searched, and one or two small items had been taken.'

'So what did he do?'

'Reported it to Gayfield, and explained the circumstances.'

Skinner's face darkened. 'And what did they do?'

Martin looked at him. 'They visited each locus with Mr Duff, dusted the doors for fingerprints, didn't find any, took notes, and filed them.'

'They had the names?' Skinner's voice had a cutting edge. Martin nodded. 'And they did sweet fuck all?' Martin nodded again.

Skinner turned, picked up Martin's telephone and dialled his own extension number. 'Brian, I want the names of the CID officers who attended reported break-ins at . . . ' he looked at the note Martin handed to him and read out the addresses, ' . . . on December the ninth, and I want them on my carpet on Monday morning. And tell them to come in their best uniforms.'

He slammed down the telephone. 'Let them sweat it out for a couple of days.'

His anger, as usual, went quickly. 'What about keys? Will we need warrants?'

'The keys are all safe and sound at Curle, Anthony and Jarvis. Kenny Duff will let us have them tomorrow. And there's no question of warrants, even as a formality. He's being very co-operative.'

'That's good. What did you tell him?'

'A version of the truth. That our enquiries are continuing and that we need to look through personal papers to pursue them.'

'Right. Stand down the people for today. We'll meet here at nine-thirty tomorrow morning. Now I'm off to make it up with my fiancée, and to explain why her Sunday's going the same way as her Saturday!'

49

The team was assembled in Skinner's outer office and ready for briefing when he arrived, one minute before 9.30 a.m. Martin, Mackie and Maggie Rose had been joined by two Special Branch detectives, and a young woman in uniform, whom he had not seen before.

The squad stood to attention until Skinner motioned them to sit. Martin began the introductions. 'Maggie you know, boss. You may also recall these two, DCs McGuire and McIlhenney.'

He introduced the uniformed girl. 'You probably won't have met WPC Aileen Stimson, sir. Aileen is fairly new on the force, but I chose her for two reasons. One, her station inspector gave her as good a report as I've ever heard, and two, she has a law degree.'

Skinner nodded to the girl, then rose to his feet. 'Thank you, Chief Inspector.

'Good morning, ladies and gentlemen. Those of you who are not already in the know will undoubtedly be wondering what can have led me to assemble a squad like this, with such urgency, and on a Sunday morning. Let me tell you.

'We have reason to believe that there may be a link between the deaths of Michael Mortimer, an advocate, and the first of the Royal Mile victims, and his girlfriend Rachel Jameson, also an advocate, who went under a train in Glasgow, just a few days after Mortimer's murder. Our friends in the Crown Office insist that she jumped. I don't believe that. I'm damn sure she was pushed.

'We know that whoever killed Mortimer did the other three Royal Mile jobs. For a while, that led us down a false trail, and eventually to a certain deranged individual, with a strong revenge motive. Some of you know that much already. But recently, we found evidence that Mortimer's briefcase had been tampered with after his death, and that Jameson's had been stolen from the scene of her murder. Now, to top that, we have discovered that the flats of both victims have been entered and searched.

'So it looks as if the killer was after something from Mortimer and Jameson. We have to find out what that was. Once we know that, we should know why they were killed. From there it should be a short step to whoever did it.

'Between us, we are going to cover every inch of the personal and professional lives of Michael Mortimer and Rachel Jameson. We will go through their papers looking for anything that is at all odd or out of place. I can't give you a more detailed brief, but you're all bright people. You'll know it when you see it. Chief Inspector Martin will allocate duties.'

He sat down.

Martin stood up and faced the team. 'Thank you, Mr Skinner. On this operation there will be three search locations, and you will divide into three search units.

'DI Mackie and DC McIlhenney will examine all of the papers and effects in Mortimer's flat. DS Rose and DC McGuire will search Miss Jameson's place.' His eyes swung towards the uniformed girl. 'You, Miss Stimson, will be based at the Advocates' Library, going over yet again all of the instructions with which the two victims have been involved over the last eighteen months. I've placed you there on your own. We have already been through these papers, and so, frankly, I don't expect to find anything. But we must go back one more time. This is a discreet operation, and if you're alone, we can give you the cover of a research fellow. With your legal background, you'll be able to talk to the advocates without attracting suspicion.'

He turned to Skinner. 'I've agreed this with Peter Cowan, boss.' The ACC nodded his approval. 'Aileen, your reward is that you can have the rest of the day off. But meet me here tomorrow morning at 8.15 sharp, in suitable civilian clothes. That means sober dress; nothing that will raise the blood pressure of any passing judges!

'The rest of us will start now. Brian, Maggie, here are the keys. The addresses are on the labels.'

He threw keys on rings to Mackie and Rose. Each key ring was weighted by a Dundas & Wilson card, encased in plastic. Each card bore the practice logo and an address.

'While you are picking your way through the paper, the boss and I will be digging into the past of both victims, looking for skeletons in their cupboards.'

Martin finished and sat down, returning the floor to Skinner.

'One last word, although it's a long one for you lot. Confidentiality. Outside of this room, no one, apart from Peter Cowan at the Faculty of

157

Advocates, knows the full nature of this enquiry. So if word leaks out, I'll know where to look. So no discussion, even among yourselves in the pub. Keep it tight.'

He looked around the circle of faces before him. 'Any questions?'

No one spoke or moved.

'Right, let's go to work.'

50

Skinner sank into his swivel chair, swung his feet up on to the desk, picked up the telephone and punched in the 041- number which Martin had written out for him.

After a short delay, the call was answered by a man, a man with an old, tired voice. 'Hello, Jimmy Mortimer.' The tones were gruff, the accent broad Clydebank.

Skinner introduced himself and explained the purpose of his call.

Jimmy Mortimer grunted. 'Hm. Yis still don't hiv a bliddy clue, hiv yis?'

'We have lines of enquiry to follow, Mr Mortimer, and one requires that we talk to your son's friends, all the way back to his schooldays. So if you can help me, I'd be grateful.'

'Look, mister, ma son's new friends wis all lawyers, and he didnae even have much time for them once he took up wi' yon poor lassie. Round aboot here, when he wis a laddie, his best pal was Johnny Smiley. Nice lad. Always aboot the hoose. He's a teacher noo; works in Port Glesca High, ah think. Oor Michael said he wis livin' in Langbank. Is that ony guid tae yis?'

'It'll do for a start, Mr Mortimer. Thank you very much.'

Skinner clicked the line dead and called up the switchboard operator. 'ACC Skinner here, Olive. I'd like you to do a bit of detective work for me. I want to speak to a Mr John Smiley, he's a teacher, and he lives in Langbank, Renfrewshire, but I don't have an address for him. He is, or rather was, a friend of a Mr Michael Mortimer. See if you can find him for me, please.'

'Yes, sir,' said the crisp clear voice at the other end of the line. 'How are you spelling that name?'

'Good question. Try S-M-I-L-E-Y or S-M-I-L-L-I-E. No, wait a minute. It's the West of Scotland; first try S-M-E-L-L-I-E.'

'Pardon?'

'I'm serious. They pronounce it Smiley. Wouldn't you?'

The operator laughed. 'No, sir, I'd change it! I'll be as quick as I can.'

Skinner was surprised when Olive rang back three minutes later. 'I've got your man, Mr Skinner. You were right; he's one of the Smellies.'

'Thanks, Olive. That's good work. Will you put him through, please.'

There was a faint click on the line. 'Mr Smellie? Assistant Chief Constable Bob Skinner, from Edinburgh. I'm told by the father of the late Michael Mortimer that you were a friend of his son.'

'Yes, that's correct. Since high school.' The accent was similar to that of Jimmy Mortimer, but the rough corners had been polished smooth, to leave a clear classroom voice. It was deep, and rolled down the telephone line like an advancing fog.

'I'll be frank with you, Mr Smellie. We have run our enquiries almost to a standstill. We are looking for any sort of a lead, and so we are talking to friends of all the victims in this series of murders, just asking about them, trying to build up a picture of the sort of people they were.'

'Where'll that get you?'

'I'll know that when I get there. What can you tell me about Mike?'

'Hah.' The single sound was laden with sadness and irony. 'What's to tell? Mike was a great bloke. The most gifted guy I ever knew. A warm kind man with a generous spirit.'

'What was he like at school?'

'He was a leader, but without being resented in any way for it. Everyone liked him, pupils and staff. He was brilliant academically, but never flaunted it. He was only average at games, but made up for it by trying twice as hard as anyone else. And if anyone had a problem, he'd always help, but never talk about it afterwards.'

'Did he stay that way? How did university affect him?'

'As a friend, not at all. But as an individual, he became more passionate, more involved with issues. He took part in all the Union debates, although he said he was doing it as part of his preparation for the law.'

'Was he political?'

'Yes and no. He always refused to join the heavy political groups. Spoke in debates as an independent. But personally, you'd probably have called him left-wing. He supported every oppressed group under the sun, South African blacks, South American Indians, North American Indians, Palestinians, Soviet Jews; you name it, if a group was under anyone's thumb, Mike would speak up for it.'

'Girlfriends?'

'In the four years that we were at Glasgow together, I remember him having two brief things then one steady relationship. That was with a girl called Liz something. It lasted till we all graduated, then she went off to study French in France, and it just sort of died a natural death.

'After that there were one or two who were fairly close. Sleeping together, but no long-term commitment either way. Mike was too keen on the law to allow it to have a rival in his life. Until he went to the Bar and met Rachel.'

'Did you see him much after university?'

'Yes, a lot when he was in Glasgow. Once he moved to Edinburgh, not so much. But we were still best mates. It was the sort of friendship where you don't need to see each other all the time.'

'Did you ever meet Rachel?'

'Of course. She was at our wedding last summer. Mike was best man. Christ, I was going to be best man at his, when they finally got round to setting the date.' Smellie's voice faltered at the memory.

Skinner allowed the man a few seconds to compose himself. 'Did you know much about Mike's professional life?'

'A bit. Not the detail. He was meticulous. Never referred to his clients by name, or discussed cases in depth. But he did tell me that he liked criminal work, enjoyed defending a client who he felt had been victimised by the police – sorry, Mr Skinner, but that was the way he put it – and really fighting for him. He had a good record too. He and Rachel defended two Chinese guys who had been charged with rape and murder. Mike thought they were carrying the can for someone else. Between them, they took the prosecution to bits, and got them off.'

'Yes,' said Skinner, 'I've heard about that case. Not one of the Crown's finest hours.

'He never mentioned any work, or any private interest even, that was out of the ordinary?'

'No, nothing that I can think of. No, never.'

'Mm.' Skinner paused. He sensed that the man was talked out. 'Thank you very much, Mr Smellie; I'm sorry to have broken into your Sunday morning.'

Skinner replaced his receiver and swung round in his chair, sliding his long legs under the desk.

So that was it. The life of Michael. Brilliant, kind, and passionate about the law, oppressed minorities, and one woman. No enemies, save for Yobatu, and he was out of the picture.

Another brick wall across the highway of progress.

161

51

As Skinner teased memories of Mortimer from Johnny Smellie, Martin, in his office, made his way gently back into the life of Rachel Jameson.

He began by calling Kay Allan, by her mother's reckoning her best Edinburgh friend. Mrs Allan came to the telephone drowsily, after being wakened by her husband. He had been annoyed by a Sunday morning call from anyone, let alone the police.

Martin introduced himself.

'How long had you known Miss Jameson, Mrs Allan?'

'About four years. We were in the same squash club, then we went to a keep-fit class together. And we went out for drinks on occasion with other girls in our circle.'

'What sort of person was she?'

'On the outside a quiet, gentle sort of person, but nobody's soft touch. I went to see her in court once. She was really forceful. It took me by surprise. It was someone that I didn't really know.'

'Did you ever meet her boyfriend?'

'Mike? Yes, quite a few times. He was a really nice bloke. The same type as Rachel, but with more showing on the outside. They were really well matched. What happened to him was just terrible. Poor Mike. Poor Rachel. To have everything, and then to have it all wiped out.'

'Did you see Miss Jameson after Mr Mortimer's death?'

'Yes. I went round the evening after it happened. She was, well, funny; very quiet, very controlled, but it was as if a big black blanket had wrapped itself around her. I couldn't reach her at all. I wasn't really surprised when she killed herself. She was keeping all the grief inside. And that's dangerous, so they say.'

'That evening, or at any other time, did she ever talk about her work?'

'Not much. She mentioned one or two criminal cases. She did tell me that she was worried about that last case. What was the man's name? McGann? McCunn? No, McCann, that was it. She said that he scared

162

the life out of her. She told me that she was sure he was guilty, but he had a defence and although she thought he was lying, she was worried that if the main prosecution witness wasn't good, he might get off. The advocate's dilemma, she called it. He didn't get off, did he, but he escaped. Have they got him yet?'

'Yes, the French police picked him up last week in Dijon. He's been charged with murdering an old woman for the sake of the forty-three francs in her purse.'

'Horrible. Rachel was right about him.'

'She surely was. Mrs Allan, did Miss Jameson ever mention anything she was working on that was out of the usual run of things; something that she might have been working on with Mike?'

The woman was silent for several seconds. 'Only the house. They'd bought a piece of land in West Linton. They were getting married next autumn and they were going to build a house.

'But work, no. Nothing at all.'

'Did Miss Jameson have any other male friends before Mike, or even while she was seeing him?'

'You can forget the second part of that question. Those two were soul-mates – there's an old-fashioned term for you. Before, I suppose she had. There was some fat wimp of an accountant tagging along when I first knew her, and she did mention once that she'd been keen on some chap at university, but that was all.'

Martin noted the two slim and unlikely leads. 'Mrs Allan, that's been a big help. I'll let you get back to sleep now.'

'No such luck! The baby's awake!' She laughed grimly, and hung up.

He chose another name from the list of friends. Marjorie Porteous had been Rachel's equivalent of Johnny Smellie, her best friend through her schooldays at St George's, and on through university. She had taken her Economics First to the City, and had married a property developer.

When Martin called the Maidenhead number, the telephone was answered by a woman with an accent redolent of Morningside, that refined but decaying suburb of Edinburgh. '652375. Marjorie d'Antonio speaking.' Rachel's mother had voiced to Martin her suspicion that the husband, whom she recalled from the wedding, had been christened Anthony Muggins, and had had swift recourse as an adult to the deed poll procedure.

'Good morning, Mrs d'Antonio.' Martin introduced himself and explained the reason for his call. At once the assertive voice at the other end of the line softened, and the accent became less pronounced.

'Yes. Poor Rachel. How can I help you, Chief Inspector?'

'By telling me about Miss Jameson and your friendship.'

'Where to begin? Rachel came to St George's when she was fourteen. You know what they say about St George's? "All they teach you there is how to write cheques."' She laughed at her quip.

'Well in our case at least, it wasn't true. Rachel and I were sort of star pupils in our year. Did our full quota of "A" levels and went to Edinburgh University together. At school, Rachel was always the popular one. Everyone thought I was a conceited little cow, and guess what, they were right, but Rachel had no airs and graces. She was head girl in our final year, and she fixed it for me to be a prefect. I got my own back on a few then, I'll tell you!'

Martin chuckled at the woman's openness. He was warming to her more and more as the call progressed. 'What about university? Did you both live at home?'

'In our first year, yes. Then my Dad bought a flat in Marchmont as an investment, and we moved in, with a succession of other girls.'

'Was Rachel active in university clubs?'

'No. Not really. We both joined the North America travel club, and spent our second summer vacation working in San Francisco, but that was all. She didn't get involved in politics or anything of that sort. She thought it was a waste of study time, and so did I.'

'If she had joined a political club, what do you think it would have been?'

Marjorie's answer came back without a pause. 'The SNP. She was very into ethnic rights. Stood up for the oppressed and all that.'

'Did she have any relationships at university?'

'With men? Just a few flings at first. Quick grope in the Odeon, that level of thing. But only one serious affair, in our third year. Her grades dipped a bit because of it. In fact that's why she had to settle for a Two-One, rather than a First; no doubt about it.'

'Do you remember anything about the man?'

'Not even his name. She called him Fuzzy; we all did. He was some sort of Arab. They met at a Union disco. Quick dance, he flashed the brown eyes and that was it.'

'What sort of a man was he?'

'I don't really know. He hardly ever said anything. He was about the flat quite a lot. I mean, he and Rachel were sleeping together, but he never strung together any more than yes, no, please and thank you, when anyone else was around. I think it might have been the fact that he was

164

so shy that attracted Rachel to him. When they were alone you could hear them yakking away through the wall.'

'What happened?'

'He left at the end of the year. But I could sense that it was running out of steam by then. Rachel told me so. She said that the trouble was his intensity, and his complete lack of humour. So he left, we went to the Côte d'Azur to work for the summer, Rachel met a big blond Swede with muscles everywhere, and I mean everywhere, and forgot about Fuzzy. End of chapter.'

'How about men after that?'

'I didn't see all that much of her after I moved south. But we exchanged letters often, and I gathered from them that there was no one serious for a long time, not until she met Mike Mortimer.'

'When did you see her last?'

'In the autumn. She came down for a weekend in September. The time before that was when I visited my parents in the spring.'

'Did she say anything on either occasion about anything unusual that she and Mike, or either of them alone, might have been involved in?'

'No. All she talked about was how happy they were, and how she would be able to take a year off from practice to have a baby when the time came, and how super everything was going to be. And then!' Suddenly Marjorie, on the other end of the telephone, burst into tears. 'What a shame. What a bloody shame. And what a waste.'

52

The cobbles roared under the wheels of the Astra as they drove through the New Town. Martin parked on a yellow line across the street from Mortimer's flat. There was an old-fashioned remote entry system on the heavy outer door. Skinner rang the bell and after a few seconds the door creaked open. They stepped into a cold, dull hallway, and went through a second door, glass-panelled this time.

'Up here!' Brian Mackie called down to them.

The two detectives trotted up to the second floor. At the top of the stairway, the DI held a door open.

Mike Mortimer's living room was furnished conservatively, mostly with reproduction items, but with one or two antique pieces situated prominently.

'Nice place,' said Martin.

'A change from your bloody Habitat warehouse!' Skinner suggested.

Mackie grinned. 'You should take a look in the bedroom. The fourposter must have cost a bob or two.'

'Does it have a canopy?' Skinner asked.

'Yes, boss. And we've checked. There's nothing stashed up there.' Mackie smiled, unable to hide his pleasure at having anticipated the question which had been bound to follow.

'We've been all over the place. All his personal and business records were in that big desk over there, or in these two cupboards. He's had them converted into filing cabinets.'

Mackie walked over to a door set in the wall to the left of the eastfacing window. He threw it open. The space behind was filled with sidehung file racks, most of them stuffed with papers and manila folders.

Skinner looked inside. 'You've got some work ahead of you. Is the other one the same?'

'There's this thing as well. We'll need to look at it.' He turned again towards the desk. The only incongruous object in the room was a grey micro-computer with a small dot-matrix printer attached by a ribbon cable. By its side was a small box with a clear plastic lid, containing a number of computer disks in cardboard holders. Mackie picked one out and showed it to Skinner and Martin. 'He's been kind enough to label all of these. All I need now is to be able to read them.'

Skinner moved over to the desk. 'I think I can show you how, Brian.' He looked at the computer. 'Yes. It's an Amstrad 8512, twin-drive, bog-standard machine. My daughter has one for her studies. Watch me.'

He ran through the start-up procedure for Mackie. 'Is that clear enough, Brian?'

'Yes boss. Thanks. Thanks for God knows how much work. Each of these things could hold a hell of a lot of files, and we'll have to look at them all.' He counted fourteen disks in the box.

'Sorry Brian, but you're right. A complete search does include our friend Mr Amstrad. Just make sure that you don't alter any of the files as you read them.'

He turned away then turned back towards Mackie. 'By the way, have you discussed your search procedure with Maggie?'

'Yes, boss, we're going about it the same way.'

'That's good. We'll pay her a visit now, to see how big a task she has.' He made the slightest move towards the door, then turned back again, as if with another afterthought. 'Brian, let's try to make life a bit easier for you. Did friend Michael have an address book, or a card index and a diary?'

'All in one, sir. He had a Filofax. A yuppie's handbook.'

His smile turned watery as he remembered the black leather personal organiser which Martin always carried, and felt the green eyes boring into him. Skinner picked up the gaffe and laughed. So did Martin. Eventually Mackie, looking relieved, joined in. From the desk he picked up a heavy brown leather binder secured by a strong clasp. The initials 'MM' were picked out in gold leaf in the bottom right corner. He handed it to Skinner.

Rachel Jameson's flat was also in a New Town block, but different in style to that of Mortimer. In estate-agent terms, it was a typical Edinburgh garden flat, in the basement of what had once been an entire house on four floors. Its entrance was below street level, accessed by a short flight of steps. French doors opened from the living-room on to a small rear courtyard, which Rachel had brightened with an array of hardy shrubs and flowers, set out in earthenware vessels. Skinner noted, with amusement, plants set in two tall chimney-pots, scavenged, no doubt, from a demolished building.

167

Like Mortimer's flat, it was part home, part office. Rachel's files were contained in two steel cabinets which stood, as Maggie Rose showed Skinner and Martin, in a deep cupboard off the hall.

She pulled open the four drawers in the two low cabinets.

'Fewer documents than Mortimer,' Skinner remarked.

'She seems to have been a very neat person, sir. I've been right through this flat, while Mario . . . '

'Who?'

'DC McGuire, sir. His first name's Mario.'

'Jesus Christ, what a mixture. Ice-cream and Guinness! Sorry, go on, Maggie.'

' . . . while Mario sorted out the papers. I've been trying to judge what sort of a woman this was. To imagine myself as her, in fact.'

'Very good. So what sort of a picture have you formed? Describe yourself to me.'

The red-haired woman hesitated, took a deep breath and began. 'Well, sir, as I've said, I'm very neat. My files are in such good order because I've summarised all my older ones and destroyed a lot of paper, or archived it in the cellar at the front under the pavement, which I've had water-proofed.

'My diary is meticulous. So are my personal habits and my dress. I use good quality soap and shampoo, not over-priced designer stuff. I bathe or shower at least twice a day – and perhaps not always alone, because there are three big towels on the heated rail. I buy most of my bras, knickers and tights at Marks & Spencer, and my working clothes at Jenners. I use storecards and chargecards rather than cash or cheques, with direct-debit arrangements with my bank.

'I'm reserved and elegant, but I can be a bit sexy too, because I have a collection of rather more exotic underwear, and one or two designer evening dresses that are guaranteed to attract attention. I'd say that I like sex, but only as a shared experience. By that I mean, if I may be blunt, that I like making love but not screwing. When I dress sexy it's for my partner's pleasure as much as mine.

'My reading list shows that I'm a very thoughtful person. I don't throw books away. Some I read over and over again. I like Tolkein, I like Leon Uris. I like Solzhenitsyn. I like Tom Sharpe's early novels, the ones that take the piss out of the South African police, but I ignore the rest of his stuff because I think it's sexist.

'My taste in music is broad, but I'm no musician. I like strong memorable melodies, from Mozart to Mendelssohn, or Marley to Morrison. It says what I think as well as how I feel. There's a Marley CD on my player right now, with three songs programmed – this is true, sir, it must have been like that since the last time she walked out – "Buffalo Soldiers", "Get Up, Stand Up", and "Redemption Song", all of them strong political statements.

'As an advocate, I'm part of the establishment. Yet when I consider my taste in literature and in music, I have to admit to myself that I'm drawn to the side of the poor people. I'm for what I regard as good against evil, and some of my beliefs and causes would be regarded as pretty left wing. If I felt something strongly enough, I'd go all the way. I have the determination to do that.'

'You sound like quite a lady, Rachel Jameson. Are you a strong person?'

'Yes, I think I am. Not physically brave perhaps, but morally strong.'

'Are you loyal?'

'Absolutely. If you're my friend, you're my friend for life and I'll do anything I can to help you.'

Skinner looked down at the serious face. 'Are you sure that none of Maggie Rose has crept into this analysis?'

She smiled. 'Quite sure, sir. I like Georgette Heyer, Len Deighton, Wet Wet Wet and Joan Armatrading. My favourite clothes are denim. As for sex, I prefer reading about it to doing it. I'll give to the RSPCA, but not Greenpeace. I'm an out-and-out realist, not a closet idealist. We couldn't have been less alike.'

Skinner continued to study her for a few moments. 'Maggie, I have a feeling that you have just given this investigation its first big push forward. I don't know why, or how, but I do.'

Then he swept back to business. 'That's what you've picked up from her knicker drawer and record collection. Does anything shout at you so far from her papers?'

'Yes, sir, one thing. We've found desk diaries here dating back to 1986, meticulously kept, with ticks for completed engagements and everything. But this year's diary is missing. Either it was in her briefcase, or it was taken from here by our man. I'd say that's more likely. The earlier diaries aren't the sort you carry around. They're detailed, the sort you would keep at base, with your Filofax for quick reference.

'Only there's no Filofax here, and I'd bet this lady had one.'

Skinner nodded his agreement. 'Could her desk diary be with her clerk up at the Faculty?'

'Not very likely, sir. The earlier ones aren't just business records.

169

There's some very personal stuff there too. They show when she met Mortimer, weekends away, and so on. There's even a date a while back, not long after she met Mortimer, with "M" and two big crosses alongside. I think I can guess what they signified. You don't leave that sort of thing at your office, do you?'

Skinner grinned briefly, bringing a slight flush to Maggie's face. 'Not personally. I'll ask Aileen to confirm that tomorrow, but I'm sure you're right. Advocates' clerks maintain business diaries for each person in their stable, and they never leave the office, as a rule.

'Have you discussed this with what's his name, Paddy Pavarotti?'

'No, sir, he didn't look at the diaries, and I didn't mention it.'

'Good. Don't. There's no need for him to know. The implications of this could be more serious than you can imagine, so don't talk about it, even to Brian.

'At this stage, only Andy and I need to know.'

53

As Skinner and Martin left the neat little garden flat, the mid-afternoon sun hung low in the western sky. Martin carried Rachel Jameson's address book. As they drove back towards Fettes Avenue, Skinner told him of Maggie Rose's discovery.

'Does she know that would confirm everything we suspect?'

'You can be sure of it. She has a fine mind, has our Maggie. She's figured out that it proves that Rachel didn't kill herself, and that the person who did has been into that flat removing any leads. She's been told in confidence, along with every one else involved in the Balerno search that Yobatu turned out to be as daft as a brush, and that he's been shipped very quietly to a laughing academy in Japan. She knows that Kenny Duff has pinned the break-ins down to December the ninth at the earliest – after Yobatu was lifted. Her mind's working away; so she can guess that Yobatu was set up. But what she can't know is how far that could lead us, to the possibility of the Foreign Secretary and the Lord Advocate being parties to the frame.'

Martin whistled. 'You don't really think that, do you, boss?'

'No, that needn't follow. As I told Shi-Bachi, there was a ring of unpleasant truth in what Allingham and Wilson said at that meeting. Diplomatic immunity is a valuable principle, and I can understand the Foreign Office not wanting that boat rocked.

'But the theft of that diary, and the break-in at Mortimer's place make it certain that we are on the track of something solid here.'

Martin turned the car into Howe Street. 'One thing, boss. Whoever our guy is, he's a really clever bastard. So why didn't he conceal the fact of the searches?'

'Yes, I'm asking myself that one. Plain carelessness is one answer. Another is that with Yobatu firmly in the frame, he didn't see the need. He couldn't have known about the wills, or the joint executor. If it hadn't been for Kenny Duff, these break-ins would probably have been reported separately, to different shifts at Gayfield. Or maybe they wouldn't have been reported at all. We've had a slice of luck there, I think.'

He paused for a moment, in reflection, and went on: 'You're right, Andy. This is an extremely clever sod, and we're back in this game only by the skin of our teeth. He's left one unavoidable lead, by stealing Rachel's briefcase, and he's made one major mistake, leaving his mark on Mortimer's.

'We've just got to hope that he's made others and that the trail isn't wiped completely clean from here on.

'You take that address book of Rachel's, and I'll take Mortimer's Filofax. Let's disregard for now every listing of full name and addresses in Edinburgh and Glasgow. Start off by looking for entries that might be unusual or cryptic in any way.'

Martin turned into the Fettes Avenue car park and pulled up beside Skinner's Granada.

The tall man climbed out. Ducking his head back through the passenger door he said, 'I'm off home. You should do the same, but don't forget your evening reading.'

On impulse, Skinner walked back to Stockbridge. At his brisk pace it took ten minutes. He and Sarah had marked their engagement by an exchange of keys. For the first time in his life, he let himself into the apartment.

'I'm home!' he called from the hall to the warm flat.

Fresh food smells drifted from the kitchen. Sarah emerged, with her hair tied high and her shoulders bare. She wore a long wrap-round apron, a pair of sandals, and nothing else. She stood on tip-toe and kissed him.

'God, I must get used to this new situation!' she whispered. 'You could have had Andy with you, or anyone.' Bob grinned and wound his arms around her, grasping a firm buttock in each hand.

'Hungry?' she asked softly. It was a loaded question.

Later, Bob wearing a leisure suit and Sarah still in her apron, but worn over a tee-shirt and denims, they cooked the meal which Sarah had been preparing earlier. They ate at the rectangular pine kitchen table, following the stir-fry with fruit salad taken from the freezer, and opting for Swan low alcohol lager rather than wine.

While they ate, nothing was said about the investigation. It was only after Bob had poured their coffee that Sarah asked him about it.

'What did you achieve today, my darling?'

'Today we've only built the machine and set it in motion. Now the hard part begins.'

He paused for a moment, staring into his coffee mug, then looked up at Sarah as she leaned across the table, her chin resting in her cupped hand.

'I made a heavy point about secrecy this morning. I told the team not to talk to anyone about what they're doing; and I meant anyone, wives and or sweethearts included. Now I want to break my own rule. I feel I've got to tell you all about it.'

Sarah dropped her hand from her chin and looked into his eyes, frowning slightly. 'Of course you do. And you should. Bob, you're not like the team. Only you and Andy know the whole story. And you think that you might be involved in something tremendous, and awful. You know for sure it's highly dangerous. You're wrapped up in it. If you don't have some sort of confessional, a safe, secure sounding board, you could become obsessive about it. This is your doctor speaking.

'But there's one other thing. I'm part of the team too. I saw what was done to those four people. I had to poke around in the mess. So I have a personal interest in seeing that this animal, whoever he is, is rounded up and put away.'

Bob smiled at her intensity, taking her hand. 'Thanks, love. I'd almost forgotten that you've been in since the dirty start of this business.'

He crossed to the fridge, took out two more cans of Swan, popped the top of each and handed one to Sarah. Across the table, he told her of the beginning of the search, of the importance of Kenny Duff's discovery of the break-ins, of Maggie Rose's perceptive analysis of Rachel, and finally, of her discovery of the theft of the current diary.

By the time he had finished, Sarah had grown sombre. 'So there was some kind of plot. And all those people were killed in cold blood, not by some crazy man. Horrible!' She shuddered.

'Let me help. You mentioned Mike Mortimer's Filofax. Let's look at it together.'

They moved through to the living room and sat together on the comfortable yellow settee. Bob opened the brown leather binding and held the book so that Sarah could read it with him. Inside the front cover, there was a card in a clear plastic holder. The words *'Happy birthday, 4/6/94. All my love, Rachel'* were written in blue fountain ink in an elegant hand. The leather still smelled new. The pages, held by a ring-binder, were arranged in four sections, diary, addresses, information and financial. Bob opened the financial section.

Mortimer had been a careful man. Every financial transaction involving payment by cheque or credit card was recorded, along with cash withdrawals, and set against receipts. Several incoming payments were marked in the ledger with the letters '*FS*'. 'What do you think that means?' Sarah asked.

'It's probably Faculty Services, the company that manages advocates' business and collects their fees. Nearly all work goes through it.'

At the end of each month the amount was totalled. Any surplus over a minimum balance of £500 was marked '*Transfer to SA*'. Mortimer had been saving over £2000 per month out of income.

'That's quite a surplus,' said Sarah.

'The taxman will want his share,' said Bob. 'All practising advocates are self-employed.

'I wonder where his savings record is.' He flicked through the rest of the financial section, but found nothing. 'This is a current account. It's his cash book, ready for his accountant to argue the case for some spending to be treated as business expenses. Somewhere there's got to be a bank-book, or a building society account, where we can cross-check these transfers.'

He left the financial section and opened Information. It began with personal details, and listed personal advisers.

'Good lad,' Bob muttered, 'this'll save us some digging.' He read down the list. 'Lawyers, Curle, Anthony and Jarvis. Accountants, Mohamed, King and Co. Insurance adviser, W. D. Kidd. Doctor, dentist, tailor. Here we are, Stockbroker, Brown Aston, Glasgow. Bank, Royal Bank of Scotland, St Andrew Square. Building Society, Abbey National, Hanover Street . . . Couldn't be better.'

The rest of the information section was made up of street maps and rail timetables, showing city destinations in Scotland from Wick to Ayr, all places where the High Court of Justiciary sits on circuit. Inevitably, there was also a map of the London Underground network.

Thumb-flip initial index markers ran down the side of the address section. Bob opened it at the first page. 'Adams, John, LlB, Aitken, William . . .' He flicked through the pages. The listings were in strict alphabetical order, except where an entry had been made after the compilation of the directory.

They read carefully through the pages. The methodical Mortimer had noted professions beside each entry. Those without such designations were, Bob guessed, purely social acquaintances. They would be the first to be followed up.

'M' and 'N' were together in the seventh section. The index made no allowance for Scotland's proliferation of 'Macs' and so the section was fatter than any other in the book. 'MacAndrew, Tailor.' began the listing, which ran through to 'MacWilliam, Roger, Bank Manager', and on into 'Mabon, Peter LIB.' The last entry on the page was 'Madigan & Co, Architects.'

Bob's eye tracked to the top of the next page. He read the first entry, 'Napley, Eleanor. Advocate.' He frowned. 'Wait a minute.'

'What's up?' Sarah's attention had wandered. She snapped back to wakefulness.

'There's something wrong here. There are no Mortimers in this directory.'

'Maybe he knew them off by heart?'

'Love, this guy has listed his girlfriend, his own office number, his building society, everyone. There's even an entry for "Lewis, John. Department store". This is more than an address book, it's a record of a life. He's not going to leave his family out.

'And what about the Dean?'

'Who?'

'David Murray, QC, Dean of the Faculty of Advocates. He isn't listed either, yet Peter Cowan is, not just as an advocate, but as Clerk of Faculty.

'Someone's been here before us. There's a page missing!'

Sarah squeezed his arm. 'Are you sure? The family couldn't be listed somewhere else?'

'They could, but they aren't.' He reached for Sarah's Mickey Mouse telephone and dialled a seven digit number. 'Andy? Bob here. Have you been into Rachel's address book yet? Well get into your wee red motor and bring it round. I want to look at it, and to show you something.'

Less than fifteen minutes later, the door buzzer sounded. Skinner picked up the entryphone receiver in the hall and pressed the button which unlocked the street door. He opened the front door just as Martin bounded on to the landing outside, Rachel Jameson's address book in his hand.

Skinner led him into the living room, where Sarah waited with three mugs of coffee and a box of After Eight mints. Skinner showed him Mortimer's Filofax, and the 'M' entries which came to a sudden stop.

'See what I mean Andy? Who's the important "M", who's been removed? Is he our man, or is it another victim, one that we don't know about; an accident, maybe, like Rachel was meant to be? Let's see Rachel's address book.'

Martin handed him the long red directory, opening it at the 'M' section as he did so. Skinner looked at it closely. The entries were less detailed than those in the Filofax, and the 'M' and 'Mac' surnames were in random order. He found Mortimer's listing simply under 'Mike' and below it a listing for 'J. Mortimer', with no address, only the Clydebank telephone number which he had used earlier in the day. There too, was David Murray's home address and telephone number. It was only when he turned the page that Skinner noticed something odd.

A long straight cut appeared, close to the spine of the book. He pressed it as flat as he could on the coffee table, and ran his finger between the pages. Suddenly he pulled his finger back as he felt the sharp pain of a paper cut. He sucked the blood which welled from the fine slit at the tip of his index finger, then ran his middle finger over the page again, crosswise this time. He bent the book open until the front and back of the red cover were touching.

'There you are. You can hardly see it, but a page has been cut out. You've got to be looking really hard to notice that it's gone. If he hadn't nicked the next page with his knife, and if I hadn't been looking as closely as I did at the "M"s I wouldn't have found it.

'So there it is. Our mystery entry has been taken out of each one.'

'Why didn't he just take the books?' Sarah asked.

'That would have been spotted, especially with all the financial information in Mortimer's Filofax. No, just take a page from each and no one will notice. That's what our man reckoned. Anyway, he thinks we've bought Yobatu. All he's doing here is housekeeping, tidying up. He doesn't really expect that there'll be a detailed search.'

'Remember, he did pinch Rachel's diary,' said Martin. 'Maybe there was too much in that for him to cut out. Have you checked the diary section of the Filofax?'

'Not yet. Let's have a look now.'

He picked up the brown leather book and reopened it. The first five months of the day-per-page had been discarded. Martin looked startled, until Skinner showed him the date on the gift card set inside the front cover.

The entries began on Tuesday 6 June, and continued daily from then on. Typically of Mortimer, they were concise, but full of detail: until Monday 20 June and Tuesday 21 June. Martin stated the obvious. 'It's not there.'

A small piece of paper was caught in one of the six steel clips of the ring-binder, snagged as the page had been removed.

Skinner stopped reading the detail of the entries. Instead, he flicked through the pages, searching for more gaps. 'October the fifteenth and sixteenth; they're gone.' He shook his head. 'A very thorough individ-

176

ual. We've been lucky to get this far. Now it looks like we're stuck again.'

'Look at the cashbook.' Sarah spoke softly from her armchair.

'Clever lady,' said Skinner. He opened the financial section, flipping over pages until he reached June.

'Very clever lady! Look at this. June the twentieth, shuttle return, Edinburgh – Heathrow. Paid by Mastercard.' He turned over more pages. 'And again. October the fifteenth. But this time it's two tickets. Did Rachel go with him this time?

'Andy, first thing tomorrow morning, I want you to use your Special Branch clout to do two things. Call British Airways and have them check the passenger listings for all flights to Heathrow on October the fifteenth, looking for Mortimer and Jameson. If Rachel doesn't show, then find out who was sat on either side of Mortimer on each half of the round trip.

'Then call Telecom. I want a printout of all calls made from Mortimer's and Rachel's telephones from the last twelve months, with the subscribers at the other end listed. They'll moan like buggery, but they can do it.'

Martin nodded. 'Anyone who's going to moan, may as well start now.'

He picked up Mickey Mouse and looked towards Sarah. 'May I?'

'Be our guest.'

Ten minutes and two telephone calls later Martin was finished. 'Airways is easy. I'll have that by 9.00 a.m. The Telecom task involves more work, but my woman there says she'll try to have what we need by midday. And she didn't moan at all.'

'Good fella. Get word to me as soon as you have anything on either one. Tomorrow morning, I'm going to break the good news to the Chief. This business has got to the point where he needs to be told.'

54

A police car took Skinner to the Abbey National Building Society for his 10.15 appointment with the manager, a small neat man, curious as to the reason for Skinner's visit.

Skinner accepted black tea in a thick, ugly cup. 'Thank you for seeing me at such short notice, Mr Needham,' he began.

'I believe that Mr Michael Mortimer, an advocate, was, until his recent death, one of your depositors.'

Needham nodded. 'Yes, that's right. And a mortgage holder.'

'I'm looking into his financial affairs. I have some of his personal records and I want to cross-check these with his account information here. I know that you have no obligation to assist me, but the matter is urgent, and the man is dead, so I hope that it won't be necessary to go through formal procedures. I'd rather keep this completely off-the-record.'

Needham held up his hand in an affirmatory gesture. 'That doesn't cause me a problem, Mr Skinner. I take it that you want the details of both investment accounts.'

'Both?'

'Yes. He had two. One was used for regular monthly transfers from the Royal Bank, as a sort of business account, I think. From memory, the balance stands at almost thirty thousand pounds at the moment. The other is joint, in the names of Mr Mortimer and Miss, or is it Ms, Rachel Jameson. It was opened in June, with a cash deposit of five thousand pounds.'

Successfully, Skinner concealed his excitement. 'Any payment since then?'

'Yes, in October a further fifteen thousand pounds was deposited, again in cash.'

'Can you give me the exact dates of these transactions?'

'Of course.' Needham rose from his chair and crossed to a four-drawer filing cabinet. He opened the second drawer from the top, looked inside, and withdrew a folder. 'Here we are. The account was opened by Mr

Mortimer and Miss Jameson on June the twenty-first. The second deposit was made by Mr Mortimer on October the sixteenth.

'I shouldn't, but I'll give you photocopies of these, and of the other account transactions for the last twelve months. Back in a few moments.'

When the door closed behind the little man, Skinner whistled to himself. Twenty grand! A tasty fee; but for what?

Needham reappeared a few moments later, and handed him a large brown envelope, sealed.

'Thank you, Mr Needham. You've been very helpful.'

'My pleasure.' He escorted Skinner to the door.

55

In the back of the police car, Skinner looked at the photocopied pages. Twenty thousand, deposited in joint names, in two tranches, after the London visits. Cash deposits, not cheques. Money laundering? A drugs pay-off? Any lawyers with criminal practices made some dubious contacts. But surely these two couldn't have been bent. Not the *Scots Law Times* Couple of the Month.

Yet there it was, and it had to be viewed with suspicion. Skinner knew that all advocates' fees were collected by Faculty Services, which took a levy off the top for administrative expenses. Could Mike and Rachel have been cheating their own company?

The searchers into files and effects were still only at the start of their painstaking tasks when Skinner called at the New Town apartments. Mackie had the tougher job, since Mortimer had been a stickler for detail. He was picking through the Amstrad disks when Skinner arrived.

'How does it look, Brian?'

'Green, boss. This bloody screen goes for your eyes. Apart from that it's bleak. There was one personal file on this thing, full of letters to relatives, thank-you notes to hostesses, and a Christmas-card list ready for printing out on labels. None of the names look promising. The others were all business records. There are actually fewer files than there might have been. Some of the disks are almost empty. If he had a filing system, I haven't figured it out.'

'Okay. Get stuck into the paperwork with McIlhenney when you're finished with that. And keep a lookout for references to a joint project with Rachel, and a cash fee.'

'Will do, sir.'

Back in his office just before midday, Skinner called Kenny Duff. 'I need some financial info on our friends, Kenny. Did either one have a private source of income? Gambling, for example.'

There was a pause at the Charlotte Square end of the line. 'I guess you've come across the joint account, and the nature of the payments. That came as a surprise to me too, when I found the account book. You understand that as executor I couldn't volunteer that information to you?'

'Sure, that's all right. You've no clue as to the source of the money?'

'None at all. It's a problem for me, I don't mind telling you. I've no way of telling whether it's earned income, a gift or, as you suggest, a win on the pools. I just don't know what to tell the Revenue, or even whether to tell them. As far as their general finances were concerned, both Mike and Rachel had good practices, and were comfortably off. Had they chosen a specialist area of civil law, rather than criminal, they'd have done even better, but neither one was short of a few bob. They were planning to sell Mike's flat to help pay for the new house, and they'd have done well out of that deal too. All that makes twenty thousand in grubby fivers even more difficult to understand.'

Skinner grunted. 'Thanks Kenny. You've been no bloody help at all, but thanks anyway.'

56

'Wait till you hear this!' Quickly Skinner told Martin of the building society account, and the cash deposits which had followed the London visits.

Martin's breath hissed between his teeth. 'Let's see if we can tie it into this.' He waved an A4 document. 'It's just this minute arrived from Telecom. I haven't looked through it yet.'

He laid the sheets on Skinner's desk and walked round to look over his shoulder. The document was in two sections, one listing Mortimer's calls, the other, those made by Rachel. Skinner handed one back to Martin.

'You check that one. Look for London numbers, private listings and ex-directories. Let's concentrate on the four weeks before Mortimer's first trip to London. See if we get the same name on each list.'

They studied the columns of numbers in silence for some minutes. When Martin spoke there was an edge of controlled excitement in his voice.

'Try this, boss. On June the fourteenth, six days before Mortimer's solo trip to London, Rachel made a twenty-three-minute call to an ex-directory number in London. The subscriber is named here as Fazal Mahmoud, address, Forty-nine, St David's Avenue, Pimlico.'

'Okay!' Skinner's tone echoed that of the younger man. 'On June the seventeenth, Mortimer made a seventeen-minute call to the same man. Let's take it forward.'

Each searched his list in silence for several minutes more. When Skinner was finished he looked across at Martin, a question in his eyes.

'Nothing else sir. No more calls to that number. How about you?'

'Consistently. One a month, each lasting no more than five minutes. Then in October, three days before the second trip, a call lasting nineteen minutes and thirty-five seconds.'

'So. Rachel is the original contact, then Mortimer makes the running, and collects the first slab of fivers. But on the second trip, Rachel goes too, so it couldn't have been anything risky, or at least Mike couldn't have thought so.'

'Yes. I wonder what Fazal's nationality is, or if his . . . '

'Wait a minute!' Martin cut in.

'Fazal. Fuzzy. Rachel's university pal told me that story about a serious boyfriend when she was a student. Some sort of Arab, she said. She never knew his real name, Rachel and the others just called him Fuzzy!'

'A pound to a pinch of pig-shit that's the man!' Skinner's voice rose.

'Let's see how good your predecessors were. Any Arab student in Edinburgh is quite likely to have wound up on Special Branch files. Come on. Let's get along to your place and see if we can find your friend Fazal Mahmoud.'

Special Branch duties include the maintenance of a discreet watch over those who might be regarded by the State as malign influences, or subversives. Sometimes, this category extends to include all citizens of certain foreign countries.

'What years should we cover, Andy?' Skinner asked as Martin unlocked the room in which the back files were stored, then answered his own question. 'Let's try '79 to '82 for openers, since Jameson was thirty-two, going on thirty-three.'

Martin nodded agreement. He scanned the labelled drawers of a bank of grey steel filing cabinets lined against the wall facing the door. Choosing one, he opened it with a small brass key.

'Let's be precise, boss. I think Rachel would be nineteen or twenty when she was involved with this guy, so let's look first at eighty and eighty-one.'

The files were labeled neatly and listed first alphabetically, then in date order. Martin found the 1980 'M' listings and scanned through them. He found no 'Mahmoud' file. He unlocked the next cabinet and found the 1981 'M' series in the bottom drawer. He flicked through the names. 'Could be, boss, could be!' he called.

He produced two creased yellow folders. 'Mahmouds, both of these.' He opened one, and read the top sheet of the papers inside. 'Mahmoud, Achmed. Iranian; Exile, believed to be in some physical danger from the agents of the fundamentalists. No that's not him.' He opened the next folder.

'You beauty!'

He scanned the pages for a few seconds, then read aloud. '"Mahmoud, Fazal, Syrian passport holder. Born Damascus 1956. Student of politics

183

and economics Edinburgh University. Matriculated October 1980. Member of Middle-East Students Anti-Zionist League. Member of University Squash Club. Residence, Pollock Halls. Known Associates Ali Tarfaz, Iraqi (see separate file), Andrew Harvey, Scottish (See separate file), Marjorie Porteous, Scottish (Nothing known), Rachel Jameson, Scottish (See separate file)."

'We've got one on Rachel!'

Martin pulled open the second drawer of the cabinet. He searched quickly through the 'H' and 'J' listings and pulled out two files. Then he unlocked the next cabinet, found the 'T' series, and quickly located a third. He opened the Rachel folder and read aloud. '"Rachel Jameson. Born Edinburgh 1961. Educated St George's School. Student of Law, Edinburgh University. Known associate of Fazal Mahmoud, Syrian. Known to have attended meetings of the Middle-East Students' Anti-Zionist League. Not thought to be a member. Nothing else known."'

He opened another. '"Andrew Harvey. Born Airdrie, Lanarkshire, 1960. Student of mathematics, Edinburgh University. Member of Middle-East Students Anti-Zionist League." – I never knew Airdrie was in the Middle-East, boss – "Also member, Student Front for Ulster Independence, Anti-Nazi League, Campaign for the Legalisation of Recreational Substances, Scottish National Party, Independent Labour Party, Edinburgh University Football Club." This guy's a bloody groupie. Let's look at Tarfaz.' He opened the third folder.

'"Ali Tarfaz. Iraqi passport holder. Born Baghdad, 1958. Student of politics and economics, Edinburgh University. President of Middle-Eastern Students Anti-Zionist League. Activities include organisation of demonstrations, fly-posting, etcetera. Surveillance reveals possible links with Iraqi intelligence officers in Europe."'

There was a photograph stapled to the inside of the folder. The man had a broad dark face. It was disfigured by a jagged, curving scar which ran round his left cheek to finish at the corner of his mouth. 'Handsome geezer, is he not?' said Martin.

'There's a later entry here, dated 1987. "Ali Tarfaz reported liquidated by Saddam after involvement in unsuccessful coup attempt." Well, it looks like we can stop looking for him in this movie.'

'Okay,' said Skinner, 'let's concentrate on Mahmoud, and let's see if we can trace Andrew Harvey, too. I suspect that'll be a waste of time, but let's eliminate him at least.'

'How do we check out Fuzzy? Through my net in London?'

'Absolutely not. You'd be bound to alert the Foreign Office, and I don't want that bastard Allingham to have the faintest sniff of this. Leave that to me. I've got a couple of sources of my own.'

57

Back in his office, Skinner pulled open a drawer in his desk and took out a small blue book, divided into sections. He opened it at 'IJ'.

The listings were initials only, opposite numbers entered in a random code which only he knew. He picked up the secure telephone on his desk and keyed in a seven digit number.

'Robbie? This is Bob S. I need a favour. Look, I know the House is in recess, but your research people in Walworth Road will be working this week won't they? Good. I'd like someone to procure for me a list of all officially accredited personnel at the Syrian interest section of the Lebanese Embassy, with their ranks or designations. Don't ask me why I need this, and I'll owe you two or three in return . . .

'No. I can't just ask the Foreign Office, for reasons which I can't explain . . .

'Obviously when you ask for this info it's for your own use. Good. Thanks a million. Yes, today would be great. Tomorrow will do, though. Call me on my ex-directory number here, or at home tonight. I'll give you an Edinburgh number.'

He dictated Sarah's telephone number.

'You've heard too. Christ, there's nowhere that the Edinburgh grapevine doesn't reach, is there. Thank you very much, I'll pass that on. Yes I do know how lucky I am. So long, Robbie.'

58

Like the House of Commons, Edinburgh University was on vacation, but its administration was working as usual. Henry Wills, the Registrar of the University, had never met Andrew Martin, but he had enjoyed a cordial relationship with Alec Smith, his predecessor. There had been occasions on which Smith had advised on political organisations within the student body. Equally, Smith's job had often been made easier by Wills' accommodating stance.

Wills was effusive in his greeting. 'Good morning, Chief Inspector Martin. I had heard of your appointment from Mr Smith, and I was expecting a visit eventually.

'Forgive me for saying this, but you look very young for the job. I have known your three immediate predecessors, and not one was under forty when he was appointed. Bob Skinner and Jimmy Proud must have a high regard for your judgement.'

Martin smiled. 'I don't know whether I'm lucky or lumbered. I always fancied this job, but I never realised how much there is to it.'

'Yes, indeed. I imagine that our occasional worries are among the least of yours.'

'From what Alec told me, the University won't be a worry at all. One thing you might watch out for, though. We have information that the Trotskyite Front are planning something against student loans. They've been a bit of a back number lately, and they're trying to make a comeback. We've had a tip that they're lining up student support for an extended occupation of the offices here, at Heriot Watt, and at Napier. It's due to start in the first week of the new term. Let me know if you need help to back up your own security. I'd rather they didn't succeed, because we'd have to crack heads to get them out, and we don't want it to get to that stage.'

'Thank you indeed, Chief Inspector. I had heard no whisper of this. We have contingency arrangements to supplement our own security as necessary, with people from outside firms. Of course if they hit all three institutions at once, even that resource might be stretched. I may have to take you up on your offer. And of course, if there is anything I can do in return . . . '

Martin smiled. 'Well as a matter of fact . . . ' Both men laughed. 'I'm trying to trace a former student, from ten or twelve years back. He's a mathematician, by the name of Andrew Harvey, birthplace Airdrie, Lanarkshire. I know your Graduates' Association is pretty tenacious when it comes to keeping track of people, and I wondered if you could point me in the right direction.'

Wills nodded. 'Leave it with me. When did he graduate, do you think?'

'Some time after 1981, I believe. It would be in character for him to have joined the Graduates' Association. The bugger seems to have joined everything else while he was here!'

Martin rose to leave. 'I know the type,' said Wills, following him towards the door.

'One thing more, before you go, and this is important. There's to be a major debate in the Union next term, on a Middle Eastern political motion. I've just heard that our pro-Palestinian lot have invited the new President of Syria to speak, as a representative of his bit of the PLO. Mind you, I don't suppose he'll be encouraged to come.'

Martin was taken by surprise. 'I hope not. But since the Gulf War, the Government has been keen to keep the Syrians on-side, so you never know.

'Thanks for the tip. I'll pass it on down South. There's a bloke in the Foreign Office whose day I'd just love to ruin!'

'Be my guest!'

59

Skinner was still in his office when his secure line rang at 6.35 p.m. He picked up the receiver and quoted the number, listening cautiously for the voice at the other end of the line.

'Bob? Aye, it's me. I've got that info you're after. The only thing is that the Lebanese don't publish a separate list of the people in the Syrian interest section. That's because they're all Syrians with Lebanese passports and they don't want to single them out for special attention from the security services, or from the Israelis. So what I've got for you are the names of all the Embassy staff. If your man's on it, you'll spot him . . . assuming that he's using his real name, that is.'

The voice on the other end of the line read out a list of names slowly and deliberately, although he knew that Skinner would be waiting for one name rather than noting them all down.

'Fazal Mahmoud, cultural attaché,' came towards the end. Skinner made no sound of recognition, allowing the caller to complete the list. 'That's it. Whoever this lad is, he must be a bit dodgy to be taking up the time of an Assistant Chief Constable, not to mention using up his favour bank!'

Skinner spoke for the first time since picking up the telephone. 'Don't worry, Robbie, I'll make it up. That's been helpful.'

'In that case,' said the voice on the line, 'I've got a bonus for you. Some of the Walworth Road researchers have contacts that are better informed than your secret police down there. The guy who gave me that list told me that the Embassy's a bit tense these days, because one of their blokes has disappeared. Diplomats vanish off the face of the earth from time to time, but usually it's because they've upset someone at home. Not this time apparently. One of the alleged Lebanese is missing without trace, and without his diplomatic passport, and no one in the Embassy has a clue where he is.'

'Which one?' Skinner's heart pounded as he waited for the answer.

'Fazal Mahmoud, the cultural attaché.'

Skinner did not respond in any way. When he spoke again it was to change the subject.

'Robbie, one more thing. Would you throw the name Ali Tarfaz at your Middle-East watchers, particularly any of them whose student days cover the late seventies and into the eighties, in Edinburgh. Nationality Iraqi. There's one other thing I can tell you about him, although just for fun, I'd like you to keep it to yourself.'

'What's that?'

'He's dead.'

60

'Come along here, Andy, please.' Martin too was working late. He was in Skinner's office two minutes after his call.

'Hello, boss, you been making progress? I won't get word on Harvey till tomorrow, but I've got some other news that might make your hair stand on end.'

'In a minute. It seems that the Lebanese have lost a diplomat from their London Embassy. They can't find hide nor hair of him. Bloke called Mahmoud. Deals in used Bank of England notes.'

A broad grin crossed Martin's face. 'Fuzzy's done a runner, d'you think?'

'Could be, and if he's our killer, why should he do that? If he is, then he set up Yobatu. And no one but us and Shi-Bachi knows that the Yobatu frame-up has been rumbled.

'No, the fact that Fuzzy's vanished says to me that he didn't do it. He's either running for his life, literally, or he's anchored to the floor of the Thames by some very heavy weights!'

Martin's smile vanished. 'Great. If Fuzzy's been taken out as well, we're at a dead stop. I've got a bad feeling about our three searches. I checked the two flats this afternoon. There's nothing so far. And Aileen Stimson called in to see me half an hour ago. The only thing that's happened up there is that she likes the atmosphere so much that she's thinking of chucking in the force and taking her law degree off to the Bar!'

Skinner laughed, ironically. 'Wouldn't you, if you had the chance? The hours aren't any longer, and the pay's a lot better, especially when it's given to you in suitcases by Syrians!'

He paused for a moment. 'Listen, it's no wonder the girl's being distracted. We've sent her up there to do what we've done twice already. Let's try something different. Ask her to get from the Librarian, very quietly, through Pete Cowan, a list of all the books withdrawn for study by Mortimer and Rachel, since the first meeting with the boy Fuzzy. Maybe their reading list will give us a hint. I know that the Advocates' Library

191

owns some of the rarest books in the world. I wonder if it has anything on its shelves that can get you killed!'

'Right, boss. I'll call her in ten minutes. She should be home by then. Meantime, the other thing I was going to tell you. Apparently there's a chance that we're going to have the Syrian President in town in a couple of weeks.'

Skinner looked up in surprise. 'Until now Syria has only been a place on the TV news. Now it's come up twice in this office in different contexts in a single day. As a copper, that's the kind of coincidence that makes my skin crawl.'

'Same here, except that the invite is in connection with a university debate, and it comes from the students. Maybe he won't accept, or, maybe the Government won't want him stirring up Middle Eastern politics here. Except . . .' He allowed the sentence to tail off.

'Yes,' said Skinner. 'Except that as far as the Middle East is concerned, we can't be sure of anything.'

'Let's keep our fingers crossed anyway. The one good thing about it is that I get to break the news to friend Allingham.'

'Then do it quick before the Chief finds out, or he'll grab the pleasure for himself. Use my phone.'

Martin dialled the Foreign Office number, without expecting to find Geoffrey Allingham in the building so late in the day. The extension rang unanswered, and so he left the Fettes Avenue switchboard number, and his own, with Foreign Office security, asking that Allingham be contacted and told to call him. Three minutes later, the telephone rang. The Whitehall policeman was stuck in a traffic jam in Cheyne Walk, and was calling from his car.

'Good evening, Martin. What's the picture this time? You haven't nicked another diplomat have you?' There was an unmistakable sneer in the voice.

Skinner broke in. 'Allingham, I have to advise you that you are speaking on a conference telephone and that this call is being recorded. Any more indiscreet and offensive remarks like that and I will personally arrange for the tape to be played to your Commissioner. Now cut the crap. Chief Inspector Martin has some information which may be of interest to you.'

Quickly, Martin related Henry Wills' story.

'I see,' said Allingham. 'My apologies for my indiscretion, gentlemen, and thank you for this news. I shall inform my Permanent Secretary. He will wish to advise ministers.'

Skinner came in again. 'We could have the invitation withdrawn, if we persuaded the University to disband the sponsoring club. Shall we do that?'

Allingham thought for a few seconds. 'Eh, no. Hold on that one, please. Ministers may regard this as a useful icebreaker with the Syrian President. He's a very new boy. Let's wait and see for a few days. Thank you again.'

There was a buzz as the line was disconnected.

'You weren't really taping that call were you?' Martin examined the conference telephone for an extra wire.

'Course not. It just seemed like a good idea at the time.'

61

It was almost 4.00 p.m. next day before Henry Wills called Martin.

'Chief Inspector, about your request. I'm sorry to have taken so long, but one doesn't want to arouse unnecessary suspicions, when one makes casual enquiries about an individual. I've got something for you now on Mr Andrew Harvey. It seems that he has turned into a very respectable citizen, an entrepreneur, no less. I gather that he established and runs a very specialised computer software design company in a place called Cumbernauld. He calls himself Harvand Systems Limited. Now there's original for you!

'Your assessment was very perceptive. He is indeed a member of our Graduates' Association. He donates about one hundred pounds every year, and he's spoken at a few careers seminars for final year maths and science students. He goes down very well, from what I'm told. Does that help?'

Wills sounded pleased, like a man expecting praise. Martin did not disappoint him.

'Very much, Mr Wills. Thank you.' As an afterthought he added, 'Any news on that other matter you mentioned?'

'Only that I heard that the Zionists have invited the Prime Minister of Israel to speak in opposition to the Syrian. He turned them down flat, apparently, and won't even allow his ambassador to represent him.'

'That might encourage the Syrian to accept, if he was in doubt.'

'Let's hope not! Dear God, imagine it!' Martin could picture Wills' eyes rolling towards the heavens.

'Thank you again for yesterday's information by the way. Securicor's shareholders can look forward to a healthy dividend. It seems that universities and colleges all over the country are hiring extra people for the week in question. I can only guess at your source.'

Martin laughed. 'That's right, Mr Wills, you can only guess!'

He went straight to Skinner's office to report Wills' information on Harvey. 'Will I check him out?'

'It sounds as if he's one rebel who's been tamed, but talk to him anyway, to eliminate him from the inquiry if nothing else. Go in with a good cover story. I want him to forget the conversation as soon as it's over, if he has nothing to do with this business.'

62

Martin found Harvand Systems Ltd in a refurbished factory unit in Wardpark, one of Cumbernauld's older industrial estates. He located the building after a few wrong turns.

He announced himself in the neat, well-furnished reception area; the girl behind the reception desk was very young. 'YTS,' Martin thought to himself.

The woman who appeared within a minute was a complete contrast. She flowed through a security door with hand outstretched. For a second he was unsure whether it was meant to be shaken or kissed.

'Hello, I'm Joy Harvey, Andrew's wife. I'm a sort of director cum general manager. I'll take you through to Andrew. He's just finishing a telephone call.'

She keyed a code into the panel beside the door and led him through into a narrow poorly-lit corridor. She walked ahead of him, tall, slim, elegant and lightly tanned. Her auburn hair shone with vitality, even under the poor neon lighting, and her body language shouted confidence. As she walked, she explained her role.

'My job in Harvand is to make it run profitably, allowing Andrew and his people to concentrate on creative work without the hassle of day-to-day domestic things like accounting, paperclips and all that.'

At the end of the corridor was a door, half-glazed with an opaque panel. Joy opened it without knocking and held it ajar for Martin.

Andrew Harvey was short, fat and bald. His gold-rimmed spectacles, with their round lenses, gave him an owlish look. As he moved from behind a huge desk to shake Martin's hand, he seemed to radiate diffidence, but then he looked directly at the policeman, who found that first impression contradicted by the strange intensity of the grey eyes.

'Take a seat, please, Chief Inspector.' The complexity of the man was compounded by a high-pitched, slightly highly strung voice, and a muted Lanarkshire accent. He led them to a conference table, just as his wife reappeared with a tray, bearing a cafetière and three mugs, each with the company logo emblazoned upon it. Martin kept his eyes on the little man at the head of the table.

'First of all, Mr Harvey, thank you for seeing me on what's really a personal matter. I belong to Glasgow University Graduates' Association. I've been asked to run a seminar on police work at a careers conference which the Uni. is running during this term. I don't know how I was talked into it, but I was. Having agreed to do it, I want to get it right.

'Henry Wills, at Edinburgh University, is a friend of mine. I asked him for ideas. He suggested that I should talk to someone who had run one of these things, and he said you do it better than anyone else he knows. Sorry to be so mysterious over the telephone, but to tell you the truth, I'm a bit overawed by the thing. It isn't exactly my line of country.'

The ingenuousness of the admission seemed to relax the little man. From the corner of his eye Martin thought that he also detected his wife's body posture relax. *Something to hide*, the policeman's instinct said to him, but the moment passed.

Harvey, assured now, smiled in Joy's direction. 'Just as well my wife's here. She can tell you a lot more than I can. She's a business psychologist by training. She plans my seminars, writes my script, designs the visual aid package, coaches me in delivery and all that.'

'Visual aids! God, does it get that sophisticated?'

Joy replied for her husband. 'No, it needn't. It really all depends upon the ability of the lecturer and in his level of confidence. Now Andrew is, by nature, a shy man. It takes a lot of personal courage for him to stand up in front of an audience. The package I put together for him is a sort of crutch to help him stay up there.

'On the other hand, you are a very assertive man by nature, for all your expression of diffidence here.'

For a second, Martin froze. Had he blown it? But he was reassured as Joy went on.

'It isn't insecurity that has brought you here. It's a desire for perfection; even if you don't know it.'

Martin smiled at her. 'Maybe I do.'

Suddenly a fragment of memory from the past tugged at him. 'You know, Mrs Harvey, it occurs to me that we must all be about the same age. I knew quite a few Edinburgh people when I was at Glasgow. Which university were you at? You weren't at Gilmorehill too were you?'

'No. I was at Strathclyde, from 1979 to 1983.'

'We overlapped, then. Did you socialise much when you were there?'

'Union dances. Daft Friday, that sort of thing. You do remember Daft Friday, don't you.' A tone of laughter crept into her honeyed voice.

'Sure do. A collection of kids in evening dress taking a long time to get plastered.'

'That's just how it was!'

'We'll all have changed a bit since then. I remember two girls called Joy. What was your maiden name?'

'Granger. What was your first name, again?'

'Same as your husband. May I be indelicate and ask, were you a blonde then?' It was an inspired guess. In fact, Martin's student vanity had been incompatible with the spectacles which he had needed then for close range vision. The faces of the girls with whom he had danced had always been blurred.

Joy beamed. 'I have to admit it. I'm sure I remember you too. You played rugby didn't you? Always bumped or bruised.'

Martin nodded, surprised.

'We were at the same party together once, out in Thornliebank.'

Martin searched his memory. Oh Lord, there was a distant night after a rugby international. Dimly, he recalled winding up in bed, for only a little while, but long enough, with a randy blonde; only of course, she hadn't really been a blonde. Could this be her? Something in her eyes told him that she was.

'After a rugby match. That's right. We had a drink together. I was on Guinness then, and you knew where it was hidden.'

Quickly, he took the opportunity to switch the conversation.

'How about you, Mr Harvey, were you at that party?' Christ, I hope not, he thought.

'No,' said the little round man. Martin could not decide whether he was amused or bemused by the conversation. 'I never got through to Glasgow in those days. I didn't meet Joy till after we both graduated. At a business seminar, actually.'

Figures, Martin thought again.

'As I said, I got around a bit. Maybe you knew some of my rugby pals there; Al Reid, Johnny Hall? Do they mean anything?'

Harvey shook his head. It was hardly surprising. The names were fictitious.

'I had a thing with a girl through there once. What was her name? Marjorie. Marjorie Porteous, that was it. Clever, but a bit of an airhead at the same time. Then there was that Arab who was always hanging around. What the hell was his name again?'

He paused. He realised, quite suddenly that the figures on either side of him had frozen, as if they were hanging on his next word. It was the sort of tension which shows itself through a mass holding of breath. For two or three long seconds, Martin drank it in.

'Ali something; like Ali Tarbrush. Ali Tarfaz. That was it. An Iraqi bloke.' Both Harveys exhaled quietly and relaxed again, imperceptibly. 'I remember; the Glasgow team used to call him Ali Macleod. He really hated that.'

Harvey looked puzzled. Martin tried an explanation. 'Ali Macleod. Ally Macleod – 1978 World Cup, Scotland team manager. Gettit? No? Never mind.'

Joy broke into a laugh which sounded slightly forced. 'Ali Macleod. That's terrible. Do you remember any of these people, Andrew?'

'I'm afraid not. None of them. But then I was very serious in those days.'

Martin decided that the time for reminiscence was over. He turned towards Joy. 'Anyway, back to this seminar of mine. Any tips?'

She nodded. 'Prepare a script so that you know exactly what you intend to say, but speak from brief notes if you can. Take a few slides along, even a short video if you have one. I'm sure the police will have one. Allocate at least fifty per cent of your time to discussion. And at the end of the session, make sure you leave behind an information pack, summarising what you said, with suitable leaflets.

'Oh yes, and if there are women in the audience, flash those green eyes at them and you can't go wrong.' She laughed. Her husband did not.

Martin stood up to leave, and thanked them both. Joy led him back to reception, and walked with him to the front door.

As he turned to take his leave, she said quietly, 'Thanks for your discretion. I remember that party pretty well now, and I remember you, Andy, very well indeed.' As they shook hands, she slipped him a business card. 'If you fancy a replay sometime, give me a call.'

He smiled at her. 'I may just do that.'

Joy laughed. 'Goodbye then. And good luck with your seminar.'

63

As Martin and the former Joy Granger were recalling their previous close encounter, the secure telephone rang once again in Skinner's office.

'Hello, Bob. About that supplementary question you asked me. It was a cracker.

'I threw that name at all the Arab watchers, and one of them all but shit himself. It seems that your man Ali Tarfaz is very heavy duty indeed; only you're right, he is dead.

'The way the story goes, Ali Tarfaz was an intelligence operative. He was planted in the UK as a student around 1980 and did well for himself. He was moved on to West Germany, and then to Brussels. Then, the story goes, in 1987 a few middle-ranking soldiers hatched a plot to overthrow the government. It failed. Saddam, as you might expect, was not best pleased. Not a nice man when annoyed. The plotters were all strung up on poles and left to rot. The intelligence community, which was said to have been in on it, was heavily purged. And among those shot was one Ali Tarfaz.

'Now this is where the story becomes legend. After the blood had been mopped up, Saddam appointed a sort of supremo, with powers of command over the military, and over all intelligence operations, everywhere. That man's name was Rashoun Hadid. He was never, ever photographed, or seen by foreigners.

'Naturally the Israelis developed a great interest in Hadid. Mossad lost two men just trying to take his picture, never mind kill him. But eventually, after, it's said, a wee bit of torture of a captured Iraqi spy that they're not keen to admit, they came out with a story. According to Mossad, the man who informed on the 1987 plot was your pal Ali Tarfaz. Far from being given a bullet as a reward, he was given a new identity, and the job of Intelligence supremo. The guy who was shown on television facing the firing squad was an obscure so-called political detainee called Rashoun Hadid, whose crime was that he had been caught fucking a general's wife.

'So if the Israelis are to be believed, and they usually are, your boy Ali Tarfaz has done very well for himself. Impressed?'

'By him or by you?'

'Both. But there's a postscript. The Israelis track this boy's movements all the time, looking for a clear shot at him. Well just recently, they were forced to admit that they had lost track. They don't know where he is, but they believe that he's either out of the country, or out of the picture. They reckon that he's either had a bust-up with his boss and been liquidated for real this time, or he's away on some very serious business. Either way, the Israelis would love to know, so if you've come across him under his old name, you could win yourself a whole barrowload of Brownie points.'

'You can forget that, Robbie. I don't know where he is. The name came up in an enquiry into events past, that's all. And if I did know where he was the Israelis would be the last people I would tell. I'm here to stop murders, not to set them up.'

'You're not wrong there, Bob. If the Israelis find this guy, he's dead. And probably if other people find him too.'

'Such as?'

'Such as the CIA. They'd love to take out the big guy in Iraq. If they could pot his right-hand man, it'd be the next best thing. Remember the supergun. Your pal Ali was right in the middle of that business. He's supposed to have signed the purchase orders for the parts, using different names, but the same pen and ink.

'Maybe the project is still active. Maybe he's away trying to buy more steel pipes!'

'If he's trying to buy steel tubes, he's not in Scotland! Look, thanks Robbie; your pals have been very helpful. Tell them that if I find Rashoun Ali Tarfaz Hadid, I'll kick his arse and send him home!'

64

Superintendent David McKinstery was twenty-five years older than Andrew Martin. Many officers of his age and stage are sticklers for form, but he was one of the exceptions. His years in Strathclyde Special Branch work had taught him that dividends can be earned from co-operation. If a brother from another force called him with an odd request, he would never ask why.

'Hello, young Andy. Good New Year to you.' The voice on the telephone was soft and friendly. 'How are you getting on in the job?'

'It's hectic, Mr McKinstery, but I'm enjoying it. You'll be busy yourself, with these bloody student occupations. How many targets have you got on your patch?'

'Six, I reckon. The two universities, Glasgow Poly, Queen's College, Notre Dame and Paisley Tech. They've all made arrangements. Of course if it leaks back to the Trots they may switch their attack to the FE colleges, and there aren't enough security guys to cover all of them. We'll just have to see how it goes. What can I do for you anyway, young man? You havena' just called to compare notes on Bolsheviks.'

'No, you're right,' said Martin. 'I wonder if you could check your back files, say between 1979 and 1984, and see if you have anything on a girl called Joy Granger, Strathclyde University. Associates, politics, anything odd.'

'No problem, I'll get a DC to look her up. That's G-R-A-N-G-E-R is it?'

'Yes, there's probably nothing there. We're doing a vetting job on her husband and we just want to cross-check her.'

'I'll call you back within an hour.' Martin thanked him, hung up, and called Skinner's secretary to see if the ACC was free.

'Yes, Mr Martin. He's waiting for you, in fact. Come right along.'

Two mugs of coffee stood on coasters on Skinner's desk.

'Sit down, Andy. How was the other New Town?'

'Interesting, sir. For a start the Great Joiner Harvey is a boring wee fart. He knows about maths and computers and bugger all else. Or at least that's the impression he tries to give. His wife, on the other hand, is a power lady. She runs his company and his life. I've asked Strathclyde to check out her background. She was a student at the same time as Harvey, at Strathclyde, though. They say they met after university.'

'Any possible connection?'

'Could be. I claimed to have been bonking Marjorie Porteous, Rachel's pal, at university, and I threw some names of people at him. He denied knowing Marjorie Porteous, but I got a strong reaction when I mentioned an Arab bloke, without putting a name to him. He and his wife both seemed to be on the edge of their seats. But as soon as I mentioned the name Ali Tarfaz they both relaxed.'

'Did they, by Christ! He's not a man to relax people.' Skinner recounted Robbie's legend.

Martin stared at him. 'So what have we got here?'

'Two Middle Eastern students of different nationalities, each in Rachel Jameson's university circle; each one goes on to become an intelligence operative. One of them, it seems, makes payments to our two dead advocates then vanishes, the other one just vanishes.

'We've got to believe that Fuzzy is involved in some way in the murders, or he's joined the head count himself. The coincidence factor says that Ali Tarfaz could be somewhere involved too.

'Boss, how long can we keep this thing to ourselves?'

'I don't know, Andy. But let's try, for as long as we can. I want a tail on Harvey, and his wife, since you thought that they were sensitive to the mention of an Arab. Although it's off our patch, you can handle it from your own resources. I'll tell Strathclyde what we're doing, not why. And I'll go and see someone else.'

'Who's that, boss?'

'A man in New St Andrews House. You'll have heard of him.' Martin nodded, his face serious.

'By the way, Andy, I've got some more stirring news for you. Remember our friend the Syrian President? He's said "yes", and so has the Foreign Office.'

'Magic, just bloody magic. When?'

'January the eighteenth. Apparently it's a special debate, sponsored by the Palestinian lobby, on international brotherhood! Allingham's coming up tomorrow with a Lebanese, at least that's what they say he is. I want the two of you to agree all the security arrangements. The

203

"Lebanese" will report back to Syria.'

There was a knock on the door. 'Yes.'

Skinner's secretary appeared. 'Mr Martin, your office buzzed to say that Superintendent McKinstery called on your private line.'

Skinner pointed to his secure telephone. 'Call him back.'

Martin punched in the Strathclyde number. 'Mr McKinstery? Andy Martin.'

'I've found your lassie, Joy Granger. I don't know what she's like now, but she was a busy wee girl at the Uni. She was in the Socialist Workers' Party, that's how we've got her on record. She didna' half get around. Saw more pricks than Jocky Wilson's dartboard, according to this file. She was chairperson of a pro-Palestinian, anti-Israeli outfit, and linked up with like-minded idiots in other universities. Some of her listed contacts were in Edinburgh, others in Aberdeen.'

'Can you read me the Edinburgh names please?'

'Sure. There's three of them. Andrew Harvey, Fazal Mahmoud, that's spelled F-A-Z-A-L. M-A-H-M-O-U-D, and Rachel Jameson. Is one of them your target?'

'Yes,' said Martin, ending the call with thanks.

'So what have they got?' Skinner asked.

'They lied to me today. Told me that they didn't meet till after they left university. According to Davie McKinstery's files, Joy helped to run an inter-university pro-Palestinian league of some sort. Fuzzy Mahmoud and Rachel are both listed among her contacts.'

'Then get that tail in place, now, Andy. From the sound of things they didn't suss you, but don't take any chances.'

'Okay, boss, I'm on my way. Will you square it with Strathclyde for me?' Skinner nodded as Martin left the room.

65

There is a small anonymous room in New St Andrews House, a monstrous office block perched on top of a seventies shopping mall.

Skinner entered the grey concrete building through its inadequate revolving door. His warrant card took him past the security guards. 'Know where you're going, sir?' one enquired. Skinner nodded.

Hugh Fulton's door bore no number. It was not listed in any office directory, nor was its occupant. Officially, neither existed. The real Hugh Fulton was a tall, broad man in his mid-fifties. Streaks of ginger still mixed strongly with the white of his hair. There was no sign of thinning on top. As he stepped from behind his desk and extended his hand, Skinner recognised the questioning gaze in the big, brown eyes.

He had met Fulton for the first time on a Senior Command Course at the Scottish Police College at Tulliallan, when the big Aberdonian, then an Assistant Chief Constable in the Grampian force, had been one of his toughest inquisitors. A few weeks after that encounter, Fulton's resignation from the force had been announced. No explanation was offered other than the bald statement that he was 'taking up another post'.

Only a handful of civil servants, and senior officers, Skinner among them, were allowed to know what Hugh Fulton's 'other post' was. Within his tiny circle his title was 'Security Adviser to the Secretary of State for Scotland.' In fact his role was much broader than this, involving all matters that were the subject of 'D' Notices, and many other situations too sensitive even for that category. Fulton was not seen in public, and reported in Scotland only to the Secretary of State and to the Permanent Under Secretary, the head of the Civil Service in the Scottish Office. Nationally, he reported only to the Prime Minister, the Cabinet Secretary, and to the Director General of the security service, MI5.

'It's been a year or two, Bob,' Fulton's voice boomed out. 'I've followed your career with a personal interest since that time at Tulliallan.'

'That's very flattering, and surprising. I thought I blew bits of it.'

'Everyone did. We set some unsolvable problems to see who came up with the most pragmatic solutions, and kept the damage to a minimum.

'Now, why do you want to see me? It's only our college connection that got you through that door you know. You're the first serving policeman who's ever been in this room.'

Skinner looked around the small grey office. It was shabbily furnished; its two windows, treated on the outside with a reflective coating, overlooked the conference suite and food hall in the central courtyard of the huge circular block. Skinner sat down in the uncomfortable low-backed tubular chair to which Fulton pointed.

He matched the directness of the man's approach.

'I'm probably the first serving Scottish policeman to have the President of bloody Syria land on his patch at only a few days' notice. I want to talk to you about his security. I want to know from the start that if I need outside help, then I'll get it. Also, the FO is sending up a clown called Allingham to liaise with my Special Branch. I want it made clear to them and him that we are not running this operation on a committee basis, and that my force is in overall charge of the situation.'

Fulton nodded. 'The last point has already been made. I know about Allingham. He's a wanker. He has no connection with the system I work in. His job is to escort diplomats around, and carry messages. I know he got up Proud Jimmy's nose last time he was here. He's been warned not to do it again.

'As far as outside help goes, I've already made arrangements for SAS personnel to be made available to you. You'll want them, I imagine, at the airport, the debating hall and the hotel.'

'I should think that's right. It's an evening debate, or I'd have him flown out straight away. Since we're going to be stuck with him overnight, I'll use a small hotel that'll be easy to protect. The Norton, maybe.'

'Yes, that's a sound choice. The soldier boys will contact you within the next few days. Anything you need, you've got.'

Skinner stood up. 'You've told me everything I wanted to hear, Hugh. I've no need to take up any more of your time.'

But the big Aberdonian did not rise from his chair. He placed both hands palms down on the table.

'All right, I give in. I'll ask. What the fuck is going on with this secret investigation of yours?'

Skinner had wanted to find out how far Fulton's network stretched. That question was answered. Now he wondered how much he knew. He played the game for a little longer.

'Which investigation do you mean?'

'Come off it, Bob. You know bloody well. I mean the people you've got digging into the affairs of Mortimer and Jameson, and that girl you've had under cover in the Advocates' Library. What's it all about?'

'Look, Hugh, as far as I'm concerned those two people you've mentioned are the victims in unsolved murder cases. Too fucking right I'll go through their papers if I think it relevant.'

'The Crown Office doesn't agree with you about Jameson. They've got her on the books as a suicide.'

'Bugger the Crown Office. I know bloody well that she was pushed under that train, and so, I'll bet, do you.'

'Come on, Bob. You got your Jap, but the politicians wouldn't let you keep him. What are you trying to do now, flush it out into the open?'

'I was fed my Jap, but I can't swallow him as the killer any more. I know he didn't do it. D'you hear me? I know it. So what I'm doing now is following up unsolved murders on the basis of new evidence.'

'Then why are you using your head of Special Branch as coordinator?'

'Confidentiality. Yobatu – the late Yobatu, by the way, if you didn't know – was framed. My enquiries are being conducted as discreetly as possible because I don't want the person who did the framing to know that I don't buy his version any more. Quite frankly, Hugh, I've come to you now – and yes, this is the other reason for my visit – because I am now at a stage at which I may need your help in certain areas. There are indications that the international intelligence community may be involved. Is that plain enough for you?'

Fulton lifted his hands from his desk, clasped them across his stomach, and leaned back in his chair.

'Bob, I knew most of what you were up to before you walked in here. I've listened to what you've said. Now you listen to me, and take my advice. Drop this thing. You've had a result, even if the punters don't know it. You traced Yobatu, and the killings stopped. What more do you want?'

Skinner leaned across the desk.

'Hugh, you might have listened, but you didn't bloody hear me. Yobatu didn't do it. I have new evidence that points in another direction.'

'Yes, the money.' Fulton caught the flicker of Skinner's eyebrows. 'Yes, I know about that. A retainer, that's all. Paid by the Syrian government through an intermediary in the Lebanese Embassy to secure the advice of two excellent advocates in Scotland, and in Europe. Paid in secret because that's the way the Syrians do all their business.'

Skinner decided to test the depth of Fulton's knowledge. 'But why those two?'

'I have no idea, but why not? Two bright young people, ambitious, with marriage plans and so maybe prepared to accept an instruction that was a bit unorthodox, even slightly against the rules of the Faculty, for hard, untraceable cash.'

'What use is an advocate who can't appear in court?'

'I told you, they were buying legal advice, that's all. Bob, hear me again. Drop it. There's nowhere else to go. That comes from me at this stage, but if necessary it can come from on high. Give it up.

'Do you know what they say about Bob Skinner? "The game's got to be played by Skinner's Rules, right and righteous, all the way."'

'Bob, sometimes you've got to bend in this world. There's another rule book too, you know. It runs to three words. Know what they are? "Adapt and survive." Understood?'

Skinner's anger seemed to fill the small room. 'Hugh, if that was a threat you can shove it. You've been cooped up in this big concrete hen house for too long. You've forgotten you were ever a copper.

'I've seen these people that are just names to you. Mortimer, our half-cremated wino, poor wee Mrs Rafferty, and young PC MacVicar with his blood all over his new tunic and his throat open in the moonlight. I know that the bastard who killed those people is still running about free. I'm not going to stop until he's locked up, and no one, absolutely no one, is going to get in my way. You're right, this game is being played to my rules, and Skinner's rules say that the bad guys pay the price. You can take that message as high up the tree as you like, or dare.'

He turned on his heel and crashed out of the room, slamming the anonymous door behind him.

66

'We've been warned off, Andy. Hughie Fulton, big Aberdonian shitbag that he is, told me to be happy that we can lay the blame on Yobatu, and to leave it at that. Friendly advice from a father figure, with a threat lying not far behind it.'

'What did you tell him?'

'What do you think? I told him to get fucked. I've had bodies littering this city, one of them a copper, and neither powers nor principalities are going to prevent me finding out who put them there.'

'What will he do?'

'Try to lean on the Chief, I expect. Jimmy'll back me for a while, but when the blackmail starts, no knighthood, that sort of thing, leading up to heavier threats, I don't know whether he'll hold out.

'The thing that narks me most is that Fulton knew about our investigation. Somewhere, he's got a spy. He knew about the money, and he suggested an explanation, one that would sound plausible if you ignored the fact that there are dead people involved. He knew about Aileen Stimson's job, and he knew that you were coordinating things.

'If we're going to continue with this operation it'll have to be tighter than a fish's arsehole. You, Andy, I'd trust with my life, and I'm as sure as I can be of Brian Mackie. What do you think about the rest?'

Martin thought for a few moments. 'I'd vouch for Maggie Rose. She's rock-solid, doesn't panic, and loves the job. The DCs are two of the closest guys you'll ever find. Good company, great talkers in the pub, but never giving anything away, and even more important, great listeners to everything going on around them. The four of them, Brian, Maggie, McGuire and McIlhenney, all have one other thing in common. They're single.

'Since they don't have any steady partners, there's no danger of pillow talk being passed on by accident, by some daft wife or boyfriend to a mate in the supermarket queue or in the pub.'

'What about Aileen Stimson?'

'We can't rely on her. She isn't committed to the force any longer.'

'You're right. Her cover's blown too. Either one of those things would disqualify her for me. Pull her out.'

Skinner sat upright in his chair. 'So our team is six. No one else. Wrap up the searches at the two flats and report to me on the findings. Then arrange for our people to take over the Harvey surveillance. No word on that yet?'

'No, it's business as usual for them. No odd moves at all.'

'Good. That means they didn't catch on to you.

'One other thing. I want our team, no one else, to work on the Syrian security job when it happens. When he was still in a dealing mood, Hughie Fulton promised me all the special back-up we'll need. The boys from Hereford and all that.'

67

The report which Martin brought to Skinner was bleak. Neither of the search locations had yielded a single clue to the reason for the secret payment to the two advocates.

'It's a dead end, boss. Nothing on paper, or on Mortimer's computer disks. I've given Kenny Duff his keys back. As far as I'm concerned he can carry on with winding up the estates.'

Skinner considered this for a few moments. 'Okay. Tell him we've finished with everything, except for Mortimer's briefcase, and the other items that we have in the Productions Store.

'Are the team here?' Martin nodded. 'Let's have them in.'

The four detectives came into the room. Skinner invited them to sit. 'Well, people, you're probably all bored stiff by now. I'm sure you all see this as a complete waste of time.'

McGuire shook his head.

'Come on, Mario,' said Skinner. 'I sent you hunting wild geese. That's what you're really thinking, isn't it?'

With a slow, wry smile, McGuire nodded his head.

Skinner smiled back. 'Well that's tough on you. Sometimes it comes with the warrant card and the nice suits we get to wear!

'But seriously, I've been impressed by the way that you lot have done the job, regardless of the boredom. You worked well and methodically as a team. That's why I want us all to work together on one of the most sensitive security jobs we've had in this city since the Pope stood under John Knox's statue. Andy, will you explain, please.'

Martin stood up from his seat in the corner. 'Question. Who is Hassan Al-Saddi?'

He looked from face to face. 'No? Well, for the past six weeks or so, Mr Al-Saddi has been President of Syria. He took over following his predecessor's enforced resignation, having been the strong man behind the scenes for some time before that.

'He is a hard-liner, and believes that the previous incumbent was soft in his attitude to the West, and conciliatory towards Israel. Since he came to power there have been signs of a shift in the balance in the Arab world; the PLO have certainly become noisier. Get to know the name, and that face.' He handed round a large black-and-white photograph. 'On January the eighteenth you're all going to be involved in protecting him when he visits Edinburgh.'

Martin described the detail of the Syrian's visit. 'Syria doesn't have an embassy in this country at the moment. Later today, a Lebanese diplomat and a guy from the Foreign Office will arrive to look over the route, the hotel and the venue. Mario, you'll drive the boss and me to meet them at the airport, and then take them to the Norton House Hotel and the MacEwan Hall. I've already had a quick look. All three places appear to give us the minimum security problems. Everybody on the team will be allocated specific tasks for the visit once the Lebanese representative is happy. That's all I have to say for now.' He resumed his seat.

'I have a few things to add on the other matter,' said Skinner. 'Call it a bonus. All that boring time you've spent going through those files wasn't in vain after all. The Filofax and the address book which Mr Martin and I took away have given us a lead. That lead has taken us quite a way.

'For example, we now know that our two victims were paid twenty thousand pounds – that's right, twenty big ones – in two cash instalments; paid, it seems, by a diplomat who, by a coincidence, bearing in mind the previous item, happens to be Lebanese, with strong Syrian connections. We have to consider the possibility that this transaction was linked in some way to the murders, and that this man, might be our killer. I'd like to ask him politely whether he is or not, but I can't. Not just because he's a diplomat, but because he's disappeared.

'We know too, that this same bloke has a past connection, a student relationship at Edinburgh University, with Rachel Jameson. We are further aware of a link between the pair of them and a one-time student radical, now turned businessman – and boring wee fart, according to Mr Martin – called Andrew Harvey.

'Mrs Harvey, who was around then, too, has for some reason, been telling us porky pies about those days. In current circumstances, I hope you'll agree that all that is very interesting. So we're keeping a close eye on Mr and Mrs H. at the moment, as the only members of this wee group who are alive or otherwise available. I want you four to take over that surveillance, and to be ready to follow wherever it leads you.

'I'll say this once more. I want you to keep this enquiry absolutely secret.'

He looked slowly from face to face. 'I'm going to tell you this only because I trust you all implicitly. There are people in high places outside this force who know something of our enquiries, and who don't like them one wee bit. In fact, I've been given a heavy hint to lay off, for reasons which I believe to be political.'

His eyes swept the room again, catching the concern in the four faces. 'I've never been a politician. I don't really know what the word means.

'This is still a multiple murder enquiry, for all the cloak and dagger. I expect the pressure to get tougher. If it does, I'll handle it. All I ask of you is total discretion. Nothing on paper. Report orally to me or Mr Martin. Unless it's most urgent, use the phone rather than police radio.'

He paused, and looked every officer in the eye, in turn. 'Having told you all that, I'm offering you an exit. If anyone thinks that this is too heavy for him, or her, or worries about career prospects – and I won't deny it, if this thing goes really badly south that could be a worry – they are free to opt out right now. No comebacks.' He paused again. He looked again at each officer. 'Well?'

Brian Mackie stood up, a gesture surprising in its formality. 'Sir, over the past four days, we've all, well we've come to know Mike and Rachel. And none of us will ever forget young MacVicar, or the others. We're all as determined as you are to catch the animal who killed them.'

Skinner's smile was one of gratitude. 'You're all good people. Stick with me on this I won't let you down.'

68

Allingham and the Lebanese diplomat, who was introduced as Mr Feydassen, arrived at Fettes Avenue just after 4.00 p.m. The Foreign Office policeman was on his best behaviour when Martin showed him into Skinner's office. The Lebanese a small, swarthy man, seemed nervous, overawed by his responsibility.

Skinner did his best to put him at his ease, explaining that, since Edinburgh was a capital city, visits by heads of state, with their attendant security requirements, were commonplace for his force.

'This visit is shorter than most. Mr Martin has been over the route, and we have chosen a hotel which will be easy to guard for the brief time that our guest is with us, and which we believe offers a suitable standard of comfort. You're booked in there tonight, so you can judge for yourself. Tonight we will drive over the route which the President will cover. Then we will look at the Hall in which he will be speaking.'

Mario McGuire drove them back out of town, heading west as if towards Edinburgh Airport. But instead of heading straight through the complicated Maybury roundabout system, he took the right turn leading to RAF Turnhouse.

'This is the original Edinburgh Airport,' Skinner explained. 'It's still used by the Queen's Flight. Security here can be as heavy as we like. This visit won't be announced in advance, but with a university and its students involved, we have to assume that it's going to leak.'

Feydassen turned towards him in alarm. 'Your newspapers will report it, you mean?'

Skinner shook his head. 'No. They'll keep quiet, in exchange for full reporting facilities at the debate. The press will be handled by the Scottish Office information department; all the media in the hall will be vetted by us.'

The car left the airfield and turned once again towards the city centre, taking the Western Approach into Lothian Road, and winding through the Grassmarket, beneath the towering floodlit bulk of Edinburgh Castle, perched in splendour on its rock.

As McGuire drew the Granada to a stop outside the MacEwan Graduating Hall, Skinner turned to Feydassen. 'On the evening of the visit, the President's car will be led by motorcyclists, and will be followed by another carrying Mr Martin and three other officers. I will be in the President's car. My colleagues and I will all be armed.'

'You *will* use outside people, won't you?' asked Allingham.

'Of course. The RAF regiment will be responsible, as usual, at Turnhouse. Both the Hall and the Hotel will be secured by a detachment from the Special Air Services.'

Feydassen smiled. 'That is most satisfactory, Mr Skinner.'

Henry Wills greeted the party at the entrance to the debating hall. He explained how it would be set out on the night, indicating the areas to be reserved for press, television and radio.

'As I told you,' said Skinner, 'every journalist and television technician will be approved by the Scottish Office people, and supervised by them. Their fixed locations make life easier for those of us on the security job.'

Twenty minutes later the group left for the hotel. They took a different route, taking the A71 to the city by-pass. McGuire drove smoothly through the Gogar roundabout, and three minutes later, drew up outside the Norton House Hotel, set in wooded countryside, more than half a mile back from the main road.

'As you can see,' said Martin, 'this is a small hotel. There will be no other guests on the night. With only a few men, we can turn this place into a fortress.'

Feydassen looked at Skinner and Martin in appreciation. 'Gentlemen, I am reassured. As Mr Allingham said, you are very thorough. I am happy that my Embassy's client will be in your safe hands.'

69

Skinner left Martin to dine with the visitors. McGuire drove him home to Stockbridge. Sarah was back into the full swing of her practice, and of her police work. When Skinner let himself in, he found her sprawled on the couch, still wearing a heavy tweed jacket, with a woollen scarf wound around her neck. The gas fire was still warming up.

'Hi, love, busy day?' He leaned over and kissed her neck, above the scarf.

Sarah nodded. 'A real bugger, as you Scots say so eloquently. Began with a heroin overdose in Leith, and ended with a ten-year-old kid in Muirhouse coming home from school to find his mother with her head in the gas oven. Life as it is really lived, or died, as the case may be. How about you?'

Bob shrugged his broad shoulders. 'Oh, just humdrum stuff. Threatened one minute by a man I thought was a friend. Soft-soaped the next by someone I had down as an enemy. Just a typical day in the life of a hard-working polis!

'Let me open a medicinal bottle of something and tell you the details.'

They sat on the sofa, Sarah in the curve of Bob's arm, Haydn's Miracle Symphony on the CD player, and sipped smooth white wine. Yet, instead of unwinding as the music and the grape did their work, Bob grew more tense.

'Hey, big boy, steady down! Is this Syrian job more tricky than you're saying?'

'No, don't worry about that. Allingham's had his card marked. If everyone does their bit it'll be a dawdle. No, it's the other thing.'

With mounting outrage, he told Sarah of his visit to Fulton.

'He told me just to go along with the Yobatu story. Can you imagine that? I know that our man's still out there; it's bloody obvious, and yet he told me to lay off. I tell you, Sarah, it stinks.'

'And what are you going to do?'

'What do you think?' He almost shouted at her for the first time in his life. 'Sorry, love, I must learn to leave these things outside.'

'No, I'm sorry, that was a silly question. But what will Fulton do? What can he do?'

He kissed her on the forehead, and some of the tension seemed to leave him. 'He'll huff and he'll puff, but he can't go public. He might try to lean on Proud Jimmy, to get him to order me to pack it in. He'd have to lean pretty hard, but it's possible. He could use the Crown Office to try to stop me.

'In theory he can't do anything. Hughie Fulton is a non-person, the sort of guy that Le Carré and Len Deighton write about.'

Sarah looked at him, and he saw a hint of fright in her eyes. But quickly she turned it into a joke. 'What, licensed to kill, do you mean?'

Bob looked at her, unsmiling. 'Listen, Doctor, I'm licensed to kill if it comes to it. Far more so than Fulton. I carry a police warrant card and I'm a high-rated marksman, trained to take people down, like everyone on my Syrian team.

'Fulton isn't like that. I think he smells something that might embarrass his masters, and he's trying to cover it up. Remember, the ex-Lord Advocate, the Foreign Office, and probably our own Secretary of State had Yobatu hustled out of the country on a stretcher; now he turns out to have been innocent, there may be no more to it than Hughie trying to save his bosses' blushes. What makes me mad is that the man was one of the best policemen in Scotland. A real Blue Knight. Now he's just an arse-licker!'

Sarah put a hand on his chest. 'All right. Now forget him. Tell the Chief about your meeting and put it out of your mind. Just do it your way . . . but don't get obsessive.

'Now, let's discuss weddings!'

70

Mackie and McIlhenney sat in a plain Ford Transit van, watching a big red-brick villa on the edge of Cumbernauld's Westerwood golf course.

Mackie had watched the couple leave the Harvand factory half-an-hour earlier, in a black Toyota Supra Turbo, and had followed them home. The curtains had been drawn at once, masking the light. Mackie had a feeling that they were in for a long night, until Maggie Rose and McGuire arrived at 6.00 a.m.

An hour later, their talk of football, and Scotland's sad exit from the US World Cup Finals exhausted, McIlhenney voiced a thought which had been in Mackie's mind. 'Why hasn't the boss got us a phone-tap, sir? We might not get anything from it, but at least it'd give us something else to do.'

Mackie smiled. 'Nice one, Neil, but I don't think he'll wear it. I'll ask him, but I'm sure the answer will be that if we called in an engineer from Telecom, that'd be someone else who'll know about the operation. Anyway, this is just a line of enquiry. If guys like you were given your head we'd be living in a police state in no time at all!'

In the dark, McIlhenney smiled. 'Aye, great, eh!'

Just after 11.00 p.m. the ground floor light went out. A few seconds later there was a sudden blaze of light from an upstairs room. Joy Harvey appeared, framed in the window as she drew the curtains.

'Fine piece of woman that,' said McIlhenney. 'I wonder how that wee chap manages all on his own?'

'From what I've heard, he's had a bit of help over the years!'

71

The first full working week of the New Year drew to a close in unseasonally mild weather. Saturday morning came in a flood of sunshine, with a hint of warmth rather than the frost which normally accompanies cloudless January skies in Scotland.

For the stake-out team it was business as usual. The only break from routine came when Andrew Harvey left home alone in the Toyota. The Transit van was parked 200 yards away in the drive of an unfinished house at the top of the cul-de-sac in which the Harvey villa was situated.

When Harvey cleared the house, Maggie Rose slipped from the van and gunned her MG Metro, parked out of the line of sight, into life. She had the Toyota in view as it reached the roundabout leading to Wardpark and Castlecary, but there were no surprises in store. Harvey drove straight to the factory, and drew up in its car park, alongside other vehicles. Six-day working, thought Maggie, the software business must be doing well.

Joy Harvey left half-an-hour after her husband, in a red Ford RS 2000 with a new 'M' prefix. McGuire followed her at a distance in the Transit. He was led into a covered car park beneath the sprawling Cumbernauld Town Centre.

As he pulled up, he saw Joy, her long legs carrying her at a brisk pace towards the Asda foodstore. He waited for a full minute before strolling absent-mindedly towards the supermarket. He took a trolley, and wheeled it casually along the first aisle, an inconspicuous unaccompanied male, one of several, picking items at random from the shelves. He spotted her easily, as she moved purposefully from section to section. Her trolley was almost filled to capacity with food, toiletries and kitchenware. 'Those two fairly go through the groceries,' McGuire muttered to himself. Eventually he saw her head towards the checkout, the trolley overflowing. He left his, and retraced his steps, as if to pick up a forgotten item. Then, slapping his jacket and swearing softly, as if he had forgotten his wallet, he spun on his heel and walked quickly out of the store.

He was back in the Transit, observing the Ford through its wing-mirror, by the time Joy returned. Eight Asda carrier bags were crammed into the trolley. She folded down the back seat and began to pack the car. McGuire noted that one of the carriers appeared to be filled entirely with toilet tissue and kitchen rolls. Two others contained cartons of orange juice, milk and various soft drinks. Another was full of fresh fruit.

Before she had finished loading her car, McGuire started the van and drove off. He was back on station well before she returned home. He called Maggie again.

Her car-phone rang out, then was answered. 'How's it going, sarge?'

'Quietly. Our boy's at work. How about you?'

'We've been to Asda. Joy did a food-shop. Enough to feed a family of six for about a month. Are we sure that this pair don't have kids?'

'Or maybe a house-guest?'

Harvey returned home just after 1.00 p.m. He left the Toyota parked in the driveway. The RS 2000 stood in the open garage, apparently unpacked. Ten minutes after Harvey's arrival, Maggie drove quietly up the slope and parked her car in its original position. She checked to ensure that no one was watching, before slipping back into the Transit.

McGuire handed her two large rolls, packed with tomato, lettuce and salami.

'Thanks, Mario.' She examined the filling. 'Is this your Italian side coming out?'

'Course not! The McGuires of Kilkenny were the salami eaters. The Corrieris of Milano were far too keen on their fresh breath to touch stuff like that. Their tastes lay in other areas!' He flashed her a caricature of a lecherous grin.

'You should be so lucky, constable!'

'Yes, Sergeant, but you'll have to contain yourself. Look. Our birds are flying!'

The double garage door was closing automatically. Harvey stood by the open hatchback of the Toyota, five Asda carrier-bags bulging in his hands. He lifted them with difficulty into the car, reached up on tip-toes and slammed the tailgate shut. Joy locked the front door and walked quickly out. She climbed into the driver's seat. Her short fat husband clambered in on the passenger side. They saw a puff of exhaust smoke, then the white reversing lights came on and the sleek black car backed out of the drive-way.

'My car, Mario come on!'

'Okay. Don't forget the bloody rolls!'

220

The Toyota was clear of the cul-de-sac before Maggie had reversed out to follow it. She was three hundred yards behind when she saw it swing left, and circle the roundabout at the foot of the hill to join the A80, heading towards Stirling.

She tailed them, still at a safe distance, as the A80 became the M80, then watched half-a-mile later as the Toyota veered left to join the M876. Joy maintained a steady eighty-five miles per hour.

'Christ,' said McGuire, 'if she puts her foot down in that beast, it's goodbye to us.'

'Don't you believe it, cowboy, this wee thing can go too. Anyway, if the worst comes to the worst, we can phone in and have them stopped for speeding.'

Maggie drove skilfully, matching the Toyota's speed. She kept other vehicles between her and her quarry, but always stayed close enough to observe the options taken at junctions. Eventually the M876 merged with the Edinburgh-bound M9.

'Where do you think we're going?' McGuire asked.

'God knows. Could be the bloody football. Is it Hearts or Hibs at home today?'

'Oh, aye, and was that their half-time piece that Harvey loaded into the boot? Anyway, I hardly see the wee man as a rabid Hibs fan? No, it could be they're heading for the Bridge. Will I call in?'

Maggie nodded and handed him the car-phone. He punched in Martin's home number. A girl's voice answered.

'Hello, miss. Is Chief Inspector Martin in?'

'He's shaving. Hold on, I'll call him. Andy!' A second later she came back on the line. 'Sorry, who's that?' McGuire introduced himself. 'It's DC McGuire,' she called. 'Sounds as if he's travelling.'

A few seconds later Martin came to the telephone. 'Hi, Mario. What's up?' McGuire explained. And as he did so his earlier guess was proved right. The Toyota headed for the Forth Road Bridge. Maggie followed, tucked behind a maroon Sierra, from which a green and white football scarf trailed.

'One other thing, sir. Joy bought a hell of a load of groceries this morning, and they loaded more than half of them into the car before they left.'

'Okay, Mario, that's good work. Call when you get where you're going. I'll wait here for you.' His tone changed as he spoke away from the phone. 'Sorry, Janie. Can't be helped.'

Then he was back. 'I'll call Brian Mackie and tell him that the caravan's on the move. Tell Maggie not to let them twig her.'

'Would you like to tell her yourself, sir?'

Martin laughed. 'No, maybe not. Good luck.' He hung up and checked Mackie's home number. The DI took some time to answer the call. When he did so he sounded as if he was rubbing the sleep from his voice. But he snapped awake quickly as Martin explained.

'Stay by your phone, Brian, until we can establish where they're going. Call your mate and have him ready in case you have to move fast. And when you do head out, make sure you have a full tank. You'll be heading north, but at the moment it could be anywhere.'

There was no answer from Stockbridge when he called Skinner. He dialled Gullane, and Sarah answered. Bob, she said, had gone for a short-notice round of golf. Martin told her what had happened.

'I'll call the boss when they arrive wherever they're going. Pending further instructions, I'll do no more than maintain the surveillance. So long.'

He put the telephone back in its cradle and turned back to Janie. 'Might as well put on a record. We could be here for a while.'

72

And then the telephone rang.

'Oh, fuck!' Andy swore only in moments of extreme stress.

'Not until you answer that bloody thing!' She rolled away, reached out an arm and handed him the telephone.

Maggie Rose spoke. 'We've arrived, sir. We're in Earlsferry, in the East Neuk of Fife. The Harveys seem to have a weekend cottage here. McGuire called directory enquiries. They're on the phone here. The house is called Earl's Cottage. It's on the beach.

'It'll be difficult to keep it under observation, and impossible from the car. But we can get a clear view from the beach. There are hardly any people about. Most of the houses must be holiday places; there's no sign of life in any of them. No lights, no smoke from the chimneys.'

'How long have you been there?'

'Ten minutes, no more. Mario's down watching the house now.'

'Can you remember if the Harveys' house has a chimney?'

'Yes. It's a newish place, two storeys. There's a big picture window upstairs and a big feature chimney up one wall.'

'Was it smoking when they arrived?'

'It was, sir, it was! There must be someone else in there!'

'Steady on, Maggie.' He swung his feet out of bed and sat on the edge. 'Don't get too excited. There could be a local who comes in to light the fire before they arrive. Keep the house under surveillance, and I'll contact DI Mackie. He and McIlhenney will bring up an overnight bag for you two. They'll do tonight. You book into a hotel or a B and B or something, and relieve them again in the morning.

'And, Maggie, book in on a Mr and Mrs basis. Remember this is a secret enquiry. I don't want you looking out of the ordinary, and any couple booking separate rooms in a place like Earlsferry on a Saturday in winter will surely do that.'

Maggie snorted at the other end of the line. 'McGuire's just going to love that!'

'You can handle it, Sergeant. Pull rank on him if you have to.'

'Rank isn't all I'll pull!' The line went dead.

73

Earlsferry sits alongside Elie on a wide bay which looks across the Firth of Forth to the beaches and hills of East Lothian. The gloaming of late afternoon had begun to obscure the coast opposite when Maggie Rose rejoined McGuire.

He was seated on a bench, his left arm looped along its back, ostensibly looking out to sea while covering the only exit from the Harvey cottage. He was in view himself from the far side of the picture window on the upper level of the house. Twice he had seen Joy Harvey framed in the glass.

Maggie sat down beside him and linked her arm through his. She relayed Martin's orders. McGuire smiled awkwardly, surprisingly embarrassed.

'Huh,' she said, 'you might show a bit more enthusiasm.' She pulled him to her and spoke into his ear. 'Let's try to play the part. Any sign of movement from up there?'

McGuire looked over her shoulder. 'Damn all. I've seen her a couple of times, but no one else. We're a bit open here, but we can see the gate. What do we do if they go out, split up?'

'No we'll have to stick together. We're here as a couple, so we can't keep dashing off in opposite directions all the time.'

'I thought that's what real couples did!'

74

Maggie and McGuire were no longer on their bench when Mackie and McIlhenney appeared, moving quietly down the lane, each clad in dark donkey jackets over thick polo-necked sweaters and police uniform trousers. They moved carefully in the dark, looking first towards the house, then at the moonlit beach.

'Here, sir.' Maggie Rose's voice came from behind a clump of sand dunes. She and McGuire had moved from the beach as darkness had approached, to a point from which they could view both lane and house, without being seen from either.

Mackie and McIlhenney sat on the sand beside them. McIlhenney laid a brown paper carrier bag against the dune. 'Thermoses and sandwiches,' he explained to McGuire, who said nothing, but reached into the bag and brought out a half bottle of OVD rum.

'What's this then, hair tonic?'

'It's okay for you pair,' McIlhenney grumbled. 'We're here a' night.'

'No action?' Mackie asked.

'No, sir,' said Maggie. 'The upstairs curtains have been half drawn, like you see them now, since about four-thirty. The room's dimly lit so we've only seen figures moving about; only two as far as we've been able to tell. No one's been out since they arrived. The car's never moved.

'Do you want us to hang about for a while in case they get off their mark?'

'No, Maggie, that's all right. It's after eight now. They're not going back to Cumbernauld tonight. If they decide to go to the pub we'll just let them get on with it, unless more than two of them come out.

'Your case is in the boot of my car. It's parked behind yours. Which hotel will you be in, if we do need to contact you?'

'We'll book into that big grey one just off the main road. I think it was called "The Beachview".'

226

'It would be in a place like this. Okay, off you go. Be back here for eight sharp.'

75

The Beachview Hotel was a big rambling building, probably Victorian in origin. They entered through a newly built bar, in which three drinkers sat, each alone at his table. McGuire asked for reception and the barman pointed towards a doorway. 'Through there, sir and round to your left.'

They followed his directions and found the check-in desk in a comfortably furnished hall. Two elderly ladies sat in chairs in the far corner, watching a large television set which needed an adjustment to its colour control. McGuire rang a brass bell, and seconds later a fresh-faced girl appeared.

'Can we have an *en-suite* room for the night, please?'

'Certainly, sir.' She smiled at him, a shade knowingly. 'Double or twin?' He looked at Maggie.

'Double,' she said, returning the girl's secret smile.

McGuire signed the register and the girl handed him a key. 'Room 211 sir. Up the stairs and to your left. Dinner's being served now, until ten o'clock. Breakfast starts at seven-fifteen.'

'Even on Sunday?' McGuire sounded surprised.

'It's for the golfers. We don't finish until ten, though, so you've no need to rush.

'The dining-room's back through the bar, then straight on.'

Room 211 was clean and fresh and the fittings in the *en-suite* bathroom, though old-fashioned, were high quality, with a six-foot bath. Maggie plugged in the stopper and turned on the taps.

'I was going to ask for a twin, you know,' McGuire said, plaintively.

'Sure you were. We've got to keep up the act, anyway. I know you'll have slept on the floor before now, being as cosmopolitan as you are. Or that bath looks big enough for you.'

She flipped open the catches on the suitcase. 'Let's see what Brian's brought us.'

She looked in. 'Marks and Spencer best. Shirt, Y-s and socks for you, heavy sweater, skirt, underwear and etceteras for me. What else?

Deodorant, make-up, ok, shaving kit, toothbrushes and paste, shampoo, even a hairdryer. Presumably the SB slush fund paid for this lot.

'I'm going to grab a quick bath.'

She found a newspaper in the bag, passed it across to him and disappeared into the bathroom. Mario glanced at the front page. He stretched out on the bed. Idly he glanced into the small suitcase, looked again. No nightclothes. He laughed, loudly enough for Maggie to hear through the heavy bathroom door.

76

It was just after nine o'clock when they walked downstairs, Maggie clutching Mario's arm tightly. She had changed into the skirt, and the heavy, but close-fitting sweater. The lipstick was pale for her, but not too bad.

The service was swift, which was as well, since they were both hungry after a hectic day. It had been a long time since those rolls.

As they finished their meal, Maggie took Mario's left hand in her right. The dining-room was empty save for an elderly couple who were eyeing them surreptitiously. She leaned over, and nibbled his ear. As the couple looked away, Mario smiled.

Maggie spoke softly. 'You know, it's a fact: people always forget couples like us. You'd think we'd stand out, but we don't. Other people find us embarrassing and look away. Just like that pair over there.'

They declined coffee and moved through to the bar, which was much busier than before. 'What would you like, love?' Mario said in a voice clear enough to carry, as they took a table facing the door.

'I would love a Bacardi-and-tonic, please, darling,' she answered in a throaty voice which, for a moment, she hardly recognised as her own. He went over to the bar, where the efficient barman had already begun to pour Maggie's drink, and asked for a pint of Belhaven 80 Shilling ale for himself.

Waiting, he glanced around the room. His eyes stopped for a split second at a table near the entrance, then moved on, his expression unchanged. Joy and Andrew Harvey were seated there. She was sipping a lager, he was staring at a large whisky, and at three empty glasses which stood beside it.

He carried the drinks back to Maggie. He slipped into the bench seat beside her, then, without warning, pulled her firmly against him and kissed her. Their heads together, he whispered. 'You can't see them from here because of those blokes in the middle of the floor, but our pals are sat right opposite us. We'd better put your invisibility theory to the test.'

'Mm,' she replied, and flicked her tongue into his ear. A tremor ran down the length of his body, and he was, very suddenly, very hard. 'What's the worst job you've ever had?' she whispered to him, and suddenly he was racked with silent laughter.

Then the men in the middle of the floor moved in towards the bar. Maggie glanced across. Five empty glasses remained on the table. The Harveys had gone.

They finished their drinks, and had two more, before Maggie tugged at Mario's arm. 'Come on, big boy,' she said, loudly enough for the couple at the next table to hear, 'I don't want you getting too plastered.'

They left the bar, again arm in arm, and made their way back to room 211. Without a word, Mario disappeared into the bathroom, to return the beer which he had rented for the evening.

When he came out, Maggie was waiting, naked, in the darkened room. 'Well, which side of the bed do you sleep on?'

He drew her gently to him. 'Sarge,' he whispered. 'You're out of uniform.'

77

It was still dark when they returned to the beach next morning.

If Mackie sensed a change in their body language, he said nothing. He and McIlhenney were both tired, irritable, and ready for the road.

'They went out last night, together, on foot,' Mackie said. 'Came back about eleven o'clock, arguing. He was a bit pissed, I'd have said. Apart from that, nothing at all. If this thing lasts for another day, you two can't pull that hotel cover again. I'll have the Transit recovered and we'll bring it up tonight. That way we can split the night duty. Right, we're off.'

They disappeared into the lessening gloom.

They found that Mackie had left behind a thick travelling rug. They settled into their inconspicuous hide as the sun rose on another fine, warm day. The Harvey cottage stood curtained against the light.

They sat in silence for a while. Then Mario drew her down on the rug beside him. They kissed again with the ease and comfort of lovers.

'Once this job's over,' said Maggie, 'I'll make sure we're never assigned together again. If I was caught with my hand in your pants, it would set the advance of women in the force back twenty years!'

'That's fine, but watch who you do work with. Us Italians are notorious for our jealousy, and us Irish are even worse.'

She ruffled his black hair. 'Just as long as I don't find out you've got a wife and three kids!' They were still laughing when they heard the sudden roar of the Toyota.

They spun round on the rug, and saw the sleek black car reverse fast out of the driveway and power up the lane. At the top, it turned right. They heard tyres squeal as it raced off, heading in the wrong direction down the one-way street.

Mario started to jump up, but Maggie held him back. 'Wait. The job is surveillance of the Harveys. We couldn't even see who was driving. It could be back in a minute, for all we know.'

'Sure. Maggie, in a place like this you don't go for the Sunday papers

232

at seventy miles an hour, the wrong way up a one-way street. That car isn't coming back, and we've lost it. I think we should call Andy Martin for instructions.'

78

Martin answered the telephone on the second ring. Maggie Rose was slightly out of breath. 'Someone's just bombed off in the Toyota. Don't know who; we couldn't get a clear view.'

'Is your cover blown? Have they spotted you?'

'They must have. Whoever was driving that car was going like Ayrton What's-his-name. We couldn't see how many people were in it. Everything happened so fast. But I don't think it was Joy at the wheel. I followed her all the way up here. She's a really good driver; very smooth.

'What do we do now?'

Martin thought for a moment. 'Knock the door. If anyone answers, spin them a tale, and piss off. If not, go in. But make sure that no one else sees you.

'Check it out and call me back. And be careful. Remember, this is a dangerous one.'

'Understood, sir. She pressed the 'end' button on the car phone.

'Come on, Mario, let's take a look. Let's see if the Harveys are receiving guests or if they've just stepped out for a bit. Just in case there is someone in there, let's have some daft story. "Our car's broken down and we need help. Where's the nearest garage?" That'll do.'

They crept quietly to the side door of the house. It was lying ajar. Mario walked round to the back and looked through the kitchen window. He was unable to see below work surface level, but there, in view, was Joy's upturned purse.

He went back to the door, and stepped halfway through. He called, 'Hello.' There was no reply – only the smell of fresh coffee, and something else.

'Wait here,' McGuire told Maggie, taking over the command role without thinking. Something in his voice made her obey without a second thought.

He stepped into a small laundry room, with washing machine, tumble dryer and a sink along one wall, and cupboards lining the other. A second open door faced him. He moved into the kitchen and saw what was lying there. He half turned to run out again, but caught himself in time, before betraying his panic to Maggie.

Joy lay stretched out on her back, her head in a pool of blood. A red trickle led from a hole above her left eye. Her hair, above her ear on the right side of her head, was matted with blood and brain tissue from an exit wound. McGuire knelt beside Harvey, who lay on his side. The front of his blue pyjama jacket was dark red, and the bullet hole in his temple stood out vividly. Blood had sprayed along the line of cupboards against which he had fallen.

McGuire closed the door on Maggie, and went quietly through the rest of the house, praying to himself that there had been only one killer. He found the master bedroom, with its two crumpled beds. There was a second bedroom next door, though nothing to indicate that it had been occupied. But the room still smelled of its tenant. McGuire looked at the bed. On the pillow there were several black hairs.

He sprinted back to the kitchen and through to the laundry room, averting his eyes from the carnage on the kitchen floor. Maggie stood there, white-faced.

'Let's get the fuck out of here, now,' he said. They stepped out into the driveway and looked about. There was no one in sight.

In the lane, McGuire made towards the street, but Maggie held him back. 'No, we've got to get that rug.'

They went back to their sand dune and picked it up. Then they walked away from the house towards the end of the beach, from which rose a grassy outcrop, with an ancient ruin as its main landmark. They left the sand behind and circled back towards the Metro: just another couple out for an early morning stroll.

They had not spoken since they left the driveway. In the car, Maggie turned to McGuire. He was shaking. 'Mario, are you all right? Tell me what was in there.'

'The Harveys. Shot to fucking bits. Let's get out of here now, and call Andy Martin on the move.'

'But shouldn't we tell the Fife police?'

'Yes, Sergeant, we should. But we're not going to. Think about it. If we call the local bobbies, we're blown, in a big way. We do what Andy Martin tells us, nothing else.'

She thought about it for a moment. 'There's no chance they're still alive?'

'Maggie, their brains are all over the floor.'

She looked for a moment as if she might be sick. 'All right, let's go.'

As Maggie drove away from Elie, heading further east towards St Monans and Anstruther, anywhere, just to put distance between them and the cottage of death, McGuire called Martin. He described the scene in detail.

'The guy must have been in the house all the time we were watching it. He could have been there for a while. Judging by those groceries, he could have been planning to stay a while longer.

'Something must have happened for him to panic badly enough to kill them and run for it.'

'If it's who I think it is,' said Martin, 'he's twigged us. He's spotted you on the beach, or they've told him about my visit. If it makes you feel better, I think that's more likely.

'Look, I want you to stop at the first phone-box you see on the way back to Edinburgh and call in a 999. Anonymously. Then get back to Fettes Avenue. I'll tell the boss, and we'll meet you there.'

79

Skinner was at home catching up on paperwork when Martin called. 'Boss, something's happened in Fife. We need to see you in the office. Can you come in, now?'

'Give me forty-five minutes, Andy, and I'll be with you.' He and Sarah left Alex to lock up the cottage when she returned to Glasgow that evening for the start of term.

'Bye, Pops. Bye, Sarah.' Alex saw them off from the front door. 'Oh, Dad, I nearly forgot. There's something I was going to ask you. Call me when you get a chance.'

'Okay, Baby.' He kissed her quickly on the cheek and climbed into his car. Just over half an hour later, he strode into Martin's office. 'What's the panic, Andy? Have our people been spotted?'

'If they have, it's by the wrong man. The Harveys are dead in their holiday place in Elie. It seems they had a house guest. Maggie and McGuire saw their car go flying out of the drive and off like a bat out of hell. They called in, and I told them to take a look. The Harveys were in the kitchen, dead. Finished off with close-range head shots, Mario said.'

'They didn't hear gunfire?'

'No, and it was quiet there. He must have used a silencer. Maggie and McGuire are on their way back, and the other two are waiting for them downstairs.'

'Did anyone else see them?'

'No. Not as far as they know. All the houses seem to be owned by week-enders, and they all looked empty. Apart from the Harveys'.'

'Did they call the locals?'

'Yes. An anonymous shout once they got clear. If they'd called in on the record, we'd have blown the enquiry and had some awkward questions from the Fife Chief Constable. I did what I thought was best.'

There was a knock on the door. 'Come in,' Martin shouted, and Maggie and McGuire entered, followed by Mackie and McIlhenney, looking tired and dishevelled.

'Hello, you lot,' said Skinner. 'An eventful weekend, I hear. Sit down and tell me about it.' He noticed that Maggie and McGuire were still pale-faced, and he took in the dark stain on the knee of the detective constable's slacks.

McGuire caught the glance. 'The kitchen was like a knacker's yard, sir. There was blood and stuff all over the place.'

Skinner looked at Maggie Rose. 'Did you get any sort of a sight of the guy when he got away?'

'None at all, sir. It all happened very fast, and that car has tinted-glass windows. We watched the place in daylight and darkness; occasionally the Harveys would appear at the window, but no one else. We saw them, or at least Mario did, in the hotel bar last night. There was no one with them.'

Skinner sat silent for several seconds. Eventually he swung round in his chair. 'So where does that leave us? Without a warm lead, for a start, and with our killer on the run and probably safe again by now.

'So who was it in the house? It could have been Fazal Mahmoud. He's missing from the Lebanese Embassy. He's either running scared because someone zapped his two advocates, or he did it himself, and now he's tying up loose ends. On the other hand, he could be Ali Tarfaz, alias Rashoun Hadid, another old university type. He's dropped out of sight too.

'On balance, based on Andy's interview with the Harveys, I think it's Mahmoud. But I'm sure of one thing. Our man did the Harveys because he thought they'd been rumbled. If he was lying there waiting to get them, he'd have done them as soon as they arrived yesterday.'

He picked up a pencil from the desk and spun it between his fingers.

'Alongside all this activity, we've got this Syrian visit on our hands, next Friday, Mahmoud's boss, for Christ's sake. We have to consider the chance of a connection between that visit, these murders, and our two wandering Arabs, and whether there could, in it all, be a threat to the President.' He looked around the room. 'Any thoughts on that?'

McGuire spoke up. 'Only this, sir. If our guy is after the Syrian, then he isn't going to run far.

'He's lost his safe house, so he'll need to find somewhere to lay his head for the next five nights. He's not going to hang on to that Toyota for long either. Where he dumps it could give us a clue to where he's heading.'

Skinner nodded. 'Let's just assume that he'll head for Edinburgh, if he isn't here already. We check now, and again and again if we have to, every hotel and guest house in the city. Start with the wee ones first. Andy, you allocate lists.

'Mario, get on to communications and pick up a couple of radios. Fife will figure out that the Harveys' car is missing. They'll put out a description. Monitor radio traffic till you hear they've found it. We could keep track of him by following a trail of car thefts.'

He turned to Mackie and McIlhenney. 'Brian, Neil, on you go home and catch up on your sleep. We can start the guest-house check in the morning. That's all, folks. Be back in this office at 9.00 a.m. tomorrow.'

As the four left, Skinner said to Martin, 'Andy, has McGuire passed his Sergeant's exams?'

'Yes, boss. He's in the queue for a job.'

'I think I'll put him into Gayfield when this is over. They could use another good DS there.

'Oh yes, and split Maggie and Mario up in future.'

He walked over to the window, where a radio sat on a small cabinet and tuned in to Radio Scotland. The news jingle came up after a few minutes.

The first report concerned the deaths of three children in a house fire in Glasgow. The second described the aftermath of violence following the defeat of Celtic by St Johnstone in a Premier League match. The third followed up on a Sunday newspaper story on the latest argument over the Scottish Parliament. Finally, the announcer paused, and his voice took on a graver tone. 'We are just getting reports that detectives in Fife have gone to a house in Earlsferry following an anonymous telephone call. Earlsferry is a popular holiday resort, and the house is believed to be one of many owned by families from the West of Scotland.'

The bulletin had barely finished when the telephone rang. Martin picked it up, listened, grunted, nodded, said 'Quick work,' and replaced the receiver.

'That was Mario. They've found the Toyota abandoned in Cupar, near the bus station. And there have been no other thefts reported anywhere in Fife since Friday night.'

Skinner picked up the telephone. 'Where was he calling from?'

'CID room, I think.'

Skinner dialled an extension number.

'McGuire, is Sergeant Rose with you. Good. Put her on. Maggie, I want you two to go down to the bus station and watch all buses arriving from Fife. If you see anyone of Arab origins, carrying luggage, tail him to his final destination, but do not arrest him. You'd better be armed, just in case. Come up here and we'll give you SB firearms.'

80

Maggie and McGuire spent three hours in the Metro watching buses pour in from all over the UK. Three of them were from Fife, but none of the passengers looked even remotely Arab. Eventually, they were ordered to stand down.

When they returned their pistols, Martin told them that they would be in different locations for the Syrian visit. Maggie would be at the hotel with Neil McIlhenney, McGuire with Skinner, Martin and Mackie at the MacEwan Graduating Hall.

Maggie made a show of indignation. 'Why is that, sir? Mario and I work well together.'

'The boss says so. End of story.'

McGuire smiled. 'Have to make the best of it, then. Come on, Sergeant, and I'll treat you to the best spaghetti in town.'

As they left the headquarters building, Maggie was still frowning. 'Where is the best spaghetti in town anyway?' she asked grumpily.

The Italian in McGuire smiled again. 'My place. Where else?'

81

Skinner was about to leave the office, when he remembered that Alex had asked him to call. He dialled the Gullane number. The sound of his daughter's voice always gave him a lift.

'Hi, Babe. What was it that you forgot to ask me this morning?'

'It's probably nothing, but remember you said this morning at breakfast that, on some case or other, your guys had to check an Amstrad like mine. You said that all the disks looked more or less empty.'

'Yes, so what?'

'Well, did whoever did the checking know about the limbo files?'

'What the hell are limbo files?'

'I thought not! It's a software oddity. When you erase a document, you don't can it completely, at least not at first. All you do is take it off the menu. As it fills up with live files, the disk makes room by jettisoning the dead ones. But until that happens, they can still be recovered.'

'So you're saying that if someone had tried to wipe a disk, he might still have left something on it?'

'Yes, that's right.'

'Clever girl. How do you check them?'

'As I remember, you press the option key. Then you press another, F5 I think, and it lets you bring the limbo files back, ready for reading, printing, editing, anything you like.'

'Alex, that's great. I'll have them re-checked. If we find anything I'll put you up for an OBE or something.'

'A law degree will be just fine. I must go now. Love you, Pops. Take care.'

82

Martin rang Kenny Duff at 8.45 next morning to arrange for another look at Mortimer's word processor. 'You're just in time,' he said. 'The family asked me to give some things to the Social Work Department, or to charities, and that will be one of them.'

The team all arrived promptly. Mackie and McIlhenney looked refreshed; Maggie and McGuire looked even more tired than they had the day before.

Martin told Mackie to begin with Yellow Pages, and to split the hotel and guest-house entries into groups. 'Then pick up a copy of the B-and-B list from the local tourist office and allocate that too. Do everything by telephone at first. We'll never get through them all otherwise. Let's keep the story simple. We can only check one name, and that'll be Fazal Mahmoud, Lebanese. We say that he is a freelance journalist, touring in Scotland. We need to speak to him because there's been bad news at home. We tell people to call us at once if the man checks in, but not to mention our call. This is because we don't want him to panic before we have a chance to break the news. Happy with that?'

Mackie nodded in agreement.

'Well, go to it, and good luck.'

The weather had broken when Skinner and Martin arrived at Mortimer's flat. It was cold and depressing, dead like its owner. Skinner switched on the computer, and loaded the software. Eventually, the menu appeared on the green screen.

He loaded the first data disk, and followed the procedure which Alex had explained to him. He pressed F5. The screen changed, and additional files appeared, each with the word 'limbo' after its title. He performed the recovery drill, then chose a document and pressed E for Edit followed by Enter. The file related to a holiday booking.

'This could take a long time,' he said to Martin. He had no great expectations. But it was part of the search, and it had to be done, even if it meant a long, boring day staring at a computer screen.

As superstition would have it, his third choice was the lucky one. He slid the thin plastic wafer into the drive slot and pressed the disk change button. The menu appeared on the screen. 'Not much on this one,' he muttered to himself. There were only three small files on the menu, each titled by a surname, month and year. He guessed that they probably related to criminal trials.

He pressed F5. The choice of options was displayed. He told the machine to 'show limbo files' and pressed the Enter key.

Seven new files flashed up before him, each one styled 'Limbo'. Each was named 'Israel', and was followed in sequence by a number from one to seven.

Skinner sensed Martin tense, then stand bolt upright beside him. Carefully, making certain not to press the wrong button and erase them forever, he recovered the documents.

When the 'limbo' tag had disappeared from the screen, he checked the size of each document. They ranged in size from 15K to 88K. He totalled them. In all, the 'Israel' series occupied 327K of memory, more than one third of the disk's respectable storage space.

He sent the cursor to 'Israel 1', and pressed E for Edit followed swiftly by the Enter key. After eight long seconds of clicks and hums from the computer and its printer, the screen changed.

Martin yelled aloud. Skinner grinned broadly, but stayed in his chair. The two detectives read, incredulous, Skinner moving the cursor to scroll the pages.

The green lettering was clear and precise, to match the language of the document.

It began:

The Case against Israel

'An opinion for the Governments of Syria, Lebanon, and Iraq by Rachel Jameson, Advocate, and Michael Mortimer, Advocate, on the legal basis for the foundation of the State of Israel.

This opinion establishes, beyond what its authors believe to be reasonable doubt, that the signatories to the Treaty and Declaration by which Israel was established in 1948 as a so-called sovereign state, acted without any legal jurisdiction or authority, and in contravention of the principles and practice of international law and of many treaties stretching back over the centuries.

It will demonstrate that the Jewish tribes had no prior right to the territories which they were allocated in 1948, and that the so-called ancient Jewish homeland was never more than territory seized by force by bands of nomads and held, for a time, against the will of its native occupants.

It will demonstrate that Israel exists as a state today only by force of arms and oppression, and that there is no basis in law for its occupancy of any territory, not just the occupied territories in Gaza, on the West Bank and in Jerusalem, on the Golan Heights, and in Lebanon, but of any of the lands which it now controls, when this is set against the justifiable claims of the descendants of the people who were the original indigenous occupants of the land known as Palestine.

This opinion will be followed by notes on differences in the methods of presentation required for the presentation of the case to the United Nations General Assembly and Security Council, the International Court of Justice in the Hague, and the European Court of Human Rights in Strasbourg.

Warmth was beginning to return to the room from the log-effect gas fire set in the fine, high, marble-topped fireplace. Skinner took off his jacket, draped it over the back of his chair, as he and Martin settled down for a long read.

Long before it was over, their eyes were smarting from the strain of the screen. Martin removed his contact lens and put on his spectacles. They were mesmerised by the detail which was spread out before them. Each had a policeman's grasp of the law, and could follow the complex arguments.

Through them all, there emerged with clarity, a powerful case for the eviction of the Israelis from the government and domination of the land they now called home, and for the right of settlement and enfranchisement to be extended to all Palestinians as well as to all Jews, leading to free elections in time.

The conclusion of the document was that since the Israelis had followed a systematic policy of oppression of the Palestinian population, and since it was clear that they would never grant this right of free settlement, or amend their constitution, the just solution of the Palestinian problem, on the basis of the precedent established in 1948, could be enforced by the nations in the region, acting in concert.

After three hours they finished reading. The documents, in total, were over three hundred pages long.

When they had finished, Skinner leaned back in his chair. His face was drawn. 'Jesus Christ,' he whispered to Martin, 'this is dynamite!'

He looked at the dot matrix printer. It had a tractor feed for loading fan-fold paper. He looked around the room, and found eventually, under the desk, a deep box of computer paper. It was almost full.

Clumsily he fed the first sheet into the machine. He pressed the key marked 'Printer' and found a new menu. He set the printer to run on continuous stationery.

It took almost five hours to run the full series of documents. Throughout that time, Skinner sat by the printer like a father-to-be in the labour ward. It had been dark for two hours by the time the print-run came to an end.

They looked at it in wonder. Could this be the Holy Grail? Could this really have cost all those lives? It was, at the end of the day, no more than an excellent piece of research, and a seemingly sound, if controversial, legal view, which any one or two among hundreds of advocates in Scotland, and thousands beyond, might have prepared. Yet, it seemed, it could kill. It had killed. It was still killing.

In a desk drawer Martin found some brightly-coloured Christmas wrapping paper. Neatly he packaged the discovery. Skinner withdrew the disk from the drive and slipped it, with the system disk, into his pocket.

They left the flat ostensibly as they had found it, but in fact relieved of an awesome secret.

83

It was 7.00 p.m. A hard rain drummed against the window of Skinner's office.

'Either Mortimer hid the files himself, or whoever broke into the flat thought that he had wiped them out. Whichever it was, this is the link. That's what the twenty grand was for.'

'It answers that question,' said Skinner, 'but it throws up others. Just for a start, why them?'

'Probably because Fuzzy knew that Rachel was loyal to the cause. Mortimer gets involved because he was loyal to Rachel.'

'Some machine, this Fuzzy. He comes back into the lives of Rachel and the Harveys after all these years, and he uses them. Now they're dead, and it looks as if he may have killed them all.'

Martin broke in. 'But why kill anyone over this. It's a good piece of work, but other people could do this research and reach the same conclusion. It's been written for use, not to be kept secret, so why kill the authors?'

'I don't know. I'm not convinced that friend Fuzzy did that anyway. But they are dead, and they sure were killed. Maybe the Israelis found out and decided to clean out the whole house. Maybe Fuzzy's on the run from them.

'No, my guess is that this is only part of something very big indeed. When we find Fuzzy we might find out what it is.'

84

But finding Fuzzy was easier to order than to achieve, with no photo to aid identification, and only Marjorie Porteous's thirteen-year-old description to go on. 'Slim, quiet, good-looking chap. Brown skin, dark hair, dark moustache. That's all I can remember.'

The hotels yielded nothing. The few bed-and-breakfast houses open for business in January reported only sales reps as overnight guests.

'Check them again, and every day from now till Friday,' Martin ordered.

Skinner briefed the team on Tuesday morning on the discovery in Mortimer's files.

Mackie looked embarrassed. 'Sorry, boss,' he said. 'I should have found that.'

'Bollocks,' said Skinner dismissively. 'You're a copper not a computer man.'

To keep the team active, Martin sent them out to make their second round of checks in person, rather than by telephone. 'Remember that cover story. We're trying to trace him because of trouble at home.'

After the four had left, Skinner picked up his jacket, and motioned to Martin to follow.

'Where are we going?'

'We're going to the airport to meet a man. We wear these so he'll recognise us.' He pinned a small gold lion badge into his lapel, and handed one to Martin, who fastened it to his tie. The lions were sometimes used by Special Branch and protection officers to indicate to each other that the wearer was armed.

The visitor approached them quietly as they stood at the bookstall opposite the British Midland arrival point.

'Mr Skinner, Mr Martin? I'm Maitland.' He spoke in flat clipped tones, with no trace of a regional accent.

The man stood just over six feet tall. He might have been around thirty

248

years old. He was clean-shaven, and his dark hair was close-cropped. His eyes were blue, as clear as a bell, and he wore the fading tan of someone recently returned from a spell in a seriously hot place. He wore a well-tailored, double-breasted suit of navy-blue worsted, with a thin vertical stripe.

He did not give the impression of physical power, but when the two policemen shook his hand they found a grip like a vice. His carriage was his most impressive feature. He walked out of the terminal building, between Skinner and Martin, with lightness, grace and perfect balance, as if his feet were hardly touching the ground.

Maitland had introduced himself in a confidential fax to Skinner as the commander of the Special Air Services detachment which had been assigned to provide cover for the Syrian President during his visit. He had not mentioned his rank, but Skinner knew that in the SAS, that was not important.

Martin drove to the Norton House, where the three were met by the manager, an immaculate man named Adrian Doyle. Skinner described Maitland as 'a security adviser who will be here during the visit'. Doyle, who had previous experience of VIPs, asked no questions.

He guided them round the hotel. In the first-floor suite which had been set aside for the Syrian President, Maitland made a careful check of the angles of view through the double window as they related to the position of the main items of furniture. He opened a window and checked for drainpipes or other climbing aids, and found nothing. Leaning further out, he surveyed the roof above. He confirmed that there were no points of access to the *en suite* bathroom, other than the door from the bedroom.

Eventually he turned to the expectant Doyle. 'It looks secure, but I'd like you to move the bed to that wall. We legislate for everything, even the sort of fanatic who will empty a magazine through a curtained window if he can't find a better opportunity. At the moment the bed is in the line of fire from those trees over there.'

Doyle smiled. 'There will be no difficulty about that.' He took them back to the entrance hall and left them to explore the hotel grounds alone.

The grass and trees were wet from the previous night's rain, but Maitland was prepared. He produced a nylon coverall from his bag in Skinner's car, discarding his jacket before slipping it on. His black leather shoes were replaced by trainers.

'No need to come with me, gentlemen. All I'll be doing is checking the terrain, and identifying all the possible firing points.' He disappeared into the woods.

When he emerged silently behind Skinner and Martin fifteen minutes later, the coverall was dripping wet.

'You've made a very good choice,' he said, as he stepped out of the garment. 'I will have twenty men here. With that number, I could keep a fly out of this place.

'When are the technical people installing the listening devices and cameras?'

'Thursday,' Martin replied.

'Good. I'll advise them on siting the video cameras. My men arrive on Thursday too. I'd like to do a rehearsal of the whole operation that evening, including the Hall. Can we check that out now?'

Their visit to the MacEwan Hall was quickly concluded. Henry Wills was there to greet Maitland, but he left as soon as the welcome was over, with what Martin read as a tiny shudder of distaste for the man and his business.

The SAS leader checked the outside of the building for entry points. Then he inspected all the doorways leading into the Hall itself.

'Piece of cake. You clear the building a few hours in advance and the specialists do the bomb search. No admission until an hour before the kick-off. Everyone entering is frisked, and all bags are searched. But no metal detectors.'

Martin was surprised. 'Why not?'

'This is a student audience. They'll be wearing all sorts of odds and ends. Big belt buckles, bracelets, all sorts of stuff that would set the alarms ringing. We'd never get them all in in time.

'You put four good people here doing thorough body and bag searches. If anyone tries to smuggle a gun in they'll find it.

'My unit will cover this place easily. We'll cover all entrances to the building, and doorways to the Hall itself. None of the students will know we're there. Even you won't notice us.'

They drove Maitland to Redford Barracks, on Edinburgh's southern outskirts, where he and his men were to be billeted. As Maitland jogged the few yards from the car into the long imposing building, Skinner looked after him for several seconds.

'That, Andy, is probably one of the most dangerous men you will ever meet.'

Suddenly Martin was aware of his own lack of experience. He began to understand the reason for Henry Wills's quick exit.

85

Skinner was packing his briefcase when his door opened. He looked up, surprised, as the bulky figure of Hugh Fulton came into the room.

'Well, Bob, having a good week?' The big man's voice was heavy with sarcasm.

Skinner was needled into responding in kind. 'I didn't think you could find your way into a police office any more. What can I do for you?'

Fulton's tone softened. 'You can listen to me. I'm worried about you. Look, man, there are times when singlemindedness and dedication can be bad for you. You certainly didn't do the Harveys a lot of good, did you?'

Skinner's face was impassive.

'What do you mean?'

'You know what I mean. Andrew and Joy Harvey, the couple who were shot dead in Fife on Sunday. You had them under observation. Your people were spotted and the Harveys were popped. Fife CID are, as they say in the tabloids, baffled. But we're not, are we?

'Bob, when I asked you to drop it, I had my reasons. You ignored me. Now two more people are dead. I'm asking you again. Let it go. Please.'

Skinner looked the man in the eye. 'You know a hell of a lot about this case, don't you? The name Fuzzy doesn't mean anything to you by any chance?' Fulton looked puzzled, until he added, 'I'll bet that Fazal Mahmoud strikes a chord, though.'

Colour flooded into the other man's face.

Skinner continued: 'Is this guy radio-active or something? I have reason to believe that he might be responsible for eight murders, and you tell me to lay off him. I don't believe what I'm hearing.'

Fulton's voice was soft. 'Fazal Mahmoud didn't kill anyone, Bob, until your people in Fife got too close.'

Skinner walked around his desk to stand in Fulton's face, setting him on his heels with the power in his eyes and the anger in his voice. 'Are you telling me you know who did kill those people?'

251

'No, man, I'm not saying that.'

'Well, Hughie boy, you seem to know everything else. If you don't know who, you know why. And you know why Fuzzy's running around out there, ready to kill to avoid being traced. Give me a reason why I shouldn't hold you here until you tell me.'

Fulton laughed. 'Don't be daft. You can't touch me. All the same, I will give you a reason. Fife CID have five sets of prints, one in the laundry room, the other four all through the house. They're looking for three people, not one – no Bill Howey didn't tell you that, did he – and you and I know that two of them are members of your force.

'Of course they don't know that. They think they're looking for a couple who left behind a set of crumpled sheets in Room 211 of the local hotel, paid cash and checked out next morning, just before the Harveys were killed. He signed the register as Mr Robert Martin, by the way. Very inventive.

'Your halo isn't shiny any more, Bob. Skinner's Rules are being bent all over the place. You're even concealing information about a murder from a fellow officer. Give this one up before you ruin your career, and more.'

Skinner's anger had abated, but his eyes, and his voice were still rock hard. 'Hughie, I'm not interested in your threats, or your plots. As far as I'm concerned, you can play spy-versus-spy for the rest of your fucking life.

'I'll give up when you give me the man who cut off Mike Mortimer's head – no, Hughie, don't cringe; that's what he did – and shoved Rachel Jameson under a train. The guy who was prepared to kill three people at random, just to put us off the trail. You may or may not know who he is, but I'm damn sure you know what he is, and where his orders come from. Give him to me!'

Desperation shone from Fulton's eyes. And to his surprise, Skinner saw real fear there too. 'I can't do that Bob. There's a big game going on here, and you can't imagine the stakes.'

'Then get the fuck out of my office. And don't you ever threaten me again, Hughie. Not if you like being able to walk upright!'

86

Maitland's SAS detachment arrived at Redford Barracks in two closed army trucks just after the Thursday morning rush hour from Colinton had subsided, and the last of the Mercedes, Rovers and BMWs had left for the city centre.

They unloaded their equipment, showered, and changed into civilian clothes before assembling in a briefing room where Maitland, Allingham, Skinner, Martin and the four members of their team were waiting. Allingham told them, for the first time, the reason for their sudden posting to Edinburgh.

Maitland pulled across a Sasco flip chart and threw back its covering sheet to display a diagram showing the area surrounding the Norton House Hotel. He explained the lay-out and identified key points on which the detail would be concentrating. A second diagram showed a floor-plan of the area where the President's suite was located. He described the locations represented by each of the plans.

Next, he displayed a vertical section of the MacEwan Hall. The points of access to the building and to the debating hall itself were all labelled.

'This is the easy part,' said Maitland. 'We will be in civilian clothes on this one, gentlemen. Each of the external entry points will be guarded by one man. There will be four of you inside the Hall, each with a clear line of fire covering the whole room. Mr Skinner, Chief Inspector Martin, and their colleagues Inspector Mackie and Detective Constable McGuire will be around the President, and they will be armed. You will take action only if you are convinced that they are unaware of a potentially lethal threat, or if they are not in a position to prevent an attack. Each of you will wear a gold lion badge when you enter the Hall. The police officers on search duty will recognise this and will neglect to frisk you . . .

'I will deal with any questions after we have recced the sites.'

They travelled in a white-liveried Lothian Charter bus. They might have been taken for a visiting football side, an appropriate comparison, since teamwork was the essential factor in both occupations.

The Norton House was empty of visitors. All other bookings had been diverted to the Royal Scot, just over a mile away. Maitland briefed those men involved in securing the hotel.

'This is the more difficult job, given the dark and those woods. The assignment at the hall will be handled by twelve men. The eight men handling perimeter security here will be in place from midday, under the command of Mr Hoskins.' Maitland nodded towards a small ginger-haired man seated on a couch near to Skinner and Martin.

'Sergeant Rose and Detective Constable McIlhenney will be here throughout the afternoon, and until the President eventually departs.'

The two, unsmiling, nodded acknowledgement.

'The visit will not be announced in advance. The media will be told at 4.00 p.m. on the day and special lapel badges will be issued to selected journalists by the Scottish Office Information Directorate. This is a sample.' He held up a buff-coloured tag with a short purple cord attached. 'The three press officers will wear green tags, like this.' He held up another sample.

'We will travel to Redford by coach, to arrive no more than thirty minutes before the President. As soon as his plane is given landing clearance, we leave the barracks in a chartered bus. Comments from anyone?'

He looked towards Skinner and Martin, who raised a hand.

'Aren't you cutting your arrival at the Hall just a bit fine?'

'If we arrive any earlier, we will be obtrusive. I don't want the students to twig us. Most of them will be little Lefties, and if they spot an SAS presence at a university event there could be trouble.

'They might even mob us, and that would be unfortunate.' He smiled at Martin, fixing him with his gaze.

87

When Skinner returned to his office, he found a note from his secretary on his desk. '*At lunch. CC called, asked if you could spare a minute on your return.*'

Skinner called to check that Proud was still there, then walked the short distance to his office.

'Hello, Bob. Come along in. Coffee?' Skinner nodded. 'Sandwich?' Proud jerked a thumb towards a plate on his desk. Skinner helped himself to a BLT as the Chief handed him a steaming mug.

'How did your recce go? Do you see any problems?'

'Just like you'd expect with the SAS boys – like clockwork. There's no way that anyone will get near our guest without being spotted. No one will have a go at this man and walk away from it. But of course, political assassins don't care about walking away. If there's a fanatic out there, he'll have a chance.'

'And is that what you're after in this investigation of yours, Bob – a fanatic?'

'No, Chief. I'm after a cold, calculating devious bastard who kills for a purpose.'

'And this Arab chap? Does he fit into that category?'

A slight smile flicked the corners of Skinner's mouth. Had Proud Jimmy been nobbled? 'Fuzzy? No, I don't think so. Yes, Fuzzy's a killer but he's not the one I'm looking for. He's a loose cannon. Somebody's wound him up and let him go.'

Almost dreamily, he continued in a soft voice, 'No, there's someone else, someone much more heavy duty than him.' Abruptly he looked Proud straight in the eye. 'What did Fulton tell you?'

The Chief looked slightly furtive. 'He told me that this man Mahmoud was on the run from his own people because of some political thing, and that Fulton's outfit was keeping out of it.

'He said that you had picked up a false trail linking the man with Rachel

Jameson, that by chance you had got too close to him, and that he had panicked. He said that Mahmoud murdered the people who were hiding him, that pair that were shot in Earlsferry on Sunday. And he said that you're still after him. That's what he said.

'And he asked me – no that's the wrong word – he told me, to nail you and Martin to your desks for a while.'

'And will you?'

'Should I?'

'That depends upon whether you like the idea of people in your town, one of your men among them, being killed for politics.'

'That's what you think?'

'That's what I know, Chief. There's a wee bit of what Fulton told you that's true. Fuzzy Mahmoud is on the move, and I want him. But not because he killed our five people. He didn't. There's a hell of a lot that I know that Fulton didn't tell you. I think I even know some things that he doesn't. Unless you order me otherwise, I'm going to keep it all to myself, to protect your position if nothing else. I'm a loose cannon in this thing too, Chief. Let me stay that way!'

Proud looked at Skinner long and hard. 'Bob, if something goes wrong here, like as not I'll be in the firing line along with you.'

Skinner sighed. 'I know that, Jimmy. And I've no right to expect it of you.'

The Chief's solemn face broke into a sudden, sunny smile. 'I've never liked that big Aberdonian bastard Fulton. The man keeps saying that he doesn't exist. Well, if that's the case, then he couldn't have been in my office this morning. And if he wasn't, then you're not here now either, and this conversation hasn't happened. So away you go then, before I notice you!'

88

The Syrian President's Boeing 737 touched down at RAF Turnhouse at 7.00 p.m., dead on time. The evening was cold, dry, crisp and moonlit. Skinner and Martin bounded up the steps into the aircraft. Mario McGuire remained on the runway. All three were armed with Browning automatic pistols, and wore lion badges.

Allingham was waiting at the door. He was white-faced. For a fleeting moment, Skinner felt sorry for the transplanted pen-pusher.

'Don't worry, man. It'll be over soon,' he said in reassurance.

The rear section of the aircraft was screened off. Allingham led the two policemen through.

'Assistant Chief Constable Skinner, Chief Inspector Martin, may I introduce our guest: His Excellency Hassan Al-Saddi, the President of the Republic of Syria.'

The man who turned to face them was short and squat, in early middle age. He stood between two escorting diplomats. He wore an olive green uniform, with heavy badges of rank on the shoulders and rows of medal ribbons on the left breast. The tunic was beautifully tailored. The cut emphasised the thickness of the President's chest and the width of his shoulders. The impressive picture was topped off by a black and white chequered headdress held in place by a black circlet.

But all the style of his dress could not hide the real man. Skinner had met many killers in his time, and he recognised another in the President of Syria. There was no laughter in the face. Instead, the grim set of the jaw and the hard gleam in the brown eyes emphasised that this was a man with no conscience, and with the will to succeed whatever the cost in other people's lives.

'Welcome to Scotland, Mr President,' said Skinner, formally. 'We are operating to a tight schedule, so there will be no ceremonial at the airfield. We will drive straight to the Hall. There you will be met by the Lord

Provost, and by the President of the Edinburgh University Students' Union, who will chair the evening.

'As I believe you know, the debate is run on British Parliamentary lines. The motion is "That this House believes that a Palestinian state should be established without delay". You will be invited to sum up, in favour of the motion. You can expect to be called to speak at around 9.00 p.m. The debate is scheduled to end by 9.30.

'As soon as the result is declared, and before the Hall is emptied, the Chairman will lead you from the Chamber. From there you will be driven to the Norton House Hotel, where you will spend the night. Be assured that you will be under armed guard throughout your stay with us. Have you any questions?'

Al-Saddi shook his head, jerking the headdress into sudden motion. 'No. I know the programme for the evening, and I have every faith in your security arrangements. Let us go.'

Skinner led on to the floodlit runway, which was guarded by men of the RAF Regiment, armed with automatic rifles. Three cars were lined up close to the aircraft. At the head of the small convoy, two motor-cycle policemen in day-glo tunics straddled powerful BMW bikes.

Martin held open the rear door of the second car, a black Mercedes limousine. Al-Saddi stepped in, followed by his equerry, a tiny nervous man in a dark grey suit. Martin followed him into the long car and perched himself on a jump seat, his back to Al-Saddi. Skinner steered Allingham towards the lead car. As he climbed into the front passenger seat of the Granada, its blue light whirling on top, he shouted to the motor-cyclists, 'Okay, boys, move out. Lights and sirens all the way!'

He jumped into the car and slammed the door shut. With McGuire in the third vehicle, the convoy swung out through the airfield gates. As it did so Skinner picked up the hand-microphone which hung from the car's radio transceiver. 'Blue One to HQ. Patch me through to Blue Two.'

'Understood Blue One. Blue Two on line.'

'Blue One calling Blue Two. Package on the way. Over.'

'Blue Two receiving.' Brian Mackie's eager voice seemed to fill the car. Skinner adjusted the volume. 'The venue is filling up. Searches proceeding smoothly and without trouble. The crowd seems quiet, sober and responsible. The press are in position, with their escorts. There's only one problem: there's no sign of the bloody military!'

89

On the darkened square at Redford Barracks, Maitland assembled the twelve men who were to guard the MacEwan Hall. Their eight colleagues were, even then, positioned invisibly around the Norton House, each clad in a black tunic and carrying a rifle with a wide, round night-sight on top.

The soldiers wore a variety of civilian dress, some in denim jeans and bomber jackets, some in overcoats. Each man carried a Walther automatic in a shoulder holster.

A white mini-bus stood nearby, its passenger door open.

'Gentlemen, let us go to work,' said Maitland calmly, quietly, but with chilling purpose and authority.

One by one they climbed on board the vehicle. Maitland, in black slacks and a Daks sports jacket, brought up the rear. The bus, with a military driver at the wheel, pulled out of the Barracks and headed towards the centre of Edinburgh.

Colinton Road ends at a complicated junction, known popularly as Holy Corner because of the three churches which seem to glare at each other across the roadway. The white bus was about three hundred yards from the traffic lights, with the driver easing his foot slightly on the throttle, when there was a roar from the left. Just as it passed Napier University, a big modern college building, incongruous among the grey tenements, terraces and villas of staid, conservative Morningside, an old, battered Land-Rover came roaring out of its car park.

The heavy green vehicle skidded and smashed full tilt into the front nearside corner of the bus, which spun out of control, crashing, as the driver jammed on the brakes in vain, into a grey Montego parked on the other side of the street. The engine roared in neutral for a few seconds, then spluttered and died.

'Bastard,' shouted the bus driver. Blood streamed from a cut on his forehead where it had slammed into the window. Several of the soldiers had been thrown into the aisle, and one looked slightly dazed. All but he had drawn their weapons in an instinctive reaction. The man next to the passenger door forced it open and looked out. The Land-Rover was slewed across the road, empty, as its driver, a slim youth in jeans and a dark sweatshirt, sprinted away into the night. The soldier was about to jump from the bus in pursuit of the escaping man when Maitland stopped him.

'No, Jones. Leave it. It's police business. A drunken bloody student, I imagine. Dismount, boys, and haul this damn thing out of the roadway.'

Already the traffic was beginning to tail back in both directions from the accident.

'I'll go into the college and call for a replacement vehicle.' Maitland disappeared into the cloistered entry to the Polytechnic.

When he reappeared five minutes later, the squad had manhandled the bus from the middle of the roadway to a position which allowed the traffic to pass. The build-up was clearing slowly.

'Well done, gentlemen. Another bus is on its way. However, the delay means that the Hall will already be well filled. By the time we got there, the debate would be well under way. Our entry, in our baggy jackets would be rather conspicuous. Therefore we will have to trust to luck and the efficiency of the police security. You will divert to the hotel and take up position there. Jones, when the new bus arrives, re-direct it to the Norton House. I will contact the police and advise them of the change. See you at the hotel.'

He disappeared into the night.

90

The motorcycle outriders carved a path through the evening traffic for Skinner's small motorcade, leading it through South Gyle towards the Western Approach Road. The cars were passing Murrayfield, the national rugby stadium, when the radio burst into life once more.

'HQ to Blue One, Blue Two. Traffic reports a hit and run on Colinton Road, in which a bus carrying a group of men has been disabled. Over.'

'Blue One acknowledges. Blue One to Blue Two. That's just magic. Are your uniforms deployed around the Hall? Over.'

'Blue Two affirmative. Over.'

'We'll have to make do then. Blue One out.'

But within seconds HQ was back on air. 'Message for Blue One. Caller advises that in view of accident delay his unit will divert to second site and take up position there. Over.'

'Blue One acknowledges. Please advise Blue Three of change of plan.'

91

The motorcade pulled up in close order at the entrance to the MacEwan Hall. Skinner, McGuire and Allingham jumped out first and surveyed the area. Latecomers were still pressing into the Hall, each one being carefully frisked by uniformed police officers.

Mackie stood in the doorway. 'Okay, Brian?' Skinner called. When the inspector nodded, he opened the door of the Mercedes limousine. Martin stepped out first, and stood close to Skinner, looking around. Mackie and McGuire took up position just beyond them. Martin leaned back into the car and spoke quietly to the President. Al-Saddi climbed out immediately, followed by the tiny, trembling equerry; the four policemen formed a shield and rushed them up the few steps, towards the three people who stood waiting for them. The Lord Provost of Edinburgh stepped forward and introduced himself. Al-Saddi shook his hand.

'May I present the Rector of the University, Mr David McKnight.' The Rector of Edinburgh University is elected by the student population to chair the University Court, and David McKnight was an articulate and politically outspoken professional footballer, something of a folk hero. He was captain of Hibernian and Scotland. His suit was beautifully tailored. He shook Al-Saddi's hand firmly, not in any way overawed.

'Welcome to Edinburgh University, Mr President. Please allow me to introduce Ms Deirdre O'Farrell, the President of the Union and Speaker for this evening's debate.'

Deirdre O'Farrell was a tall, fair-skinned, flame-haired girl. Even in the pseudo-Parliamentary robes of her office she retained an air of authority. Her expression indicated that she walked in no one's shadow, not even that of a visiting head of state.

She spoke with a soft Dublin accent. 'I'm pleased that you could come, Mr President. I am only sorry that your Israeli counterpart has declined to join us.'

'That is of no matter to me. What I have to say is for the ears of the world, not for him alone. Shall we go in?'

The party turned into a small procession, led by Deirdre O'Farrell, with Al-Saddi, McKnight and the Lord Provost following in that order. They threaded their way into the hall, where the other speakers were waiting.

As they did so, they were followed by a sudden press of students. Several of them by-passed the search in the few moments it took to regain control. Among them was a small swarthy man, older than the rest, with a three-day stubble emphasising the grimness of his marred face.

92

A place of honour had been reserved for Al-Saddi at the head of the 'Government' benches on the Speaker's right hand. Mackie and Martin sat at the Clerk's table. McGuire took up position at the main entrance door. Skinner faced the Speaker, beside a television camera. He looked around, trying to peer into the far reaches of the panelled Hall, but was dazzled by the television lights.

The debate opened in fine formality. The motion was proposed by Bernard Holland, a left-wing Labour Member of Parliament, whose fame leaned towards notoriety because of his support for a number of organisations, including the PLO, which, either openly or by reputation, were involved in terrorism. Holland knew the niceties of Parliamentary debate and his speech, powerful in its delivery, brought a sense of reality to the mock event.

He set out his stall from the start, declaring his support for the Palestinians, and challenging the Israelis. 'They of all people, Madam Speaker, a nation landless for two thousand years, should understand the plight of the people of the State of Palestine, who for too long have been in the wilderness. There is room for all. Let them live together!'

Holland sat down to applause that was warm, but which stopped short of being thunderous. He was followed by another Parliamentarian, Sir Sidney Legge, MP, a veteran of thirty years at Westminster, and a leading member of the Board of Jewish Deputies. He was a small grey man, but he spoke with surprising power.

'Madam Speaker, I regret most sincerely that I must urge this House to reject the motion. For once, the gentleman opposite is correct. We Jews appreciate more than any other the plight of the Palestinian people, and we wish them well in their efforts to find a permanent home. But the State of Israel will not be that home. Nor will we allow its security to be put at risk. For that is the real issue here tonight, Madam Speaker, and that is why that gentleman is among us.'

Dramatically, he thrust out his hand, pointing directly at Al-Saddi.

'He is a sworn enemy of Israel. He comes here tonight not to argue the case for Palestine, but to sow, if he can, the seeds of the destruction of the Jewish State.'

The little man thundered on. 'Since the nations of the world recognised Israel's claim to its homeland over forty years ago, we Jews have been attacked on four occasions by people like him. Four times they have sought to take what is ours, and four times they have been taught painful lessons. It may be that, being bad students, our neighbours have forgotten the lesson yet once more. Let us hope not. But with people like that gentleman opposite,' he glowered again at Al-Saddi, 'in places of power in the Middle East, I fear that it is the case. Let us hope that tonight, he has come to listen, not to threaten. It would be as well for him.'

As Sir Sidney sat down, the audience, ringed around the participants in the debate rose in applause. Skinner looked across at Al-Saddi. He was impassive; only in the tightness of the mouth was there a hint of anger.

The exchanges boomed back and forth across the Chamber, not sustaining the weight of the opening salvos, but nevertheless holding the audience and maintaining a fine air of tension.

The case against the motion was summed up by Herbie Clay, a Los Angeles Jew who was one of the world's leading comedians. He performed out of type. For once, no one rolled in the aisles when he spoke.

'Madam Speaker, my parents left Europe for America because they had a simple choice. It was either to leave their homeland or be murdered by a regime which is not dissimilar in outlook to that of the gentleman opposite. Madam, I am sorry that I cannot keep to your Parliamentary tradition by using the word 'honourable' to describe him.

'Millions of my cousins, my brethren, did not have the chance which my parents had. They did not escape. They died. The State of Israel was founded by the survivors of the genocide. Others returning to lands from which they had been expelled by force, determined not to be driven out again.

'Like my Right Honourable Friend, I sympathise with the people of Palestine. I hope they find a home, and soon. But not in my back yard. What about Syria, Mr President? At the rate at which your people have been disappearing since you came to power, you must have room for them. Or what about Lebanon? If you don't actually own it, at least you hold the lease, and at a peppercorn rent too. Why not sub-let a piece to the Palestinians?

'Madam Speaker, as my Right Honourable Friend has said, the Palestinian homeland is not the real issue here. What we are discussing tonight is, as it always is, the existence of the State of Israel. And when the gentleman opposite rises to speak, I am sure that will become all too clear. Well, Madam Speaker, let those who threaten us never forget their mistakes of 1948, of 1967, of 1973, and of 1991, when the world stood by us. Next time the cost of such a foolish misjudgement might be much higher.'

For a second after Clay resumed his seat the audience sat silent, stunned by his unexpected grim eloquence. Then they burst into an ovation which continued until Deirdre O'Farrell called for order.

Finally, President Hassan Al-Saddi was invited to sum up for the motion. He stood up, bowed stiffly to the Chair, and at once his presence filled the room.

'Madam Speaker, I am a blunt man. I do not have the glib tongue of these ladies and gentlemen opposite, who have dismissed the plight of my Palestinian brothers with their fine words. But I have come here tonight to listen to the bluster and threats of these Jews, and to face their insults, as a sign to the world that we people of the front line Arab states, whatever difficulties might arise between our individual nations, are no longer afraid, and that we have recovered our pride.

'For too long, my predecessors in office have paid lip service to the plight of the brave Palestinian people. We have given them our support and little else. When they have become a nuisance in one place, like Lebanon, like Jordan, they have been moved on, like a herd of cattle. We have always put our own interests over theirs. I say that of Syria, my own nation. And, as I say it, I am ashamed of the rulers who went before me.

'But now I say to the people of Palestine, have hope, for Al-Saddi is with you, and Syria is with you, to the death. And my brother in Iraq, whose cause I recognise tonight and to whom I pledge myself in Holy Alliance, although beset and under siege by the world, he joins me in this promise. Together we will win back for the Palestinian people that which was theirs. We have the right on our side. We know this, and we will defend our cause in any court in the world. Morally it is just. Legally it is sound. The finest lawyers have told us that this is so.'

Suddenly Al-Saddi brandished in the air a thick sheaf of papers, bound together at the top with an India tag. The hair at the back of Skinner's neck began to tingle. Opposite, he saw Martin stiffen in his seat. Neither had to be told what those papers were.

'Tonight, with the law at my back and in my hand, I put the Israelis on notice. This is the last chance that they will be given to return to the people of Palestine the land that was stolen from them.

'Once President Kennedy told the people of Berlin, "I am a Berliner". Today they are all free. Tonight, I say to the people of Palestine, "I am a Palestinian". Soon, not tomorrow but soon, they too will be free.

'But there will be a price.

'The State called Israel was founded as our American friend has reminded us, after a holocaust. Let us hope that it does not take another to regain Palestine for its people. But if it does . . .' he paused ' . . . then so be it. We are ready and our cause is just!'

The terrible warning boomed out into a stilled hall. Six hundred people knew that they had just heard a declaration of war, a promise of destruction by a man who was as ruthless as any of history's great tyrants. As Al-Saddi sat down, there was no applause, only an awful silence.

Madam Speaker broke the spell by calling upon the House to vote upon the proposition.

The motion was put by the Clerk. 'All in favour say "Aye".'

On the side of the proposers many, Bernard Holland notable among them, sat silent, chilled by the threats of Al-Saddi. When the 'No' vote was called, the word roared out in the hall, voicing the horror of the gathering.

Deirdre O'Farrell declared that the motion had been defeated.

Hassan Al-Saddi's portentous face darkened still further. He glared across the floor at Sir Sidney Legge and Herbie Clay, who sat smiling softly. There was a bustle at the back of the hall as two television camera assistants left with their cassettes, ready to break around the world the news of the Syrian President's sudden and sensational announcement of alliance with Iraq, and his ultimatum to Israel.

Deirdre O'Farrell stilled the hubbub even as it arose. 'This House stands adjourned.'

She rose from her chair and slipped down to lead the procession from the Hall.

Skinner and Martin moved into the passage to keep it clear. Mackie and McGuire rose and flanked Al-Saddi as he took his place behind the Speaker, and in the tension, behind David McKnight.

Skinner nodded to Deirdre O'Farrell, and the Speaker's procession began to wind its way towards the doorway.

And there, waiting, was a man with death in his hands.

93

Fazal Mahmoud was trembling as he approached the MacEwan Hall. He had come so far, risked so much, and done such terrible things. He was ready for his moment, but one barrier remained.

Possibly he could complete his mission from where he stood, but with so many people milling around, and at night, his chances of success would be slim.

No, thought Fazal; I must be inside. He checked his watch; it was 9.18 p.m. Inside the building, Al-Saddi had risen to his feet.

Four police officers, in uniform, the quartet who had carried out the body searches, were ranged across the door. Four more stood around the three cars parked close to the steps. The motorcycle men waited at the end of the exit road.

Fazal stepped towards the Hall. He wore clear spectacles. He was dressed in jeans and a bulky parka, partly zipped over an open-necked check shirt with a white tee-shirt showing at the throat. His hands were deep in the pockets of the parka, and he was slightly hunched over as he walked. Back home in Syria, he had been trained to adopt a body posture which made him seem not just of no significance, but almost invisible in a crowd. Tonight, however, there was no crowd – only a few people making their way through the cold January night, most of them bound for or coming from the Royal Infirmary.

Not looking at the police officers, as they stamped their feet on the paving slabs to stimulate the circulation, he drifted towards the steps. If no opportunity to enter arose, he would linger there, insignificant, until a chance came.

But just as he drew near, the policeman closest to him, a red-faced, heavily-built sergeant in uniform, turned towards him. 'Evening, sir. Can we just stop there a minute.'

Fazal's hand slipped through the slit in the pocket of the Parka, and found the grip of his Uzi.

94

Someone else was watching the Hall, pressed in the dark shadow of the building. And he was watching Fazal Mahmoud as he sized up the situation and decided on his gamble.

The girl still squirmed in his grasp, trying to bite the hand clamped over her mouth. She had been walking through George Square, a student on her way home from the library, when he had grabbed her in the dark spot between two street lights, pulling her round the corner into the shadow.

It was his strong left hand which was clamped over her mouth, the forearm crushing her breast as he held her with her back towards him. His right arm encircled hers, the hand trapping her left wrist and holding her completely immobile.

He watched the unfolding drama of the Hall, the police and Fazal Mahmoud.

Suddenly he moved. His right hand left her wrist, and in a single powerful move, ripped her blouse open. Then, a blurred second later, a knife was in the same hand. She felt it slash through the waistband of her skirt. For a second, the left arm relaxed, and she spun out of the man's grasp, her skirt falling loose round her ankles.

She gathered her breath and screamed, a second before the knife cut her chin. Involuntarily, her arms flew up, and the knife slashed again, across her exposed belly. She screamed again, louder this time. She stumbled back, screaming a third time, and waiting for the next blow of the knife.

It never came. The man was gone, melted away into the darkness. As the girl screamed yet again, feeling the warm blood running down her neck, her chest and her legs, ten uniformed police officers, two in motor cycle gear, sprinted towards her.

95

As the police sergeant turned towards him, and he grasped his gun, Fazal knew what he must now do. He must take this man down quickly, rush into the Hall, and complete his mission before the other police could react.

Then he would throw the gun down – to be hailed, when the full story broke, as the saviour of the free world.

His hand moved to withdraw the gun as the bluff sergeant moved towards him. 'I'm sorry, ma mannie, but you can't go in . . . '

The rest of the sentence went unsaid – and the sergeant lived to see his wife again – as the screaming began. The big policeman turned away from Fazal and rushed off after his colleagues towards the source of the disturbance.

Fazal Mahmoud slipped quickly and quietly up the steps and into the Hall. A few seconds later, a second figure turned towards the building from Teviot Place, and followed him inside.

96

The procession had almost reached the end of the passageway when Fazal appeared. Deirdre O'Farrell had stepped to one side, to allow her guests to leave, as the *burr* of the Uzi sounded from the doorway, masking a hoarse cry in Arabic.

In a second, the air was ablaze with gunfire. Fazal's burst of fire was slightly high at first. One of the first bullets caught David McKnight in the head. The million-pound footballer was dead before he hit the ground.

Mario McGuire's gun was already drawn as he leapt in front of the Syrian President. Two bullets caught him high in the chest, throwing him backwards in a spray of blood.

Al-Saddi, Fazal and the third man were hit simultaneously.

A red hole, slightly bigger than a caste mark, appeared suddenly in the middle of the President's forehead. The black-and-white headdress was tossed wildly by the bullet, as it cleaved its exit.

Fazal jerked around as the returning gunfire concentrated on him, Mackie and Martin each emptying their magazines into the human marionette.

The third man did not even get off a round before Skinner shot him dead with two bullets through the heart.

As the procession was nearing the doorway, Skinner's eye had scanned the crowd. Suddenly it had focused hard when a dark-skinned, unshaven man had jumped out of his seat, his hand probing inside his leather jacket. Even as Fazal appeared, shouting and firing, the man had pulled out a pistol and brought it up to a marksman's firing position.

In the second when Skinner pulled the trigger of his Browning, the realisation came to him: he's aiming at the doorway, not at Al-Saddi!'

But he was already committed. The man went down.

As the firing ceased, the hysterical screams throughout the Hall turned to frightened whimpers. Many of the audience, instinctively, had dived for the floor at the very first shots. Now as the firing stopped, and the reek of cordite filled the air, they began to stand up, staring in shock at the figures sprawled in the passageway by the door.

Bodies littered the floor: some still and bleeding, others simply crouched in terror.

Skinner, moving towards the doorway with his pistol still at the ready, called out to his men one by one.

'Mackie.'

'Okay.'

'McGuire.'

Silence.

'Martin.'

'Okay.'

He looked quickly at the body in the doorway. It was still twitching slightly, as its dying brain sent out random, pointless messages. Skinner kicked the Uzi into a corner, and turned back towards the aisle.

The three victims lay in a row. McKnight was first, his body twisted on its side. McGuire lay behind him, but McGuire was still moving. Blood bubbled from his chest, the sure sign of a lung shot.

'Andy.' Skinner barked the order. 'Ambulances, quick. Everything they've got!' But Martin was already speaking urgently into his radio.

Skinner stepped across to McGuire and crouched beside him. He inspected the wounds, then put a hand on his shoulder. The man's expression begged for reassurance. Skinner spoke to him with more confidence than he felt.

'It's okay, son, just take it easy. The Royal's right next door. You've copped a good one, but you'll be all right. They'll have you fixed up in no time.'

He moved beyond, to Al-Saddi. The President was now a closed chapter in history. His eyes were open, but they had no lustre; none of the cold, hard anger which had shone from them only a few minutes before. The headdress had fallen away, the head was tilted slightly backwards, and a thin line of blood traced from the bullet wound into the receding hairline, eventually running into a spreading puddle on the floor.

Skinner became aware of a thin, soft wail alongside him. Looking over his shoulder he saw the tiny Syrian equerry on his knees, keening over his leader's corpse.

He rose to his feet, and joined Martin, who was still talking urgently into his radio, ordering all available men to seal off the Hall.

Sobbing was audible now from various parts of the auditorium, so

Skinner raised his voice. 'Attention please, everyone. I must ask you to remain seated, exactly where you are, for the moment. The Hall will be cleared as soon as possible and in an orderly way, once we have taken statements and personal details from everyone here. Now, is anyone else hurt?'

Two voices answered. Herbie Clay had been hit in the arm by a stray shot, but the bullet had passed right through. He remained conscious and calm. A girl student had cut her head badly in diving to the floor, and her boyfriend had fainted, thinking she had been shot.

'Help is on its way. If there are any medical people in the room, either qualified or students, will they please render assistance to the injured.'

A handful of people came forward, among them two nurses in uniform and a young man in a white coat.

Skinner walked back to the doorway, where Mackie stood over the fallen Fazal, whose twitching had finally ceased.

'Brian, get on to HQ on the radio. Andy's called up all the available uniforms, but I want every CID man on duty in Edinburgh here within the half-hour, to take statements from these people before they leave the building. Then get outside, and find out why those fucking clowns on the door let a man with an Uzi just wander in here.'

Mackie nodded and began to speak into his radio. Skinner turned to find Michael Licorish, the senior of the Scottish Office men, standing at his shoulder.

'Bob, the media want to know if they can leave to file their stories.'

'Sorry, Michael, not for the moment. I want total security on this for the next hour at least. I must give the Foreign Office time to do what it has to with the Syrians. You know what the Middle East is.

'You can confirm to your people that the President is dead. So are David McKnight, and two armed men of Arab appearance. One of my men, Detective Constable McGuire, is badly wounded, and Herbie Clay has sustained what appears to be a flesh wound. There's also a girl with a badly cut head, but she hasn't been hit.

'You could remind the people also that this is now officially a murder enquiry, and that they should bear in mind the rules and requirements of the courts in terms of reporting. That isn't a threat or anything, just advice.

'Oh, and one more thing, can you ask the TV guys if they recorded all that? If they did, I'd like to review their footage as soon as possible.'

Licorish nodded. 'Sure, Bob. I'll ask them. But you'll get them clearance as soon as you can?'

'As I said, give me an hour.'

Skinner turned back and bent over the body in the doorway. The man had been hit in the chest by several bullets. The face, which now wore the yellow pallor of death, looked young, peaceful and oddly beautiful. But a lake of blood had spread beneath the corpse, like a dark blanket.

'So, Fuzzy – and it is you, isn't it – you've shown yourself at last. But why in Allah's name did you do it? And who gave you your orders – not to mention your Uzi?'

He rose and walked up three steps to inspect the man he had himself shot. The body was sprawled along the bench from which he had risen. He stared into the dead face: the eyes were cloudy, and the stubble on the chin was dark against the pallid skin. A long, ragged scar curved round the left cheek, ending at the corner of the mouth.

'Well, Ali Tarfaz – and going by that scar, it's you right enough – I wish you could tell me what the hell you were doing here, although I can have a good guess at it.'

Suddenly he remembered someone else, and he looked around the Hall. The Foreign Office man was sitting alone on a bench to the right of the Speaker's chair. White-faced, he stared straight ahead. He looked stunned by the slaughter, but Skinner was in no mood to be gentle.

'Allingham!'

The man took a few seconds to react, but eventually he rose and walked, trembling slightly, towards Skinner, who motioned him out of the chamber.

'My friend, I have this feeling that you're not as surprised by this business as the rest of us. I think you might know something about it. If you do, you're going to tell me before this night is out. Believe that. For now, I want you to call your panic number in the Foreign Office and tell them that we've managed to lose the Syrian President . . . before they see the whole thing on telly!

'Then, I want those two Arab stiffs in there positively identified. I believe that one is a Syrian named Fazal Mahmoud, registered as a Lebanese and working out of their Embassy. I'm nearly certain that the other one is, or was, a man known as Rashoun Hadid. He's only the head of Iraqi Intelligence, that's all. Just what the fuck he was doing here, I'm not certain. He may have been sent to hunt Mahmoud, or just to mind Al-Saddi, or both. Whichever, he finished second.'

As he spoke, he watched Allingham intently, looking for any sort of a reaction. There was fear in the man's eyes, and Skinner was sure he saw him flinch slightly at the mention of Fazal's name.

274

He turned towards the entrance as Mackie reappeared with two uniformed constables.

'Sir,' the inspector called across, 'there's something funny outside.'

'Tell me later, Brian. For now, leave those two lads to guard the door. Then take Mr Allingham here to a private telephone. Once he's finished, bring him back to me. And don't let him out of your sight.'

'Yes, boss.' Mackie escorted Allingham away.

An ambulance crew appeared at the top of the steps, and Skinner led them into the chamber, pointing to the fallen McGuire, who was being tended by the young man in the white coat. 'There, boys. Be quick.'

The detective constable was still conscious. Martin crouched beside him, speaking quietly, keeping up his confidence. Skinner called out to the other two casualties.

'Mr Clay. Miss. Can you walk? If so, would you please get yourselves into the ambulance outside.'

Both Herbie Clay and the girl began to move slowly towards the door, each escorted by one of the nurses who had come forward earlier. Clay was clasping his arm tightly, as if afraid it would fall off. The girl pressed something white to her head. As they neared the door, a second ambulance crew appeared to help them away.

McGuire was lifted up carefully and placed gently on a stretcher. Just before they carried him out to the ambulance, he grabbed Martin's jacket with one bloody hand. He spoke weakly, his voice whistling occasionally. 'Tell Maggie I'm going to be all right. I'm glad you sent her to the other place.'

Skinner stopped the man in the white coat. 'Will he make it?'

'He should do. He's been shot through the lung, but the bullet seems to have exited. There's another one in his upper chest somewhere. It smashed his collarbone and must have lodged in muscle. But the guy's as strong as a bull. He'll pull through.'

'Good man. Go on after him, then. Andy, you go, too. Look after all three. Make sure that Clay and the girl get everything they want.'

'Right, boss. Do me one favour, will you. Break it to Maggie Rose, but as gently as you can.'

'Sure.'

More police had begun to arrive. The senior man present was a uniformed superintendent from the St Leonards station. Skinner called him over.

'Hello, Jack. Good to see you. I want you to run this. CID people will be arriving from all over the place. I want everyone in the Hall interviewed and released as quickly as possible. No one gets in at all – and no media get out until I say so.

'Will you also please let the Press Bureau know that if they have any calls about this, they should say that an incident has occurred in the MacEwan Hall and that details will be released as soon as possible. Clear?' The Superintendent nodded. 'Good, get under way.'

Skinner took his slim two-way radio from his pocket and pulled out the aerial. 'Blue One to HQ. Patch through to Blue Three please.'

The line clicked. Maggie Rose's confident voice sounded through the small speaker. 'Blue Three acknowledges. Over.'

'Blue Three, listen closely. Your package has been damaged and will not now be delivered. Your companions are ordered to return to their digs, their leader to join me here. Understood? Over.'

There was a short pause. 'That is understood. Companions will be so ordered. But be advised, Blue One, their leader is not here, only his deputy. Over.'

Where is the bastard, then? Skinner thought to himself. To Maggie Rose he said, 'Message received and acknowledged. Please ask local group leader to organise his own transport.'

Skinner then dropped the code. 'You should be aware that Mario has had an accident. He is badly hurt but he'll be okay. You are authorised to go to ERI. Leave your oppo to supervise shut-down of your location, and to advise its management. Over.'

There was a longer pause this time. 'Blue Three acknowledges. You confirm that this location is no longer relevant, yes? Over.'

'That is correct. Brief your colleague and get along there. Blue One over and out.'

Skinner flicked the transmitter off, then had second thoughts.

He called Headquarters again. 'Blue One. Please raise the Chief by telephone and patch me through. Over.'

A minute later the connection was made. Proud came on line. 'Chief, just listen, no questions. I'm on site at our main event. We have a worst case scenario. Please get here fast.'

'I'm on my way.' The line went dead. Skinner put away his radio and looked around the auditorium. The uniformed superintendent had taken control efficiently. The crowd had calmed down considerably, and were seated in small groups. Detectives had begun to gather statements. Police stood around the four corpses.

Skinner summoned over the Scottish Office information man. 'Michael, once a few more CID boys arrive, I'll detail a couple to clear your people and get them out of here. But I still don't want the news released until the Foreign Office has had a chance to act on it.' He checked his watch. It was three minutes past ten. The Press Association man can be processed first and let go, if he guarantees not to file copy before 10.45.'

Licorish nodded. 'Fair enough. You won't be able to keep it tight any longer than that anyway. Your man's gone to the Royal with gunshot wounds. You know what that place is like.'

'Yes, you're right.' Skinner shook his head. 'Christ, what a bloody night! You try to plan for every possibility, but there's no way you can. If a determined fanatic with a gun has luck on his side . . .' His voice trailed off for a second, then snapped back to normal.

He called the superintendent over and told him that the next detectives to arrive on the scene should take statements from the media. Then he turned back to Michael Licorish. 'Right, let's talk to the photographers and the TV guys.'

The press were gathered in a group between the two television cameras. They included two stills photographers.

'Did you two get any pictures of the action?' Skinner asked.

The taller of the two shrugged his shoulders. 'I *might* have. When it all started, I ducked. But I stuck my camera up, held my finger down, and let the motor-drive run out the film. I won't know until I process it.'

He looked at the other photographer, who nodded. 'I did the same, but I doubt if I got anything. Denis is a lot taller than me, and I ducked bloody low, I'll tell you!'

'Let's see what you have, then,' said Skinner. 'You two grab a CID man, tell him I sent you. Give him your names and office numbers, tell him you didn't see anything, then get back to your darkrooms and process those films. But send any stuff you have back up to me by midnight. Fair enough?'

'Fair enough, Mr Skinner,' the taller and older man replied for both. They set off in search of a detective.

Skinner turned next to the television crews. 'What about you gentlemen? Do you have anything in there?' He gestured towards the cameras. As he did so, he realised for the first time that the strong blue television lights were still switched on.

'Turn those things off, someone.' Two lighting engineers threw all the switches. The Hall seemed suddenly dingy, and much cooler.

'We can take a look right now,' said one of the cameramen. 'I had a fair view from this position.' The cameras were set a few yards back from floor level, two or three feet above the head height of the passageway that had recently become a shooting gallery.

'Ray here was a bit naughty, of course. As usual he took his camera off its fixed position. He was right behind you lot when the shit started to fly.'

The other cameraman looked sheepish. Skinner threw him a mock glare. 'I'll let you off with a yellow card this time . . . *if* you've got some decent footage. Let's have a look – but on my own, if you don't mind.'

One of the technicians plugged a cable into the back of Ray's camera, which had now been returned to its tripod. He linked it with a monitor and checked the battery levels at each end of the line. The cameraman rewound his cassette at high speed, as the technician switched on the monitor.

The first pictures, taken as the camera was balanced on the man's shoulder, were shaky, but soon they steadied. Skinner found himself watching a side view of the procession as it snaked its way out of the Hall. A dark shadow moved across in front of the lens, blacking out the screen for a second. That was probably me, he thought.

The angle of view changed as the cameraman stepped out into the passageway, looking almost directly towards the door. Skinner saw Deirdre O'Farrell step away to the right, to allow her guests to depart, her Reeboks contrasting garishly with the bulky robes of her office.

And there he was.

Fazal the assassin.

The fusillade began.

The *burr* of the Uzi sounded louder through the monitor's speaker, and Fazal's cry in Arabic was almost completely drowned out.

Even as he watched the shooting start, Skinner saw himself, staring intently up into the crowd to the right, then reaching into his open jacket for his Browning.

He made himself concentrate on the main action. He saw David McKnight as he crumpled and fell to the floor, his talent, his charisma and his life all snuffed out in a second.

He saw Mario McGuire leap across in front of Al-Saddi, then slump backwards as the bullets hit him.

And then three things seemed to happen simultaneously.

He saw himself snap off two shots towards his target in the audience.

He saw the President's head jerk back as it was devastated by the bullet.

He saw Fazal begin his dance of death as Martin and Mackie, standing up in the face of the Uzi, concentrated their return fire upon him.

And he saw something else.

'Stop!' Skinner shouted. The cameraman was startled, but after a second the image froze. 'Rewind, please.' The picture zipped back. 'Stop. Now forward again, please, but frame by frame, if you can do that.'

Again he viewed the trilogy of death, but this time in slow motion. Almost simultaneous, but not quite.

His shots seeming slow and deliberate this time.

Mario McGuire taking his hits, and going backwards like a man beginning a complicated high-board dive. A fine red spray from his back, below the right shoulder, as one of the bullets exited.

Fazal's first contortion as a red hole appeared in his chest, the Uzi beginning to droop in his hand.

Al-Saddi's head dress jerking up, as it filled with the bone and brain tissue blown out by the bullet.

And, surely in the same moment, a flash in the darkness of the doorway.

'Stop.' This time the order was more controlled. 'Back one frame, and freeze.'

The picture wound back, like a reversing snail.

'Yes!'

There it was.

A light in the darkness and a puff of smoke. And behind it, framed for that millisecond in time by the tiny flare of the gunshot, alone in the entrance hall, was a black shape: a tall, slim, short-haired, perfectly balanced silhouette.

'Maitland!'

97

The name escaped from Skinner's lips in a whisper.

He sat and stared, as frozen as the image on the screen, his gaze unmoving and unblinking. Even as a shadow picture, the grace of the man was unique. The perfect killing machine.

Michael Licorish, a decisive man by nature, did not know what to do. He gazed at Skinner as he sat there wide-eyed and suddenly white-faced. For a moment, the poetic thought came to him that the Assistant Chief Constable looked like a man who had seen something so horrible that it had turned him to stone.

Skinner stayed motionless until Licorish, his resolve regained, began to move round from behind the monitor. And then Skinner's right hand shot up, palm outward, in a sudden clear command to halt. For one of the few times in his life Licorish was suddenly, and irrationally, afraid.

Skinner reached forward with his left hand and switched off the monitor. Then he stood up and looked at Ray, the cameraman. 'I must have that tape.'

Something in his voice forbade argument. Without a word, Ray removed the Betacam cartridge and handed it over.

'Yours too,' said Skinner to the second cameraman. The second cassette was also handed over. The two men looked to Licorish, testing his willingness to intercede for them. But they found no response.

'You will square it with our bosses, won't you,' said Ray. 'And we'll get them back sometime?'

Skinner looked him straight in the eye. 'Forget that these ever existed. You've already sent film out of here tonight. And if your editors ask if you have film of the assassination, then blame Michael here. Tell them he wouldn't let you move to follow the procession, so you didn't have a view. But, from this moment, forget these tapes.'

The two men stared at Skinner, reading his deadly serious expression, and they nodded.

At that moment they were joined by their reporters. 'What's wrong?' asked one, a tiny blonde girl.

'Nothing at all,' replied Ray.

'Bob!' Sarah's voice carried to him across the Hall. Skinner turned and they moved towards each other. When they met, she clasped him tight.

'Thank God you're okay. All they would tell me was that there'd been shooting, and to get here fast. And when they call me, that usually means a body. I was scared to death. You're all right, aren't you?'

He smiled and hugged her close. 'Yes, love, I'm still in one piece. But there are four people lying around here who ain't, and who won't be ever again. So you'd better take a look at them. The man we were hunting was the one over in the doorway.'

'I'll get to it. But where's Andy?' The anxiety was still in her voice.

'He's at the Royal.' She started in alarm. 'No, he's all right, but Mario McGuire's been shot. Andy's gone with him – and with two other casualties.'

'Are they bad?'

'The other two are superficial, but Mario was hit twice. They think he'll make it, though. Now, love, I must go. Did you see Brian Mackie on your way in?'

'Yes, near the entrance. There was another man with him looking terrified.'

Skinner smiled again, grimly. 'Good. Off you go and look at those four poor bastards.'

'Which is the President? Oh, he'd be the one in uniform. And who's the young man?'

'David McKnight, the footballer. He was hit first. The other two are our hits.'

As he said the words, he shuddered. He was talking about death with the woman he loved, and about a man he had just killed. He was talking about the part of the job which put his life in danger. The shudder turned into trembling.

Sarah read the signs. 'Bob, sit down.' He obeyed. 'Did you kill one of those men?'

He nodded.

'This isn't exactly the South Bronx. Have you ever shot anyone before.' This time he shook his head.

'How do you feel about it? Think, and tell me. Say it out loud. Admit it to me. Don't keep it inside.'

Skinner sat in silent thought for several seconds. Then he looked up, and into her face. 'I feel a lot of things at the moment. I'm glad that when it finally came down to it, I was able to react in the right way, and that my men and I were brave enough, and well enough trained, to stand up there, and do what we had to do.

'I've killed a man. But he had a gun, and he was going to use it, so he killed himself in a way. What worries me is that I'm looking into myself for remorse, but as yet I don't see any. What sort of a man are you marrying, eh, Doctor?

'Where I do feel remorse, it's because I've failed. It was my job to keep that Syrian brute alive, and now he's dead. The world might be a better place for it, but right now, that's immaterial as far as I'm concerned. He was in my hands and I lost him.

'How the Christ did my people let a man with a fucking Uzi just walk in through the front door? That was the only way in. Everything else is sealed.'

By now, Skinner was speaking to the night, but Sarah answered him.

'Maybe your people were helping the girl.'

'What girl?'

'One of the men – the one over there with the silver on his hat – was telling me that it'd been a hell of a night. "First some girl is attacked and cut up by a maniac, right outside, then all this happens." That's what he said.'

'The *ba . . . astard.*' The word hissed through Skinner's teeth, its first syllable dragged out. Abruptly he stood up. All the shock and self-recrimination had gone, and fury came back to the surface. Sarah, better than anyone, could sense it.

'What is it, Bob? You think that your Arab over there attacked the girl just to draw the police away from the door?'

'Don't ask me any questions, love. Not now. I have to keep this to myself.'

She was suddenly afraid. 'Be careful, my darling.'

He kissed her softly and left the Hall.

He found Mackie and Allingham standing near the entrance. Sarah had been right: the man looked frightened.

'I've done what you asked, Mr Skinner. By now the MOD will have put all forces in the Mid-East on the alert. Next, the Foreign Office will inform the Syrians. It's always difficult to predict how these people will react.

'Now I'd like to get away from this place!'

'Shut up. You're going nowhere till I say so.'

282

He turned towards Mackie, and gestured over his shoulder with his thumb. 'Brian, tell me how friend Fuzzy got in here with a fucking Uzi. What's this story about a girl?'

'That's how, sir. A girl was attacked just along the road there. She's been taken to hospital, slashed on the face and body. Superficial though. She was walking home when she was grabbed from behind and pulled into a dark corner. The guy pulled a knife, but she said she got loose, and he cut her. She started screaming, and all the uniforms just ran over at the same time, even the sergeant in charge. You can't blame them really.'

'*Who* can't! Where's that sergeant? Brian, this was a fucking kid-on. Someone gets the soldiers sidetracked on their way here, then pulls this stunt so that the front door leading right in to Al-Saddi himself is left lying wide open. This is our man from the Royal Mile. Exactly his style. This guy kills and maims without a second thought, but there's always a purpose.'

'And that wee dead bastard Fuzzy did all that?'

'That's what us simple coppers are meant to think. But you and I know better, Allingham, don't we? This is another fucking stitch-up!'

For a second, Allingham's face was illuminated with pure terror, and in that instant Skinner knew with absolute certainty that he was right about it all.

Allingham fought for self-control. He blustered. 'You're crackers, Skinner! You've botched this whole affair. Last time you arrested an innocent Japanese diplomat. Now you've allowed the President of Syria to be shot, and you're peddling some ridiculous conspiracy theory to divert attention from your own incompetence.'

Skinner smiled at him: it was a strange smile, a savage smile. 'You knew, Allingham, didn't you. "An innocent Japanese", you just said. But when you and I first met, after Yobatu was arrested, I was convinced he was guilty and you couldn't get him out of the way fast enough. Now I can *prove* he was innocent, but only a handful of people close to me know that. So how come you do, too? You knew all along, my son, didn't you. And Hughie Fulton had me believing that you were too low down on the food chain to be let into secrets like that.'

Allingham was chalk white. 'You're mad.'

'You'd better hope I'm not, mister. You and I are going somewhere very quiet for a chat. No one else is coming. It's going to be just you and me. And you're going to tell me the whole story. I've got most of the bits of the jigsaw in my head, and I think I can fit them together. You're going to help me with the last few pieces. Most of all you're going to tell me about Maitland.'

'You can't make me go with you.' The man turned despairingly to Mackie.

The Inspector shook his balding head. 'I wouldn't bet the house on that, Mr Allingham.

'You'll need a car, boss. Why don't you take the one that Mario and I came in. It's unmarked. I think the Merc would be a wee bit conspicuous.'

'Fine, Brian. When I'm gone, nip along to the Royal and find Andy. Tell him that Mr Allingham and I have gone down to the coast to sort things out. And tell him this, too. If either of you sees that man Maitland, disarm him and lock him up. Be very, very careful. Give him no opportunities. Just lock him up. And if he as much as looks at you the wrong way, don't hesitate. Shoot him.'

He turned again to Allingham, who had backed away into a corner. For a moment, Skinner thought the man was going to shout for help.

'Let's go. You've got some talking to do. The rules on your side of the street are new to me, but I'm learning fast. Move!'

He hustled the man outside, into the cold January night. The three cars were still parked in front of the Hall. Their drivers, two policemen and one civilian, stood talking together. The policemen stood to attention as Skinner approached.

'Keys please, John.' He held out a hand to the driver of Mackie's car, a blue Sierra.

'Sir!' The constable handed over the keys without another word.

'Get in, Allingham. Front seat.' The man obeyed, his shoulders drooping in submission and a look of hopelessness on his face.

Skinner started the engine. But, before pulling away, he looked into the face of the man on his left.

'I'll tell you what I think, my friend. I think that you're scared shitless. You're involved in something that's just too big for you to cope with.

'You leave the Met for what you think will be a nice cushy job as a sort of diplomats' baby-sitter and general bum-wiper. Then all of a sudden it starts to get more than that. You're involved in the dark side of international relations. People start getting killed. It's all part of a serious Intelligence operation, and a state secret, but those nosy coppers up in Scotland won't cooperate. You see, they've got this aversion to their people being chopped up and shoved under trains and stuff like that. And now the whole thing's a mess. It's out of control, and you find yourself up to your arse in hedgehogs. You know the truth and, as recent events tell you, that could be fatal.

'Well, chum, this is your way out. You're going to point me at brother Maitland, and I'm going to see that he's put away. I don't care much whether it's done in private or in public, but he's got to be locked up.

'We're going for a drive to my place. It'll take us about half an hour to get there. You've got that time to consider your position in all this. And you've got that time to make up your mind to tell me the whole story. You're going to tell me anyway. I'm not pissing about here. There's the easy way, and there's the hard way. I don't want to have to beat it out of you. That's strictly against my rules. But as I said, I'm on your side of the street now, and if I have to, I will. Now I'll shut up and let you think it over.'

He slipped the car into gear and moved off, out of Bristo Square, turning back towards George Square, past the open-air car-park, towards the main road. As the Sierra turned left into Potterow, a nondescript elderly Ford Escort, its locks worn smooth with age and easily picked, pulled gently out of the car-park.

It followed the Sierra's turn into West Nicolson Street, past the Pear Tree pub, its customers overflowing into the beergarden as the Friday-night crescendo gathered momentum, and the student survivors of the MacEwan Hall massacre began to arrive.

It kept the Sierra's tail lights in sight as it headed through Holyrood Park, towards Edinburgh's eastern suburbs, and beyond, to East Lothian.

98

Skinner was as good as his word on the drive to Gullane. He was silent all through the journey, throwing only the occasional glance at Allingham. Once or twice, in the headlights of on-coming vehicles, he could read the despair written on the man's face.

The drive in the dark took the half hour that Skinner had forecast. There was no street light near the cottage. After drawing to a halt, he allowed the Sierra's headlights to illuminate the front door, while he unlocked it with Chubb and Yale keys.

He stepped into the entrance hall, switched on the light, and deactivated the burglar alarm. Then, leaving the Yale off the latch, went back to the car, switched off the lights, and motioned to Allingham to precede him back to the cottage. Inside, he pointed him towards the living room. As the man obeyed, Skinner closed the front door behind them.

The house was chilly. Skinner turned on the gas fire at full power. He pulled the heavy, lined curtains across the windows and across the double patio doors, and stood for a minute in silence with his back to the heat, facing the door to the hall. Allingham had slumped on to the long green leather couch to his left, where he sat, staring at his knees.

'Right, chum,' Skinner said abruptly, rousing the man from his contemplation. 'Your moment has arrived. I don't really want to get blood and snot all over my upholstery, so save us both a lot of pointless grief and tell me the whole story.'

He walked over to his hi-fi stack, to his right on the wall facing Allingham, picked up a cassette and slipped it into the tape-deck. He pressed the RECORD button.

For a second or two, a last faint gleam of defiance showed in the Londoner's eyes. Then it was gone. He sighed long and deep.

'Okay, Skinner, okay. How much do you know?'

'I know that Mortimer and Jameson were working together to develop a legal case to invalidate the Declaration which set up the State of Israel.

I know that their paymaster was a man named Fazal Mahmoud, an old lover of Rachel Jameson from her student days. He was a Syrian then, but currently is – or was until tonight – trading as a Lebanese out of their Embassy in London.

'He's been missing for a while. Last weekend we tracked him down to a house in Fife, where he was being sheltered by two other old university chums. They were a couple named Harvey. We found the link and watched them. They led us right to him. My people were careful, but somehow Fazal discovered that the Harveys had been rumbled. When he did, he shot them dead on the spot and made a run for it. He's been underground since then – until tonight.

'He was the man with the Uzi. I believe that he was set up by your outfit as the assassin of Al-Saddi. The reason ties in somehow to the Mortimer-Jameson document. But I haven't put that quite right. The real point is that he was set up to take the blame for the assassination. Poor old Fuzzy was your Lee Harvey Oswald, with us cast in the Jack Ruby role.

'For Fuzzy had back-up – back-up from Maitland. Maitland wasn't sent up here to protect Al-Saddi. He was sent up to make sure that he was killed; if necessary, to kill him. Just as he killed Mortimer and Jameson. Just as he killed three innocent people in Edinburgh to set us on the trail of a maniac. And just as, at the very start, he killed Shun Lee, a piece of advance planning to help us fit Yobatu into the frame when the time came.

'His first job tonight was to get Fazal into that Hall with his Uzi. So he arranges an "accident" for his SAS unit, to keep them away from the very operation that he has planned. Then he attacks and cuts up a young girl, to lure the police away from the door of the debating chamber. Finally, he follows Fazal inside, unnoticed, through the open door. And when Fuzzy opens up with his Uzi, hitting everyone and everything but his target, he stands in the darkness behind him and puts Al-Saddi away with a single shot from a silenced pistol.

'In concept and execution, it was awful and brilliant. But he made one huge mistake, although he couldn't have known it at the time.'

Skinner produced one of the Betacam cartridges from the right-hand pocket of his jacket, and waved it in the air.

'He allowed himself to be filmed. If he hadn't done that, then neither I nor anyone else would ever have cottoned on.'

He paused for a second, allowing Allingham to take in what he had said. He placed the cartridge on a long rosewood coffee table.

'That's what I know. But there's a big piece missing, and that is: *why?* What was the brief to Mortimer and Jameson involved with that made it so lethal?

'Tell me, Allingham. Tell me now.'

The white-faced man lifted dark, haunted eyes and looked into Skinner's face.

'Don't make me. I warn you, there are some things that it's safer not to know. Man, I'm police, like you. I lived in your world not so long ago. But now I'm part of another where, as you said, the game is played in a different way, where the stakes can be whole countries and millions of lives. In that game, rule number one is this simple: there are no rules.

'When it's a matter of protecting the state, even the planet, you do what is necessary. That's why we have Maitland. There is no one better than him at doing what is necessary.

'He isn't SAS of course, not in the sense of being a regular officer. He was Special Boat Services once, at the time of the Falklands, when his unique talents were first noted during certain operations on the South American mainland. Now he works with the Special Forces on occasion, but on a consultancy basis.

'Maitland isn't his real name, by the way. He was Captain Lawrence in the SBS, but that may have been false too. But whatever his real name, he is, shall we say, the principal executive arm of the Security Services.'

'You mean he kills people that the Government wants out of the way?'

'Not the Government. The politicians don't know about him, not even the Prime Minister. Although the Security Services report to the PM, there are some things that even he isn't told. That he can't be told. For example, the fact that he himself, the whole Cabinet, and the entire Opposition Front Bench are kept under permanent surveillance.'

Skinner whistled. 'Holy Shit!'

'It gocs back to a standing order given by Macmillan after the Profumo Affair. He told them to do it forever, as standard practice, and never to refer back to him or any of his successors on the matter.'

He paused. 'But that's got nothing to do with this business. As for Maitland, very few people know about him. Those who are aware of his existence sometimes refer to him as "The State Executioner".'

Allingham looked into Skinner's face. 'Now that you know more about him, do you still want to know the rest of it?'

Skinner's eyes were hard as flint. His voice was soft, but filled with power and a terrible menace. 'Friend, it's as simple as this. Your man Maitland recently killed seven people, of whom only one could possibly be described as an enemy of the State. He's a cold, calculating murderer, without a thought for the sanctity of life. I recognise the fact of the existence of your secret set-up, but I don't recognise its right to exist. There's only one society in this country, not two. Your man Maitland is an outlaw. I'm the posse.

'Now. Tell me *why*.'

Allingham sank back into the big green couch, shaking his head.

'Doomsday.' The word seemed to crackle. 'That's what it's all about. The brief which Mahmoud gave to your two Scots advocates was going to be used all right, but as a defence.

'For over a year now, the Western Intelligence community has had whispers that Syria and Iraq had settled their blood feud in private, and had come to a secret understanding on cooperation against Israel. The CIA weren't too worried at first. They thought that the UN and the coalition air forces had pretty well emasculated Iraq's nuclear and chemical capacity. But gradually doubts crept in. Recently the satellites have picked up some movements between Syria and Iraq that were highly suspicious. And some other odd things have been noticed in the mountains to the north of Iraq, where the intelligence community has always suspected that they had kept a top-secret store of goodies.

'A few months ago, our friend Fazal Mahmoud contacted his old flame Rachel Jameson, and offered her a commission. Miss Jameson, as you will be aware, was a PLO sympathiser in her student days. It seems that she kept that allegiance. When Mahmoud telephoned her and asked her to meet him to discuss business, she told her fiancé, Mortimer. She must have told him the whole story, because Mortimer didn't fancy the idea of Ms Jameson having clandestine meetings with one of his predecessors, and so he took over the negotiation. It seems that he was pro-Palestinian, too, because he agreed to accept the instruction on a joint basis.

'We knew about the meeting in advance of course. Mahmoud was under routine surveillance, and that involved a telephone tap. But we knew very little of what it was about. After that first meeting, the trail went cold for a while. Naturally, the spooks kept a weather eye on the two advocates, but since they didn't seem to be involved in any extra-curricular activity, it was concluded that the instruction from Mahmoud must have been purely academic in nature.'

Skinner held up a hand, interrupting the narrative. 'Wait just a minute. They kept them under observation? On my patch? Without me knowing?'

Allingham looked at him nervously. 'It was done through Fulton. There are resources outside the police force, Skinner.'

'That's being brought home to me. Were any of my men involved?'

'No one currently serving. That's all I'll tell you.'

'We'll go into that later. Go on.'

Allingham lit a cigarette and drew deeply. Skinner handed him a rarely used ashtray.

'As I said, the trail went cold. But then, in October, Mahmoud contacted me.'

'He contacted you?' Skinner was surprised.

'Yes. Most of the diplomats know me as someone to whom they can speak off the record as well as officially. They think of me as a chum. You think of me as a sort of escort. What they and you don't know is that I'm also a part of the Intelligence services. I maintain my baggage-carrier cover rather well, don't you think?'

He carried on without waiting for Skinner's answer. 'Anyway, Mahmoud was in a fearful state. He asked for a meet under total secrecy. I set it up. Mahmoud was an experienced intelligence operative, but he wasn't the top man. The Syrians run quite an extensive undercover operation through the Lebanese Embassy. He showed me a signal from Damascus to his head of section. He had read it, although it was not for his eyes, and had taken a secret copy.

'It was encoded, but he translated it for me, using a secret cipher that not even Langley can crack. It turned my blood cold.

'It made it clear that the Iraq-Syria love-in story was true after all. The signal briefed Mahmoud's head of section on a joint operation called Day of Deliverance, a plan jointly drawn up by Al-Saddi and the Iraqi leader.

'On that day the Iraqi-Syrian Alliance, which had been forged by Al-Saddi even before he made himself President, would launch a pre-emptive strike against Israel, using Iraqi Scuds and Syrian aircraft. The weaponry would be chemical, not nuclear.

'Everyone knows that Iraq had stored chemical weapons and wasn't squeamish about using them. We thought they had all been neutralised, but not so. The real stuff and Iraq's last-resort nuclear weapons were holed up in that mountain store. What no one knew either, until we asked and the Russians confirmed it, was that, during his mercifully brief reign in the Kremlin, Andropov supplied the Syrians with some very sophisticated chemical weapons as a deterrent against, of all people, the Iraqis. He did it to keep them from drifting into the American camp.

'On the Day of Deliverance, massive strikes using these weapons were to be made against Tel Aviv, Haifa, Eilat, and all the populous areas of Israel. Only Jerusalem, Gaza and the West Bank would be spared. There, supposedly spontaneous armed insurrection would break out. Simultaneously, there would be a chemical-backed conventional attack across the Golan Heights, using paratroops to encircle the defending garrison. They anticipated little or no resistance there, once news of the attacks on their cities had reached the Israelis.

'The legal arguments, commissioned by Mahmoud and prepared by Jameson and Mortimer, were to be used as a sort of second strike. On the Day of Deliverance, petitions based on their work would be presented in the International Court of Justice, and in the United Nations itself. They would seek to have the 1948 Declaration set aside as invalid. The Syrians were sure that, on strictly legal grounds, they would succeed.

'In other words, the case prepared by Mortimer and Jameson was to be used to justify an act of genocide in the eyes of the world.'

Skinner sat down in an armchair, his back to the door. He was stunned by what Allingham had just told him.

'But what about the Americans? Wouldn't their first reaction be to bomb the shit out of them?'

'But would they be allowed to? Al-Saddi and the Iraqis thought they had that one figured out. The Americans and the rest are onside with the Arabs only to defend Kuwait, Saudi and the Gulf oilfields – not Israel. Anyway they only have enough ordnance out there to fight Iraq, not Syria as well. History tells us that the Yanks don't think too quickly when it comes to strategic adjustments.

'Al-Saddi and his new ally reckoned too, and rightly, that no Arab state, not even the Saudis, would allow its territory to be used as a base for the defence of Israel. The Americans and the other Allies would be completely exposed. They could not resort to nuclear retaliation. The Saudis would order us out. We would have to withdraw, or else fight a war against the whole Arab nation, and ultimately the whole nation of Islam – with limited resources and thousands of miles from home. By the time the UN got its act together, it would all be over. Iraq and Syria allied would control the whole region overnight. All that the Americans could do would be to garrison Turkey, and probably occupy Saudi. But offensive operations would be a non-starter.

'Finally, as an insurance policy, Syria and Iraq were going to arrange for widespread native unrest to break out in all the Islamic republics in Asia.

'So there you have it. An enormously sophisticated operation, brilliantly conceived by totally ruthless men, which would lead to the occupation of all Israeli territory. The Israeli survivors would be rounded up, interned, and expelled, or worse. Once the chemical contamination had been cleared, ostensibly the land would be settled by Palestinians, and renamed Palestine. But it would be ruled by the Syria-Iraq axis, just as the whole of the Arab world, even the Egyptians, the Iranians and the Libyans, would dance to their tune.

'With the bulk of the global oil resource in the hands of a unified, militant Arab League, with Al-Saddi and the Iraqi leader at its head, the consequences for the rest of the world would be unthinkable. We would be talking about economic enslavement. That, Mr Skinner, is the secret. Are you happy now?'

Skinner was thunderstruck. And this unbelievable tapestry of world domination had been unfolded before him in his own living room, for Christ's sake.

'You say that Fazal contacted you in October?' he managed at last.

'Yes, after he had taken delivery of Mortimer and Jameson's brief.

'As I told you, the man was in a fearful state. He was, to be sure, pro-Palestinian. But in the final analysis he was also sane, and a humanitarian. He asked me what could be done to stop the madness.'

'So what did you do?'

'First, I double-checked with the experts on the cipher which he had used. It was the real thing, the Syrian Supercode. That meant that the document was genuine. It also let us crack the code without the Syrians knowing.

'That done, we contacted the CIA. A conference was held within forty-eight hours. The situation was assessed, and an agreement was reached. It was clear that Al-Saddi was the key. He was the driving force, quiet and deadly, not brash and boastful like the Iraqi. He had taken Syria into the deal, and dragged his military with him, but it was reckoned that if he could be eliminated, they would fold and the whole operation would fall apart. The CIA said that if Al-Saddi could be taken out, then they could control what happened next.'

'Why didn't your people just tell the Israelis?'

'Good God, man, we couldn't do that.' Allingham sat bolt upright. 'If the Israelis had found out about this, there's no doubting what they'd have done. They'd have got in first. They'd have nuked Damascus and Baghdad, even though that would have set off the biggest Holy War the world had ever seen. Even now the Israelis must never know.

'The Yanks felt that we were best placed to take the lead in sweeping up, since the leak had come to us, since our nationals were in a sense involved, and since we were less polarised than them. They expressed the view that the necessary executive action should be coordinated by us. And, of course, the Yanks had heard of Maitland – even used him on occasion. Our Director General agreed. Maitland was called in.

'Skinner, you have to believe me. When he appeared, I had no idea what he was, or what he was capable of. I thought that he would give your two advocates a good talking-to, warn them off, and tell them to forget all about it. Then, I thought, he would take care of Al-Saddi on his own ground. But no, that's not his style. He never leaves possible loose ends – or loose tongues. Never.

'The whole plan was his, including the trail that led to Yobatu. We had files on Mortimer and Jameson from Day One. We knew, and so he knew, about the Chinese case. The very first thing he did was to kill Shun Lee, and cut his balls off. That was Maitland's idea of forward planning. Then he set about silencing Mortimer and Jameson, and eliminating any trace of their work. You know the rest of that part of the story.

'Then Maitland set out to nail Al-Saddi. We knew from the document Mahmoud showed me that the Syrians were looking for a platform somewhere in the West, just before the big day, so as to launch their propaganda campaign. We knew that Al-Saddi himself would take it up.

'Maitland and I saw Mahmoud together. He wouldn't talk to anyone without me there. Maitland scared the shit out of him; he told him that as a Syrian he had a sacred duty to put an end to the madman Al-Saddi. He also told him that if Mahmoud refused, then he Maitland would, with regret, have no option but to pick up the telephone and spill the whole story to a friend of his in MOSSAD. Goodbye Damascus, hello Armageddon.

'You know, Maitland would really have done that. He told Mahmoud that he must activate the student network that he ran still in Edinburgh, and set up this debate. He told him to ensure that a personal invitation was sent to Al-Saddi. He said that with the Syrians still publicly on the side of the angels, against Iraq, it was quite natural that our Government would roll out the red carpet for him.

'Finally, he told Mahmoud to go missing until the debate itself. He warned him that the Syrians, the Iraqis, our people, anyone might come after him. He gave him a gun, and told him to keep in touch and not to be caught. When we found out through Fulton that you were back on the trail, Maitland went up to Fife, while Fazal was holed up there alone, and gave him the name and photograph of everyone in your team, including you.

'Maitland saw him again on Monday, to give him the Uzi. He was

293

checked into a prearranged bolt-hole address in Perth. Fazal explained that he had shot the Harveys after they had let slip that they had been visited by your man Martin. He took a peep outside, saw two people on the beach, and that was that.

'Mahmoud's mission was to show up and kill Al-Saddi. Maitland told the poor bastard that the armed police guard would be briefed to miss him when they shot back. After he had killed the President, Fazal was to throw down his gun and be acclaimed as the saviour of the free world.'

'And he believed all that?' said Skinner.

'You saw for yourself tonight. He must have died a disillusioned man. He performed his sacred mission and was blown away for his trouble.'

'But in the end, Maitland had to do the business himself.'

'That was always his intention. He couldn't leave it to luck. He always knew that you would have a better than even chance of dropping the Arab before he hit Al-Saddi. He only wanted him there to get a few shots off and to carry the can – to be, as you said, Lee Harvey Oswald.

'He had a back-up plan, you know. If tonight had fallen through for any reason, Al-Saddi's plane would have exploded in mid-air tomorrow, shortly after take-off from Edinburgh. But this one was so much neater. Beautiful in a dreadful way.'

Skinner held up a hand. 'Didn't the Syrians get worried when Mahmoud went to ground?'

'Their section head in the Lebanese Embassy did, to be sure. We fed them some disinformation to the effect that Mahmoud had been gambling, badly, and was on the run from some rather nasty creditors. I don't know if they bought it. The only thing I do know is that the section head passed a message, to Damascus, to be passed on to someone in Baghdad, telling him that Mahmoud had vanished. I can't think why that was.

'We had them all under close observation, of course, but there was no sign of the operation being aborted. The opposite in fact. Al-Saddi was enthusiastic about the debate. He had them all jumping through hoops. Biggest mistake of his life, eh.'

'There's one flaw in Maitland's plan,' said Skinner. 'Al-Saddi was shot by a pistol, not an Uzi. That will show up at a postmortem, or we'll find a strange bullet in the hall.'

'He thought of that. Before he gave the Uzi to Mahmoud, he fired some rounds from it. If a bullet was dug out of Al-Saddi, and from what I saw, that's unlikely, the plan was to swop one of those for it before they did the ballistics tests.'

'Who in Christ's name would arrange that?'

'Why, Fulton, old boy.'

Skinner was stunned. 'Fulton! How much does that bastard know?'

Allingham smiled weakly, enjoying his discomfiture. 'Everything, Skinner, everything. Maitland told him the whole story.'

'And he went along with it?'

'He didn't have a choice! He isn't bullet-proof. He was, or rather is, as scared as me. Once Maitland lets you in on one of his operations, you guard his secret with your life. Literally. If he ever finds out that I told you all this, he'll kill me.

'As for you, you're not one of the magic circle. If he ever finds out that you know the whole story, you're dead too.

'I'd destroy that video tape if I were you, and fast. I promise you, the man has an amazing eye for detail, and he never leaves a loose end.'

A cold fearful thought formed in Skinner's brain, sending an icy hand down to grip his stomach.

'The doctor who examined McKnight and Al-Saddi is a scene-of-crime specialist. She knows all about the effect of different calibre weapons. She'll have seen the back of Al-Saddi's head blown off, and know that he wasn't shot with an Uzi.'

Allingham looked at him. Something in Skinner's voice brought the fear back into his eyes.

'Yes,' he said slowly. 'Maitland thought of that too. She'll have an accident. Very soon. Within the next twenty-four hours, I'd guess.'

The rage exploded in Skinner. Awful images of Sarah flooded into his mind, wiping away all his restraint. He jumped from his seat and grabbed the man by the lapels, hauling him to his feet. In the same movement, he butted him between the eyes.

'Where is he? Where will I find him? Tell me now or I'll cause you more pain than you can ever imagine?'

Blood poured from Allingham's broken nose, as Skinner held him upright. But his stunned gaze was focused over the big detective's left shoulder. His eyes widened and the mouth dropped open.

'Here I am, Skinner. Here I am.'

99

Even as the quiet voice spoke, there came a strange, firm thumping sound, like a baseball whacking into a catcher's glove.

Allingham's right eye, and the back of his head, exploded in a reddish-grey spray. The impact of the soft-nosed bullet jerked him out of Skinner's already loosening grasp, and hurled him backwards on to the couch. His body convulsed for a few seconds and was still.

Slowly, Skinner turned to face Maitland, and the smoking gun, wondering all the time whether he himself would hear the sound of the shot that killed him.

The man stood framed in the doorway. Skinner looked for madness in the eyes, but found none. Instead he saw an expression which was a mixture of pleasure and icy control.

He saw the silenced pistol, held in two strong hands, and levelled at his head.

'You knew I'd take the bait, didn't you. You even left the door on the latch. It's too bad that our late friend here made you forget yourself. But however did you think you'd *know* when I arrived?'

'There's a loose board in the hall. Squeaks like hell. Everyone hits it the first time they come here. Not you, though.'

'Come on, Skinner, you didn't think I'd just rush into the trap, did you?'

Maitland smiled at him. He lowered the gun slightly, pointing it at his heart, and moved past the two-seater couch into the middle of the room.

'You're a tenacious fellow, aren't you. Tell me, when did you realise that I was your man?'

'I had a twinge when your bus was involved in that accident. That was a bit sloppy. But I'd never have put it together if I hadn't seen that television tape.'

Maitland's eyebrows rose.

'Ah, so you didn't overhear that part. Yes, your biggest mistake. You've made four or five, but that was the clincher, underestimating the resolution of these new generation TV cameras. They can catch a mouse winking in the dark, or in this case a shadow framed in the flash of a single gunshot.'

Skinner looked Maitland straight in the eye and smiled. He forced his body to relax, ready for any half-chance.

'Still, you timed it perfectly. Deserved to be on TV.' He amazed himself by laughing.

'But it will never be shown, will it. Not if that's what I think it is, lying on the table.'

Maitland took his left hand from the gun and pointed at the cartridge.

'Thanks, Skinner. You've saved me a tricky job by bringing that along. Now do one more thing for me. Take your pistol from its holster, incredibly carefully, and put it on the table too.'

Skinner shrugged his shoulders – and regretted it as he saw Maitland's eyes narrow and his finger tense on the trigger of his gun.

'Why should I? You'll kill me anyway.'

'But not yet, old boy, not yet. And people will do anything, you know, for just one more minute of life.' His voice hardened. 'So, do that for me. Now.'

Slowly and carefully, Skinner opened his jacket with his left hand. Using his right thumb and index finger, he withdrew the gun from the holster and placed it gently on the coffee table. As he did so, he kept direct eye-contact with Maitland and, with an imperceptible movement, flicked off the safety catch.

'So what now? Do you shoot me or do I have an accident?'

'I'll shoot you if I have to. I suppose I will at some point; you're that type of chap. But whatever happens, you and your lady doctor will have a terrible accident. In her car. I'll make sure there's plenty of petrol around. You'll both be burned to cinders.'

Skinner knew that he must hold the man's respect. He must put fear out of his own mind – in particular, fear for Sarah. That had let him down earlier. He searched in Maitland's eyes for uncertainty, looking for any sign of weakness, but finding none.

'You know, pal, you're some act. Where the hell did they dig you up from?'

'Thank you, Mr Skinner.' Maitland bowed his head very slightly. 'I accept your compliment. Since you're going to die, I'll even tell you.

'I came from the Marines to the Special Forces. All my past records have been destroyed, of course. I did my thing in the Falklands, and after that I went on to become something of a cult figure in Ireland. Remember

297

the shoot-to-kill policy?' He laughed, lightly. 'Well, I was it. But I was too efficient, and the politicians took fright. Pity. Anyway, round about 1985, I left the SAS payroll and became a sort of freelance, working on very special projects only, at a very special rate of pay.

'I only insist on a few things. It is understood that once I am given an assignment I will accept no recall orders. Any mess that I make is cleared up after me by other people, people like your chum Fulton. Also, it is written in stone that any colleague who betrays any detail of an operation will end up like silly old Allingham there. Instantly. No appeal. Bang.

'Fulton told me about Skinner's rules. But it's amazing what you can achieve when you play to a set of rules like mine. You should try it sometime, my friend.' He laughed. 'I'm sorry, you should have tried it! You wouldn't like to join me in my work, would you? You'd really be very good. Why not let me win you over to the dark side of the force? I work quite a bit on the international scene, you know. I have some very free-spending clients in Colombia, and if I had a partner I could take on more contracts. Of course, your ladyfriend would still have to go, but you and I would do well in business together.'

Skinner controlled himself with a great effort. He shook his head. 'No, my son. It wouldn't work. I was never made to be the sorcerer's apprentice. I'd want to be the fucking sorcerer. Once I'd picked your brains and learned where your contacts were, you'd have to go.'

Maitland laughed again. 'You really are a killer at heart, Skinner, aren't you. If you hadn't become a copper, if you'd taken my route, you'd be absolutely terrifying. I've got the gun, so I can tell you this. You even scare me a bit, and no one's ever done that before.'

Skinner's response was heavy with irony. 'Sure, you look really fucking nervous. But tell me this. Why kill all those people? Why so brutal?'

'That was your fault. I researched you, you see. I realised that my cover story for the elimination of Mortimer and Jameson would have to be very special to fool you. By the way, there was never any question but that Mortimer and Jameson had to go. Everyone linked to Mahmoud had to disappear before the assassination. If he hadn't killed the Harveys, they'd have had a gas explosion.

'Anyway, the Royal Mile Maniac was created in your honour. But I couldn't just leave it at that. I knew that you would never give up, so I threw in a culprit. Yobatu *san* was perfect. A samurai freak who regarded it as an honour to be framed! His turning up at the McCann trial was an incredible bonus. When he headed for the same train as Rachel, I decided to take care of her there and then. It's not that difficult, you know, at the end of a winter day on a crowded platform. No one ever sees anything. My original idea was that she would take an overdose, in her grief.

'The Yobatu cover was perfect. It should have worked. But you're a cynical fellow. You don't believe in perfection! That was my only mistake.'

Skinner laughed out loud. 'Oh no.' He saw Maitland's eyes crease with annoyance for a second. 'That wasn't your only mistake. Not by a long shot. You must learn about limbo files, for a start. You must learn to take your gloves off when you open briefcase locks. You must learn never to steal single pages from books.

'You're good, but you could improve your attention to detail.' He laughed again.

This time the anger stayed in Maitland's eyes. 'Enjoy it, Skinner. Laughs can turn into screams.

'There's one other thing I want to know. Tell me and I'll kill you quick. Hold out, and I'll shoot you in the balls and let you enjoy *that* feeling for a while. You shot another Arab in the Hall tonight. I saw you, through the doorway. Who was he, and why was he there with a gun?'

Skinner gave an unforced smile. He was amazed to find a glow of self-satisfaction spread over him.

'Okay, I'll tell you. Ever hear of a man called Rashoun Hadid?'

Maitland's eyes widened in surprise.

'Yes I thought you would have. Well, I'm guessing some of this from what Allingham told me. When Fazal disappeared, his section head in London told Damascus, and Damascus told Baghdad. They weren't sure that they had a problem, but the stakes were so big that Hadid decides to play ultra-safe. He knows Mahmoud. They were students together in Edinburgh, when Hadid was called something else. So he slips out of Iraq and comes over here, ready to shadow Al-Saddi, just in case Fazal does have something spectacular in mind.

'And tonight, when Fuzzy appears with your Uzi, there's Hadid in the audience with his gun out, ready to pop him and get away, no doubt, in the general confusion. Only he was unlucky.

'So, Maitland, it turns out that we have both been playing on the same team. You get Al-Saddi, and I zap the head of Iraqi intelligence, the big chief's right-hand man.

'There we have it. You've done your thing and I've done mine. We can bet that, even as we speak, the Stealth bombers will be overflying Baghdad, and the brown-trousered Syrian military will be aborting the

Day of Deliverance. The world saved from another fascist threat, thanks to a fascist like you and a dupe like me. So that's the full story.

'Now let's stop pissing about! Do you really think I'd have led you out here without lining up my back-up first? Martin and Mackie were both ordered to give you a fifteen-minute start, then to follow you out here. They have keys. Right now, Andy's probably in the kitchen, and Brian in the hall, just waiting for my shout.

'Shoot me, son, and you don't leave this house alive. Drop it. We'll give you a warm room and three square meals a day for the rest of your life. We'll even let you tear the wings off the occasional pigeon.'

Now Maitland smiled again. The gun hung by his side now, ready to swing up in an instant. The name of the game was death, and they both knew it.

'I'm sorry, but I've got to do you now, old boy. You'd be too dangerous if I took you out there into the dark. And you can't bluff your way out of it. Your men are like brothers to you. You know the risks, and you wouldn't expose them.'

'Bollocks! I kept them out night after night in the Royal Mile, chasing your shadow. You're a lone hand, Maitland. My lads and I are a team, we trust each other, we take risks for each other. You can't comprehend that, can you?'

Somewhere, far back in the cool grey eyes, Skinner thought he saw an edge of uncertainty. He edged closer. Time to chance it all, he thought, for me, but most of all for Sarah; if I don't stop this man now, we've both had it.

He only had one hope, and that was the oldest, the corniest trick in the book. He glanced suddenly towards the kitchen door. 'Okay, boys, come in now!'

But Maitland was too good to take the bluff. His eyes never left Skinner. The gun started to come up, slowly. The cold, killing smile spread.

Bob Skinner had never believed in miracles. His personal creed encompassed only goodness and logic, and left no room for the concept of a higher power. So, when the crash of the loose shelf and its contents – falling off the wall after all those years – sounded from the kitchen, he was almost as surprised as Maitland.

But he retained sufficient presence of mind to react as soon as the grey eyes swung towards the door.

His left foot arced up in a kick, more powerful than any he had ever made. His life hung on the race between his strike and Maitland's gun, as it swung up towards the firing position.

It was almost a tie. As the outside edge of the heavy black shoe smashed into his elbow, dislocating it and smashing the ball of the joint, Maitland squeezed off a shot. Even as he followed through, and as the silenced Walther flew across the room to crash against the wall, Skinner felt the bullet rip through his right thigh and burst out in a tangle of flesh.

But when death threatens, pain is a distraction to be ignored. Skinner knew that, even with one arm, this man was lethal. He threw himself to his right, carried by the momentum of his kick. He snatched the Browning from the coffee table and levelled it at Maitland.

'Stop!'

Maitland, too, was ignoring his pain. He was halfway across the room, reaching for his lost gun with his left hand, when he heard Skinner's command, and felt the tangible force of his aim upon him. He stopped in mid-stride, and turned slowly, his right arm hanging smashed by his side, and a look of terrible exultation on his face.

'So, old boy.' The voice was steel-hard and controlled. 'It's stalemate. What do we do now? They won't let you try me, you know.'

Skinner looked at the man. His thigh burned as it pumped blood, but his mind was cold as ice. He thought of Mortimer, his head lying on the pathway; he thought of Rachel Jameson, of PC Iain MacVicar, and of the others. And then he thought of Sarah, burned to a crisp in her car.

'No, Maitland, they won't, will they? This game's got to be played by your rules – to the very end.

'Rule One: adapt and survive. Goodbye.'

No fear, only surprise, registered on Maitland's face as Skinner pulled the trigger. The bullet went through his heart.

There was no real need for the second shot, but Skinner took no chances. After all, this man was very special. It was wise to ensure that he was very dead. And so as Maitland's legs buckled and he slumped to his knees, he took careful aim, and fired again, taking him in the SAS death spot, in the middle of the forehead. The body crashed backwards on to the pale green Wilton.

Skinner stood over the dead pile of flesh and bone that had been Maitland. He stared at the body, stunned, until the pain in his leg forced itself into his consciousness, pulling him back into the world.

He threw his gun on to the couch beside Allingham's sprawled corpse, noting for the first time, that the room smelled foully of shit.

He yanked his black leather belt from its loops and buckled it around his thigh, above the wound. Then he took the poker from an ornamental fireside set, a wedding present from many years before, and used it to form an efficient tourniquet.

He hobbled over to the hi-fi stack and picked up the one-piece telephone which lay there in its cradle. Its cord stretched as far as the two-seater couch. He sat down, carefully, holding the tourniquet tight, and patched in Hatch One, his short code for Fettes Avenue. The switchboard took longer than usual to answer, but eventually Skinner heard the friendly businesslike voice of the night-duty operator. 'Police Headquarters.'

'This is Skinner. Give me the Chief, wherever he is.'

More than two minutes went by before Proud's anxious voice echoed down the line. 'Bob. Where are you? The Foreign Office has made an announcement, and the press are breaking down the doors here looking for more.'

'Give them the minimum. Tell them that there were two assassins, and that they were both killed by police. Tell them about McKnight – if we're clear with next of kin. But tell them that anything else will have to be channelled through the Foreign Office.'

'I'll do all that, but you still haven't told me where you are, or what's up.'

'No, and I don't think I'm going to. Just do one more thing for me. You have a contact number for Hughie Fulton. Use it. Tell him to be in my office in one hour. Don't ask him, Chief. Tell him. Tell him that Skinner said so.'

'All right, Bob. I'll do that. I'll see you there too.'

'No!' Skinner's sudden yell down the telephone startled Proud. 'This is between that fat cunt Fulton and me. I know it all now, Jimmy. You must not be involved. Believe me.'

Proud could hear the pain in Skinner's voice. 'Okay, Bob. Do what you have to do. Are *you* all right, though?'

'Yes, Chief, I'm okay. Now is Sarah still there?'

'No. She finished up and went home about ten minutes ago.'

'Okay. Thanks, Chief. For everything.'

He laid the telephone face-down and loosened the tourniquet. The bleeding had virtually stopped. 'Good. No arterial damage. And no broken bones, by the feel of it.' He made a conscious effort to stay matter-of-fact as he examined his wound.

He then called Sarah.

'Bob. Are you back at your office? All Brian would say was that you had gone off somewhere with Mr Allingham.'

'No, love, I'm in Gullane. There's no one else here. Listen, Sarah, I've had a wee accident. Just a scratch, but I want you to have a look at it for me. I just need a bit of first aid. Meet me in my office in about forty minutes. I've got a very important date, and I want to be properly patched up for it. Oh, and bring along a pair of slacks for me, there's a girl.'

He hopped and limped through to the bathroom and took a pack of cotton wool, a roll of tape, and a pair of scissors from the cabinet. With the scissors he cut through the right leg of his trousers, exposing the area around the bullet-hole. The entry wound was small and neat. But the area where the bullet had exited was shredded. Each was crusted with dried blood, and the mess at the back of his thigh still leaked a little. He packed each hole with cotton wool, securing it roughly with tape.

He eased his way back to the living room, and through to the kitchen. The floor was a mess of shattered crockery, from the collapse of the life-saving shelf. He smiled through the pain. 'Thank God I'm not a DIY freak.'

Leaning on any available support, he hauled himself back into the living room. He picked up his Browning and returned it to its holster. He thought of taking Maitland's Walther, but left it lying on the floor. Instead he picked up the video cartridge and replaced it in the pocket from which he had taken it a lifetime earlier. He turned off the gas fire and started towards the door – before remembering the tape-deck. The cassette had run out. He removed it, slipped it into an inside pocket of his jacket, and left the house in darkness.

There were no lights in any of the surrounding houses. The double glazing provided an efficient sound-insulator, and no one had heard the shots.

He eased himself behind the wheel of the Sierra, and found that he could work the pedals without too much pain, and without having to put weight on the wound.

He had not gone far when he was hit by a sudden, desperate need to speak to Alex. Luckily, the car had a phone.

Alex sounded wide-awake when she came on line, her voice echoing on the car speaker.

'Hi, Pops. Why the hell are you calling at this time of night? I'm just in. Jenny and I were up at the Rusty Pelican.'

'You haven't heard any news then?'

'No. Why?' Alarm sounded in her voice.

'Don't get them in a twist. There's been an incident tonight, and some people have been shot. But I'm fine, and so's Andy.'

She was unconvinced. 'You don't sound fine.'

'Well I am. Now listen, are you coming through tomorrow?'

'Yes, of course.'

'Well don't go to Gullane. We won't be there. Come to Stockbridge. Okay?'

'Okay, Pops.' She began to ask what the big mystery was, anyway, but thought better of it. 'Now, if you promise me that you're really fine, I'll get some sleep.'

'Promise. Love you. Night.'

As he ended the call, he thought, suddenly, that he had been within half a second of never hearing that voice, or Sarah's, ever again. He felt hysteria lurking within him. To keep it at bay, he smiled savagely in the dark and fixed his thoughts on Hughie Fulton.

100

The drive, normally thirty minutes, took fifty. Skinner drove at a steady pace, keeping the pain in his leg to a minimum.

The wound was still leaking blood when he reached Headquarters. Mackie's overcoat lay in the back of the Sierra. He threw it on, and walked, as evenly as he could manage, into the lift.

Sarah was waiting for him in his inner office, seated in the big swivel chair behind the desk. She jumped up when he hirpled into the room.

'Oh my God, darling. What's happened? You're grey!'

He threw the overcoat on to a chair, and she saw his leg. Her hands flew to her mouth. A scream started, but she choked it off.

'Bob! That's a gunshot. Who did it? Are you hurt anywhere else?'

Skinner gave her what was meant to be a reassuring smile. To Sarah it resembled the clenched-teeth expression of someone trying very hard to hold himself together.

'Don't worry, love, it's a flesh wound. I've had a talk with the bloke, and he won't do it again. Let's use the Chief's bathroom.'

She helped him along the corridor to Proud's suite. Skinner opened the door with a key from his collection, and motioned her in ahead of him.

In the white-tiled bathroom, she cut off the bloody trousers. Gently, she removed his makeshift dressing. Then, using surgical spirits which burned with a cold fire, she cleaned the wounds, front and back, and washed the leg.

'Bob, you *have* to go to hospital.'

'I know, but not just yet. I have to see this man.'

She took out a syringe and injected anti-tetanus serum straight into his thigh. Then she placed a powdered lint packing over the raw wound, and bandaged the leg from knee to crotch. As she worked, he talked to her continuously to keep his mind off the screaming-pitch pain.

'Tell me, Doctor, did anything strike you about those two head wounds you examined tonight?'

'Yes. I meant to ask you about that. They were caused by different weapons. The younger man was killed by a light-calibre bullet. But Al-Saddi's brains were blown out, literally. He was hit by something heavy-calibre and soft-nosed: the sort of bullet that would make a hole like the one you have in your leg, for example. If that had hit bone . . .' She stopped suddenly and looked at him, her eyes widening.

'Clever lady. You should be careful. That thoroughness could land you in trouble some day. When you write your report, I want you to forget all that detail.'

'Bob, what are you into?'

'The biggest, nastiest mess of my life, my darling. But it's almost over now.'

He saw no need ever to tell her of the danger in which she herself had stood hardly an hour before. She looked into his face and decided to press him no further.

When she had finished dressing his leg, she helped him into the sharply pressed grey slacks which she had brought from the apartment. He kissed her, and as he held her close, he whispered in her ear, 'I'm so glad I found you. If anything should ever happen to you, I'd be finished.'

Sarah saw the trauma in his eyes. She knew that when he was ready, he would tell her the story.

'Go, my darling,' she said, 'and, as always, do what you have to do. Whatever it is.' Her eyebrow raised in a familiar movement. 'And as soon as you've done it, have someone drive you straight to hospital. Call me the minute you get there. Doctor's orders.

'Oh, by the way, Andy called just as I was on my way out. McGuire was still in surgery, but he's going to be fine. Andy's staying there with Sergeant Rose, until he comes round. What's Maggie Rose doing there anyway?'

Skinner smiled. 'Let's just say she's off duty.'

Sarah kissed him again, and ran off downstairs.

101

In his office, Skinner took a bottle of brandy and a glass from his cabinet and poured himself a stiff measure. He made to put the bottle back, then changed his mind.

He took off his jacket, draped it over the back of his swivel chair, and sat down, carefully, behind his desk. The Browning was still in his shoulder holster.

He was halfway through his second brandy when Fulton's bulk swept into the room, full of bluster.

'Who in God's name do you think you are, Skinner! You preside over the assassination of a visiting head of state, and then you have the temerity to summon me to your presence!'

Skinner's hand was rock steady as he took the gun from its holster and slammed it down on the desk. But inside he felt shaky. He knew that sooner or later, shock, loss of blood and brandy would get to him. This had to be done fast and hard.

'Shut the fuck up, Fulton! I'll tell you who I am, my non-existent friend. I'm your worst fucking nightmare come true. I'm the man who shot Liberty fucking Valance, that's who I am!

'You can fix things, so they tell me. Well you'd better fix this. In my cottage in Gullane you'll find two stiffs. One of them is our pal Allingham – that's Allingham of the FO. He was shot by the same gun that killed Al-Saddi, and you can guess who fired it, can't you. The other stiff is your late colleague Maitland. You know all about Maitland, Hughic, don't you. You should; I'll bet you wake up screaming every time you dream of him.

'Well you can forget him. The hitman got himself hit. Did you know that he was going to kill Sarah? Did you?' Skinner roared the question at the big man, his right fist grasping the automatic, his finger curled round the trigger.

Fulton's belligerence had vanished. He shook his head violently. 'No, Bob. Honestly, I didn't know that. You must believe me!'

'God, man, you'd better pray that I do! For that's what he said to me. He actually stood in my living room and told me that. As matter-of-fact as you like. And he thought that, having heard that promise, I'd let him walk out the front door. Fatal mistake, that was.

'So your bogeyman's dead. You're safe from him. Now here's the bad news. You're not fucking safe from me, Hughie. For I *know*. I know the whole stinking story from beginning to end. I know that Maitland, the state executioner, killed all those people – and I know why. And, with all of that, I know that you were an accessory, after and maybe even before the fact of all those murders.

'I know what the stakes were in the game, Fulton, and so I know it's got to stay secret. But it stops here, and it stops now. I have proof that Maitland shot Al-Saddi. I have a copy of the document that Mortimer and Jameson died for. They're both well secure, but if anything unexpected happens to me, they'll both go public.

'And one thing more. If anything, the slightest mischance, should befall my nearest and dearest – Sarah, Alex, Andy, any one of them – then you, fat man, are fucking dead! You've lost one bogeyman, Fulton, but you've found another. You've just as much reason to fear me as you had to fear Maitland. After all, which one of us is lying right now in my living room with a bullet in his head?

'As far as the Day of Deliverance is concerned, you can mark that down as mission accomplished, in spades. The Syrian is dead, and your masters have their Lee Oswald. They've even got a bonus. If they ever identify that second dead Arab, they'll see why. Tell them to try looking in Iraq.'

Skinner picked up the Browning and waved it at the man before him, seeing him cringe backwards as he did so.

'My most sincere advice to you, Hughie, is this: retire. Go away. Get the fuck out of the sewer you work in. I'd rather not see you again, because if I did, I'd start to think again of all those dead people. And the devil inside of me that wants to shoot you where you stand might just win the argument next time. So quit, Hughie. Piss off. But before you hang up your cloak and dagger, there's just one more thing you have to do.

'I'm going back to my cottage on Sunday. That's tomorrow now. When I do, I want to find it clean and spotless. I want Allingham gone. I want his blood and shit off my sofa, and I want his brains off my wall. Maitland, too. I want his mess cleaned up. That shouldn't be too difficult, should it, Hughie, since he's like you: he never existed anyway.

'Spotless, man, spotless. I don't want Sarah or Alex ever to find anything that might have been a bullet hole, or a bloodstain. I love that house. I'll never forget what happened there tonight, but I don't want anything left to remind me. Except for the shaky shelf in the kitchen. Leave that as it is, for luck!'

Skinner heaved himself to his feet, the gun still in his hand.

'And now, my fat friend, as Fazal Mahmoud might well have said . . . imshi!'

Epilogue

When Bob, leaning on a stick, limped into his cottage just after midday on Sunday 22 January, it was immaculate.

'Have you had cleaners in here?' Sarah asked him.

'Yes. We both work hard enough. I fixed up some springcleaning through someone at the office.'

'Well they did a good job, whoever they were. Could we get them for Edinburgh?'

Bob laughed a strange laugh. 'You never know what people'll turn their hands to when they retire. But I think this was a one-off.'

Sarah and Bob were married, under an awning in their garden in Gullane, on the sunny afternoon of 21 April.

Sarah was given in marriage by her father. Alex and Andy were bridesmaid and best man. Among the guests were Chief Constable and Mrs James Proud, Detective Inspector Brian Mackie, Detective Sergeants Maggie Rose and Mario McGuire, and Detective Constable Neil McIlhenney.

Not one of them, not even Andy Martin, had ever asked Skinner what had happened on that explosive night – after he and Allingham had driven off in the dark towards Gullane.

Only Sarah knew of the weight that he was carrying. Long after his leg had begun to heal, she felt him toss and turn in the night. Occasionally he would awaken in a lather of sweat, and once or twice with a scream dying on his lips. But she never asked. She waited for the shrapnel buried in his soul to work its own way to the surface.

Three nights into their honeymoon, they sat over dinner, gazing at the stars above L'Escala. Until then, Bob had been bright, happy and never more attentive, but now Sarah sensed a tension in him, stretched to bursting point.

310

'Love, I think you should tell me now. I'm your wife, and if something makes you wake up trembling in the night, I want to know what it is.'

And so he told her. He told her the whole story of the night that he had finally discovered that there was a world where Skinner's rules of honesty, fairness and mercy did not apply; the night when he had been forced to look into his own character and learn the depth of the ruthless streak that lay within him.

'Do you know what Maitland said? He told me that I'd be a sensation in his line of work. And d'you know what? The fact that we're sat here, and he's buried in an unmarked hole in the ground somewhere, proves just how right he was. What sort of a guy am I, Sarah?'

'That was an awful man, a terrible creature. But he finished the job he was sent out to do. Al-Saddi died, and the Day of Deliverance went with him. There was a clear, warped logic to everything he did. All the victims – he saw them as casualties, necessary to his success. There are two million people alive in Israel who would agree, if they knew the story. But ask Iain MacVicar's mother. What would she say?'

'And you, Bob. Do you think you're a casualty too? Is that what's eating you?'

'Probably. I got into this job because I believed that I knew the difference between the good guys and the bad guys, and I knew what I was. Now I don't know that any more, not for sure. All I do know for sure is what I'm capable of.

'Skinner's Rules! I broke them along the way, and in the end I broke the biggest commandment of all. I was warned off, but I ignored it because I never doubted that what I was doing was right. Then I found that I was in a place where right and wrong were immaterial, and where only results mattered. And the really terrible thing is, I survived there. I took Maitland on, on his own terms, on his own turf, and I won. That makes me just like him, doesn't it?'

Sarah answered the question in his eyes, as she took his hand and entwined his fingers in hers.

'Bob, if you had lost, and Maitland had come for me, and we were both in Dirleton Cemetery instead of sitting under that big full moon up there if that was how it had turned out, would Maitland have been sitting somewhere agonising about it?

'The hell he would!

'When good faces evil, it doesn't win through being nice all the time.

311

It wins by being brave, and it wins by being right.
'And take it from me, Skinner. The good guy won.'

Now you can buy any of these other bestselling books by **Quintin Jardine** from your bookshop or *direct from his publisher*.

FREE P&P AND UK DELIVERY
(Overseas and Ireland £3.50 per book)

Thursday Legends	£5.99
Gallery Whispers	£5.99
Murmuring the Judges	£5.99
Skinner's Ghosts	£6.99
Skinner's Mission	£6.99
Skinner's Ordeal	£6.99
Skinner's Round	£6.99
Skinner's Trail	£6.99
Screen Savers	£5.99
Wearing Purple	£5.99
A Coffin for Two	£6.99
Blackstone's Pursuits	£5.99

TO ORDER SIMPLY CALL THIS NUMBER

01235 400 414

or e-mail <u>orders@bookpoint.co.uk</u>

Prices and availability subject to change without notice.